BREAD AND A STONE

By Alvah Bessie

Fiction: Alvah Bessie's Short Fictions (1982)
One for My Baby (1980)
The Symbol (1967)
The un-Americans (1957)
Bread and a Stone (1941)
Dwell in the Wilderness (1935)

Non-Fiction: Spain Again (1975)
Inquisition in Eden (1965)
Men in Battle (1939)

Anthology: The Heart of Spain (editor) (1952)

Bread and a Stone

ALVAH BESSIE

Chandler & Sharp Publishers, Inc.
Novato, California

This edition of
BREAD AND A STONE
is dedicated to the memory of

Mary Burnett &
Helen Clare Nelson

Library of Congress Cataloging in Publication Data

Bessie, Alvah Cecil, 1904-
    Bread and a stone.

    Originally published: New York: Modern Age
Books, c1941.
    "Published in cooperation with Shire Press"--
T.p. verso.
    I. Title.
PS3503.E778B7   1983   813'.52   83-7488
ISBN 0-88316-553-8

This book is published in cooperation with Shire Press,
P.O. Box 1728, Santa Cruz, California, 95061. All inquiries
regarding subsidiary rights and licences should be directed
to Shire Press.

About BREAD AND A STONE

Although this is a story about a murder, it is more than a murder story. It is the moving and exciting story of a man who tries but who is never able to overcome his start in life.

Life really begins for Ed Sloan when he marries Norah Gilbert, attractive widow and schoolteacher, stranded with her small child in an eastern village. To win the love of such a woman, a woman of culture and grace, is a wonder beyond understanding; to become a second father to six-year old Katey is happiness beyond imagination.

Ed Sloan had received nothing from the world — no family, home, money, education — not even a steady job or enough to eat. But he was born with the capacity for becoming a fine human being, with strength and gentleness, kindness and sensitivity; he was capable of boundless love and self-sacrifice. As Norah Gilbert awakens and nourishes these qualities in him, Ed's life really begins. He is determined to hold on to this new life.

Then the police arrive to take Ed away for what appears to have been a particularly brutal murder. With terrifying swiftness, Alvah Bessie's novel carries us through events leading toward a tragic climax — through the pain of a long court trial which eventually brings understanding. It is a blunt story, simply told, packed with suspense. Written with compelling sincerity, BREAD AND A STONE presents a frightening picture of a man caught up by society in a chain of circumstances too strong for him to break.

Received with broad critical acclaim upon its initial publication on the eve of America's entry into World War II, BREAD AND A STONE remains as vital and as revelant now as it was then.

1

SLOAN CLOSED THE DOOR to the upstairs bedroom and set the basin of hot salt water on the floor by the bed. It was a cold night, and he could hear the wind howling across the meadow and around the house. He sat on the bed and took the new white sneaker off his left foot carefully, pulled off the white woolen sock, and set his foot, bandage and all, in the steaming water. It took a moment to soak through, and then immediately it was too hot, and he lifted his foot, baring his uneven teeth in a grin. "Christ," he said under his breath, then eased the foot back in again.

Norah won't be sore, he thought, if I don't help her with the dinner. He heard Katey in the next room, calling, "Mommy, come and say good night," and he heard Norah reply from downstairs, "Go to sleep, darling, I said good night to you." He leaned back over the bed with his foot still in the water, like the doctor said, and reached for the button on the radio. It took a moment to warm up, buzzing all the time, and then the music came loud and he kept turning it and a voice said, "—at his press conference today. The President said—" and Sloan thought, That ain't what

I'm looking for, and he switched the set onto the short wave.

The short wave wasn't very clear; there was always too much static, but he could sometimes hear the airplanes saying, "La Guardia tower from Stearman eight, eight, two, eight, go ahead," or "TWA one, five from Newark Tower, go ahead," and sometimes they even said where they were, like, "Floyd Bennett tower from AA three, Orange three thousand, landing at Floyd Bennett, go ahead." He liked to listen to the airplane signals and imagine he was flying the big airliners into port; but that was a hell of a thing to be thinking now, he thought, and he turned the dial slowly until the Shoreline police wave came in.

The monotonous voice was saying, "Car number 5, proceed to 41 Maple Street, tenement fire; Car number 5, proceed to 41 Maple Street, tenement fire." What's the good of listening to that? he thought; that's Shoreline, and there ain't no station up the road in Polk or Low Hill where they'd be sending from. We're way out in the country here. But he continued to listen, feeling the heat on his injured foot through the bandages. There were long buzzing silences and then the voice came in again, saying, "Car number 2, proceed to Post Circle, street fight; Car number 2, proceed to Post Circle, street—" he stopped listening.

It ain't no good, he thought; they're not going to put that on the air, not them; they're smart enough for that. Lots of folks got radios these days, and lots of them listen to the police calls. It ain't the kind of thing they'd put on, and even if they did, they'd use a code number like they sometimes do, Car number 7, proceed to 82 Willow, signal Y, signal Y. Signal Y must mean something they don't want the folks listening in to know about, he thought.

I won't listen to the damn thing, he thought, and switched the set back onto the broadcasting waves, tuned in a station that was playing music, and turned it up loud. He sat on the edge of the bed and looked at his foot soaking in the water, and he could see the dark stain on the bandage. Wonder how long it will take to cure up; shouldn't be very long, it ain't a bad one. He thought he heard her calling, and he turned the radio down and standing up with one foot in the basin, he leaned forward and opened the door. Dinner must be ready, he thought.

"Ed," she was calling, and he said, "Yes, Mom?"

"Ed, there're some men here to see you."

He straightened and took his foot out of the water. He sat down on the bed and carefully pulled the dry sock over the wet bandage, and he put the sneaker on his foot. He had to lean against the door going out of the room, for the foot was mighty sore and he couldn't help but favor it. Well, he thought, here it is, brother; this is the business.

He leaned on the wall going down the stairs, and when he came into the room he saw the men. One of them was short and thin and the other was tall and heavy, and the short one said, "Ed Sloan?"

"That's right," he said.

· · · · 2

HER FACE WAS RED FROM
the heat of the oil range; she could feel the redness of her
face, and the heat. The child Katey called from upstairs,
saying, "Mommy, come and say good night," and she called
back, "Go to sleep, darling; I said good night to you." She
could faintly hear the sound of the radio upstairs in the
bedroom and knew that Ed was lying there, listening to it
as he had listened so intently during the past week since he
came back from New York with the new Chrysler his
brother had loaned him. She felt a slight resentment that
he was not there to help her with the dinner, to lay the
table as he always had since they were married almost a
year before.

For the week since he had come back with the new car
and the injured foot, he had been worrying her. He wanted
to be on the move all the time; he wanted to take them
riding in the new car, saying, "Ain' it a beaut? Listen to it
hum. Wish it was mine." They had been riding all that
week, to no apparent purpose. He took them north into
Massachusetts and down to New York; they drove into
Rhode Island and once even into southern Vermont, leav-

ing early in the morning and getting back after dark, and there was a new restlessness about him that she had not seen before. He has something on his mind, Norah thought; if he wants to tell me, then he'll tell me.

She turned to call him to come down for dinner, when she saw the car drive into the dooryard. Her heart suddenly leaped into her throat, and she put her hand to her breast, thinking, What's the *matter* with you? but there was something about the determined faces of the two men that said to her, as loud as any words, *Now it has come; now it's really come!* They were a comical pair to look at, coming across the yard to the door, a tall heavy man and a short thin man, and they knew that she saw them and stopped at the door as she approached, wiping her hands on the apron.

"Yes?" she said.

"This where Ed Sloan lives?" one said, and she said, "Yes."

"You Mrs. Sloan?"

"That's right, won't you come in?"

They said, "Thank you," and they walked right through the kitchen into the dining room and looked around them. The tall man stood holding his hat in his hand, and the short thin man with the soft brown eyes and the more determined face looked at her and said, "We'd like to talk to him, if you don't mind."

"Certainly," she said, and went into the living room, calling toward the head of the stairs. "Ed," she called, and then she had to call again, louder, for the radio must have drowned out the sound of her voice. She heard the radio turned down and knew the door was open and heard him say, "Yes, Mom?"

"Ed," she said, "there're some men here to see you," and

the radio snapped off and she finally heard his limping foot-steps coming slowly down the stairs. She turned to look at the men, but they avoided her eyes until they saw Sloan enter the room, when the short one said, "Ed Sloan?"

"That's right."

"We want to talk to you," the short man said. He turned to Norah, whose hands were still gripped tightly in the folds of her apron, and said, "A child was run over in Shore-line." He gripped Sloan by the arm, and Ed turned to look at his wife and smiled at her.

"Don' worry none, Mom," he said.

"A child!" she said, with a sick feeling, and then she thought, But that's impossible; I was in Shoreline with him yesterday, we were both in Shoreline; he said he wanted to look at some tools, and he paid the bill for the lumber we got this fall, and he got a haircut and we sat in the car and waited.

The three men went out of the house and she saw Ed and the tall one get into the car, and the short thin man came back.

"I'm sorry, Mrs. Sloan," he said. He showed her a badge. "I'm from the state police." He handed her a card that she did not look at but held stupidly in her hand.

"There was a fight upstate, and a man was killed. We'd like to ask your husband some questions. We'll be back." He turned then and left her, and she saw the car drive away. Then she looked at the card in her hand. It said, *Corp. Gordon Slattery, Troop B, State Motor Police, Low Hill Barracks.* She heard the car skid on the gravel as it turned into the road from the driveway. Now you're alone again, she thought. Now you've lost your second—non-sense! she thought. Stop it! But they told you so; Bill Hogan said; Ella Horton said; you said yourself—stop it!

she thought, and said it aloud, "Stop it," then heard Katey calling from upstairs.

"Yes, dear," she said, "I'm coming." She hurried up the stairs into the bedroom across from her own, and the child was sitting up in bed.

"Who came in a car?" the little girl said, and she answered, "Some men to see Ed."

"Why do they want to see him?"

"I don't know, dear. Go to sleep," she said. "Ed will be back."

"Were they soldiers?"

"No, dear; I want you to go to sleep now." She tucked the covers in around the child; it was cold in the room, and she felt herself shivering and went quickly downstairs again into the kitchen. She looked out the kitchen door into the dark yard, switched on the outdoor light for a moment, turned it off. When the light was on, she had seen nothing but the bare, frost-hardened earth and the winter-stripped trees near the barn and the low stone wall around the apple orchard. The darkness had been dissolved for a short radius around the house, but the night beyond was much darker.

She sat on the kitchen stool by the oil range and unconsciously stretched her hands toward the warmth. What shall I do now? she thought, and the voice spoke in her, saying, You *must* have known it, even though you didn't want to know it. Why do you suppose Ella Horton? and Bill Hogan? But you *knew* that instinctively yourself. She went into the living room, and on the bookcase near the window she saw the picture of Ben in his French Air Force uniform, and she could hear Ed speaking again.

"That's a nice photo," he said. "I think you ought t' have it out where the little girl c'n see it. He was her dad."

— 7 —

"Yes," she had said, "you're right; I don't know why I ever put it away." How little Bill Hogan knew, or Ella Horton, or anyone else for that matter.

She picked up the telephone and said, "Long distance." No, she thought, no, you shouldn't call him, but then the operator said, "Long distance," and she said, "I want New York. Chelsea 6-4201, Mr. Hogan." She heard the operator say, "Through Shoreline," then, "New York, Chelsea 6-4201." The New York operator repeated the number, and she heard the bell ringing, and Alice answered it. The New York operator asked for Bill, and Alice said, "Just a moment," and then Bill was there.

"Bill," she said, "this is Norah Gilbert."

He laughed, "Sloan, don't you mean, Norah?" and she said, "That's right."

"Bill," she said, "if it should be necessary, could you come out here and get me and Katey and bring us into town tonight?"

"Has something happened?" she heard the voice say, with an inflection that meant, *I know it has,* and she said, "Yes."

"Anything you can tell me?"

"No."

"When do you want me to come?"

"It may not be necessary," she said. "But if it is—it's a lot to ask—could you?"

"Why—yes," she heard him say. "I'll start now."

"No," she said. "I'll call you. If you don't hear from me, you'll know it's all right."

"All right," he said.

"Don't worry. I can't say anything now. But I'm all right, Katey's all right."

"O.K., I'll wait to hear from you."

—— 8 ——

"Thanks, Bill," she said.

She hung up the receiver, weariness suddenly spreading through her back and limbs like a hot flood. She sank exhausted into a chair, whispering, "I can't stay here whatever, I can't stay." She must have sat there a long time, staring at the photograph of Ben Gilbert in his wartime uniform. She thought of him, of the splintered propeller in the closet that he had brought back from France, of the bitterness of his face when he spoke of the war, and how he had gone, a romantic youngster, to help save the world for democracy.

"That isn't the way it turned out," he used to say. "And I can understand this son of a bitch Hitler for that matter." He didn't want to talk about it, and he never flew again.

Four years ago, she thought; is it that long? In the three years of their marriage she had developed a slight resentment against his bitterness. He had never been able to surmount it; he had never put it in its place.

My God, she thought, what're you thinking about? She rose from the chair, her hands at her sides, and stood in the middle of the room. What shall I do? she thought; I must do some—then she heard the car coming into the driveway again and walked slowly toward the kitchen, seeing the men coming, the tall, heavy man and the short, thin one, again.

"What is it?" she said.

The short man licked his lips and said, "Your husband's being held for murder, Mrs. Sloan. I'm sorry. It's got nothing to do with you. Do you mind if we take a look around?"

"No," she said, "of course not. My daughter's asleep upstairs."

The tall man went upstairs, and the thin man sat on the

kitchen stool and looked at Norah. "Sit down," he said. She drew up the kitchen chair and sat facing him.

"What can I do?" she said.

"Has he been away from home recently?" the short man said.

"Why, yes," she said. "He was away the week before this last."

The man was writing in a notebook, and she thought, Isn't he supposed to say, Anything you say may be used against you? But he didn't. Instead, he said, "How long was he away?"

"He must have been away four days."

"Did he say where he was?"

"He went to New York State to try to raise some money on a mortgage."

"Did he raise the money?"

"Yes," she said.

"How much?"

"About two hundred dollars, I think. He paid most of the bills with it, the grocer in Coney, the butcher, the telephone, the lumber in Shoreline, the milk, the coal man in Stiles."

"You didn't use to have a car, Mrs. Sloan."

"It's his brother's car," she said.

"I see."

The tall man came down, said, "Should I go in the kid's bedroom?"

"No," said the short man, "leave it alone." He rose, putting his notebook in his back pocket, and Norah followed the two men up the stairs into her bedroom. The tall man started to rummage in the bedclothes, and his companion said, "Leave the lady's bed alone, Joe." Instead, the man called Joe looked through all the drawers, through the closet where Ed's few cheap worn clothes were hanging, even at the shoes in the closet. He picked up one shoe and put it in his overcoat pocket. There were two boxes on the dresser, and he opened one.

"Leave the lady's things alone," the short man said, and he asked Norah if she would please come downstairs.

In the living room he sat on the couch and offered her a cigarette. "I'm sorry this had to happen, M'am," he said. She didn't take the cigarette.

"A friend of mine's coming tonight," she said absently, her hands clasped tightly together. "Would it be all right if I took the little girl and went to New York? She goes to school down the road. I wouldn't want her to find out what happened when she goes to school on Monday."

"That's all right," Slattery said. "Did Sloan have a pistol?"

"A pistol?" she said. Something in the back of her mind was trying to claim her attention, but she could not grasp it. "I think I saw something that looked like a pistol," she said. "I never touched it." She heard the other man coming down the stairs. He had a pistol in his hand, and he was grinning. He held the pistol out to Slattery.

"Where'd you find that, Joe?"

"In his coat pocket in the closet," said the tall man. He held it out to Slattery, who took it. Joe grinned. Slattery looked up at his colleague and said, "This ain't no pistol, Joe." He hefted it.

"It's a toy," said Joe, "but I'd hate t' have anybody poke it in my ribs at night. I'd sure reach."

"Ever see this, Mrs. Sloan?" the corporal said.

"I think so."

"Ever see another one?"

"No," she said. She was still sitting on the other end of

———— 11 ————

the worn sofa in the living room, and she noticed that the man called Slattery was looking at her hands. She looked down, saw that the knuckles were white. She looked up at him; he smiled.

"You don't have anything t' worry about, Mrs. Sloan," he said. "If you leave tonight, let me know where you'll be. I gave you my card."

"Certainly," she said. "Of course."

"How long have you been married?"

"Since last March."

"You were married before, weren't you?"

"Yes," she said.

"Didn't you used t' teach school in the academy over Olds-way?"

"I taught there part time till last spring."

"Your husband, I mean Mr. Gilbert, he taught there regular."

"For about a year—until he died," she said.

"I see," he said. "Well, Mrs. Sloan, try not t' worry too much. If you go 'way, leave your door unlocked."

"Certainly," she said, "of course." She held out her hand as the man named Slattery rose from the sofa, put the toy pistol in his side overcoat pocket. He looked at her.

"I don't know no more than you," he said. "There was a man killed over Morrisford-way." He paused, then said, "You been having a hard time making out since you and Sloan got married?"

"Yes," she said, thinking, Don't tell him anything; why should you tell him anything? He has no right to pry into your life.

The two men left (one of them driving the new Chrysler) and the sense of desolation settled upon her again. It was December, and the ground outside was bare. There had been a little snow, not much, and the dry leaves rustled in the wind that swept down the lightly wooded hill and across the meadow behind the house. The roof still leaked in the upstairs storage room; Ed never did fix that leak, she thought. Now. She walked up and down in the room, then reached for the telephone again. She got the Hogans' number in New York. Bill answered immediately, his voice anxious.

"Can you make it?" she said.

"Yes. I'll start right away."

"Take it easy," she said. "There's no hurry."

"Is there anything you can tell me, Norah?"

"Not a thing."

"I'm starting in fifteen minutes."

Mechanically, she went to the upstairs storage room and brought out a number of cartons that had been stacked there when she and Ben first rented the house five years before. She had not wanted to come away from New York, but it was the only appointment that was offered him. He was just as disappointed about it as she had been; they were almost two years married, and he had taught before in universities, but those days were gone forever, he said. He was a lonely and disillusioned man with many violent impulses; it had not been a happy marriage. She had been attracted to him out of some persistent youthful romantic impulse toward a war bird who had been an "ace." "In French they call it as," he said, "as-s-s-s." You could not make much money in a small-town academy; it was hard to save.

She took the cartons downstairs, then went up again into her bedroom. She removed some clothing from the drawers, her own and Katey's; she went to the closet and brought out two clean house dresses, changed into her only good suit. She looked at the meager wardrobe that was about the only possession of her second husband, saw the old pair of sneakers on the floor, the toes curling upward. She felt the sleeve of his cheap, unpressed coat, then closed the closet door. From her writing desk she took those documents and letters she had saved over the years, some pamphlets and articles Bill Hogan had written or sent to her. Under an old hat on the closet shelf, she found the cardboard box Bill had given Ed Sloan on Labor Day. She lifted it. It was tied with a string, was very heavy.

All these things she brought downstairs and packed in the cardboard cartons, thinking, It was beginning and now it's over; I know it's over. I have done nothing wrong, she thought. There's nothing I have done that's wrong. She could hear that voice again, the voice on the party line, saying, "Heard where that Gilbert woman in your house has took up with Ed Sloan." The women's voices had laughed, and one had gone, "Tch tch!" and Norah had hung up the receiver quietly so that the women would not know that she had accidentally listened in. She felt that she was blushing, and she felt the same sense of shame that a person might experience who witnessed an indecent act in public. Let them talk, she had thought at the time, a lot they know. They have to have *something* to talk about. And it's lonely living in the country. Nothing ever happens.

That thought made her laugh as she sat in the armchair in the living room, in front of the new coal stove Ed had bought only a few days before with the money he had brought back. It suddenly occurred to her that he had not spent a cent of that money on her, not even for a pair of hose that she badly needed; all of it had gone to settle bills; there were so many. He had not even bought a toy for the child, and she had thought that that was strange, but she said nothing about it. There was something on his mind, and she had been mildly frightened, she recognized now; yes, she had been very frightened by something that she could not put her finger on.

The inside voice said, Stop thinking now, stop thinking. She rose from the chair and got a pail and a brush and some soap powder, filled the pail from the kettle that was always on the range, cooled the water with a dipper from the other pail, and started to scrub the kitchen floor. When she had finished the kitchen floor she started on the dining room, then the living room, and finally the stairs. She was exhausted; she had been counting in rhythm with the strokes of her brush, one-two-three, one-two-three, but she knew she could not finish the entire house. She left the pail at the foot of the stairs and started to repack some of the things in the cartons. It was not that they were not packed well enough; only that she had to keep on doing something. But it was impossible; she sat down with a scarf in her hand, limp in the armchair.

She was still sitting in the chair in front of the stove, the scarf in her hand, when she heard the car coming swiftly into the yard and thought, Here they are again, but it was Bill Hogan. He took off his hat as he came in the house, his face worried. He's getting bald, she thought. She looked at his short, stocky figure.

"Norah," he said.

She rose from the chair and said, "Well." Then she was crying, and Hogan had his arms about her awkwardly, patting her on the back, thinking, The bastard has deserted her already; that's what I thought he'd do. She turned away, out of his arms, gestured to the sofa, but he did not sit down. She sat down herself.

"Well," she said. Then, "It was good of you to come."

—— 15 ——

He waved his hand. "What happened?"

"Ed was arrested."

"When?"

"Tonight," she said. "Just before I called you."

"What for?"

"For murder."

"What?" he said. He felt his heart in his throat, and as he looked at her he wondered how she could be so calm, so self-controlled. Murder!

"I don't know anything," she said. "Only that they came and took him away, said they were holding him for that. He was away a few days last week."

Hogan looked at her, wet his lips, said, "Where's the gun, Ben's gun?"

"It's here."

"Here! Where is it, let me see it!" he said. He automatically put out his hand, saw her point to a carton on the floor. He bent and looked in it, saw the cardboard box he had packed and tied with a string a couple of months before, lifted it. It was heavy. He stood with it in his hand, turned to her.

"Where was it when he was away?"

"Here."

"Are you sure, how can you be sure it was here?"

She sighed, said, "When he was gone longer than he said he would be, I felt a little uneasy, and I went to the closet where he kept the box and lifted it; it was heavy."

"You didn't open it?"

"No, but it was in the box."

Christ, he thought; this is no place for this thing to be found! He nodded to her, went out the kitchen door, opened the door of his new car, and put the box inside the dash-board compartment. He came back in again.

"Would you like a cup of coffee?" Norah said. She moved to the stove, turned up the oil flame, shook the coffee pot. She turned to her friend and said, "Is Alice alone?"

"She's all right," Hogan said.

Norah sank into the chair and put her hands to her head, saying, "Oh, God, this is an awful mess; this is a terrible mess." Hogan stood over her, patted her head. He got cups and saucers out of the cupboard, poured the coffee, offered her a cup. She sat drinking it, smiling at him.

"You can say it," she said. "I know what you're thinking. You can say it."

"I have nothing to say, Norah," Hogan said. "You're our friend. I hope you think we're yours."

"I know you are."

"It's only—" he said and paused.

"I know," she said. "You told me it couldn't work. I don't hold it against you. I'm not even angry at Ella Horton for calling you that time. She's a friend, too; she was worried about me; but neither of you can know—neither of you."

"Don't talk," Bill said. "Relax if you can." He looked into his coffee cup, thinking, Of course it couldn't work, and you should have known it. When a woman's grown up she ought to think twice before she marries a man she knows nothing about. But it's none of my business, he thought; it's none of your business, Hogan. He heard her speaking and looked up at her.

"Just because a man's uneducated, has no job, is dead broke—" She did not finish her sentence, but put the cup down, said, "I guess we should be going, Bill, if you don't mind."

—— 17 ——

"Of course," he said. He gestured at the boxes. "You want me to take these things along?"

"Please," she said. "It's only some clothes, personal papers."

He was glad to have something to do, to be busy coming in and out of the house, loading the cartons into the rear of the convertible car. He half expected a police car to come down the road and turn in at the house, but the night was cold and still outside, fresh and tangy as it never is in the city. He drew a deep breath and thought, I'm awfully tired. He saw her tacking a note outside her door with a thumb-tack and putting out a milk bottle with a note in it.

Inside again she said, "I guess I'll have to leave the food— but maybe you can use it."

"Leave it," he said, and she went upstairs to get Katey.

Hogan moved up and down in the kitchen. He turned off the oil range, went into the living room and saw that the dampers on the coal stove were closed part way, the windows closed and latched. He picked up the picture of his friend, Ben Gilbert, held it to the light and looked at it. The face was much as he had remembered it from their days in France together; there was the old, familiar deep-blue uniform and the round pill-box hat of the air-force officer. There was the mustache he grew in France, to look more French. He was smiling, and his hand was on the heavy pistol at his belt. Hogan put the picture down when he heard her coming down the stairs with the child wrapped in a blanket. The little girl was waking up, and she smiled at him.

"Hi there, toots," he said, and the little girl said, " 'Lo, Uncle Bill." She had been taught by her father to call him uncle, and on the rare trips he and Alice had made to visit

Norah since her husband died, she had always called him that.

"Where're we going?" Katey said.

"To New York, dear."

"It's late at night, isn't it, Mommy?"

"Yes, dear, it's late."

"Oh, goody!" the child said, her eyes suddenly bright, her face lit with the excitement of adventure. Then she remembered and said, "Where's Ed?"

"He had to go away for a few days."

"You'll be asleep in five minutes in the car," Bill Hogan said, and Katey said, "Bet you I'm not. Bet you I'll stay awake all night till morning."

"Bet you a lollypop," said Hogan.

Norah laid the child on the sofa while she got into her coat and hat. She took a look around, thinking, This is the end of it, now it will be no more; I'll never come back to this house again. She picked the child up again and started moving toward the door.

"I'll put out the lights," Hogan said.

In the car, Norah sat with Katey on her lap and looked into the darkness outside the window. She could see the dim bulk of the house and the low stone wall that surrounded the apple orchard. I loved that house, she thought. She caught her breath as they started down the gravel driveway toward the road, for a wild house-cat had suddenly appeared in front of the car, its eyes blazing in the headlights. Hogan automatically braked the car for a moment, and the cat leaped into the scraggly underbrush that bordered the narrow drive.

"Damn!" he said, "I've stalled the bloody thing."

The cat's eyes flashed once more in the darkness and then were gone.

3

■　　■　　■　　■

THE ROOM IN THE LOW
Hill barracks was full of smoke and the attention of the
men in the room was concentrated on the tall man sitting
in the chair. He was slumped in the chair, as much as a
large man can slump in a hard chair; his legs were crossed,
and his wrists were still cuffed together.

Captain Fenster, who sat in the chair opposite him, with
the other men grouped at random around the room, looked
at the man. There were the same shifty eyes he had seen
so many times before; there were the powerful forearms of
the manual laborer. There was the same surly expression of
the professional; and despite the healthy skin, there were
suggestions of the sickly pallor of the man who had been
in stir.

"You're a handsome cuss," he said to the man. Sloan
didn't answer.

"All right, take your time," Fenster said. "We've been on
this case a week now, and we got all the time in the world."

Sloan said nothing; he kept his eyes focused on the
floor when he didn't glance at the new sneaker on his left
foot.

"A pretty boy," said Fenster. "You did a good job on that Gilbert woman, all right. Thought she had a poke o' dough; only you got foxed that time."

Sloan looked at the detective with contempt; said nothing.

"You might as well get it over with," the captain said. "She spilled the beans."

"She didn' say nothin'," Sloan replied.

Fenster looked around at the other men. "He talks," he said, grinning; the others laughed. "The cat didn't get your tongue after all, did it, Ed?"

"Name's Sloan."

"You're Ed to me," said the detective.

"I never seen you in my life."

"No, but you saw a lot just like me, brother." He dropped his cigarette on the floor, ground it out with his foot. He took out a pack of Camels, lit one, offered one to Sloan.

"I never smoke," said Sloan.

"You're a liar," said the captain. He glanced at Sloan's fingers.

Sloan didn't answer. "Take it," said Fenster, "it ain't doped." He shoved it in Sloan's open mouth till the man gagged, spat it out.

"Take off the cuffs," Fenster said, and a trooper unlocked them.

Sloan rubbed his wrists, looked up at Fenster, who was standing over him, looked down again. If you want a story, he thought, I'll give you a story, you lowdown sonofabitch. He opened his mouth, then closed it.

"Where'd you get the new Chrysler, Ed?" said Fenster.

"My brother lent it t' me."

"Who's he?"

"He's a Navy aviator, went t' China last week on duty."

"Uh-huh," said Fenster. "You used to be a flier yourself, didn't you?"

"Yeh."

"That's what I thought," said Fenster. "All right. Your brother lent you the car to keep for him when he was in China."

"That's right," said Sloan. "He was at the Coast Guard airport in New York. I seen him there las' week."

"Did he lend you the dough, too?"

"What dough?"

"Oh, s . . . , Sloan," said Fenster. "We've checked on every cent you spent since you got back from your little trip last week. Your wife—"

"She don' know nothin'."

"How you know she don't?"

Sloan didn't answer. Instead, he said, "I went t' York State t' raise some money on a mortgage; I own a house down there."

"Where?"

"Near Peekskill."

"Who held the mortgage?"

"Don' know his name."

"Got a paper?"

"No."

"Where was the office?"

"In Peekskill."

"Ever hear of a man named Jim Baldwin, owns a flour mill near Morrisford?"

"No."

"You're an ex-con, ain't you?"

"So what?"

Fenster nodded to the trooper, who snapped the cuffs back on Sloan's wrists. He grasped Sloan's heavy, dark hair

and pulled his head back. Fenster took the butt of his cigarette and inserted it gently in Sloan's nostril; Sloan writhed
in the chair, snorted and expelled the butt.

"Cut it out!" he shouted.

The trooper was still holding him by the hair, and he
tried to get up to relieve the pain; with his other hand, the
trooper punched him in the stomach and he sat down
again. He coughed; his eyes rolled; he bit his lip.

"All right," said Fenster. "You know all the tricks.
Maybe I should teach you a few new ones we thought up
since you got out of the pen three years ago."

He glanced at the men who were standing and sitting
around the room, silent, their eyes on the man in the chair.

"I don't like to waste my time on a heel like you, Sloan,"
he said. "You're a small-time crook and you know it. You
got your hooks in that Gilbert woman—she was a decent
woman before you come along."

"Never mind her," Sloan said. "She's outta this."

"Out of what?"

Sloan did not reply. The trooper had let go of his hair
and he was leaning slightly forward, staring hard at the
large, heavy man who was talking to him. His eyes were
red-rimmed, and he had not shaved that day. His foot hurt.

"Have to hand it to you," Fenster said. "You made a
honest woman of her."

"Keep y'r dirty mouth shut, cop," Sloan said, and the
detective walked over to him and slapped him across the
mouth with the back of his hand. His lips bled, and he
licked them.

Fenster picked up a shoe and held it under Sloan's nose.
"This your shoe?"

"Don' know."

"It matches the other one, don't it?"

"What 'f it does?"

"Take a look at it." He held it in front of Sloan's face, so close that in order to focus his eyes Sloan would have had to look cross-eyed. He didn't look at it. Fenster took out a pencil, ran it through two holes in the upper part of the shoe and held it up for the other men to see.

"Clean through," he said. "An' this lug says he stepped on a spike!"

Sloan didn't reply.

"Where's the gun?" said Fenster.

"I threw it away."

"Oh, you *had* a gun. Why'd you throw it away?"

"I didn' have no license f'r it."

Fenster laughed. "A guy knocks a man off to get a car and throws the gun away because he don't have a license for it!"

The other men laughed and shifted in their chairs, shuffled their feet.

"His wife said he had a brace of guns, Captain," one of the men said, and Sloan thought, I don't believe she did. Anyhow I don't know if she did or not. And until I know what she said I ain't saying nothing. They got nothing on me; they can shove me around because I'm a stiff. All right.

Fenster took out of his pocket the toy pistol Slattery had given him. He held it up, said, "What did you have this cap pistol for, Ed?"

"I used t' stick up banks with it," said Sloan and grinned.

"Say, Captain, there *was* a bank stuck up over in Shoreline, couple weeks ago," one of the men said, and Fenster impatiently said, "I know, I know." He looked at Sloan.

"You know a guy named George Goreski?"

"Met him once," Sloan said, and thought, Oh, Christ, what's the use?

—— 24 ——

"Where?"

"In Deerfield."

"That'll be all," said Fenster. "My wife's waiting supper for me."

He nodded at Slattery and the other men and left the room. Slattery got a straight chair and sat down in front of Sloan and looked at him.

"Look, Ed," he said, "you might 's well save us all this trouble. We know enough as it is to burn you. Your woman told us plenty, but we didn't need her, either. We know you were away last week. Last week a man named Jim Baldwin was knocked off near Morrisford. He had a 1940 Chrysler, the same one that's standing outside; want t' see it?"

He paused, but Sloan was looking at his hands, so he went on. "We found Baldwin; he was shot full of holes. He was carrying about three hundred bucks. You bought a car over in York State for seventy-five bucks, got some tags for it, left the car to be painted, put the tags on the Chrysler. You were pretty dumb, Ed. You were plenty dumb t' think you could get away with that. You were plenty dumb t' hang around for two days an' talk so much. Two people saw you riding with Baldwin. Half a dozen people remember you limping around. Goreski saw your gun; you showed it to him, asked him—"

"You can' pin it on me," said Sloan. "I didn' do it."

"Who did it?"

"Don' know."

"You were there."

"No, I was in New York."

"You want we should go t' work on you, Ed?" Slattery stood up and held out his hand. Another man put into his hand a short length of rubber hose. Slattery smiled at Sloan, who swallowed and looked him in the eyes.

"You c'n make a guy say anything with that," he said contemptuously.

"You're damn tootin'," said the corporal. "So why not say it first? I don't like t' beat no man."

"I got plenty friends," said Sloan. "You better not hit me."

"They can't hear you, Ed."

"Don' hit me," Sloan said, leaning back in the chair. Then he got up. Slattery pushed him back in the chair, and the trooper held his hair again.

"Don' hit me, you yellow-bellied bastard!" Sloan shouted.

■　　■　　■　　■　　*4*

As HOGAN'S CAR PASSED through Rye, then Port Chester and Ford going north again on the crowded Boston Post Road, he felt more and more uneasy. He made it a point to make irrelevant remarks, however, about the ugliness of the highway and the crowded traffic conditions, partly out of a conscious desire to distract Norah, partly out of a growing necessity within himself to be reassured.

When they had got into town Sunday night, he had taken the box, surreptitiously, into the bathroom, so his wife Alice would not notice it, and with nervous fingers undid the cord that tied it. He was relieved, therefore, to find that the gun was wrapped in exactly the way he remembered having wrapped it a month or so before. He took it out of the cloth, stripped it down, and was still more easy in his mind when he smelled it and saw that it was clean and oiled.

Now, as they rode north on Number 7 toward Low Hill, where Norah had been told by long distance telephone her husband was being held, he was becoming uneasy about it again. He looked at her; she was chewing gum. He admired her; she seemed to have perfect control over herself, barring the understandable collapse after they had arrived in the city that night. A horrible experience, he thought, and shuddered.

She turned and smiled at him and said, "You're being damned good to me, Bill," and he smiled back. "I have no right to involve you guys in this mess, but there was no one else to turn to."

"Norah," he said, "about that gun. We have no way of being sure it wasn't used."

"They didn't say anything about a gun being used."

"Well," he said, "suppose we leave it this way. It was dumb of us to bring it into town. I have no license for it, you know. So—" he paused. He wasn't exactly sure that he knew what to do, and he didn't want Norah to get the idea that he was afraid of what he had done or was trying to worm out of whatever slight responsibility he had assumed.

"What shall I say if they ask me about it?" she said.

"Say?" he said. He drew breath, eased his foot off the accelerator, pressed it down again. Here goes, he thought.

—— 27 ——

"Say nothing about it unless they mention it. If they mention it, you can say yes, your former husband had a gun. Tell them where it came from. Tell them I kept it for you after he died. Tell them I brought it back when your second husband asked for it. Tell them the truth," he said, "but don't volunteer any information."

She was worried. She could not remember whether she had admitted ever seeing another gun beside the toy, but she put it out of mind.

"O.K.," she said. "Things can't be much worse than they are already."

Then they were silent as the silent miles moved by the car, South Foremouth and North Foremouth, Burgess. Outside Low Hill they stopped at a diner to get a cup of coffee. Hogan said he would look for a newspaper, and across the road he found a small shop with papers on display. There was a banner headline:

POLK MAN HELD FOR MILLER'S MURDER

EDWIN ALBERTS SLOAN
TELLS ABOUT SHOOTING

BUT CLAIMS A FRIEND FIRED
THE FATAL SHOTS

BUT HE SHARED LOOT

BLOODSTAINED CAR OF VICTIM
FOUND IN HIS POSSESSION

HAS WOUND IN HIS FOOT

Hogan stood outside the diner in an angle where Norah could not see him and hastily scanned the front-page story.

(By A Staff Reporter)

Following a trail that led through the YMCA hotel in Deerfield, State Motor Police brought an investigation into Meadow County yesterday afternoon that led to a farm house near Polk, where they arrested the man they charge with the murder of James T. Baldwin, 56, of Morrisford, Baconsfield County, widely known upstate flour miller.

Baldwin was found shot to death last Thursday in the Baconsfield County section of the State forest. He had been missing since last Sunday, the day, police believe, he was murdered. A member of a searching party of volunteers and WPA workers discovered his body stuffed under a small bridge on a lonely mountain road.

Charged with the crime is Edwin Alberts Sloan, 34, of Polk township, who lived on the old Abbott farm, now owned by Mrs. Ella Horton, and leased by Sloan and his wife. He is in the Low Hill jail, where he was questioned again last night by the arresting officer, Corporal Gordon Slattery of the Low Hill sub-station, and Captain Harry Fenster. Circumstantial evidence from this end points a strong finger of suspicion at Sloan.

Hogan tucked the paper in his overcoat pocket and went into the diner. Norah looked at him and said, "Did you find one?" and he said, "I don't think you'll want to read it now, Norah."

She held out her hand, however, and he gave it to her. She spread the paper out on the table, looked at the headlines, and rested her face in her hands. "Oh, God," she said.

"Keep your nose down, Norah," Hogan said.

"I'm all right," she said. She handed the newspaper to him across the table and said, "Excuse me, Bill." She moved to the end of the diner, where there was a sign that said LADIES. He looked at the paper again:

In his cell last night Sloan vigorously denied killing Baldwin or even knowing him. Police in Baconsfield County, however, told this reporter over long distance telephone this morning that Sloan had been seen in the miller's car a short time before the murder. Sloan, who admits to being an ex-convict, has lived on the Meadow County farm since he was married last March, at the Methodist parsonage in Polk by the Reverend Franklin Halstead a few days after he obtained a marriage license at the county bureau.

His wife's name on the application was Norah S. Gilbert, 35, who had been married previously to Benjamin Gilbert. Mr. Gilbert taught Romance languages in the Olds Academy for one year in 1936 before his sudden death. She has one child by that marriage, and for the three years following her husband's death held a part-time teaching appointment at the same school. Her arrangement with the school was not continued after last spring. She formerly lived in New York City, where she married Gilbert, who had been a pilot in the French Air Force during the World War. This angle of the case is interesting, for it was pointed out that on his marriage application Sloan listed himself as an aviator, and he blames the murder on "an aviator who lives in New York and is attached to the Coast Guard station in Brooklyn." He gave police the name of this man, and this angle is being investigated this morning in an effort to locate the aviator described by Sloan.

When the murder was described in last Friday's Deerfield papers, the Reverend Elwood Proctor, who is connected with the Young Men's Christian Association hotel in that city, gave police some information which connected Sloan with the case. A man of Sloan's description had spent many nights at the YMCA hotel during the past three years, and he told the clergyman . . .

"Shall we go?" Norah said, and Hogan hastily folded the paper and put it in his pocket. They inquired their way to the motor-police barracks and parked the car. It was a small frame building, and they passed through a narrow hall into an office. There was a young man in state trooper's uniform sitting at the reception desk and a much older man in his shirt sleeves was at another desk in the overheated room. A map of the state was on the wall.

To the younger man who looked up and smiled Norah said, "I'm Mrs. Sloan." The older man looked up.

"Yes?" said the young trooper.

"I spoke to someone here—Mr. Slattery—on the phone from New York yesterday, and he said I could have permission to see my husband; they're holding him for—" she could not complete the sentence.

"Sloan?" said the old man, placing his spectacles on his nose. "Tom, tell the captain."

The young man left his desk and went through a door into another room. The older man gestured to Norah and Hogan to take a seat in the straight chairs against the wall and said, "I think they've taken your husband back to Baconsfield County, where it happened."

He looked curiously at Bill, who sat with his hat in his lap and smiled at him. Two or three men in uniform came out of the inner office and walked through the room, glanced casually at the two newcomers, and went into the hall. Hogan was feeling uncomfortable; his throat was dry, but he swallowed and said nothing. The door to the other office opened and a large man came out.

"Mrs. Sloan?" he said.

"Yes," she said, rising.

"Would you mind stepping in here?"

Hogan rose also, advanced toward the man. He did not want to be left alone, and he felt it would be better for Norah if he could come in with her.

"My name's Hogan," he said to the large man. "Friend of Mrs. Sloan. I—"

"I'll talk to you in a minute, if you don't mind," the man said and started back into the inner office. At the door he said, "What was the name?"

"Hogan," Bill said. "William Hogan."

The door closed, and Bill took the newspaper out of his pocket and started on the inner page again:

Last night in the Low Hill jail Sloan admitted that he lied when he told the "spike" story. This morning he told police that he was with "this friend of mine from New York," whom he had known for about five years, and that they went to Baconsfield County together. Sloan said that he wanted to place a small mortgage on a house he owned near Peekskill, New York, but the friend wanted to run up here first. While in Baconsfield, Sloan said, they met the mill operator and his "friend from New York" held him up. Sloan told police that he tried to separate his friend and the miller, and, in the attempt, was shot through the left foot. His story from this point on is very confusing.

He told Corporal Slattery that his "friend from New York" shot the mill operator with a pistol that had a black barrel and a pearl handle. In a coat pocket in Sloan's bedroom last night police found a white-handled cap pistol similar to those used in attempted holdups many times. The real pistol, police believe, was tossed away. . . .

Hogan's eye was caught by a sentence down the page: "We have been hard up, that's true," Mrs. Sloan told police. He heard the door to the hallway close and looked up at the old man, who was looking at him and who said, "I'd like to see that paper, young man," and stretched out his hand. Hogan smiled at being addressed as "young man" and reluctantly held out the paper.

The young trooper, who was leaning against a filing cabinet, said, "That's this gentleman's paper, Major," and the major said, "That so?" and looked at him again. "Hmm," he said and folded the paper carefully and put it aside. "I'll take care of it," he said. "What's your name?"

"Hogan."

"Oh, yes," said the Major, as though he knew something he preferred not to mention. Bill could hear Norah's muffled voice through the door, and then the door opened and the large man came out and closed it carefully behind him. He looked at the man sitting in the chair.

"Your name is Hogan?" he said.

"That's right," Bill smiled.

"Where's Sloan's gun?" Captain Fenster said.

Bill heard himself say, "What gun?" Then he knew definitely that he had said the wrong thing; that he could not lie to this man, no matter how he tried. His heart thumped, and he looked at the man, waiting to hear what he would say. Fenster stared at him, and his tongue moved in his cheek.

"Oh," he said. "What gun, eh? I suppose you don't know there was a gun in that house?"

"Why, yes," said Hogan, "I did. But it wasn't Sloan's gun; it was mine—"

"Oh," said Fenster, "it was your gun?"

"That is," said Hogan, "I was keeping it, I brought it—" he stopped.

"And where is it now?" said Captain Fenster.

"It's in New York."

"Oh," said Fenster, "it's in New York. Where in New York?"

"At my apartment."

"I see," said Fenster and opened the door to his office. He nodded to Norah, who came out into the outer office. Her face was pale, and there was an apologetic expression on it as she looked at Bill. She lifted her hand and sat down next to him.

"There're some men coming from over Morrisford-way," said Fenster. "I'll have to ask you to wait till they get here. They'll have some questions to ask."

He looked at Hogan, smiled, and said, "Why did you have to lie about that gun?"

5

. . . .

OLD ELLA HORTON HAD
told her, Norah remembered. She thought of Ella as old,
but she couldn't have been more than forty-five at the
outside. But she was one of those women who look old
long before their time. She could remember her saying,
"There's a man does handy work for me, name o' Sloan."
That was a year ago this spring, Norah recalled; she had
even seen the man when she passed the Horton place to
get the bus that took her in to Olds, those days she had
work to do. He was working in the fields early that spring,
stripped to the waist. And she remembered this, because it
was not usual to see farm workers in New England who
took off their shirts in the field.

"I'll send him up soon's he finishes with our plowin',"
Ella said. "He could do the shinglin' for you."

"There's no hurry," Norah said and did not add what
she was thinking: If I could pay for the shingles, Ella could
take it off the rent; and if I could pay something on the
rent, Hortons would pay for the shingling themselves. Old
Sam Horton might be bed-ridden, but he must have some
money put away by the looks of the way they kept the

place up and the fact that they rarely pressed her for the twenty-dollar rent.

She had a feeling they would have liked her to move. The Gilberts had not made any real friends in the neighborhood, for ever since they had moved to Polk in 1935, they had kept pretty much to themselves, resisting invitations to participate in community affairs. Ben had a mildly sarcastic way of speaking that almost invariably rubbed people the wrong way. But the school had no complaint about his work. He did his job and minded his own business, and his scholars learned the languages he taught. But when he got home on the bus from Olds, he said that he was home, and he didn't want to go out again. "*J'y suis, j'y reste,*" he used to say. Unlike his wife, he seemed to have a definite dislike for people.

Later that spring Ed Sloan came up the narrow road from the Horton place, driving a small truckload of shingles. He came around to the back door, wearing a white sleeveless shirt and a carpenter's duck cap, and the first thing Norah noticed about the man was the powerful musculature of his arms.

He touched the cap with one finger, said, "Miz Horton says how I should shingle y'r roof."

"Why," said Norah, "I didn't order any shingles."

Sloan grinned, showing his uneven teeth, and said, "These shingles was layin' 'round the place, not doin' nobody no good, so I told her we c'd use 'em on y'r house."

He drove the truck around past the house and started to unload the shingles, stacking them in even rows. Katey stood by the truck watching him. She watched him as he set up a scaffold on one side of the house with two-by-fours he found in the old shed, and she asked him a lot of questions that he did not answer. It took him the best part of a week to shingle the roof. During part of the time Norah had some classes at the academy and had to call in Sally Prago, the fifteen-year-old daughter of a poor farmer who lived up on the hill, to keep an eye on Katey while she was gone. Sally had bright, dark eyes and was wise beyond her years.

"That man you got workin' on your roof," she said. "He's a bad 'un."

"Why?" said Norah.

"Dunno," said Sally, "but folks hereabouts says he's a bad 'un. Ain't got no place of his own, runs all 'round the country."

"There's nothing wrong with that, Sally."

"Dunno," she said, and went home with the half dollar Norah had paid her for minding the child. Katey was nowhere in sight, and her mother went outdoors to look for her. She walked toward the shed where Sloan had been stacking the remaining shingles and the two-by-fours that he had used, and she heard his voice and stopped to listen. She could not make out what he was saying, but through a broad crack in the wall of the shed she could see Katey's blue overalls, and then she heard her squeaky voice.

"What then?" the child said, and her mother moved closer to the shed.

"Why then the pollywog that didn' have no tail looked at the other pollywogs an' says, 'You guys don' need t' think y'r so smart 'cause you got tails an' I ain' got a tail—' "

"Didn't he really have a tail?" Katey said.

"He really didn' have no tail at all," Sloan was saying, "an' that made him feel bad 'cause nobody likes not t' have what everybody else has got, even if it's on'y a tail."

"So what did he do?"

"Nothin' to it," the man said. "He hid hisself un'er a lilypad an' when a certain pollywog come along that he didn' like—his name was George—he come out an' he snapped his tail right off. Then he waited till one by one all the other pollywogs inna pond come swimmin' by, an' one by one he snapped off all their tails, so that none of 'em had a tail an' then they was all alike."

"That's not a very nice story," Norah said, walking into the shed, smiling, and Sloan rose from the block of wood on which he had been sitting. He blushed.

"Why didn't the pollywog go out and buy a tail?" Katey said.

"He didn' have no money," Sloan replied and started to walk out of the shed.

"Would you like to wash up and have a cup of coffee?" Norah said.

"No, thanks," the man said, and he was gone.

She was sorry he had gone, because she would have liked to talk to him. She would have liked to talk to someone, and she sensed that he was carrying a loneliness that matched her own. When Katey had gone to bed that night, she stood and looked into her mirror and heard herself talking out loud. A pretty pass, she thought. When you get to talking to yourself, you've lived too long alone.

She sat in the chair in her downstairs room and stared at the bookcase on the other side of the room. There was not a book she had not read; there was not a book she cared to reread. She had exhausted the meager roster of activities that people engage in who live alone. She had done sewing and knitting and embroidery; she had played solitaire, even to inventing variations on the game. She had tried to write and had played around with sketching; she had worked cross-word puzzles and anagrams and cutouts that, when put together, made a pattern. She listened to the radio, and she played on the small piano they had brought from New

York; she had even taught herself to improvise. She had pondered long over her life with her dead husband, whom she had always liked and admired, even though their union had not been blessed by such love as one reads about in books. She had written long letters to her daughter and had thought of writing enough of them to make a book, but when she reread what she had written, even though it had been written out of singular emotion, it seemed platitudinous and far from sound. (Now she thought she heard someone moving outside the house, and went onto the porch. No one was there. I must be getting the jitters, she thought.)

In the course of that summer Sloan worked for her several times. He put in a small garden and came up every afternoon to tend the weeds. He built a small henhouse and gave her advice about the care of chickens. Katey followed him around like a dog and had taken to accompanying him on some of his routine chores around the Horton place. She rode on the manure spreader that spring; she rode on the hay wagon that carried in the first summer crop, and Norah was delighted that the child had found a companion, even though he was so much older. Sloan did not seem to mind her tagging after him, and he told her innumerable stories that he made up as he went along.

It had been weeks before Norah succeeded in getting him to come into the house and sit and drink a cup of coffee. She had recognized that she was making what might have been called "advances" to the man, and she thought, And what's the harm? It's good to have another human being to talk to; it's good to talk to a man. What ever happened to me, she wondered, that at the age of thirty-five, I have so few friends in the world?

Her father had died when she was a child, and her

mother survived him by four years. The aunt who had brought her up had died the year she was graduated from college. There was a series of jobs to keep herself alive— proof-reading and office-work, a stretch in the theater till she found out she had no talent as an actress, the urge to see the country. She had lived in New York and Philadelphia, in Washington and Boston, on the East Coast and the West. In retrospect there was no point and there was no direction.

I'm a woman without talent, she thought; but I'm a good woman; I have no harm in me; there's something I could do. When Ben had said, "Let's get married; there's no sense in playing around like this. Let's settle down and have a home," she had thought, What more could a woman want? Back of it there was a decency, both in Ben and in herself, that couldn't be denied. We were good people, she thought—he was a good person, even if he would have disapproved of this man sitting here, of my being what he would have called "intimate" with him.

She looked at the man in the old trousers, the battered shoes and the sleeveless shirt who sat uncomfortably in the chair across the table from her. He held a saucer in his gnarled hands, and his body was twisted with embarrassment. He had a high color and deep gray eyes that looked at her steadily despite his reticence.

"You get lonesome livin' here alone," he said.

She started, then laughed and said, "Once in awhile, sure, who wouldn't?"

"Don' you have no friends?"

"Sure," she said, "lots of 'em—all over the United States. I never see most of them."

"You been t' school, learned a lot o' books."

"Too many," she said. "What makes you so curious?"

"I like t' study out people, find out about 'em. I met a lot o' folks in my time, all over the world. You see me workin' in the field down at the Horton place, you don' know who I am."

He paused and said nothing for a time. She did not answer what he said, for she wanted to see if he would overcome his embarrassment.

He licked his lips and said, "I seen you." He didn't continue, and she didn't know what he meant, but she let the subject drop. Instead, to make him feel at ease, she began to talk about herself. He listened with his head cocked on one side, not looking at her for a time, but with a faint smile upon his lips. She told him the general story of her life, or as much of it as she wanted him to know. She told him about Ben; went upstairs and brought down a picture of him in his air-force uniform. He looked at it and smiled.

He held the picture and said, "This guy cared a lot f'r you, didn' he?"

"I guess he did," she said. "Why do you ask?"

"Anyone c'd tell it from the picture."

She laughed. "The picture was made years before we met."

"That ain' what I meant."

He put the picture down, rose from the table and said, "I got the milkin' t' do now," and added, "Good-by," and went out. He came right back again and, standing in the door, he said, "You know what folks'd say 'f they seen me comin' here."

"I know," she said. "Does it matter to you?"

"Not t' me," he said. "I got a bad name a'ready. To you."

"Why have you got a bad name?" (She thought of Sally Prago.)

"Ast no questions," he said. "I tell you no lies. On'y I

—— 41 ——

c'd spin you a yarn sometime that would make y'r hair stand on end."

Then he was gone, and somehow the loneliness was even greater than before. She did not see him for a month and Ella Horton told her he had gone away, but he came back late one afternoon in early fall, riding a new bicycle he said he had bought in Shoreline, and she was so glad to see him that she said, "A bicycle! I haven't ridden a bike in years!"

"Hop on," he said, and she straddled the wheel and pedaled down the driveway to the road, and up the road past Hortons' to the main road, then turned around without falling off and came back down again. Ella waved to her from her window, and she waved back and almost lost control of the machine, then went through the light growth of trees back up to the house.

"You're good," he said, grinning. "I'll show you a trick."

He mounted the bicycle and, holding the handle bars, yanked the front wheel off the ground and pedaled around the dooryard on one wheel. He fell off and scraped his elbow, and she insisted on bathing it with peroxide.

"Where'd you learn to do that?" she said.

"Inna circus. I once traveled with a circus."

"Go on," she said.

"Sure," he said, "I was a trick clown in Sells-Floto once."

"I don't believe you."

"I c'd tell you more, but you wouldn' believe that neither."

They sat in the living room after Norah had put Katey to bed and made some whole-wheat sandwiches with lettuce and tomato and cucumber in them, and some tea.

"There's not much to eat in this house," she said.

"You get paid good over t' the school, Olds-way?"

"No," she said. "I could manage more easily if the work were steady, but it's only part time."

"You c'd mebbe learn me t' speak good English."

"Why not?" she said.

"I never had no education."

"That's not important."

"You don' think so?" he said. "Lots o' folks do. What you do inna summer when school ain' keepin'?"

"That's the hardest time," she said. "I save a little from what I make—I've made preserves the last few summers and sold them around the neighborhood."

"I know," he said. "I et some once. I know a lot about you you don' think I do. You don' know nothin' about me."

"All right," she said. "Suppose you tell me about yourself?"

"I didn' like t' tell it, 'cause o' y'r husband," he said, "but I was a flier once myself."

"A pilot?" she said and lifted her eyebrows.

"You don' want t' hear about it," he said.

"Sure."

"I was inna Army," he said, "till a few years ago. I cracked up a ship down Kentucky."

He lifted his trouser leg, revealing a long, gnarled, white scar. "An' that ain' all," he said. "Fog-flyin'. I cracked her up against a hill; got a piece o' steel in my head still," he said, pointing to his forehead between the eyes. "The stick went right in my stomach. Guy with me got killed."

She shook her head and bit her lower lip, and suddenly she heard Ben's World War stories all over again; she had always felt those stories in her body—the giddy soaring and the centrifugal bank, the rattle of the machine guns as he described them, the pilot gritting his teeth, the burst of

—— 43 ——

crackling flame and the falling plane, the heavy, black smoke trailing like a plume from heaven to earth.

Ed was standing at her side, his hand timidly on her shoulder. "Keep y'r nose down," he said. "I tol' you I shouldn' have ought t' say it."

"It's all right," she said, "go on."

She smiled at him, tentatively touched his hand. He went back to his chair and looked at her, his large hands clasped on his knees, his back bent.

"I was over a year inna hospital," he said. "They wanted t' git me back again."

"Do you want to go back?"

"Not on y'r life," he said. "I'm scared. I los' my nerve."

She wondered how much of what he had told her was true, and she looked at him, but he was not smiling; he had a distracted light in his eyes that she had seen in many men and many women in many places. She remembered a man who had lived in a furnished room next to hers in Seattle. He was a small man who wore high heels and had had his trousers lengthened in the hope of concealing them. He was a foreigner, and he always bowed to her when they met in the hall, and he too had just such a look in his eyes.

"You haven't had an easy time, have you, pal?" she said.

"What the hell?" he said. "Who has? I made plenty in my time; would surprise you. Made it an' pissed it away— excuse me," he said, and they both laughed.

"Owned a service station once, owned a auto agency— Studebaker; used t' race cars, drilled oil wells, joined the Army. Brother o' mine's in the Coast Guard air force, down Pensacola-way."

He got up and walked up and down in the room. He stood at the window and looked out into the night. He felt that he had said too much to this strange woman, and he did not intend to say any more. Norah could feel him closing up, and she knew the reason for his sudden silence. She sat where she was, however, and did not move. She waited till he turned around, and then she smiled at him. It was not coquetry but encouragement; she wanted him to know that wherever he had been, whatever he had done, he could consider that she looked on him with favor; that she recognized his independent and valuable existence as another human being; that she was not trying to pry, but neither was she cutting herself off from him, or from anyone. She was not exactly certain that he understood what she was feeling.

"I'll see if Katey's covered," she said. "The nights are beginning to get cold."

He grinned at her and watched her as she mounted the stairs, then sat down in the chair by the table and picked up a magazine. He looked at all the pictures, but he was aware that he was not really looking at them with particular interest; he was listening for her to come down again. When she came down, he stood up and said, "I'll be goin' now."

"Come again—Ed," she said. "You don't mind if I call you Ed, do you?"

"Hell no," he said, "Miz Gilbert."

"Norah to you," she said, and he replied, "I might have a hard time sayin' it."

"Try it."

He opened his mouth, then said, "I'd ruther not, if it's alla same t' you."

He smiled at her, his head on one side. "I got a house down near Peekskill, New York," he said. "If I ever git my hands on a car, I'd like t' take you down t' see it, some time, if you'd go with me."

"I'd love to go some time."

"It ain' a much," he said.

She said nothing.

"Well," he said, "I'll be suin' ya one o' these days." He nodded toward the upper story, said, "You got a right smart young 'un there."

"I like her," Norah said.

"She's a caution," Sloan said. "Kin ast more questions inna minute than I c'd answer inna week. Besides, I ain' too smart, you know."

"Oh, you'll get by."

"Mebbe," he said. "But I'm nuts about y'r kid. Wish she was mine."

He closed the door behind him, and she heard the bell of his bicycle as he coasted down the driveway into the road back to Horton's place.

■ ■ ■ ■ *6*

THEY SAT IN THE OUTER office side by side. The older man who had been addressed as Major had gone home for the day—it was about two o'clock—and the tall, heavy man named Fenster was in his own office. They could hear him talking through the wall.

They did not say much to each other, but they both knew there was a guard on the door into the outer hallway, although they had not seen him; and although the young trooper who sat at the desk was scrupulously paying no attention to them, they knew he was listening.

Then Fenster's door opened, and he came in with several other men and said, "All right, Mr. Hogan."

Hogan took off his overcoat and laid it on top of the filing cabinet, placed his hat on top of it. He glanced at Norah and smiled, and she lifted her chin with a slight gesture. He walked toward the door and it was opened, and he was accompanied up the stairs by the men, some of them in front of him, and some behind. At the top of the stairs they directed him into a large room that was apparently a dormitory for the troopers; there were several cots and various items of clothing and equipment hung on the walls. There was a large wardrobe with a full-length mirror. Fenster introduced him to one of the plain-clothes men, but as usual, he could not catch the name. The other men looked at him, and Fenster placed a chair in the middle of the floor, indicating that Hogan was to sit in it.

He looked around at the seven men who were in the room and who arranged themselves in a rough open square about him. It's like a moving picture, he thought; the psychology was obvious—isolate him in the middle of an open space and make him feel uncomfortable. He *was* uncomfortable; he was aware that his hands were trembling and that there was a strained sensation in his chest. It reminded him of the first time he had climbed into his Nieuport near the western front and knew that he was going on patrol. (Combat maneuvers were not actual combat.) The unknown was just around the corner, and he was becoming aware that he had made a serious mistake.

"Now, Mr. Hogan," Fenster said, "Lieutenant Partrick here would like to hear all you know about that gun."

Hogan looked at the man Fenster had indicated; he was seated on the edge of a cot. He had a heavy, hawk-like face, the nose was strong, the eyes were cold. He had a toothpick in his mouth, and he looked as though he could not easily be impressed by anything. Fenster's face, in contrast, seemed blurred and out of focus, soft.

"That's simple," Hogan said, fishing for a cigarette. "The gun used to belong to Ben Gilbert, Mrs. Sloan's first husband. He died about four years ago. Kept it as a souvenir, I guess. He was a pilot in the first World War, French Air Corps. I was in his outfit, knew him from college days at Dartmouth. I didn't know he'd kept the gun till after he died, when Norah—that's Mrs. Gilbert, Sloan I mean—asked me to keep it; she was nervous having it around the house, afraid the little girl might get hold of it."

He paused, tapped the ashes off the cigarette. He could feel the perspiration creeping in his armpits and thought, What the Christ am I getting nervous about? I didn't do anything. He looked at the men. A short, thin man was taking notes; Fenster was looking at his shoe; Partrick sucked his toothpick and looked at him. Hogan gestured with his hand.

"After Norah married Sloan—I came up with my wife and child to visit. Sloan asked me if I would bring the gun the next time we came, said there were some skunks and porcupines around."

Hogan laughed nervously. "I told him if he could hit a skunk with a .38 automatic he must be a dead shot. I'm pretty good myself, but I could never do that. That's funny," he said, "I never thought of that—I mean—a couple months ago when I brought the gun, that day we had some target practice. I fired it, my wife fired it, Norah fired it, but Sloan didn't."

He felt that now he could not stop talking; he knew that now he would have to say something that made sense, because he was aware that he was not making very good sense.

"Anyhow," he said, "we must have fired about fifteen-twenty rounds. I stripped the gun and cleaned it, oiled it, wrapped it in a cloth I had, put the whole thing, holster and all, back in a box."

"What sort of a box?"

"It was a book box, a box you mail books in. I tied the box up. I remember when I was cleaning it, Sloan was sitting next to me. I said, 'Beautiful, isn't it?' meaning I thought it was a fine piece of mechanism. Sloan shook his head and said, 'I don't like the things.' I tied it all up tight and Norah put it away, I guess."

He took out another cigarette and lit it from the butt, and he could not control the shaking of his hands. He knew that the men saw his hands shaking, and he thought, What can they make of *that?* One of them handed him an ashtray, which he held on his knee.

"What else, Mr. Hogan?" said Fenster. Partrick said nothing.

"Well, nothing much," Bill said, "except that Sunday night Mrs. Sloan called and asked me if it should be necessary, could I come down and get her and her daughter and bring them to the city. I asked her what had happened, and she said she couldn't tell me on the phone. I had a feeling something had gone wrong, naturally. That must have been seven o'clock. She called back an hour and a half later and asked if I could come. I did. She told me her husband was being held by the police—"

"Did she tell you what for?"

"Why, yes," he said. "For murder. She didn't know anything about it. Naturally, I thought of the gun and asked where it was. She said it was there. I knew she didn't have a license for it, and I didn't think it would be a good thing to be found—"

"Why not?"

"Well," he said, and paused. "Well—I felt responsible about it, and I don't know, it was pretty dumb of me I guess, but I didn't know anything about a gun being used, so I brought it to New York with me. It's there now. I'm sure it wasn't used; I examined it. It was cleaned and oiled and wrapped exactly the way I left it when I was down there."

"You say you knew something was wrong, Mr. Hogan. How did you know that?"

"I didn't say I knew, I said I *felt* something had gone wrong."

"Why did you feel something went wrong?"

"Well—Sloan isn't like Norah's, Mrs. Gilbert's, first husband—I didn't know anything about him. I don't think she knew much about him either. He's an uneducated man, and she's a cultured, intelligent woman. I didn't exactly think she should have married—"

"You're a good friend of hers?"

"I've known her ever since she married my friend Gilbert."

"You was in love with her yourself?"

"No, of course not."

"Then what business was it of yours who she married?"

"Well," said Hogan. "I don't suppose it's any of my business, but she's a good friend of mine."

"Did she ask for your advice?"

"No."

"Did you try to stop the marriage?"

"I tried to talk her out of it."

"Why?"

"Well," he said, "I have nothing against a man because he's uneducated or poor, in fact I have nothing but sympathy for Sloan—" That was a foolish thing to say to these bastards, he thought.

"You're a communist, ain't you?"

"No, I'm not."

"Make a good living from your writing?"

"Not very." He thought he would like to switch the subject, so he said, "How did you know I was a writer?"

"We saw a book you wrote over at the place. About flying in the last war. You didn't approve of it, did you?"

"Why, no," he said, "but what's that got—?"

"All right, skip it, only stop kidding us, Hogan," Fenster said. "You lied once about the gun— 'What gun?' you said —and you're lying now."

Hogan swallowed and said nothing. Then he said weakly, "I'm not."

"How long did it take you to drive up to Polk Sunday night?"

"About an hour and a quarter."

"That's pretty fast, ain't it?" said Fenster. "You were in pretty much of a hurry."

"Well, naturally, I thought something had gone wrong."

"What did you think had gone wrong?"

"I don't know, I didn't think."

Partrick took the toothpick out of his mouth and rubbed his chin. "When did you bring this gun to Sloan?" he said.

"About two months ago, this fall."

"When did he ask you for it?"

"Last summer, must have been in July—July Fourth, matter of fact."

"He didn't tell you he wanted it to pull a stickup?"

"Of course not."

"Why of course not?"

"Well, if he was planning a stickup," Hogan said, "would he have told me about it?"

"He might," said Partrick. "Especially if he cased it with you."

"You knew they were broke?" Fenster said.

"Of course—I used to send Norah a check once in a while, when I sold a story, could afford it."

"Why?"

"I told you, she was a friend of mine—we knew she was hard up since her husband died; matter of fact, they were hard up before he died, but since then she's had a pretty tough time."

"You knew Sloan claims to be an aviator—what was the name he gave us?" Fenster said, turning to the short, thin man who was taking notes. "The man he said did the shooting?"

"Logan," Corporal Slattery said, looking at Hogan with his soft brown eyes. Hogan opened his mouth to speak, remembered that he had not been accused of anything yet, and shut it.

"What were you going to say?"

"Nothing."

"You still fly?" Fenster said.

"When I have the money."

"Now," said Fenster, "you're supposed to be an intelligent man, a writer. Now just listen to the story you told us, and see if you'd believe it if you saw it written in a book. You're a man with no money. So were the Sloans. You're a good friend of theirs. They're hard up. You have a gun belongs to her husband. He asks you to give it to him and you give it to him. He goes out and knocks a man off with that gun, swipes the car, and takes a few hundred bucks off the stiff. We don't know where all that dough went yet. For all we know you got some of it. In fact, the first story he told us, you did the shooting."

"*I* did?" Hogan said. "Why . . . he's lying. I can't—" The dirty low-down bastard, he thought, the lousy son of a bitch.

"We bring him in—he left a trail a mile wide from Morrisford to York State, and back again. He lied like hell. Had a bullet hole in his foot, said he got it stepping on a spike. Then he said he got it when you plugged this guy and he tried to stop you. Gave us your name."

"He gave you my name!"

"Your name's Logan, ain't it?"

"Hogan."

"Said you gave him the gun, cased the job with him, and he was to take the rap if he got caught. You knew he was an ex-con, didn't you?"

"No, I didn't."

"Sure, he's got a record a mile long, ever since he was a kid fourteen. He's a bad egg, that boy, we know him."

"Why would a man do a thing like that?" Hogan said. "Hell, I've been hard up most of my life, but I'd never think of sticking a man up with a gun."

The men in the room smiled, and Fenster said, "The motive's plain enough—he wanted the money." He scratched his head. "What was I saying? Oh, yes. O.K. His wife sends for you the minute he's nabbed. You come running up here in record time, she tells you there's been a murder, you take the gun and the woman and the kid and run to New York with it."

"How do you know it's the gun that was used in the murder?" Hogan said.

"It's a German gun, ain't it?" Fenster said.

"Yes."

"Nine millimeter, Luger, clip holds eight cartridges?"

"Yes."

"Had a piece of black friction tape on the grips?"

"Yes."

"That's the gun all right," Fenster said.

"Christ," said Hogan. "All the way to New York I had an impulse to throw the damned thing in the bushes."

"You did, eh?"

"It was pretty dumb of me, all right. If I'd done that—let me call my wife in New York and have her deliver it to the police there."

"We'll take care of that," Partrick grinned. "We don't use the telephone. The New York Homicide Bureau's got the case now. They'll send someone around to your house all right, and the gun better *be* there."

"If I'd thrown it away," Hogan said, "I'd sure be in hot water."

"You're in plenty of hot water now, brother," Partrick said, smiling. . . .

. . . "Your friend thought maybe you'd better come upstairs, Mrs. Sloan, where you can lie down," said Slattery.

"Thank you," she said. "I guess I'm pretty tired." She followed the corporal up the stairs, and she decided that she liked him; he'd been very decent to her. She wondered how poor Bill was making out; she could hear the men in the other room, hear his voice speaking with the urgent tone she knew so well. She thought that perhaps she should have paid more attention to him the last time she heard that tone of voice; but that was oversimplified, and what was past was past. I couldn't have done anything else, she thought.

In the empty room that had a few narrow cots against the walls, she lay down, and Slattery closed the door behind him. Through the wall behind her head she could hear the men talking, but it was difficult to make out the words. Then they stopped talking and she could hear them coming down the hall, and she sat up.

They came into the room, six of them, and sat down in various places. They asked her if she minded if they smoked, and they offered her a cigarette, which she accepted. Slattery was with them, and he had a notebook, in which he was apparently taking notes on what she said. I have no intention of lying, she thought; what is there to lie about?

"Now, Mrs. Sloan," they said, "about that gun. You told the arresting officer here"—Fenster nodded at Slattery—"that you didn't know your husband had a gun."

"No," she said, "no—I believe I said I had seen a pistol. I don't know anything about pistols, I never touched it."

"Have you ever fired a pistol?"

"Well, yes," she said, and thought, My God, what have I said!

"When was that?"

"When Mr. Hogan and his wife were visiting us, about two months ago that must have been."

"Didn't Mr. Hogan bring a pistol to your house?"

"He did."

"It belonged to your husband—Mr. Gilbert?"

"That's right."

"And Hogan brought it because your second husband asked him to?"

"I didn't know that. I told Ed not to ask for it. He asked me if Bill—that's Mr. Hogan—would bring it if he asked for it. And I said I didn't want it around the house, and he coaxed me until I said, 'You know how I feel about that,' and he said, 'Don't worry.' "

"You just said you didn't *know* your husband asked for it."

"Did I say that?" she said, passing her hand across her face. "I don't remember saying that. I meant—"

"Never mind what you meant. On Sunday night you said you didn't know your husband had a gun, but you *did* know he had a gun, and you knew it was in the house, because Hogan brought it there, and you fired it, and you put it away in a box in a closet—"

"No," she said and glanced at Slattery, who seemed nervous and was biting his lips.

"I give you my word of honor," she said, "that I didn't think of it. I was upset. I simply didn't think of it at the time. Yes, I knew it was in the house, put away, and when Ed was gone longer than he said he'd be, I was worried, and I lifted the box. It was heavy, so I thought the gun was there."

"Listen, Mrs. Sloan," Partrick said, fishing for a new toothpick, "you want us to believe that when the officer came and arrested your husband for murder, and you knew there was a gun in the house, you never connected that gun with the murder—"

"I never."

"—and you knew the officers were searching the house for a gun, and you simply didn't remember that gun was upstairs, and they came downstairs with the toy gun and asked you if you'd ever seen another, and you said no, didn't you?"

"No."

"You *didn't* say no when they asked you if you'd ever seen another gun?"

"I knew I'd seen a gun, but I didn't know the one I'd seen was—" she paused, wet her lips, and said, "Would you mind if I stretched out a minute? Would you please give me a minute to rest, otherwise you're likely to find me on the floor."

"Go ahead," Fenster said. She lay back on the bed and closed her eyes and put her arm across her face. I don't know what to say, she thought. I don't know what to think. She counted slowly and silently to one hundred, then to two hundred. While she was still counting someone touched her, and she opened her eyes and drank the glass of water Slattery had brought her. He looked grateful to her; she could see that he was glad she had not mentioned the fact that he had instructed his companion not to "touch the lady's things." She smiled at him.

"What were your relations with Mr. Hogan?" Partrick said.

"I'm telling you the truth," she said. "So help me God I'm telling you the truth. If I can't tell you any more it's because I don't know any more and I've *told* you—"

"What were your relations with Mr. Hogan?"

"I don't know what you mean."

"Was he your boy friend?"

"Of course not," she said. "He was my former husband's friend; he's been a friend of mine for seven years."

"Did he like Sloan?"

"I don't know."

"Did Sloan like him?"

"I think so, yes."

"Did Hogan know you were broke?"

"He helped me occasionally."

"After you were married, too?"

"Occasionally."

"You didn't know your husband was going to pull a holdup?"

"No."

"He didn't tell you when he came back?"

"No, I could see he was trying to tell me something, but no."

"You thought he got the money on this mortgage?"

"Yes."

"You thought he owned a house?"

"I *saw* it."

"You thought the car belonged to his brother?"

"He said so."

"You never met his brother?"

"No."

"What do you think of Sloan now?"

"I love him," she said. "He was kind to me." Her eyes were wet. "He was kind to my little girl." She looked at Partrick and said, "Have you any children?"

"Naw," he said. . . .

. . . The trooper who was guarding Hogan sat sidewise in a straight chair, holding a detective-story magazine on his lap and a cigarette in his mouth. There was a tiny gold cross in the lapel of his dark blue suit, and Hogan could not take his eyes off that cross.

"Yeh," said the trooper, "this guy Sloan had us on the run all right."

Hogan did not answer. He was walking up and down in

the room (his legs ached), smoking one cigarette after another. It was dark outside now; the men who questioned him had left him and come back again and left him and come back again many times. Each time they came, he sat in his chair in the middle of the room and answered questions. Then they left again. I suppose they're checking my story against Norah's, he thought. Christ alone knows what she's said. He had heard her voice through the wall of the room, pleading, urgent, strained.

"Well," the guard said, "maybe you'll write a story about it some time."

"If I ever get *out* of this mess," said Hogan.

The guard laughed, shook his head. He lit a new cigarette, turned to his magazine, and said, as an afterthought, "He'll burn."

"What do you think made him say I did the shooting?" Hogan said, and the trooper looked up at him.

"Who knows?" he said. "He lied like hell at first. Said he threw the rod away, an' we said, O.K., tomorrow we'll go over the road from Morrisford to Polk, an' you can find it. That was Sunday night. Yesterday he switched his story, said the gun was in his house. We took him there, it wasn't. By that time we didn' believe nothing he said. He said his wife must of took it. He lied like hell till this morning. So we—we interrogated him," the guard said, tripping over the long word, "an' he come clean. He's no good, that boy. Poor white trash like we got a lot of in the mountains. You oughtta see the way they live. Get outta hand once in a while, but we know how t' keep 'em in line. Ain't had much trouble with 'em for a year or so. We sent out a flash to New York for his wife, but she wasn't there—she was on her way down here with you, I guess," he said, looking at Hogan. "So we just sit an' wait an' here you are."

"If I knew anything about this business, do you think I'd walk in here?"

"No, I don' suppose you would of," the trooper said.

Hogan looked out of the window into the dark street beyond. The Chrysler was still standing in front of the house, and the new Ford convertible he was buying on the installment plan was parked behind it. He wondered what would happen if— Then the door opened and the short, thin man with the soft brown eyes came in and said, "Well, New York has got the gun."

"That's good," Hogan said, thinking of Alice and her frightened face. "I told you it was there."

"Yeh," said Slattery. "It was there all right; good thing for you." He looked at Hogan and said, "I wish t' hell you hadn't taken it t' New York. They're gonna hold you anyhow. They're not satisfied with your story."

"May I phone my wife?"

"You can do that later," Slattery said. "You may go t' Baconsfield tonight."

"Baconsfield," Hogan said and swallowed. That was on the western border of the state.

"They're pretty burned up over there," said Slattery. "The guy that got bumped off hired a lot of folks in his flour mill; now it's shut down."

Hogan saw a picture in his mind and immediately blanked it out. But I didn't, he thought, I don't, this is *insane*. He saw Norah come in the door. Her body was drooping, and she sat down in a chair near him and sighed. She looked at him and shook her head.

"Bill," she said. "I'm sorry, Bill." Her eyes were red from weeping. "What will happen to the baby now?" she said.

Hogan said, "Don't worry, Norah."

She put her face in her hands, then shook her body and

—— 60 ——

sat up again. He offered her the last cigarette he had and crumpled the package.

"Don't worry none," Slattery said. "Things'll get straightened out. They're callin' the Major now t' find out what t' do." *That* stupid bastard, Hogan thought.

Ten to twenty years, he thought. It's ridiculous. I didn't do anything but a stupid thing; we didn't either of us do anything that was wrong. Surely they would, *should* believe the truth when you tell it. Surely they should know when you're telling the truth, even if you did pull a dumb stunt and even if you did get nervous when they questioned you, anyone would get nervous, you can make an innocent man look guilty as all hell with that stuff. A pure technicality. Like their saying, "You lied about those phone calls, Hogan. You said she called you at seven and eight-thirty. That's a lie, because we didn't bring him *in* till eight-thirty."

That stumped me, he thought. "I don't know when you brought him in," I said, "but I know that was the time she called." Then they went away again. That bastard, he thought; it's one thing to sympathize with a guy because he's down and out and another to have him involve you in a murder. Ten years for a technicality, concealing the evidence of a crime, accessory, Sullivan law. How was I to know? My feeling about that guy was right in the first place, he thought; my feeling was right. I don't want to be mixed up in this, he thought; I don't want to have anything to do with this. You should have thought of that before.

They all came into the room again, and Partrick, the man from Morrisford, was grinning. He offered Hogan a cigarette and said, "Well, you know, we could hold you for this, Mr. Hogan, and I don't know what would happen to you if we took you over to Baconsfield County. The folks back there are seein' red. It's only a small county jail, and you'd be the only prisoners there, you and Sloan and his wife."

He looked at Norah, who sat with her hands clasped in her lap, her underlip caught under her teeth. "You co-operated with us," Partrick said, "an' we're gonna co-oper-ate with you. We're gonna let you go now, but I want you to keep in touch with us." He handed his card to both Norah and Hogan. "This thing can be reopened any time."

Norah was staring at him wide-eyed. Tears were form-ing in her eyes, and Hogan felt quite sick.

"You mean, you're not going to hold us, both of us?" she said, and Partrick nodded.

"That's right," he said. "I think you're telling a straight story, an' I'll take a chance on it."

They must have a confession, Hogan thought. He stood up. Partrick put out his hand, and Hogan grasped it. Norah shook hands too, and all the cops were smiling at them both.

"Next time you pick up a gun, Mr. Hogan," Fenster said, "you want t' be sure it ain't loaded." They all laughed.

"You want to see your husband?" Slattery said, and Norah looked at him.

"Is he here?" she said incredulously, and Slattery said, "Sure, he's been here all day."

They all left the room and went down the stairs. In the hallway, they stood talking while Norah went into the room and closed the door. She was not gone long, and when she went in Hogan could see that the room was white with smoke. She came out, dry-eyed, and nodded at Hogan, and he asked Partrick if he could see Sloan.

"Sure, go ahead," the detective said.

Hogan walked to the door and opened it and saw that the room was full of men. On a low, worn sofa Ed Sloan was sitting slumped into himself, his wrists manacled. He had a three-day growth of beard, and his eyes were red. He looked up at Hogan, and tears ran down his face.

"I'm sorry," he said, and Hogan bent over him, put his hand on his shoulder and squeezed it. He couldn't find any words to say, and he was aware that the men in the room were looking at him with amused curiosity. He patted Sloan's shoulder; the man seemed completely broken; his facial muscles were fagged and drooping, his mouth hung partly open.

He looked up at Hogan and said, in a low voice, "Take good care o' her."

■ ■ ■ ■ *7*

Norah had shown Ed Sloan the propeller in the closet. He took it out and looked at its splintered blades, the two bullet holes that were visible.

"Cripes," he had said, "but he sure wrapped it up."

"I don't know why he brought it back," she said.

"I know," Ed said. "He brought it home t' remind hisself."

They went downstairs and found little Katey still sitting in the large galvanized wash tub that Norah had bought when they first moved to the country. She had splashed water onto the linoleum flooring and was leaning out, reaching for the soap.

"It hopped out of my hand," she said.

Sloan picked it up and gave it to her, and Norah said, "Get out now, dear, and dry yourself. It's time for bed."

"I don't want to go to bed," the child said. "I want to sit up and listen to you talk. You talk too much."

"We sure do," Norah said, and Ed laughed. They sat in the kitchen watching the child dry herself and get into her flannel pajamas with the feet.

"I feel like a bunny," Katey said.

"You are a bunny," said Sloan. "On'y y'r ears ain' big enough."

"Aren't," Katey said.

"O.K.," said Sloan, "aren't," and walked into the living room.

Norah knew he had been hurt by the child's correction, but she couldn't help smiling. Katey had picked it up from her mother, because Sloan had asked Norah to correct him when he made an error. But while he had asked for it from the mother, he could not take it from the child.

But when Norah walked through the living room with Katey on her shoulder on her way to bed upstairs, Sloan looked up from the paper he was looking at and said, "Goo' night, Miss Bunny. Don' forget t' keep y'r ears inside a covers, they might get froze off."

"Good night, Ed," said the child and waved.

Sloan looked around the room; it was bright and warm. This is the life, he thought; this is the way it should be. What'd old Miz Horton think if she could see me, or

George Goreski, or any of them for that matter? The hell with them, he thought. They don't know nothing. But sitting now in the warm room, he got a funny notion. It was winter now; he could hear the wind howling around the corner of the house, drawing in the chimney, and the world was outside and he was inside.

It was different sitting here in this house, that he could imagine for a moment was his own. It was a house where he was free. He could walk around in the room and talk and sit and smoke a hand-rolled cigarette and be a different man than he was down at Hortons'. There, it was true, he ate with Mrs. Horton and carried dinner up on the tray to old Sam Horton, who was twenty years older than the woman and bedridden.

The old man was a crab at that. He would look squint-wise at Sloan when he brought the tray and say, "You back in these parts again? I thought you was gone f'r good." Ella would come into the room, and the old man would say, "This man been makin' cow eyes at you, Ella? I'll whup him if he do." The old man was a pain in the neck, Sloan thought, and his house never gave a man the feeling that he was at home. Here he felt at home. Here he felt free. Here—but it wasn't good to get the idea that he had something. He didn't have it at all. It was like a dream, he thought, the woman treating him like he was as good as her. Not like old Ella Horton, who was kindly enough; only when she wanted something done, she didn't say please, she just said, I want this or that.

When Norah came downstairs, Sloan said, "I got a funny notion sittin' here, like it was the first time in my life I was ever warm."

"I know what you mean," she said.

"It ain' true that it's the first time I was ever warm, but I got t' feelin' that."

He looked at her, sitting there on the couch across the room from him, and the sense of being separate began to go away again. He didn't understand her very well. He watched her instead of understanding her, as an animal watches its master for signs of disapproval. He expected at any moment to catch a look in her eyes that would mean, You can go away now; I don't want you around here any more. He was always waiting for that look, that he had seen in many people's eyes, and he would not have been surprised or particularly disappointed had he seen it. But instead, Norah always acted as though he wasn't any different from her. She talked to him about things that had happened to her, about the things she would have liked to do. She listened when he talked, as though he had something important he could tell her and as though she could really learn something from what he said.

"I'm glad you come up here, Ed," she said. "I'm glad you feel you have a place to go. It must be pretty lousy down the road."

"It ain' so bad," he said. "They let me fix up the tool shed in the barn with a cot an' a old chest o' drawers an' a table, an' I got a little air-tight stove. I put tar paper outside the shed an' banked it, like I banked y'r house here, an' it's right warm, but it ain' like here. It must be good t' have your own home, like this."

"I don't own it, you know. I rent it."

"How come you never went away after y'r husband died?"

"There was no place to go," she said. "I have no folks; I have no money, and I guess I got sort of frightened to go back to the city and start over again with nothing at all. There isn't much I can do."

"You could mebbe teach, like you do over here."

"No," she said. "It's not the same in the city. I never had any special training as a teacher, and even if I had a license, there're thousands of teachers who can't get appointments in the city."

"I don' see why it should be that-a-way," he said. "There mus' be loads o' kids that ain' got no schools, an' loads o' schools that ain' got enough teachers."

"It's the same all over," she said. "Farmers without farms and workers without jobs and people without food and food rotting in the warehouses, and doctors without patients and lawyers without clients."

"Yeh," he said. "You should know the half of it."

She smiled at him and they sat silently in the room, listening to the wind in the chimney. She made coffee, and it was a good feeling to have a guest in the house, someone for whom she could do something; something that would please someone. It occurred to her that perhaps she had been just as dead as Ben, ever since he had died. The inertia of living had claimed her; she had just gone on living because she had been doing it all her life, and even the child Katey had not been enough to compensate her for the sense of futility and emptiness. It wasn't that she had lost a mate, she thought, a man she adored and who had taken half her life away when he died and left her with only half a life. It was as though he had never been, and she had never been herself; she had been cheated. In some way she had never related herself to herself, had never created herself, found her place and followed it. It was like being a disembodied spirit.

But to sit in a small, warm room with another human being was good. Especially to sit with Ed, as he had taken to coming up every night after he had had his supper, and after the evening chores were done at Hortons'. He came up the road on the bicycle, ringing the bell as he turned into the driveway. She had taken to listening for the bell and had been disappointed those nights it did not ring.

He was different from any man she had ever known. He was not of her class, for one thing, but that was not the important thing. The important thing was the intimation of a deprivation such as she had never met in any other person. He whistled in the dark. He fended her off continuously; he would never let her get at him. What is he afraid of? she thought—but that had been late in the summer. Now he was opening up; now he did not seem to distrust her quite so much.

It was a wonderful and lovely thing to watch another human being flower, to know that inside the physical frame of the person who sat across the room from you, there was a personality distinct from your own, formed in a different way, with a different background of experience and habit, and to see that personality emerge, little by little, as a snail pokes its head out of its shell, its tiny horns waving tentatively, quick to withdraw.

She brought the tray into the living room, feeling the heat rising strong from the register in the floor, blowing her skirt. She could hear him down in the cellar stoking the old furnace with the wooden chunks she had bought, rattling the doors. It was like Ben being alive again, but different. Then he came up again and she poured the coffee into the thick white cups and said, "How many sugars, Mr. Sloan?"

"Three if you don' mind, Miz Gilbert," he said, grinning.

"Nuts to you, Mr. Sloan."

"The same t' you," he said, "an' many of 'em." His hand reached for her wrist, and he squeezed it.

"Cut it out, brother," she said.

She was slightly dizzy. Her legs were suddenly weak and her knees trembled, and she wanted to throw her arms around him, but she moved quietly away from him, smelling that scent again, an odor of the male, that moved her in a way she had never been moved before. Think of what you're doing, she thought, before you do it. Make a decision, yes, but be sure before you do it that you *want* to do it, and *why* you want to do it. Play square. It must not be because you've lived so long without a man; it must not be because you're so lonely; it must not be because you're desperate for human companionship, affection, and don't know which way to turn.

"Well, pal," she said. "What do you think about the war?"

"I'm agin it."

"Is that all you think about it? Have you listened to the radio? Don't you think Hitler and his gang have got to be licked?"

"What else is there t' think about it," he said, " 'cept that I'm agin it? Sounds like one gang o' crooks tryin' t' muscle in on another. But I don' know much about these things. I can' talk. But nobody will git anything outta it that's any good."

"All right," she said, "we'll talk about something else."

"Anything you say," he grinned. She got up and reached for a book from the shelves against the wall. She opened it at random and said, "Do you like poetry?"

"Dunno nothin' about it."

"Anything," she said.

"Anything. I used t' know the 'Cremation o' Sam McGee' once, by heart." He started to recite:

"The Northern Lights have seen queer sights,
    But the queerest they ever did see,
Was that night on the marge o' Lake Lebarge,
    I cremated Sam McGee.
Now Sam McGee was from Tennessee . . ."

He stopped and scratched his head. "I f'rget the rest,"
he said.
    "See if you like this better," she said, and began to read:

"O wherefore was my birth from heaven foretold—
no," she said—
    "Why was my breeding ordered and prescribed
    As of a person separate to God,
    Designed for great exploits; if I must die
    Betrayed, captived, and both my eyes put out,
    Made of my enemies the scorn and gaze;
    To grind in brazen fetters under task
    With this heav'n-gifted strength? O glorious strength
    Put to the labor of a beast, debased
    Lower than bondslave! . . ."

"I don' rightly understand it all," he said, "but it sounds
strong. It sounds like the man was feelin' bad."
    "He was," she said. "It's about Samson—you remember,
from the Bible story. The man who wrote it was blind
himself.

    ". . . O dark, dark, dark, amid the blaze of noon;
    Irrecoverably dark, total eclipse
    Without all hope of day!
    O first created beam, and thou great word,
    'Let there be light,' and light was over all;

—— 70 ——

Why am I thus bereaved thy prime decree?
The sun to me is dark
And silent as the moon,
When she deserts the night
Hid in her vacant interlunar cave.
Since light so necessary is to life,
And almost life itself, if it be true
That light is in the soul,
She all in every part; why was the sight
To such a tender ball as th' eye confined?
So obvious and so easy to be quenched
And not as feeling through all parts diffused,
That she might look at will through every pore?
Then had I not been thus exiled from light;
As in the land of darkness yet in light,
To live a life half dead, a living death,
And buried; but O yet more miserable!
Myself, my sepulcher, a moving grave,
Buried, yet not exempt
By privilege of death and burial
From worst of other evils, pains and wrongs,
But made hereby obnoxious more
To all the miseries of life,
Life in captivity
Among inhuman foes."

She looked at him and he was watching her face. He smiled, but the smile did not remain long. Then he laughed and said, "Did you ever play like you was blind when you was a kid?"

"Sure," she said.

"When I was a kid I used t' play like I was blind an' deaf an' dumb. It scared the pants off'n me."

"I know."

"Someways I feel that I'm really blind," he said. "An' I know I can' talk at all. I never knew nobody that I c'd talk to an' tell things to. When I was a kid my stepfather used t' beat me, an' I run away from home a dozen times."

"You could talk to me," she said, knowing now for the first time, and in no specific way, how deeply he was distrustful, even of her. Instead of talking, however, he said, "I got it—

> "Now Sam McGee was from Tennessee
> Where the cotton blooms an' blows.
> Why he left his home in the South
> T' roam 'round the Pole, God only knows.
> He was always cold, but the land o' gold
> Seemed t' hold him like a spell;
> Though he'd often say in his homely way
> That he'd sooner live in hell.

"You want I should go on?" he said. "Mebbe I could say it all."

"No."

"All right," he said, "I won'."

He rose from the chair and came over to the sofa and sat beside her. He looked at her and took her hand, and she let him hold it.

"I was in Alaska once," he said. "Went with a group o' pursuit planes inna Army. I was in Europe, too."

"When was that?"

"Oh, a few years back. It was a secret air mission. Saw Hitler an' Mussolini."

"What do they look like?"

"Oh," he said, "just like you seen 'em inna movies.

Talkin' an' stickin' out their jaw. Little guys, both of 'em, look scared."

"I imagine they are," she said. "They must have bad dreams."

"I wouldn' know that," he said. "You like me, don' you?" He pressed her hand.

"Yes, Ed," she said, "I do."

"Don' know why you should," he said. "I ain' much good."

"You've been in trouble with the Army, haven't you?" (It was a shot in the dark, and she wasn't at all sure she should have said it.)

"You hit it there," he said. "An' that ain' all."

She ain't like the other woman, he thought, not even a little bit. She don't look like the kind that would let a man down, but there's no telling.

"You don't have to tell me anything you don't want to," she said, and he said, "I don' aim to, Mrs." They laughed.

"Don' never tell a woman nothin' you want t' keep quiet," he said, smiling.

"That's right," she said. "They're all alike. Men always get the dirty end of the stick."

"I'll tell you a secret anyhow," he said. "Tit f'r tat."

He bent toward her, and she inclined her head. He kissed her gently on the ear and she turned her face to him and he kissed her tenderly on the mouth, as though he were afraid of her.

"That's a nice secret," she whispered. "Do you know another?"

"Yeh," he said. "I do."

8

■　■　■　■

HE WAS GONE BEFORE
dawn; she had felt him rise and heard him dress in the
darkness, and then she had felt him bend over the bed and
kiss her lightly on the cheek. She pretended to sleep because she did not quite know what to do or say, but she
did not sleep after he left. She heard the bicycle tires grit
softly on the gravel of the driveway, and there was the
faintest tinkle of a bell, and she had smiled.

She lay there thinking of him, of what he had done and
what he had said. She tried to drive from her mind any
comparisons with Ben, but they would return. Strongest
of all these comparisons was the nature of Sloan's approach
to her. Always she had felt, after her marriage, that Ben
had approached her out of a sense of obligation and with
little lust. He had even hinted to her at times that there
was no fire left in him; he was a tired and a beaten man.
"Something went out of me during the war," Ben had said.
"I've needed women, but there was always more hunger
than love. It's not my fault, Norah," he said.

It was too early, she felt, to say that this was love, but
it looked that way to her. There were many complicating

factors, she knew; aspects that might readily be interpreted as wishful thinking—her need for a man, Katey's need for a father, the necessity for a focus and a direction that she had left too long suspended. What in hell do you intend to do? she had thought. You're not really a teacher; you're not earning enough money to do more than barely keep the two of you alive; you can't stay here forever; you're marking time.

But with Ed Sloan, and in one night, she felt, she had known more of tenderness and passion, of true intimacy of body and spirit, of companionship, than she had experienced in the three years of her marriage with Ben. Nor could she put her finger on the truth of this. What was it he had said as they first lay on the bed together and she had felt his body shuddering? What did it matter what he said? He said, "I don' know how t' make love, Norah; nobody never teached me."

If she had thought that he would understand, she would have laughed uproariously. There was nothing, she felt, that he did not know, instinctively. What did he say afterwards? She had felt him chuckling silently, and for a moment she had felt lonely and bereft, thinking, You've been cheated again, and this is nothing. But his laughter, she knew now, did not come out of any condescension. He had said:

> "An' there sat Sam, looking cool an' calm
> In the heart o' the furnace roar;
> An' he wore a smile you could see a mile,
> An' he said, 'Please close that door.
> It's fine in here, but I greatly fear
> You'll let in the cold an' storm,
> Since I left Plumbtree down in Tennessee,
> It's the first time I been warm.'"

—— 75 ——

They had both laughed, and they had both gone to sleep almost immediately, but before she slept she had lain there, soaking in the warmth of another human body that was different from the warmth you generated when you were alone; and tasting with conscious pleasure and with selfishness the sharp sense of the hardness of his long body. She drew strength from it before she went to sleep, and the strength remained with her when she awoke, feeling him rise from the bed. She was grateful for the kiss he gave her, thinking her asleep; she was grateful for the tact he showed in leaving before dawn, when someone might have seen him coming from the house. He would be doing the chores when Ella Horton came into the barn.

All that day she had sung at her housework, but the song came less easily as the day wore toward afternoon and evening, and she knew he would return. She knew, as the day lengthened, what she had to do, and when he came and the coffee was on the table between them and Katey was asleep, she said, "Well, Ed," and he smiled timidly, as who should say, I know what you're going to say, and I don't like it, but I will accept it.

"I want you to know I'm not sorry for last night," she said. She reached across the table and took his hand. "I want you to know it was right and beautiful. But life's not as simple as we'd like it to be."

"You're tellin' me?" he said.

"I'm telling you. I think you'd better go now, Ed."

"I guess you're right," he said and rose from the table, taking up the leather jacket and slipping his arms into it. The telephone rang.

"Well," he said, at the door, "I'll be suin' ya," and he was gone.

She nodded her head, thinking, that was hard to do, but

it was right. Your better sense tells you it was right, so keep a stiff upper lip now and stick by your guns and don't go soft again. You've got a way to make; it's time you made it. She rose from the table, remembering that the telephone had rung in the living room, and she picked it up before she realized that it had not been her ring.

She was about to hang it up again when something in the tone of the woman's voice caught her attention, and she listened. One of the women was Ella Horton, who was on her line; she did not recognize the other voice.

That voice said, "Heard where that Gilbert woman in your house has took up with Ed Sloan."

"Don't know nothin' about it," Ella said. (Good old Ella! Norah thought.)

"Tch, tch," said the other voice. "No tellin' what some folks will do."

Norah gently replaced the receiver; she had an impulse to run out the door and call for Ed, but instead she sat down in the chair and stared at the books in the case.

If there had been daily work to do at the school over in Olds it would have been easier for her. But her arrangement was purely on a part-time basis—no more than two or three days a week, and those days she sent for Sally Prago and got on the bus at the crossroads beyond Hortons'. She did not see Ed working in the barnyard or around the house, and one day Ella met her at the mailbox and told her.

"That fine bird o' mine flew the coop agin," she said. "Went in t' Stiles one day an' never come back." She looked at Norah and cocked her head to one side. Norah said nothing.

"Must of bothered you a lot," Ella said, "him comin' up that way all a time."

"No," Norah said, "he never bothered me."

"Folks got t' talkin'," Ella said, "but I told 'em, them as talked t' me; I told 'em to mind their own row. Whatever happened to them people from the city that used to come to see you, what was their name?"

"Bill Hogan?" she said. "They were up late this fall, you know. They may come up Christmas week again."

"New York City they live, don't they?" Ella said.

"That's right."

Then the bus came and she got on, and she was left only with a bad taste in her mouth for the conversation. Ella was getting nosey again, but that was her way. She had always wanted to know more than she was entitled to know, even when Ben was alive. But she was a good-hearted soul who wouldn't harm a fly. Norah started to chuckle on the bus, remembering the old quotation, "For Satan finds some mischief still for idle hands to do." Ella would agree with that, she thought, but it wasn't Satan who found the mischief. Bill Hogan would have said it was the economic system.

"Too bad," Bill had said, "that Ben didn't live to watch what happened in Spain. There was something he'd have gotten hot about. He'd have got so god damned mad he'd have wanted to fly again."

"Maybe," Norah said.

"He was nobody's fool," said Hogan. "Nothing's static; everything's in a process of becoming; people *learn!*" He smiled and said, "Are there any questions?"

"Lots," she said.

Lots of questions, she thought, lots of questions and very few answers. Work is an answer, but there is no work for me, for millions. That makes no sense. But you must have a focus, a center, a base on which you stand and from which you operate. Why isn't little Katey base enough for you?

She's not. You have to do something about this, she thought; you can't mark time forever. *And he said, Please close that door.* . . . You'll have to sit down, as Bill would say, and lay out a plan of action, a flight plan, such as a pilot charts when he decides to fly from A to B. True course, variation, magnetic course, deviation, compass heading, whatnot. But first you must know where you are (A) and where you want to go (B). That's what I don't know, she thought. *It's the first time I've been warm.*

There was little time to figure it all out, however, for Christmas week came and the school gave her a small cash present and the Hogans wrote they would come up one day during the holiday, and on Christmas Eve she saw Ed Sloan standing on the snow-covered road looking at the house.

Her heart pounded in her chest, and it was all she could do to prevent herself from running out of the house and through the dooryard to the road. As it was, he came slowly toward the house with a package in his hand.

"Merry Christmas," he said, and she looked at him. He still had the leather jacket, but the bottoms of his trousers were frayed, and in the snow he was wearing an old pair of sneakers. He was unshaved.

"Come in," she said.

He handed her the package and said, "It's for Katey," and they called Katey, who was playing upstairs. The child threw herself upon Ed and cried, "Merry Christmas," and he gave her the package, which she opened.

When the cover was off, Norah's heart leaped into her throat, for it looked like an automatic pistol.

"It's on'y a toy," Ed said, and the child took it and ran around the house, shouting, "Bang! bang!" It was black and had a white handle, and Norah looked at Ed quizzically, as much as to say, That's a peculiar present for a little girl.

Ed grinned. "I know what you're thinkin'," he said. "I reckon you're right, but I didn' know what t' get."

"Little girls like dolls," she said and slapped him on the back. "Never mind," she said. "You probably got it for yourself, anyhow."

He laughed. "Mebbe you hit it that time," he said. "I seen it an' I somehow couldn' git my eyes off'n it."

"Saw it," she said.

"I sawed it."

"I saw it."

"I seed it," he said, and they both laughed and she pushed him and he pushed her and they sat down roaring with laughter.

"Ef you don' like my English language, you c'n lump it," he said.

"I like it."

"You c'n lump it."

"All right, I'll lump it."

"I had a mind t' send you a picture-card, but I said, T' hell with her."

"You were right," she said.

"I said, T' hell with her, who does she think she is, the Queen o' Sheba?"

"Where were you?"

"Oh, I was down New York-way t' see my brother an' sister, an' I was here an' there."

"Where's the bike?"

"They took it back," he said. "I was buyin' it onna installment plan."

"That's too bad," she laughed. "Now we won't have anything to run into town with."

"Easy come," he said, "easy go. I'm takin' my job back t' Hortons'; they got over their peeve at me."

"I didn't know they were peeved."

Katey was put to bed, and she lay awake for hours, it seemed, calling down every five minutes to find out if Santa Claus had come; but finally she was asleep, and Norah and Ed turned to each other with a smile.

"I won' go 'way agin," he said, "less'n you want me to."

"I don't know, Ed," she said. "I'm confused. You'll have to give me time."

"I'll give you all a time inna world," he said. (Whatever comes of it, she thought, it's right, and it's clean and wholesome, it's healthy, it's good.) He did not speak again, but his kisses were so hard and so hungry that she was afraid. She strained to release herself, but his arms, she felt with fear and delight, were enormously powerful and he would not let her go.

"You don' want me t' go 'way," he said, "you don' want me t' let you go."

"Yes," she said.

"I'll let you go 'f you say to."

"Yes. I want you to go now," she said. "Are you going to Hortons'?"

"Ay-eh," he said, and she said, "Good night, pal, Merry Christmas."

. . . On the day before New Year's the Hogans came with presents for Norah and Katey, with a baked ham and a quart of good Scotch, canned goods and cigarettes, candy and Birdseye frosted vegetables.

"What did you do?" Norah said, "rob a bank?"

"No," said Bill. "I hit the Saturday Evening Post with an article." He handed her an envelope and said, "Merry X-mas, Happy New Year."

She looked quizzically at him and opened the envelope. In it there was a check for twenty-five dollars.

"I can't take this, Bill," she said, and he said, "And why not?"

"Because I can't."

"That's a woman's reason," he said, "but it won't go with me. You always said I was a misogynist; I don't respect women's reasons."

"Oh," she said, "this is Ed Sloan, Bill Hogan and his wife, Alice."

"Pleased t' meet you," Ed said and sat on a leather hassock near the register in the floor.

"Ed works at Hortons' down the road," she said.

Bill shook hands, and Alice thought, What goes on here? This Sloan was a seedy-looking individual. Where had Norah picked him up—oh, she said he worked down the road.

Ed sat there and didn't have much to say. He watched the others and listened. He had decided early in the conversation that what they were talking about didn't interest him much; books and magazines, politics and the war. He didn't know enough to talk about these things. But he listened to what they said and he watched Norah, and he came to the conclusion that these were her kind of people.

They seemed to be nice enough people, and they sure talked a lot about nothing much, and they asked him questions he could only answer with yes or no. Therefore they didn't pay too much attention to him. Katey was playing outdoors in the snow with the Hogans' little boy, Bill, who was two years her elder and somewhat disdainful. He could hear them throwing snowballs at each other and screaming, and he watched Hogan's face. He was a short, stocky man who talked a lot about Norah's husband, Ben. Norah had said he was a friend of Ben's, had been in the war with him, in the aviation. He turned to Sloan with new attention when Norah said, "Ed here used to be in the Army Air Corps."

"That so?" said Bill. Sloan nodded.

"He cracked up a ship and spent some time in the hospital."

Hogan looked at him with considerable interest. "What sort of ship was that?"

"Don' know," said Sloan. He was uncomfortable.

"North American trainer?" Hogan asked. "Seversky, Curtiss, Ryan?"

"It was a two-seater," Sloan said. "I f'rget what make."

The man's a fool, Hogan thought, and dropped the subject. He was a little annoyed with Sloan anyhow, who had been staring at him since he came in; an unprepossessing individual, he thought. Besides, he sensed that there was something afoot between him and Norah, whom he had always admired and who had always attracted him as a woman. It was a perfectly unreasonable form of jealousy, but he recognized that the reaction was common among men. The presumptive interests of his friend Ben Gilbert might have had something to do with it—by a process of extension. He decided to ignore the man.

"That guy don' like me," Sloan said when the Hogans left in the car they had borrowed and Katey had gone to bed, exhausted.

"He's a queer bird," Norah said. "You mustn't mind him."

"I didn' do nothin' to him."

"You mustn't forget," said Norah, "that he was Ben's closest friend. But that's not all. He probably doesn't like himself too much."

"He's studied in a lot o' books."

"He writes them, too," said Norah. "They'd be better

books if he could understand people with something besides his head."

"I got that," Sloan said. "People don' generally like me nohow, so's I don' blame him. He don' believe I was a pilot."

"Of course he does."

"No," said Sloan, "but it don' matter. You don' believe half I tell you y'rself. It ain' easy f'r me t' talk."

"Isn't."

"Isn't easy." He looked at her and smiled. "I got bad news," he said. "I gotta go now; I'm through at Hortons'."

"What do you mean?" she said. Most of this man is under water, she thought, like an iceberg.

"I couldn' take the old woman no more," he said. "She got under my skin. Talks about you alla time, nasty. But that ain' all; she's after me."

"Oh, come, Ed," she said, "what're you talking about?"

"No crap," he said. "She's alla time hangin' around inna barn, waitin' t' get hold o' me. Her man's been laid up f'r years, you know."

"I can understand that," Norah said, "but it's hard to believe. I don't know why."

"I tol' you you didn' believe what I said."

"I do," she said. "I believe it; why shouldn't I? Where are you going?"

"Don' know," he said.

Think fast, she thought, don't make a bad mistake. She looked at the man standing there in his scuffed leather jacket and the frayed corduroy trousers. What are you going to do? she thought. Is he going, does he really mean it, do you want him to go? She felt, knowing a little of his history, that his rootlessness was deeply ingrained; that there was as much of a necessity in him to go as there was a desire to have roots.

"You have no place to go, have you?"

"I kin allus find a flop," he said. "I gotta lotta friends." You should *let* him go, she thought, but if you do you'll never see him again. She knew this, definitely, but she did not know how she knew it. She caught her breath; the decision had come to her. Be careful, her mind said, but she silenced her mind and knew that she wanted him to stay—for a while at least, her mind said; for a little while, see what happens.

"You can stay here, Ed," she said, "any time you want to." Now I've said it, she thought; now I've done it; now I've started something. She saw a light come into his eyes, and then it was extinguished; she knew just what that meant.

"No," he said. "I thank you kindly, but I couldn' do that."

"Why not?"

"I'm thinkin' what the neighbors would say 'bout you; I don' care f'r me."

"Do you think I care what they say? Do you think they haven't said enough already? It's nobody's business but our own." She smiled and said, "You can be my hired man for a time. There's plenty of work to do around the place." Be careful, her mind said to her; are you sure that this is what you want? No, she answered, I'm not sure, but I know I want it.

"No," said Sloan. "You're mighty kind t' me."

"I couldn't make you stay," she said, "if you don't want to. If you think it's better to go, then you must go."

"It's better," he said. "I ain' like you; I ain' like y'r

—— 85 ——

husband. You been 'round these parts a long time now; people know what kind o' woman you are. You got a job. You got a little girl. I'm nobody."

"They always thought there was something queer about us," Norah said. "Even before Ben died. We never went anywhere; we rarely had anyone here. I would have liked to. They asked Ben to stand for the school board over in Polk and he turned them down; they asked him to join the Democratic committee, but he wouldn't have any truck with politics. So they left us alone."

"It ain' the same," he said. "I'm a bum."

"Are you?"

"Sure," he said. "Didn' you know that?"

"No, I didn't." She grasped him by the arms and said, "Happy New Year, bum."

"The same t' you, mum," he said, "an' many of 'em."

"We'll see what happens," she said. "We'll keep our fingers crossed." She crossed her fingers and held them up for him to see. "Did you used to do that when you were a little kid?"

"I'm allus doin' it," he said. "I allus got my fingers crossed."

"All right," she said, "is it a bargain?"

"It's a deal," he said. . . .

. . . There was a lot of snow in January, but late in February it began to thaw. The snow dripped from the eaves of the house, and the new shingling leaked over the storeroom on the second floor. It was a storage room because there wasn't enough furniture to make a guest room of it. For that matter, the furniture that filled the rest of the house was getting pretty ratty. Norah and Ben had bought it in New York, second hand, and brought it to the country with them. During the summer just past Norah had made slip covers of a cheap chintz, but the covers were worn already, and besides they could not hide the bulging springs. The place looks lousy, she thought; it's enough to demoralize a man. There was no money to buy new furniture, and credit could no longer be established. But if you wanted to, you could get demoralized more easily than that; there wasn't enough money to spare to buy a decent pair of hose, even once a month. And more importantly, there wasn't enough to get the two cavities in Katey's teeth fixed; the first she'd ever had.

The child was unhappy at the little country school up the road. She had entered in January; the school bus picked her up sometimes, and sometimes she walked the mile by herself. It was her first experience with school, and she was having a difficult time adjusting herself. Norah had taught her to read and write when she was five, and she was far ahead of her kindergarten class. But she frequently came home with tears in her eyes, and on one occasion in late February she said, "Mom, is Ed my father?"

"No, dear."

"Ben's my father."

"Yes, dear."

"I haven't any father, have I, Mom?"

"Not any more," she said. "Why?"

"All the other children have fathers."

There was no way to answer this, Norah felt, but she explained to the child that sometimes fathers died. Her own father and mother had died, she said, long ago.

"Isn't Ed my *new* father?"

"You may call him that, dear, if you want."

"I did," said Katey and started to cry again. Norah waited for the child to quiet herself, but she started to sob and said, "I *said* Ed was my father but the other children said he wasn't either, and I said Ed *was* my father and they said Ed ain't your father at all he ain't *married* to your mother. Ed lives in our house like fathers do."

"Yes, dear," she said.

"Ed *is too* my new father," Katey said. "I'll sock 'em if they say he ain't."

"Isn't, dear."

"Isn't."

Norah sighed, thinking of Ed in the cellar splitting wood. He had tried to make himself useful to her since he had moved in with his cardboard suitcase a month and a half before, but no matter how many things he did around the house, painting and puttying, splitting and hauling wood, scrubbing the floors and helping with the meals, running errands to Polk, Stiles, and Coney, he could find no way to augment their income. She did not press him to find work, recognizing in him the urgent need for a little rest. She had asked him what he could do and what he was thinking of doing, and he said, "I c'n do a mite of ev'rything. I been a auto mechanic an' a airplane mechanic; I s'pose I c'd get a job in a airplane fact'ry if I wanted, but I wantta keep away from them places, accounta there's gonna be a war."

Ella Horton did not come near the house, although she was only a quarter of a mile away. Norah saw her only when she paid the rent or made excuses for not having paid it on time, and Ella was formal, if polite. She wore a secret smile these days that infuriated the younger woman, and Norah had decided on any number of occasions to give her a piece of her mind, but she held her tongue.

She could see the way things were tending, however, in the fact that Hortons sent at least three people up that month to take a look at the house. Previously Ella had always hinted that she would like to sell the house to Norah (to Ben when he had been alive), and she intimated that she would be disposed to sell it on the easiest of terms —as monthly rent. Now three couples drove up to the door and told her that Mrs. Horton had said the place was for sale, and could they please take a look around? She showed them around the place and stifled an inclination to tell them that the house was even more run down than it seemed; that way, she could keep her conscience clear.

Ed spoke of moving to Peekskill in the spring, where he owned a house and had a brother and a sister. They talked it over, and he said he would arrange to borrow or rent a car when they had some extra cash and drive her down to see the place. He said he had had an offer to sell it, but he didn't want to sell unless he had to. He did find some work that month on the snow plow; he cut some wood on shares with Sally Prago's father up the hill and drew it down to the house in Prago's old truck. But the actual cash income amounted to no more than the fifteen dollars a week Norah earned at the academy, and it was difficult to stretch it over the twenty-dollar monthly rental and leave enough for milk and food and clothes and cigarettes and telephone and kerosene and light.

"Ed," she said, "it's going to be tough, but we'll make out."

"I think you ought t' marry me," he said.

"No," she laughed, "I'm not sure about that yet. I don't like to be rushed into anything."

"I'm livin' here like I was y'r man," he said. "We might's well git hitched; that would shut Hortons an' the rest of 'em up mighty fast."

They chuckled together over that idea, but she said, "Listen, Ed, I've lived in small communities before, and

I know just what you mean. But I'm too old to order my life according to some other person's pattern, and if they don't like the way I live, they can lump it."

"I ain' much use t' you," he said. "There don' seem t' be no work that I can git."

"Shut up," she said. "Some day I might tell you what you've done for me." Are you sure, she thought, or are you sure?

"I can' talk t' you about the things you like," he said, "like Hogans. I like t' listen to you playin' the piano, but I don' understan' nothin' 'bout it."

"You don't have to understand," she said, "if you like the music."

"Anything you say, Mom," he said. "On'y don' say I didn' warn you."

They were in the living room, and it was raining. He was sitting with the Sunday newspaper in his hand, idly turning the pages, and she was knitting. She had unraveled an old sweater dress and was knitting a pullover; he had so few clothes to cover him.

"Read me the news," she said and silently cursed the tangled wool.

"There's a picture o' that louse Hitler here," he said. "Looks jus' like I saw him."

He did not continue; he was thinking, Now she's going to find out, and then what will she think of me? Well, he thought, I don't care what she thinks of me, it ain't my fault. I better go away from here, he thought; I'm going to have to go away sooner or later; this is too good for me. If she knew—he put the thought away and looked at her. He hoped she would be too busy with her knitting to notice that he was not reading to her. He pretended to be absorbed in the paper, but over the edge of it he watched her, and he watched the room as well. He saw that the room was clean and warm and comfortable. His mind went back to the first room he could remember in the low mountains near Morrisford. "You call those mountains?" she had said. "You ought to see the Rockies. It always makes me laugh when people in the East talk of mountains."

In those hills he had been born, he guessed, and he remembered the room with the wood range where they always spent the winters, his mother and the man that she had married after the father he had never seen had died. The windows were nailed shut in the winter, and you could barely see outside. There was tobacco-juice spit on the floor near the stove all winter long, and the steam from the green wood burning in the grate clouded up the dirty window panes. There were newspapers tacked on the wall to cover the dirty, faded paper. The table was covered with cracked and sticky oil cloth and there was a smell in the room that he would never forget.

He looked across his paper at her and thought of her sitting there and of the child that was not his, asleep on the upper floor. You sure got into something this time, he thought; it ain't your kind of thing. She's a good woman, he thought; she's like my mother. He remembered his mother vaguely, the pinched face and the steel-rimmed cheap eye glasses; not that Norah looked much like his mother, but there was something about her.

Can you do it? he thought; you went and got yourself a ready-made family. You got to work like you never worked before; you got to take care of them. Who's going to help you do it? who's going to lend a hand? Nobody but you. She needs you maybe and you need her, but you ain't really any good for her. He remembered her face during the time the Hogans were up for the day before New Year's; she had looked at him and she must of been thinking, Look what the cat dragged in! A strong man with strong arms but like a baby. A man who could do anything but don't know nothing at all. I don't know how to talk, he thought. I don't know what to say to her.

"Ed?" she said.

"My eyes hurt," he replied.

She looked at him. "Maybe you need glasses," she said. "We'll have to send you in to New York with Bill next time he comes and get you tended to. We'll get Katey's teeth fixed, too."

"It's the piece o' steel in my head," he said, touching his forehead between the eyes. "They never took it out."

"Didn't they know it was there?"

"Dunno," he said. "You know," he said, "you ought t' be awful nice t' Katey."

"I try to be," she smiled. "Katey says you're her new father," she added. "She came home from school a week ago and said the children had teased her because she had no father."

"Kids 're mean," he said, remembering. "You got no idee how mean kids c'n be."

"Oh, yes I have," she said. She laughed. "It's worse when you're beginning to grow up. I remember when my breasts started to fill out, how self-conscious I was. I used to walk along the street almost hunch-backed so nobody would look at me. I didn't know what to do with my hands, they were so big."

"You got nice—" he couldn't say the word.

"Breasts?" she said.

"That's right." He blushed.

"A little out-size," she said, "but lots of milk."

"I allus thought I'd like t' have a kid o' my own," he said. "I'd be real good to it."

"Read me the paper, Ed," she said.

"I can't," he said. "I never learned t' read."

She looked at him. . . .

. . . He heard her undressing in the dark, and he lay there with his legs held stiff and straight. Sheets, he thought. No, he thought, you gotta go, and so he lay there, hearing her undress for the last time. She undresses in the dark, he thought, because she don't know me well enough yet to undress in front of me. The same with me. I never knew a woman that well neither. The other one—that was years ago, he thought; well, not so many years. She played you mean and she played you dirty. She said, "I'll always remember you," and she wrote, but she didn't remember, at least not the way she said she would. When you came back, she said, "You can go to hell, you—" he suppressed the word. "You didn't think I'd wait for you, you ain't no good." Maybe she was right. What can you do for anybody? How can you be a husband, be a father? A *stepfather!*

Norah got in beside him, and he heard her sigh. She sighed, he thought, because life is tough and she knows it, and she's sorry already that she asked me to stay, but that will be all right, too. She's a good woman; I wouldn't play her dirty, and I wouldn't play her mean. I can't do this. She likes me right enough, he thought, but I ain't the guy she's looking for. He felt her reach for him, and touch him, and he stirred restlessly. Not tonight, he thought, even if it's for the last time; no, that would be too hard. He mumbled softly, like she had said he did in his sleep, so she would think he was asleep already. He had worked hard drawing the wood down the cellar and stacking it; she would understand why he had gone to sleep so soon. He lay there thinking, You don't belong no place; nobody would want you if they knew.

It's a good thing, he thought, that she don't know what they're saying. People in the stores in Polk and Stiles, as far away as Coney and maybe Shoreline, they must know. They looked at him with a smirk when he came in the store, or when they picked him up on the road when he was hitching into town. He felt like pasting them all the time; he felt like hauling off and letting them have it right in the kisser, saying, What the hell do you know about anything, you little punks? He never said anything; he only smiled.

But he knew what they were saying about her, and he knew what they thought of him. He'd been around those parts long enough to know. A man carries a long story with him, he thought, something like a tail hanging after him; you can't get rid of it. I want to stay, he thought, but I want more to go. I got to go. He could see the long road stretching out ahead of him, wherever it led; roads always lead to somewhere else, and that was good. There was something good about it, being free, even if you couldn't have some of the things you would like to have.

He knew that she was asleep now, and he stepped cautiously out of the bed. The floor was cold to his bare feet, and he dressed hurriedly, shivering. She stirred in the bed, and he stood frozen beside it, waiting till she should resume the deep sleep that she fell into so soon after she hit the mattress. She's been tired a long time, he thought. He could vaguely see her form in the darkness under the covers. The shoes were under the bed, and he slipped them on. They were still new, and she had bought them for him; she had sent for them by telephone, so it would be a surprise.

He hoped they wouldn't squeak. This is the best I can do for you to pay you back, he thought, for what you done for me. You done a lot for me. You made me think maybe I could be a man, but it's too late. You made me think maybe I was a pretty good guy after all, but you don't know. You're like Katey, he thought; you don't know me, nobody knows me at all and I can't tell about it.

He moved cautiously out of the room and heard Katey turn in her little bed in the next room. He wanted to go inside and kiss the child, as he had kissed Norah in her sleep, but he didn't do that. He went down the steps, one step at a time, carefully avoiding the third step from the top that he knew was loose. The house was dark downstairs, and he felt his way with arms outstretched, his fingers feeling for something that might be in the way. He moved through the kitchen to the door, and unlatched it.

It was cold outside, and he pulled the leather jacket up around his face and moved rapidly down the driveway, avoiding the gravel that was still loose despite the frozen ground. In the road he turned and looked back at the house; it was dark. He could see the curve of the low stone wall that bordered the apple orchard and the bare arms of the trees that swayed lightly in the night wind. He looked up. There was a moon somewhere behind the heavy clouds, and occasionally the clouds became translucent, and the light of the moon shone through, outlining the house more clearly.

He started walking, feeling the hard road under the new shoes; they were comfortable. At least I got a pair of shoes, he thought; they should last a time. Where are you going? he thought and smiled. He felt his face move when he smiled and thought, It don't make no difference where you go. There's nobody waiting for you there. So you could go in any direction and keep on walking till a night driver came down the main pike and picked you up. Who would pick up a man at night, a man without a suitcase even? People were afraid of hitch hikers these days; people who had money were afraid of having it took away from them. It was cold, and he couldn't help shivering.

It was dark at Hortons' place when he passed, and he stopped for a minute and looked at the house. It was well kept; there was a trimmed hedge (he had trimmed it), and the fence around the chicken yard was kept in good repair. He had done the fence mending there last spring. He touched the rails with his hand and thought, there's something you did; there's something you can do.

Suddenly he heard a voice in his ear, saying, You're running away again. He deliberately started to walk faster, but the voice kept saying *running away running away*, and he saw himself, a small boy on a road in the night (it was cold that time, too, he remembered), tears running down his face, and dripping from the end of his nose. He was saying over and over, You can't do that to me, nobody can do that to me you son of a bitch you lousy bastard you stinking lousy bum—nobody. But they done it, he thought. They done it over and over and over, and every time they done it you run away. You always run away, he thought; ain't nothing that has ever stopped you from running away. This is different, he thought; this ain't the same thing.

He was getting near the main road, and he could see an occasional headlight moving on it. When he got there, he stood at the corner where the two roads met and thought, Which way? Maybe he could get to Deerfield before morning and go to the Y.M.C.A. and he would see the Reverend Proctor and Proctor would say, Are you here again, Ed, and what do you want to do this time? Proctor would shake his head and say, like he used to say, "Ed, my boy, you got to have more determination; you got to have more sticktoitiveness; you got to know what you want and go out and get it."

What do you want? he thought. What you want is a mile behind you asleep in the bed, the two of them. What you want is not so easy to get, he thought. Why didn't you talk to her about it? Why didn't you tell her? Maybe she could of helped you get it. Maybe she would of understood. Sure, he thought, she would of understood. She could look through me like a pane of glass.

She don't know, he thought; I never told her. She don't know that long before I come there to shingle the roof, I used to walk up the road at night from Hortons' and look into her window. I seen you, he thought, I saw you, that's right. I saw you through the window, and you was all alone, and you sat there reading in a book or maybe just sitting listening to the radio that was on the table then, before you took it upstairs in our bedroom, our bedroom. That was the time. But I used to watch, and I could tell from looking at you, when you didn't know that I was looking, what you was think—were thinking about. You were alone, too.

All your life that is what you wanted, he thought, go back. No. A car was coming, and he lifted his arm, but the car went by with a high singing whine, and he said automatically, "You bastard, f . . . you with your car." He had said it many times before; it always came. Do you see me standing here? he thought, me without no place to go, and you riding in a car with a heater? He could see the inside of the car, with the shining metal parts and the neat levers and the little lights, and the cigarette lighter and the ash tray and the soft seats in it. I can drive that car as good as you, he thought; maybe you would like to see me do it!

—— 97 ——

There was another car and he lifted his arm again, and the car slowed down, but as he started running after it, it picked up speed again and kept moving. He stopped in his tracks, his heart pounding, and deliberately turned around and started to move in the opposite direction. I'll start walking back, he thought, and see if I get there. If I get there, it will mean I want to go back. No, he thought and stood still. Go home, he thought, and said it out loud, "Go home." Norah's waiting for you, he thought. Katey's waiting for you. There's a fine blue car standing in the shed, and it has lights and a horn under the hood, and in the house there are sheets, and there will be better things to come. New sheets and lots of food in the ice box and plenty of work to do if you really want to do it. I ain't afraid of work, he thought. Give it to me and I'll do it. Go out and get it, the voice said. *Make* them give it to you; say to them, I got a family to keep, I got a little girl and a woman that's waiting for me to come home to them. Do you see these hands? Do you see these arms, they're strong. Put it down in front of me and let me at it. I don't want to sit on my tail until I die.

He was still walking, and in the darkness ahead he could see the bulk of Hortons' place, the house and the out-buildings, the fence that ran around the chicken yard; he heard the chickens in the houses and the dog barking. There would be a house, and there would be a car; there would be a better house and a job and money in the bank. There would be good clothes and clean sheets and a electric razor like he had seen in the paper once and somebody had told him what it was. There would be a woman and there would be another kid around, a little kid to play with Katey, and it would be his kid and it would look like him. "Some day," she said, "I might tell you what you've done

for me." Go home, the voice said; don't be afraid no more,
but go on home. . . .

. . . "What made you think I could do anything?" Hogan
said.

"Well," said Ella Horton, smirking at him, "I knew you
was a friend o' Gilberts' folks, an' I thought mebbe you
could do something."

Hogan scratched his head; he wondered what Ella's interest in the thing amounted to, whether it was simply
good-heartedness or something else that had made her call
him. It didn't matter, he decided; the thing was certainly
serious enough.

"I don't know exactly what I can do," he said. "After all,
she's a grown-up woman with a mind of her own."

Ella looked at him. Her face was serious. "We don't
know nothin' 'bout him," she said, "but folks 're always
sayin' things."

"What sort of things?"

"Nothin' particular, just things."

"Mrs. Horton," he said. "Folks are always saying nothing
in particular about people. There's an awful lot of gossip
goes on in the world." You're talking through your hat, he
thought, and noticed that she blushed.

"Well," she said defiantly, "I tried t' do somethin'
myself."

"What?"

"I went t' the town clerk," she said, her head tilted back
and a self-righteous expression on her face, "an' I asked him
whether somethin' could be done."

"What did he say?"

"He said the same as you."

"I thought so," Hogan said. "You don't know anything

—— 99 ——

against the man, anything *definite*, do you?" He wanted to say, After all, what's wrong with a man who's just uneducated, Mrs. Horton; you're pretty uneducated yourself, you know? He didn't.

"Nothin' 'cept he's a shiftless no-good; he worked for me," she said. "I never could find him no-how when I wanted him. Always dreamin'. But he rode into town with me the other day. I said, 'Heard tell where you're gonna marry,' an' he says, 'Yeh, it weren't my idee though, it were hers.'"

"He said that?"

"Sure enough."

"All right, Mrs. Horton," Hogan said. "I'll run over there; please don't say I came to see you. I don't think there's anything I can do, but I'll find out what's going on."

"God bless you, Mr. Hogan," Ella said. "Norah's a fine young woman. I love her like she was my own, an' I hate t' see her tie up with a man that ain't got a shirt to his back."

Hogan drove slowly down the road. He had a bad taste in his mouth from his conversation with Ella Horton; he was sorry he had come down when she called, and he felt like a fool. You simply did not interfere in other people's lives. But the more he thought about it—whatever Mrs. Horton's reasons for interfering might have been—the more he thought she had something worth looking into. He wondered what in hell had got into Norah. Certainly she needed a man, but was that the best that she could find?

He drove into the muddy dooryard. The house looked dismal from the car; it badly needed a coat of paint, and there was an atmosphere of gloom about it. Maybe that's my imagination, he thought; it's early March, the day is dark, the trees are bare. Damn! he thought, and bent over to release the accelerator, which had stuck again. He switched the engine off, pulled the accelerator pedal out, and jerked on the brake-handle.

"Hi, there!" Norah said. "What brought you here?" She smiled. "Where's Alice?" She looked pretty shabby.

"I felt like driving out," he said. "She's home, doesn't feel very well. Wanted to get some air, so I borrowed this rotten jallopy and came out. "Hello," he said to Ed. "The accelerator pedal sticks; maybe you know how to fix it."

"I c'n try," Ed said, grinning and putting out his hand.

"You know Ed Sloan," said Norah, and Bill said, "Sure."

There was a pause. The sun came out.

"Let's sit on the porch," Norah said. "What's on your mind, pal?" Hogan grinned at her, at Sloan, who sat down next to her.

"Not a thing," he said. He coughed.

"Aha!" said Norah. "The plot thickens."

Hogan laughed, and Sloan laughed with him. Bill looked at the man. He had on a gray slipover, and his lined face was freshly shaved. It isn't a bad face, Hogan thought. His sleeves were rolled up, and Hogan noticed his powerful forearms. I wouldn't want to tangle with this guy, he thought. He looked at Norah, whose face was suddenly serious.

"No plot," he said, feeling a complete fool.

"How did you hear about it?"

He didn't answer, and Norah laughed at him. "A little bird told you, I'll bet," she said, and Bill flushed. Suddenly she was angry, turned to Ed, and, holding his arm, said to Hogan, "Did Ella Horton call you up?"

"That's right," Bill said sheepishly. "She got me worried."

Norah got up and went into the house, and Hogan

thought, I hope to Christ she doesn't call her. He looked at Sloan, who was watching him soberly.

"I know how you feel," Sloan said. "You're a old friend o' Norah's; you're worried about her marryin' with me."

"No," Hogan said idiotically.

"You don' need t' worry none," Sloan said. The words came very hard with him, but he felt that he must say something to this man. He knew that Norah was beholden to him.

Hogan waved his hand in a deprecatory gesture and was relieved to see Norah coming out of the house. She was smiling now, but there was an expression on her face he did not recall ever having seen before. She was an exceptionally even-tempered woman. She sat on the porch beside Sloan and held his hand in a manner that Bill felt was unconsciously defiant. She looked at Ed and smiled when he smiled at her, and pressed his hand.

Then she looked at Hogan and said, "Yes, we're thinking of getting married, Bill; we have a license."

"When?" he said, somewhat relieved.

"Maybe tomorrow, maybe not for a week, maybe in a month or two."

Hogan said nothing but looked down at his shoes. What the hell did I come here for? he thought; then he made up his mind.

"Could I talk to you alone?" he said, ignoring Sloan. Sloan started to rise, but Norah held his hand and he sat down again.

"Anything you've got to say, Bill, you can say in front of Ed."

"I have nothing to say," he said. "I just wanted to know what was going on."

"Why?"

"Well," Hogan said helplessly, "you didn't tell us or even give us a hint. After all, we've been friends a long time—" he laughed with embarrassment, said, "We'd have liked to stand up with you."

"Why should I have told you?" Norah said. "What difference does it make to you?"

"I don't see why you're defending yourself, Norah," he said. "I'm not attacking you." More and more he knew that he could not say what he wanted to say in the presence of this man, who stared at him so disconcertingly.

Very softly, very earnestly, he said, "Might I speak to you alone, Norah?"

"Hell, why not?" said Sloan, rising from the porch and rapidly walking away.

"Well?" she said.

"Nothing," he said. "Except that—listen, Norah," he said, "I don't know anything about Sloan, it's none of my business."

"That's right," she said. "It isn't; and you don't." She saw that he was about to speak again and interrupted him.

"I know what's eating you, Bill. Forgive me for snapping at you. You are a good friend of mine, that's true. I don't know what I'd have done without you."

"Nuts."

"No," she said. "I know what you mean. But there's a lot you don't know."

"What do you know, Norah?" Hogan said quietly.

"You mean about Ed Sloan?" She saw him nod. "Plenty," she said. "I'm not certain I'm going to marry him. Maybe I will; maybe I won't; I don't know. But I do know that he's been kind and considerate; I know that Katey adores him and he loves her—you should see him with her; it would open your eyes."

—— 103 ——

"Of course," he said, "but he's not your—"

"What do you know about my 'type,' Bill? Did you think Ben was my type? Do you know anything about our life together? Have you any idea how unhappy we were? I admired him; I respected him. But we weren't right for each other. Did you know that?"

"No," he said, "I didn't."

"I know what's on your mind, Bill," she said, "and since we're being so honest, how about shooting the works?"

She's getting hysterical, Hogan thought, but he said, "You may fire when you're ready, Gridley," and smiled.

"What you're *really* worried about," she said, "is that Ed didn't have a college education."

"Nonsense!"

"Don't kid yourself," she said. "You've lived all your life with your nose in a book. It's time you took a look around. You thought Ben was the man for me because we were alike. We came out of the same class. We were interested in the same things. Why should that work any better than the opposite—oh, I admit it should—but that doesn't mean the opposite can't and won't."

"I didn't say it wouldn't."

"No. But you think so. You're a bit of a snob, you know, Bill."

"Am I?" he said. "Well, maybe I am. But I'm not being a snob right now. I don't look down on any man because he hasn't had an education; everyone should have an education—"

"Damned right," she said.

"—all I'm saying is that I hope you've looked it all around, Norah, and examined it from every angle and know what you're doing, aren't rationalizing—forgive me—because

—— 104 ——

you're broke and lonely and need a companion. Christ knows you deserve one."

"No one deserves anything," she said. "You take it as it comes. I'll tell you something I wouldn't dream of telling anybody else, only because I know you're not an Ella Horton." She paused. "It's very difficult for me to say this."

"You don't have to say anything, Norah."

"No," she said, "maybe I won't; it's none of your business, Bill. It's too personal. But use your imagination and you'll know what I mean. Ed's been living here," she said, "for over a month. I know what people are saying; it doesn't make any difference to me. Would you respect me if it did?"

"No," he said. "But you've got to be practical, Norah."

"I know," she said, "make a plan, as you always say."

"That's right. You've not only got yourself to consider, you've got Katey, too. Do you think, forgive me, that Ed will be a good influence on her?"

She lifted her chin and said, "None better."

"Can he take care of you?"

"He'll find work; there's lots of work that he can do. He can do carpentry, mechanics. He's worked on and off all winter on the roads; he's got a job on the road coming up tomorrow morning—think of it, Bill," she said. "It starts at six in the morning, lasts till dark. Twenty-five cents an hour."

"That's pretty tough."

"Oh, Christ!" she said, her face suddenly in her hands. "If you only knew what it was all about, you'd understand. But you don't. You've had a pretty easy time of it, Bill, relatively speaking. You don't know what I've been through out here, alone. You don't know what it's meant, living on next to nothing. I've been trapped here—" she looked up at him, "completely trapped. This man—" she stopped speaking and wiped her eyes.

"Why didn't you let us know, Norah?" he said. "We could always have scraped up something. All you had to do was yell for help."

"I know."

"You must understand me," Bill said. "Your neighbor down the road gave me a scare. Told me all sorts of things. Said Sloan had a bad reputation, hinted at all kinds of things. I think you ought to know some of the things she said."

"For instance?"

"Well," he said, "that she'd taken Ed into town the other day, and he told her it wasn't his idea to marry you, but yours."

Norah laughed. "He doesn't express himself very well," she said. "He's not articulate the way we are—you god damned intellectuals," she laughed. "Me, too, I'm the same. We can't see the forest for the trees; it has to be all worked out in the head before we can take a step, then it's generally the wrong step. I know what he meant," she said. "It doesn't matter."

"But get me straight, Norah," Hogan said. "I'm not saying it won't work, and I'm not concerned with the class angle, if you want to put it that way. That's nonsense. But from what little you've told me it looks as though the man didn't have the *means* to make you happy—not the money, to hell with the money—but the spiritual, the emotional, the intellectual means. He's not your equal, Norah; it's not his fault. He won't be able to keep up to you—"

"I haven't made up my mind," she said, smiling. "You're a sweet guy, Bill. I'm not sore at you. I *do* think you're a little thick about people; you haven't *lived* with them enough; if you had, you'd be a better writer."

"Maybe you've got something there," he laughed.

"Think it over," she said. "I'm really a simple gal. I've always got along better with simple people, working people, people with no booklearning, no education. They're not complicated the way we are; I've always felt like a fish out of water trying to keep up with you brainy boys. It's no one's fault."

You like to think so now, he thought, and said, "Maybe you're right."

Sloan came from around the house and said, "I fixed y'r exhilerator, Mr. Hogan."

"Call him Bill," Norah said. "That's his name."

"Thanks," Bill said.

"Come on in the house," said Norah, "and have a glass of beer."

■　■　■　■　*9*

"You said there'd be work on Friday last," said Sloan.

"I know," the road commissioner said, "but there ain't. I thought I'd need a extry hand, but I don't. Mebbe tomorrow, Ed, ef you want t' show up."

"O.K.," he said. He turned and started to walk away, and he heard the men on the road machine laughing quietly, and he wanted to turn and swing on one of them, but that wouldn't of done no good. He started to walk back, but then he turned around and walked into the town; there was something he wanted to do there.

When he got back to the house, Norah was hanging out the Monday wash. It was warm that day, and the soggy earth was springy to the feet.

"You back already?" she said.

"Yeh." He went into the house and sat in the armchair in the living room.

She came in and said, "What's the matter, pal?"

He grinned at her. "Hear them spring peepers down the swamp?"

"Yes," she said.

"Make a powerful lot o' noise f'r a little frog."

"What's on your mind?" she said.

"You ready t' get married t'day?"

"Cut it out," she said. "Wasn't there any work on the road machine?"

"Nah."

"Forget it," she said. "It doesn't matter."

"You want t' get hitched t'day?"

"Why not?" she said.

He got up out of the chair and put his arms around her. "You get on y'r bes' bonnet," he said, "an' I'll go back t' town. I got a car all lined up, friend o' mine in the gas station will loan it t' me. We'll go over in style, see the Rev'rend Halstead. He's a Methodist."

She looked at him; she saw his serious face with the heavy lines, and she bit her lip. She felt that he was desperate, and she thought, Do I want to get married now; do I want to

marry this man? She saw that he needed her; that his failure
to get work again that day had something to do with his
asking her again, and she felt that the thread between them
might soon snap if it were not rewoven, reinforced.

"You mean it?" she said.

"O' course I mean it," he said, his face flushed, his brows
knit. "D' you think I'd kid you 'bout it? Or mebbe you don'
think I'm good enough f'r you?"

"Don't talk rubbish," she said. She held him in her arms
and kissed him. She laughed. "I'll keep my fingers crossed,"
she said.

"Tha's right."

"We can do it," she said. "There's no reason why we
can't."

"Can' nothin' stop us," he said, "if you don' want it to."

"I don't want it to."

"What about y'r friend Hogan?"

"What about him?"

"Didn' he talk you outta it?"

"He did not."

"I'll be back," he said and was out of the door.

In a half hour he was back, and she had changed to her
one good woolen dress and made up her face and brushed
her hair. She had Katey dressed, too; the child had come
home for lunch and was delighted not to have to go back
for the afternoon session.

"Where we going?" Katey said.

"To Polk."

They came out of the house and saw him sitting behind
the steering wheel of the old Dodge. Norah laughed and Ed
laughed, and vaulting over the door, he opened the rear
door for her.

"I'm sitting in the front," she said.

"It ain' a much," he said, "but it'll get us there an' back."

"It's beautiful," she said. "You couldn't want a better one." She reached in her pocketbook and took something out and handed it to him.

"Wha's that?" he said.

"A ring, dopey." It was her wedding ring; a plain gold band.

"I don' need that ring," he said. "I got one o' my own." He reached into his pocket and handed it to her. She looked at it, and her eyes filled with tears.

"Thank you," she said.

"I bought it off a guy," he said. "I'm sorry it couldn' be no better one."

"It's lovely," she said. She held it up and turned to him with surprise. "How did you know that it would fit me?" He reached in his other pocket and handed her a small piece of string. She laughed.

"You're a beautiful driver, Mr. Sloan," she said.

"I druv before," he said. "I been all over the country, I tol' you. Ain' no make o' car I can' drive; jus' git right in an' drive her off."

On the main road he put his foot down on the accelerator and the old car picked up speed. There was a terrific rattling knock in the engine and the car swayed from side to side and Norah held on to the door next to her, with Katey on her lap.

"Take it easy," she said, "or you'll kill us all."

"No back-seat drivin'," he said. "I like t' go fast."

"I do, too," she said, "but if we're going to get married, we want to get there first."

"You going to get married, Mommy?"

"Yes, dear."

"I thought you *were* married, Mommy?"

They both laughed and the child looked at their faces and laughed too. "Mommy's going to get married, Mommy's going to get married," she chanted, and Norah laughed until her sides ached.

I'm happy, she thought; keep your fingers crossed. She looked at Ed and saw how intent he was on the driving, how he was enjoying it. He was relaxed in the seat, almost too relaxed, she felt. He was imagining that the car belonged to him, that it was nothing uncommon for him to have a car to drive.

"Keep an eye peeled f'r the speed cop," he said, and she turned and looked behind.

"Here we go," he said, and he leaned back further from the wheel. "Get y'r nose down first," he said. "Now keep her there . . . now, ease back a bit on the stick, a li'l more, a l'il more, O.K.; feel 'er comin' off? Feel 'er comin' off the groun'?" He laughed and tossed his head back, then eased his foot off the accelerator and turned to laugh at her.

"Keep your eye on the road, aviator," she shouted, and he laughed with his mouth open.

"You'd make a hot pilot," he said, "scared o' altitude."

They drove into the small town and asked at the gas pump for the Reverend Halstead's home. He lived off the main road in a plain frame house, and they parked the car right on the road. They took Katey between them, each holding one hand, and walked up the driveway to the house. There was a bell pull, and Ed yanked on it; they could hear the bell ring deep inside the house.

The door was opened immediately, and an old man with a dilapidated face said, "Come right in, folks," He stepped aside and showed them into a large, almost empty room. There was an upright piano and a few chairs, a small table.

On the mantelpiece there were several cheap photographs of young and middle-aged couples, a few children.

"Sit right there, little girl," the Reverend Halstead said, and Katey obediently sat on an old-fashioned chair. The minister rubbed his hands and said, "I guess you folks come t' be married?"

"That's right," Ed said, and Norah nodded.

"You have the license, may I see it?"

Norah brought it out of her purse, and the minister took a pair of pince nez from his inside pocket and scrutinized the license.

"I see you have been married before, Mrs. Gilbert." He looked at her over his glasses.

"My husband died four years ago."

"Oh, yes," he said. "Yes, of course." He looked at Sloan and frowned. From his side pocket he took a small book and said, "Stand there, please."

"Don' we need no witnesses?" Ed said, and the minister looked up at him and said, "No, it's not necessary." He began to read from his book, and Ed looked at Norah, who was watching the Reverend Halstead's face. He was frightened and he was struck with awe. He looked back at the minister, who was saying, "Will you, Edwin, have this Woman Norah to your wedded Wife . . . Will you love her, comfort her, honor and keep her, in sickness and in health; and forsaking all others . . .?"

Ed watched the man's face. It told him nothing. He looked at Norah, hearing the words, "till death you do part?" He looked back at the minister, who was watching him. He opened his mouth.

The minister said, "Say I will."

"I will," he said.

"Will you, Norah, have this Man Edwin . . .?"

Sloan saw her face flush, and he watched her lips. She ain't going to say it, he thought; I don't see why she should say it. He heard her say, "I will," and the minister said, "Edwin, place the ring upon Norah's finger." He found it in his pocket, and she was holding out her hand and looking at him, and he put it on her finger and she grasped his hand and held it firmly. Then it was over, and she was kissing him and the minister put his book back in his pocket and smiled mechanically and said, "I hope you will both be very happy."

"We sure will," Sloan said. Behind the minister he saw Katey sitting solemnly in the chair, her hands in her lap, her eyes wide. He winked at her, but she did not smile.

"You folks live hereabouts?" the Reverend Halstead said. "If you don't, there's a nice hotel in town you might—"

"On the old Abbott place," said Norah.

"Oh, yes," he said, "of course, I recollect now. You're Mrs. Horton's renter."

"That's right."

Sloan wanted to get Norah and the child outside; he wanted to talk to the minister alone for a moment. He said, "I'll be right out," as they approached the door, and then he turned to the minister and said, "What do I owe you, Rev'rend?"

"Anything you'd like to give."

"That's it," said Sloan. "I can' give you nothin' now, but I kin owe it t' you, git it soon."

The minister did not smile. "That will be all right," he said.

"We ought t' go f'r a spin," Ed said to Norah, "but I ain' got no money f'r the gas."

"It's all right," she said. "We can drive into Coney and have a Coca-Cola."

"O.K.," he said, and they went down the main road. In the town she was aware that the people on the street looked at her, and in the ice cream parlor the woman who ran the place watched her curiously after they had been served. She felt uncomfortable, but she thought, To hell with them. She turned to her new husband and said, "Are you happy?"

"None happier."

"Katey," she said, "you said you wanted Ed to be your new father; now he is."

"Is that what happened in that man's house?" she said, and they both laughed.

"I may be y'r new father, Katey," Sloan said, "but you musn' forget you had another father, who was the real one."

"I won't forget," the child said, her face solemn, and Norah looking at her knew suddenly, and perhaps more completely than she had ever known before, the extent of her obligation to the child. You could do anything with children, she thought; there's nothing that can't be done to them, and they have no way of defending themselves. As the twig is bent, the tree— She looked at Ed. "We can do it," she said, and he nodded.

"Did you think we couldn'?"

"I had my doubts. It won't be easy."

"You tol' me once that nothin' easy was no good."

"I was talking through my hat," she said, "but probably that's true. Let's go, Ed," she said. "Let's go home."

"The honeymoon ain' over yet," he said. "Katey wants another Pepsi-Cola."

At the house he vaulted the car door again, and when Norah got out of the car, he said, "I heard tell you're supposed t' carry the bride inna house."

"That's right," she said.

"All right, bride," he said. "I reckon I c'n tote you."

He took her in his arms, and Katey held the door open for him. He carried her into the living room and deposited her in the middle of the floor. They embraced, and she clasped him desperately in her arms; her throat was full, and no words would come. Oh, God, she thought, I hope I've done the right thing; I think I have, there's no way of knowing. She saw the child standing in the doorway, watching them, and she broke from his arms and bending before the child said, "Mom's pretty funny, isn't she, dear? Don't you know what it's all about?"

"You and Ed got married," Katey said.

"That's right," she said.

"I'm going to catch a peeper," Katey said. "I won't fall in." She ran out of the house.

"Well, husband," Norah said.

"Well, wife."

"You don't know what you got into this time, pal," she laughed.

They sat on the sofa and looked at each other. She took both his hands and said, "We can make a go of it, I know it."

"None better," he said.

She lay in his arms, her head on his shoulder, and she sighed. He thought, She done this before, but it was different. I never done this before, but now I done it, and now I'm like all the others. Now I got me a wife and a family to keep. Before, she was taking care of me, I was the hired man; now I got to take good care of her. He kissed her cheek, and she put her hand on his face and pressed it to her. They did not speak for a time, but he heard her sigh, and he thought, She ought to quit teaching school; when I get a job she can quit.

He saw, in his mind's eye, a succession of good jobs that

he could hold; there would be planting and cultivating and haying. There might be shingling and various carpentry work to do; he could hire out by the day to cut wood or saw it, work on the roads or do the chores for someone. Maybe he could learn some new things to do, days when there was no other work. Joe at the gas station might need a helper; the blacksmith in town, or they could move. It would be good to move away when they got a little money saved up, find a place where nobody knew that she had had another husband and that he wasn't any different from anybody else. Here, he thought, we got two strikes on us already.

"Norah," he said, "we gotta move away."

"Some day," she said, "why not?"

"I'll run down Peekskill-way one o' these days, find out what I c'n do 'bout that house. I reckon I c'd sell it f'r a price."

"Would it be a nice place to live?"

"A right nice place."

"Then why not live there?" She watched his face, and suddenly she knew that she loved him. His face was serious, in much the same way that Katey's face grew serious when she was puzzled; he thinks slowly, she thought, but there's nothing wrong with the way he thinks. He was never trained to think, but you can oil a rusty machine and make it hum.

That ceremony! she thought. Good God! what a sordid business they made of it. That minister, trying to steer us to a "good hotel." She remembered how she and Ben had "eloped" to Maryland to get married, and how the houses in Elkton had huge signs in front, GET MARRIED HERE! NO WAITING! or REVEREND FOSTER, THE MARRYING PARSON. Every building housed a minister lying in wait for customers. Before that, they had gone to Connecticut, but there they would have had to wait, and when Ben had asked, "What's this about waiting for two days, can't that be arranged?" the man had said, "What's it worth to you?" It should have been beautiful, she thought.

"Mebbe it c'd be arranged," Ed said.

"What?" she said, startled.

He looked at her. "About livin' in the house."

"Oh," she said, "forgive me, I was thinking of something else."

"What was you thinkin' 'bout?"

"About getting married," she said. "About how ugly they can make it."

His face was serious. "Did you think so?" he said. "It was the first time I was married. I thought it was right pretty."

"Ed," she said. "I love you."

"Mebbe you do," he said, "but I don' think you know yet."

"What makes you say that? Why do you think I married you?"

"You're lonesome," he said. "I think you like me good enough. Mebbe you married me f'r my money."

She laughed and drew away from him with a pretense of having been discovered. "How did you catch on so quickly? I meant to hide that from you."

"You can' hide nothin' from me," he said. "I may be dumb, but I c'n tell a oak from a whiffle-tree. The minute I met you I said t' myself, This woman wants t' hook me. She thinks I got a pile o' dough."

She wrinkled her brow in mock despair. "Oh," she said, "can you ever forgive me?"

"That depen's," he said. He held her face in his hands and looked into her eyes. "You got nice eyes," he said. "You got a honest face. D' you know that b'fore I used t'

—— 117 ——

come here, I used t' come up at night an' watch you
through the window?"

"Did you?"

"I did."

"What did you see?"

"I ain' tellin'," he said, "but plenty."

Katey came in the door and looked at them sitting there.
"Mom," she said, "I couldn't catch a peeper. I guess they
don't want to be caught."

"Why not?" she smiled.

"They peep when you're far away," the child said, "but
when you come up close, they stop."

"You'd shut up y'rself," Sloan said, "if somebody was
after you."

*

In the Baconsfield County Courthouse Sloan dictated
the statement and it was read to him and they took him
back to the cell.

"Can you read?" they said, and he said, "On'y a little."

"After you've finished this and we read it to you, Ed, will
you sign it if it's all right?"

"Sure," he said.

It had taken half the day and all the night, and he was
exhausted. He had sat facing the woman who took it all
down on the typewriter. She never looked at him, and he
had thought, You think I'm a rat; you don't think I'm no
good. You think you're pretty good yourself. She did not
look at him, but she kept typing all the time that he
was talking. She's dried up, he thought.

They had driven him from Low Hill to Baconsfield to
make the statement. He sat between them, his hands cuffed
on either side. They put cigarettes in his mouth and lit

them for him, and they took the cigarettes out and knocked the ashes off them. They were nice. They could afford to be. They got what they want, he had thought on the ride. They got a confession; it's open and it's shut. They were very pleasant.

They said, "Ed, suppose you'd been picked up when you was driving that Chrysler, what would you of done?" He had looked at them and he knew what they wanted him to say.

He had set his face (but he had a smile inside him) and he said, "On'y thing t' do woulda been t' shoot it out." The dopes, he thought; they took that one; they swallowed it whole. That was what they expected a stiff to say, a gunman, a triggerman. But how could I of shot it out with them when I didn't have no more bullets for the gun? They knew that, too. It was just something to say.

So they had sat him down in the office in Baconsfield, and they had all stood and sat around, like before, only it was different, the guy called Slattery that had brought him in and Joe Reilly and the captain, Fenster, and the cop, Partrick, from Morrisford and the D.A. and a lot of guys he had never seen before, and there was the old sheriff that had come for him, Ed Fisher. Old Ed was a pretty good guy; he even has the same first name as me, Sloan thought; that's funny. He had come over from Baconsfield to bring him back, and he sat there while they all sat around and listened, and he had talked and talked and the woman had taken it all down on the typewriter.

Then after it had been finished and read back to him, they made him sign all the pages, and all the copies of the pages, too, one after the other, and because it was hard for him to write his name, it had taken a long time to do it. All the time he was signing it, his large, gnarled hand painfully making the unfamiliar marks, and ink always splattering from the pen, he was thinking of the thing they had said. "We have not made any promises to you or any threats to make this statement, have we?" "We have not mistreated you, have we; this is all made of your own free will, isn't it?" To which he had always said "Yes," or "No," whichever they wanted.

What point was there in saying anything else? They got him with his pants down. So it didn't make no difference whether he said No, you went to work on me, or No, you never did me any hurt. It was open and it was shut and they seemed very pleased that it was that way. Their job was almost done. He hated every one of them; they didn't know what it was all about; they didn't know this from that, nor how a guy could get to feel.

But he didn't hate old Ed. He thought maybe he should of, because Ed Fisher was probably like the rest of them, but it was hard to hate the old man. He had taken him in the cell and closed the door and sat down next to him.

"Well, Ed," Fisher said, "you remember me?"

"Sure," said Sloan, "I remember."

"I didn't think you would, Ed," the old man said. "It was so long ago."

"I never f'rget my friends."

"That's nice of you," the sheriff said, "your sayin' I'm your friend; that's mighty nice."

"You was good t' me when I was a kid."

"That was a long time ago," old Fisher said, offering him a cigarette. "I never thought I'd see you brung in for this."

"I never did myself."

"When was it?" the sheriff said.

"Don' know," said Sloan. "I was on'y fourteen, I reckon."

—— 120 ——

"I recollect," the old man said and sighed. "You're in plenty trouble now, Ed."

"You're tellin' me?" said Sloan. "I'll burn f'r this."

"Oh, I don' know," said Fisher. "I don' know. They'll appoint you a lawyer, you know. It's a free country; they don' kill a man without hearin' what he has t' say. You got a right t' trial. The law's just," he said.

"Yeh," said Sloan. "Sure is. Like the time I got three years f'r stealin' home brew from my brother-in-law's house. Like the time I got indefinite f'r telling the judge I'd ruther be dead than go where he was gonna send me. 'A wise guy,' he said."

"That so?" said the sheriff, rising. "Well, I gotta turn in, Ed. Anything you want I should do f'r you?"

"My foot's hurtin' me bad," said Sloan. "Mebbe you c'd send me in a doctor."

"I'll do it," Fisher said. "I'll do it first thing inna morning. You try t' get you some rest; you must be plain tuckered out."

The door clanged after him, and Sloan stood at the cell door and looked around. There was a bulb burning in the middle of the place, but there wasn't nobody else around, or else they were asleep. They had taken his shoes and given him a pair of slippers. They had taken his belt and necktie, but he thought, if I wanted to, there's a sheet on the bed, ain't there? In the corner of the cell there was a toilet seat; the place was pretty clean, but it looked like all the rest of them.

Now you done it, he thought. Now what're you gonna do? There wasn't nothing he could do but sit now. They would send in a mouthpiece and they would take him out and bring him back and there would be a lot of talking

—— 121 ——

that he couldn't understand, but it wouldn't make no difference in the end, that was sure enough.

Would she come? he wondered. He decided that she wouldn't. He decided that she must of learned her lesson, and now she would know all the things he had always wanted to tell her, but he never could. They would tell her. They wouldn't leave nothing out. And she would think, He sure played me for a sucker, and to hell with him. Could you blame her? What else could she do or say or think? But I *told* her, he thought; I said, "Don't say I never warned you," I *did* say that.

He could hear the song in his head, the one they used to sing over the radio, what was his name? I'm headin' f'r the laaaaast round-up, giddyap little dogie git along git along, laaaaast round-up. He sat on the cot, holding his sore foot in his hand, wondering. He wondered why it was he felt safe now, like there was nothing else to be afraid of now. He felt safe like you do when you come in out of the rain and get yourself dry in front of a pot-bellied stove. It was a good feeling. He lay down on the cot; it was warm inside the jail, and there was snow on the roads outside; the car had skidded half a dozen times on the way from Low Hill, and he had said, "Mebbe you want me t' drive you," to the cop that was driving, Slattery. "I c'd do a better job'n you." They weren't sore; they laughed when he said it. They got what they wanted, and that was all they were interested in. A hell of a job, he thought.

Suddenly an idea presented itself to him. Now I don't have to ask her to fill out the question sheet for me, like I was gonna have to. The questionnaire from the draft board had come the morning he was nabbed. They wouldn't of taken me nohow, an ex-con, he thought. That was the time when she saw the question sheet printed in the paper and she started to read it to me and when it said "convictions," I said you don't need to read no more, Mom, and she didn't know what I meant. That was a funny idea all right. You're inna army *now*, you're not behind a plow, you'll never get rich you son of a bitch, you're inna army now. He slept.

*

On the last day in March the Hogans had driven into the dooryard unexpectedly. "We've come to see the newly-weds," they said. There was an atmosphere of tension despite the presents they invariably brought; the cold cuts and the beer, the candy and small toys for Katey, the carton of Camels and the magazines and newspapers.

"Where's the groom?" Alice said.

"Why, he's away," said Norah. "I expect him back any time now. He went over to Peekskill to see about his house."

"What about it?" Bill said.

"Well, we were over last week to look at it," she said. "It's a lovely place, on a little pond. The people who've been living there weren't home, so we couldn't get in. But Ed went back to see them yesterday. We may move later this summer," she said. "Don't be surprised if we get rich yet."

"Nothing surprises me," Bill Hogan said. "Not these days."

"I get it," Norah said, "I get it; you needn't rub it in."

"Are you happy, kid?" said Alice.

Norah hesitated, but she said, "Never happier," and Alice thought, She's lying. Her emotions were obviously pretty near the surface these days. When Bill had told her the story, Alice had said, "I don't approve of it." "It's none

—— 123 ——

of our business," Bill had said, and she agreed. But Norah must have been pretty hard up, Alice felt, to have married such a man. She didn't remember him very well; he hadn't made much of an impression on her at Christmas time, but from what Bill said, well, hell—women with Norah's background simply didn't up and marry some uneducated farm hand, and she didn't recall that he was much like Gary Cooper or Charles Boyer, or even Ben Gilbert.

"No kidding," Norah said. "Things have been pretty tough, but we're doing all right. The neighbors didn't exactly approve," she laughed.

"What do you care?" Alice said. "So long as you've got what you want."

"I don't," she said. "Thanks for the wedding present, guys."

"Forget it," Hogan said. "It wasn't much, but the heart was there."

"I know it," Norah said. Her nose itched and she rubbed it. Alice thought, I hope she doesn't cry; but I'd sure like to know what's going on here.

While they were eating lunch Ed appeared from down the road. He was wearing a white pullover sweater, and the new shoes Norah had given him just before their marriage were pretty well broken in by now.

"Hi," he said, and the Hogans said, "Hi, congratulations."

He sat down on the porch with them and had a sandwich and a glass of beer, and Alice watched him with distaste. Bill put himself out to be friendly, watching the man's face and gradually coming to the conclusion that there wasn't much the matter with him that some affection and some friendship couldn't mend. But he was embarrassed by the role he had played up until the marriage, by the spectacle he had made of himself the day he had come running when Ella Horton called.

"How's your landlady?" he said to Norah.

"Ella?" she said and laughed. She glanced at Ed. "Why, she's been pretty good since we got married. Before that she didn't talk to us. The day after the wedding she came down with a pie; was pretty cool but friendly. She sort of had a yen for Ed, you know."

"That so?" said Bill.

My God, Alice thought, does she believe that? She looked at the man again, noting the powerful arms in the tight knitted sweater, the uneven teeth and the lined and melancholy face, the steel-gray eyes. Maybe so, she thought, but then she's a farm woman.

"Man I know," said Sloan, "over the Glover airport. Saw him on my way back."

They looked at him. It was more of an announcement than an intelligible remark, and they waited to find out what it meant. He saw them looking at him and went on.

"Promised me a ride, 'f we come over. I'd sorta like t' get my hand onna stick agin," he said. "See if I lost my nerve complete. He's hoppin' passengers."

"If you'd like to go over there, it's not very far, is it?" Hogan said. He felt some excitement stirring in him.

"'Bout sixteen miles."

"What say we take a run over after lunch?" Bill said. "Maybe I could get checked out and take the kids for a ride; what sort of ship?"

"Dunno," said Sloan. "Three-seater biplane."

"Probably a Travelair or a Waco."

"Can't you stay away from those things?" Alice said, and Bill glanced at her.

"You know I can't," he said. He was more excited at the

prospect of doing some flying than Katey, who had never been up.

"I been up lots o' times," said little Bill. "My dad took me."

The women did not want to come, so Bill took Ed and Katey and Bill, Jr., over in the borrowed car. It was a chance to get better acquainted with Sloan, and he was personally curious to find out how much he actually knew about flying. He had come to the conclusion that Sloan had never been in the Air Corps, possibly never flown; there was a lingo men picked up if they so much as hung around an airport for more than a week. On the way over, he asked some questions.

"Used to be a time," he said, "when you could get in the Army Air Corps without two years of college; no more."

"I know," said Ed, "I never went."

"How come—?"

"I got a brother inna Navy; got some pull."

"I see," said Hogan. Might be, he thought, but I doubt it.

"Didn't you get a pension after you cracked up?"

"Nah," said Sloan.

"That's queer."

"They don' like me much," Ed replied. "I took it on the— I run outta the hospital 'fore they said I was all cured up."

A deserter, Hogan thought, well, that might account for a lot of things. He decided he had asked too many questions and paid more attention to his driving.

"You folks gonna stay up here t'night?"

"Oh, I don't know—"

"Sure like t' have you," said Sloan.

They arrived at the Glover airport, which was pretty

much of a dump, Hogan saw. He noticed the pole lines to the north and south of the field, the trees that hemmed it in. There was one hangar, and the field itself wasn't too level. Sod. Sloan went around the hangar looking for someone, and Hogan held onto the two children and watched the two young fellows with the old O-X Bird biplane who were hopping passengers. He spoke to one of them, brought out his private license, and asked how much they would charge to check him out and let him have the ship about a half an hour.

"Sorry, friend," the pilot said. "We're not renting the ship, just sight-seeing."

Sloan came back and said he couldn't find the man he was looking for. "Must o' took off f'r somewhere," he said.

"Oh," said Hogan, "I thought these boys—"

"Nah," said Sloan, "I don' know 'em."

"Why don't you take a ride with the kids?" Hogan said. "You can all get in the front cockpit together."

"No," said Ed, "I'd ruther you took 'em."

"Hell, man," said Hogan, "I don't like to ride; I like to fly."

The two children jumped up and down, urging Sloan to take them, and he agreed. Hogan paid the special price of four dollars for the three of them and watched the take-off. The boy did a good job of it, using up the whole field before he took on altitude. It's different than it used to be, Bill thought; these kids take to it the way we took to driving cars. He followed the gradually diminishing plane, his hand shielding his eyes, and he recognized that he was mildly frightened, having sent both the children up together. It would have been safer—but that's nonsense, he thought. This is no time for you to be afraid of flying; there was nothing to be afraid of, after all. The boy knew his job, and the ship looked as though it had been kept in good repair.

After fifteen minutes it came in for a neat landing, and when Hogan saw it finally touch down he was relieved and sighed audibly. It taxied up to the hangar, and the children were helped out. They were excited, and he saw Sloan climb slowly out and shake hands with the pilot. He was pale.

"Want to wait for your friend to come back?" Hogan said.

"Nah."

"How'd it feel?"

"Pretty good when we was climbin' outta the field," said Sloan. "But when we got over the woods, I got scared." He shook his head.

"That's interesting," said Hogan.

"I didn' like the way that boy flew," said Sloan. "Didn' know his job."

"That so?"

"That ol' ship's a crate," said Sloan. "Expected the motor t' give out any time."

Back at the house in Polk, the children shouted and climbed on Norah and Alice.

"I went up in the airplane," Katey said.

"She was never up before," said Bill, Jr. "She was scared. I saw her face."

"I was *not.*"

"You were *too,*" said Junior. "I was looking at you."

"Where's Ed?" said Norah.

"He's outside."

The expression on her face made Hogan look out of the window when she had left the room, and he saw her standing next to Sloan, who was sitting on the ground. She had her hand on his shoulder, and it was fifteen minutes before he came into the house. No one spoke, and he excused himself and went upstairs.

"He was sick as a dog," Norah said. "It all came back to him."

"Imagine it would," said Hogan. "I'm sorry I suggested it."

"No," she said. "He wanted to do it; he wanted to see how it would feel. You're staying tonight, aren't you?"

"Why," said Alice, "you can't put us up."

"We'll manage," Norah said. "Besides, I was wondering if Bill would lend us the car to run over to Peekskill for an hour or so."

"It isn't mine."

"Of course," she said. "I forgot."

"If you've got business there, I could drive you," he said.

"We'll see," said Norah, and Alice looked at her husband with annoyance. What a sucker the man is, she thought. If I didn't know him pretty well, I'd say he had a yen for her. Norah's O.K., she thought, but this man of hers is a mess. She could hear Bill talking to her, saying, Aren't you being a bit intolerant? Yes, she would say, I am, and what's the odds? Aren't you a bit of a snob, Alice? he would say, and she would reply, Call it what you like, but people ought to have some common ordinary taste. She felt sorry for Norah; she ascribed the whole business to the fact that Norah had let herself in for a sex relationship, and the man had got his hooks in her. Probably she also felt sorry for him. She'll find out, Alice thought; she'll get over it soon enough. I don't give it six months; it was plain enough to see they had nothing in common.

So after dinner she volunteered to stay with the children if Norah and her husband still wanted Bill to drive them over to Peekskill. It wouldn't be more than three or four hours at the most. It would be good to be alone. The Sloans wanted to look at a house that Ed said a man wanted to trade him for his own.

"Mine's on a l'il pond," he said. "Make a good summer place. This guy wants t' swap a good farm with me, throw in five hundred bucks t' boot."

"Sounds like a good swap," said Bill, "if the farm's all right."

"Like t' do some farmin'," Ed replied. "Like t' have Norah quit bein' a school-marm."

"You can't make me mad," she said. "With a farm and five hundred dollars in the bank we could make a good start, don't you think?"

"None better," Sloan replied.

"We'll be rich yet, Bill," she laughed. "Come around some time when you want to borrow a couple thousand dollars."

"I will, lady," he said. "I'll put in a bid right now."

"Life's stranger than fiction any day," said Norah.

It was dark by the time they reached Peekskill and followed Route 9 up the Hudson for a little distance. Ed directed Bill, who was driving; he seemed to know the way.

"It's a good thing you didn' loan us the car," Sloan said. "I can' see at night."

"That so?"

"He's still got a piece of steel in his forehead from the crash," Norah said. "It must be pressing on a nerve."

"You ought to have it looked at," Hogan said. "That sort of business can be dangerous."

"Gives me headaches," Ed said, "once in awhile."

They followed a dirt road for a time and made several turns, one sharp turn up a hill that took them into the dooryard of a farmhouse.

"Here it be," said Sloan.

"Nice-looking place, from what I can see," said Hogan.

"Ay-eh," said Sloan.

There didn't seem to be anybody home, although they knocked on all the doors. There were no lights and all the windows were locked.

"Don' get it," Ed replied. "I tol' the guy we'd prob'ly be over t'night t' look it over. Mebbe they all went into town t' the movies."

But they could see it was a solidly constructed house. Hogan pumped some water from the well; it was cold and sweet. There was a large meadow in front of the house, a barn in good repair, and a woodlot further up the road. "House needs a coat of paint," Bill said.

Sloan said, "I'll walk up the road a piece, 'f you want t' stay here, see if the neighbors' folks knows anything 'bout where the folks be." Norah stayed with Hogan, sitting on the front porch in the quiet night.

"I want to apologize to you," he said.

"For what?"

"For making such an ass of myself the last time I was up."

"Forget it," she said. "You meant well."

"Hell is paved etc.," Hogan said. "But I want to say I like the boy. He's a nice guy."

"A swell guy," she said.

"I don't think I ever saw a man treat a woman with such —well, deference is the word I mean, consideration."

"He's sweet," she said. "He didn't get much of a break, you know. He's been kicked around a lot since he was a kid."

"I gathered that," said Hogan.

"You don't think he ever flew, do you?"

"Does it matter?" he said. "It's just that most pilots have a special terminology they use; it was strange not to hear him use it."

"He's done a lot of things that would surprise you; he was a test pilot for a time."

"That so?" said Hogan. "Who'd he work for?"

"The Army, I guess."

"I see," said Hogan.

"Nobody 'round," said Sloan, coming into the dooryard with his flashlight. "I reckon there ain' much sense in settin' here."

"What do you think?" said Norah. "I'd like to take a look inside the house before you make up your mind."

"We'll do that," Ed replied. "We'll run over agin one o' these days. I'll write 'em a letter t' expect us."

On the way back Hogan was surprised to notice that Sloan could see well enough at night to call the turns before he came to them.

"I know hereabouts," said Ed, "like the inside o' my pocket. You got good lights on this car. I coulda druv over here t'night, but I'd a hadda go a lot slower than you do."

"Hope you don't mind," said Bill. "I like to move when I'm moving."

"Ay-eh," said Sloan, "I'm with you there."

Next morning Norah rode down to the mailbox on the Hogans' running board. "So long," she said. "Make it soon again."

"We will," said Bill. "We'll come some time this summer, never fear."

"Hold the fort," Alice said. "I think you've got more guts than any sixteen women I've ever known. Good luck."

"Fiddlesticks," said Norah. "It doesn't take guts to do what you want to do."

She waved as they turned left into the road past Hortons' place, and she lowered the little flag on the mailbox. There was one letter in the box, from the superintendent of schools of Meadow County. She opened it with trembling fingers.

Dear Mrs. Sloan:

It is with regret that I must inform you that at a recent meeting of the board of the Olds Academy, it was decided, reluctantly I assure you, to dispense with your services as of the end of the spring term. Budgetary considerations, among others, made this necessary. I wish to assure you that there has been no complaint about the quality of your work, which was entirely satisfactory.

Most sincerely yours,
Elwin Fosdick, Superintendent

Humph! she thought, budgetary considerations, among others. *Among others* was the key to this mystery. She walked slowly back to the house, the letter in her hand. What did you expect? she thought. What else did you expect? You can't have any kick coming; you know a thing or two.

"Had a right good time with y'r friends," said Ed.

"They're good eggs," she said, sitting on the porch. She looked at him, where he was sitting with his hands clasped on his knees. It begins, she thought; you know a thing or two, but you should have been more prepared for this.

"What's the matter, Mom?" he said. "Did I do somethin' wrong?"

She shook her head, and he saw the letter in her hand.

"Git bad news?"

She looked at the letter, shook it, said, "No." She smiled. "We don't care, do we?" she said.

" 'Bout what?"

"About anything."

"Sure," he said. "I care 'bout you; you care 'bout me, don' you?"

"Ay-eh," she said, and he pushed her.

"You're makin' sport o' me," he said.

"How would you like me to be the principal of Olds Academy?" she said, laughing.

"Right 'nough," he said, "if you've a mind to."

She took the letter out of the envelope and read it to him. She watched his face and saw the lines deepen as he listened, and his hands clasped tighter around his knees.

"You know what day this is?" she said.

"Can' say as I do."

"It's April Fools' Day," she said.

■ ■ ■ ■ *10*

SLOAN SAT IN THE CELL with his hands clasped around his knees. There were no other prisoners at the time, and old Ed Fisher came in two or three times a day to talk to him. He could not go out of the cell, even to exercise, except on Saturdays when they let him shave and take a shower. Sometimes the sheriff would bring a checkerboard, and in the more than a month Ed had been there, Fisher had taught him how to play; but the old man always won the game, and then he would laugh uproariously.

"You don' use your head, boy," he would say. "Looks t' me, boy, like you never used your head at all."

Sloan didn't answer, but he asked the sheriff to leave the board and the checkers with him when he left, and he spent long hours working out games. He played both sides, and he found it difficult, at times, to resist the temptation to cheat himself. Nobody was looking, and sometimes he would maneuver his imaginary opponent's men into moves he knew a real opponent would have foreseen and never make. But it gave him great satisfaction to be able to jump three or four men at one move, and at such times he would say, under his breath, "That'll show ya, that'll learn ya t' make sport o' me."

He had not been surprised, the second day, when the doctor came, to find that he was the same doctor who had treated him the day of the shooting. His name was Pincus and he lived in Lemmon, where Sloan had found him early that Sunday evening. He had a pipe in his mouth when he came in the cell door with his bag, and he said, "Hello."

"Hello," said Sloan.

"Let's look at that foot."

Sloan held out the foot, and the doctor cut through the dirty bandage.

"You been having this doctored?"

"Yeh."

"Nasty-looking thing," the doctor said. He looked up at Ed and said, "This's going to hurt, so you can yell if you want to."

"Go ahead."

Pincus probed the wound, and Sloan did not make a sound. He cleansed it and bandaged it again and put his things away in the bag. He looked at Sloan; the fellow interested him.

"Look," he said, "this's none of my business, of course, but that story you told me that day—it wasn't true, was it?"

"What story?"

"About your brother cleaning a rifle upstairs, and it went off and the slug came down through the floor."

"I ain' got no brother," Sloan said. He looked at the doctor, who was smoking his pipe, and said, "You ain' got a butt, have you, Doc?"

"Sure," Pincus said, and fishing in his pocket, brought out a pack of Camels.

"Thanks," said Sloan, "that's my bran', when I got enough t' buy tailor-mades." He let the doctor light the cigarette and inhaled deeply. It made him slightly dizzy. He looked at Pincus and said, "Christ, Doc, but this's a hell of a mess." He shook his head.

The doctor said nothing, and Sloan said, "It sure is one hell of a mess, ain' it?"

"Yes," the doctor said. "Why did you do it?"

"I didn' mean to."

"You knew the gun was loaded."

"I f'rgot it was cocked."

"You went out to hold up a store, they say."

"Tha's right."

"You didn't intend to kill anybody?"

"Hell, no."

"You know how the law looks at that, don't you?"

"No."

"The way the law looks at it," Pincus said, "is that when

a man goes out with a loaded gun, he intends to use it if he has to."

"I didn'."

"What did you think would happen?"

"I thought when I flashed the gun, he'd get outta the car."

"Who?"

"The dead man, the man in the Chrysler. I on'y wanted the car t' make a getaway."

"After you pulled the holdup?"

"Yeh."

"You didn't think he'd put up a fight?"

"Would you of?"

"No. But you didn't think *he* would?"

"He was a old man."

"Didn't you think before you went out to do this job, when you put the gun in your pocket in your house, that something might happen?"

"I s'pose I did."

"Don't you know?"

"No."

"Why did you want to do it?"

"I hadda have the money, Doc," he said. "I *hadda* have it."

"I see," the doctor said. "You couldn't borrow any?"

"Who'd loan me money? Who'd gimme a job? They allus ast f'r recommendations. I ain' got no recommendations. They allus ast las' place. My las' place—"

"I understand," the doctor said. "You know you gave me your real name, don't you? We were talking about fishing and hunting for quite a time there, and when you left you gave me your real name."

"Did I?"

"Yes. Why did you?"

"I dunno," Sloan said. "You ast my name; that's my name."

The doctor rose to go and Sloan said, "You f'rgot y'r cigarettes, Doc."

"Keep the pack, son."

"Thanks," Sloan said.

"I'll be in again to dress your foot."

He patted Ed on the shoulder and called for the sheriff to let him out. So Sloan sat in the cramped cell for days with his hands folded, and old Ed came to play checkers and the lawyer came, and Ed's old wife that he called Winnie, she came too to bring him his meals, that she slid under the place in the door. She never spoke to him, except once, to say, "You sure turned out bad, didn't you, Ed?" He didn't answer.

The food was bad; leastways it wasn't like Norah could cook over the old oil range in the house near Polk. He thought of her cooking, her face red over the stove, and her grumpy, like she sometimes was. Like that time I said, Don't, and she said, Doesn't and I said, I'll say don't if I've a mind to, and she said, I thought you wanted to learn to talk proper English, and I said, To hell with it, if you don't like the way I talk I kin allus go away agin, like I did one night just before we was going to get married, only this time I won't come back. Did you run away? she said, did you really? and I said, Sure I run away and I'd do it agin if you don't like the way I talk, and she said, Forgive me, Ed, I didn't know. I was feeling mean; some days things get to be too much for me and I get to talking mean, don't pay me no mind those times, don't you pay no attention to what I say.

He wondered what she was doing and where she was, and

what she was thinking, and did the cops give her a going over, like that day. Like the first day when she was held with that guy Hogan, and they brought me from the clink across the way and they kept asking questions, so I knew she was there in the troopers' barracks, and they were asking her questions and then coming to me and asking me, and they were asking Hogan. That guy, he thought; he don't like me. Only when he come in the room that time, and I was bawling like a kid, he put his hand on my shoulder, like the Doc here did. That time he looked like he felt sorry for me. I don't want anyone should feel sorry for me, he thought; there ain't no reason why anyone should feel sorry. I give it and I take it and to hell with them. But I'll show 'em, he thought. I'll sit right here till the end and leave 'em all guess about it. Hogan don't know and neither does Norah or Ella Horton or any of them. He decided, sitting there, that he hated them all in a way, maybe even Norah. She was different, she came from a different place and they stood for something else that he didn't. They don't know me, he thought. I said to her, "You see me an' you don' know me." She didn't know what that meant, did she? No, she didn't. Did they ever wait for a handout at the Salvation Army joint or the Y.M.C.A. or the relief or the mission? Nuts to them. And I won't tell them anything.

Like yesterday, when George Goreski and his wife come, with their faces worried, but with company manners and saying, Sorry to hear about this, Ed; if there's anything we can do for you, let us know. Nah, I said, there ain't nothing you can do, but what they really wanted me to say was, You ain't got no reason to worry. You don't need to worry at all. Like I said when I was a kid to Tim Fowler and his sister, I said the same. Just because I was at your place before I done it, and you're a ex-con yourself and used to know me years ago in the Deerfield pen don't mean you got to worry. But Goreski must of told them about the gun, he thought. Yeh, it was a sure thing that Goreski was the one who described it to them, but he couldn't do nothing else, they had him on the spot, I bet. And maybe they put the heat on him. So he comes down here with his flat-faced wife and he says, If there's anything we can do, the yellow-bellied bastard. But he knows things that Norah don't and Hogan don't and none of them except maybe the cops, they know, they're nothing but a bunch of mugs themselves, would knock a guy off for a ten-cent cigar. Only they get paid for what they do, so they don't give a hoot in hell about the other guys.

O.K., George, he thought, I wouldn't say nothing because there ain't nothing to say, but I didn't tell him, he thought, and smiled. I didn't tell him not to worry, because it done me good to see the worried look on his puss, being so nice and smooth all the time and Ed this and Ed that and what can I do for you old pal old pal? Nuts to you, he thought. You can go take a flying f . . . for yourself, that's what you can do, with your flat-faced dame and your little shack and your road job and you're telling me, I'm going straight since the last time, no more for me, I learned my lesson. Yeh, he thought, and what if I should tell them—I *did* tell them, he remembered, by God I did tell them!

I told them; George said, "How much you want for the gat?" and I said, "I ain' selling it, it don' belong t' me, it belongs t' the truckin' company I work for an' we all carry guns." Holy Smoke, he thought, I *did* tell them that, and maybe that's what he's worried about, or is it something else? Well, he'll find out, Sloan thought, it'll all come out in the wash. What would a ex-con that's going straight want with a gun, a concealed weapon? He got a rifle, Ed thought, and we was all firing it that day at a mark on the hill, and maybe that's why I said to the doctor that my kid brother was cleaning a rifle upstairs and it went off and come down through the ceiling.

Why did you tell so many lies? the lawyer says, and how should I know? I just said the first thing that come into my head. I don't like that lawyer, he thought, what's his name? Farmer, he recalled. Burton Farmer, a lawyer with the name of Farmer. Come in here with a sour puss and says, I'm your lawyer, Sloan; the State appointed me to defend you, because every man has got a right to a lawyer. But I don't mind telling you I didn't much want to take the job—that's what he *should* of said, Sloan thought, because that's just what he was thinking. It showed on his face as plain as any words.

Why did you tell so many lies? Why did you tell the doctor that your foot got hit by a rifle bullet? and why—I read the statement you made, he says—why did you tell the guy in the diner that you got a couple toes cut off by your boss's kid? What a crazy story, who would believe it? and why did you tell the girl in the shoe store where you bought the rubber galoshes that a truck run over your foot? and why did you tell the guy in Peekskill where you bought the Ford that you got a broken toe where you hit yourself with a sledge hammer, did you think, what did you think?

I didn't tell him, Sloan thought. He don't like me neither, he's only got the job because they said to him, You, Farmer, go and defend this killer Sloan against the chair, and he done it. There's no real dough in it for him, what does he care? Why did you make the statement, he says? Don't you know you got a right not to say nothing until you consult an attorney? And I told him, I said, No, I didn't know that, but I never had no lawyer ever. Every time they pulled me in, for the schoolhouse and for the homebrew and for Nancy's man's car and for breaking the parole, they never said nothing about a lawyer, how was I to know? Anyhow, where would I get the money to hire a lawyer? You can always have a lawyer without no money, he said. A man accused of crime is entitled to a lawyer, this is a democracy. I didn't know that, I said. Besides it don't do no good now, it won't do no good nohow.

He got up from the cot and walked up and down in the cell. I don't trust that guy, he thought. They're all the same; they're all friends together, the defending lawyers and the prosecuting lawyers, they're friends out of court, and they talk with each other and they make deals with each other, everybody knows that. Standing up in court and shouting at each other like they was mad, and then outside they shake hands and make a deal. And with the cops too; they know all the cops. They know the cops and they know the judges and the cops know the judges too, and what chance does a stiff like me have with those bastards?

So what's the sense, he thought, him defending me when I already said, Yes, I done it, I shot the guy, I didn't mean to shoot the guy, but it's me that done it? And him saying, You know that's automatically first-degree murder and you're in a tough spot, just like the doctor said, if you go out with a gun. A automatic. Automatically is what he said. So, if I said I done it and it's automatic first degree it's automatic the hot seat and what's the sense? That ain't the point, he said, you must be defended by a lawyer, because they don't take a man's life away from him just because he says all right I done it. That wouldn't be *right*. So they're going to defend me from something I done, and burn me in the chair and *then* it will be all right and that will make other guys think twice before they go out with a gun.

The days went by slow, as they always do in jail, especially when they won't even let you out of the cell. Mr. Farmer, the lawyer, came and he went, and old Ed played checkers with him and Mrs. Ed, called Winnie, brought the food, and she began to talk to him. At first he didn't want to answer her, and he didn't answer her, because what she said was mean. She said, "You sure turned out bad, didn't you, Ed?" and he didn't answer that. But then sometimes after she had brought the tin pan with the spoon and slipped it under the door, she sat on a stool outside the door and watched him eat. The first time she did that, he sat on the cot with his back turned to her. But the second time she said, "Is the food all right?" and he said, "Yeh."

"Ed," she said, "you got no call being sore at me, I never did anything to you."

He didn't answer, and she went on. "I remember you when they brought you here when you were a kid, a fourteen-year-old kid," she said. "That time you burned the school house down."

"I didn'."

"Who did?"

"Tim Fowler."

"Who's he?"

"The kid that did it."

"I don't believe you, Ed," she said. "You always were a liar, even when you were a little kid, but we treated you right."

"Yeh," he said. "You treated me good."

"You did something bad this time," she said. "You killed a man. An old man that wasn't doing anybody any harm. A lot of people got thrown out of work when you did that, Ed. They shut down the flour mill, and maybe they won't open it again."

"That's bad."

"It's not so bad as what you did," she said. "You ought to look in your heart and ask God for forgiveness; there ain't much else that He can do for you."

Sloan didn't reply. He looked into the plate, and he remembered the Reverend Proctor in Deerfield, and his mother with the pinched face and the eyeglasses, and her prayers. He was startled to hear the woman talking about her. The woman was saying, "It's a good thing your poor mother's dead; God spared her all of this. She didn't have an easy row to hoe; I remember her."

"It was *his* fault," Sloan said.

"Whose fault?"

"Jed Alberts, my stepfather."

"That don't do you any good now, Ed," she said. "You'll have to get punished for what you did. Jed Alberts didn't do it. Jed Alberts didn't shoot this Mr. Baldwin."

He wished the woman would go away. He wished she would bring the slop when it was time to bring it, then go away and leave him alone. He looked up at her through the bars, his face set, and he saw her looking at him.

"You turned out to be a mean cuss," she said. "They tell how you were going to rob old Mr. Forsythe's store in Morrisford. He knew you all your life," she said. "He knew your stepfather too, and your mother, when you lived up in the hills back of town. He never did you no hurt."

"No," he said.

"Anyhow," she said, "I meant to tell you that your woman's coming up to see you tomorrow."

He rose suddenly from the cot and the plate fell on the floor.

"Look what you did," she said angrily. "Now you can just clean it up. . . ."

. . . Burton Farmer met Norah at the bus stop in Morris-ford and drove her to his home just out of Baconsfield. The hills rose right behind his house, and his wife was waiting on the porch. They were very kind to her; they insisted that she stay with them if she was going to stay overnight, and Farmer said he could arrange for her to see Ed at any time she wanted to.

"It's just a small county jail," he said. "Right now he's the only man there."

He took her into the little study he had built onto the house and he offered her a cigarette. He looked at her; he had learned from the police that Sloan's wife was a well-bred woman; but he had not been quite prepared for the sort of woman that he met. The more she talked, the more astonished he was at the nature of the relationship between these two, but he curbed his curiosity and asked no questions.

"I don't mind telling you," he said, "that I didn't want to take this case. The Court appointed me, but I didn't want to handle it. I have no liking for criminal cases, especially this sort of thing."

"I can understand that," she said.

"But after I'd met your husband in the jail two or three times, I began to change my mind," he said. "I began to get interested in him. I've seen his record, and I've read his statement. Would you care to read it?"

"Perhaps," she said. "Yes, I would."

There was no sense in dodging the issue. It would not make very pretty reading, but there was little enough that she could do, and she was determined to do at least that little. She felt, to her astonishment, a fundamental fear of being further involved, but she also felt a sense of obligation.

The fear was paramount, however, and she could not trace it to its source. There was the word *murder*, of course; and there was the *fact* of murder. All the connotations of this word inspired in her something close to terror. Here was a world in which the majority of human beings never had to function, a world they never touched upon. It was impossible to understand, she felt, how one human being could kill another, no matter what the circumstances, no matter what the provocation. Or was the "impossibility," she wondered, purely the result of our normal experience and the fact that acts of violence such as this were always in the tiny minority? She remembered having read once that a man had killed another man because the second man refused to pass a sugar bowl at table!

She sat in the office for the next half hour, reading the statement, while Farmer was silent in his chair. She knew that he was watching her, and she knew that she must not make a display of emotion; it would be of no assistance. The thing was horrible; it was incredible, and she seemed to see a different Ed from the one she had known during the months before their marriage and the nine months it had lasted. (Nine months—long enough to bear a child!) She had the image in her mind of watching a moving picture unreel upon a screen, but she also began to understand, at every step in the narrative, why he had done what he had done and why he had said what he had said. The poor child, she kept thinking, and wondered if she was saying it aloud, the poor, lost child.

She looked up at Farmer and placed the manuscript on his desk. "It's dreadful," she said and caught her lower lip between her teeth. "I don't suppose there's much to hope for."

"To be frank," he said, "there isn't. I'll do my best. This

is automatically a first-degree offense. Homicide committed in an attempt to commit a felony. We can try to establish a reasonable doubt—" he saw her mouth open as if to speak and anticipated what she was going to say. "A reasonable doubt that he actually intended to carry out the felony. You remember he said he had tried to take two other cars earlier in the day but lost his nerve. And we can plead his background and training. That's the usual defense," he said and sighed, "but I'm afraid it leaves people rather cold these days."

"My God!" she said, "but that's the exact truth! Surely there should be some understanding of the effect upon a human being of such forces as—" she gestured at the statement lying on the desk.

"It's the usual defense," he said. "There's no room here for a plea of insanity, do you think?"

"Of course not," she said. "Of course not." Something in her was outraged at the idea.

"A victim of society," said Farmer, clasping his hands and intertwining his fingers.

"The phrase is all worn out," she said, "but it should have some bearing. I'd phrase it, a victim of a particular type of society."

"The law is quite explicit in these instances," said Farmer. "When a man goes out with a gun, a loaded gun, it takes it for granted that if he's forced to use it, he will use it. That's very unequivocal, but don't you think it's just?"

She thought a moment and sighed and said, "I suppose it is, but it leaves so many factors out of consideration."

She was silent for a moment and then went on, as though talking to herself. "It's a terrible thing to do, to take a person's life, any person's life, for any reason. There are wars, of course; there's a war now and I suppose we'll get into it. He registered a month or so before this happened. I remember the day he registered. He couldn't read or write, you know, at least not much. They sent him a questionnaire, and I realize now why he was so sensitive about having to ask me to fill it out for him. Ex-felons aren't accepted in the Army, and he didn't want me to know about his record. I can't see any difference between one type of murder and another—yes, of course," she said. "Of course I can. But I don't understand the law at all—" She stopped as she had started, without looking at the man across from her or speaking consciously to him.

"Mrs. Sloan," he said, "the law is made for our protection, for the protection of our society. Sometimes it may seem very rigid, and sometimes it miscarries. There have been many innocent men who paid for crimes they did not commit, I'm sure of it. But the law cannot permit—"

"I know," she said bitterly. "I know what the law cannot permit. But this man—" she held out her hand, as though she were herself pleading his case before a jury. It was no use continuing, she thought; he wouldn't understand what I was saying. There's a stone wall here, she thought. There's a wall through which we'll have to smash our way. It begins with the child, she thought; you must begin with the child. A child must have food and clothing, a home with love in it, with a loving father, a loving mother, with love between the mother and the father. A man-child especially must have a father. There must be warmth, there must be security. *It's the first time I've been warm.* Certainly it was true—

"Surely it's true, Mrs. Sloan," the lawyer said, "that every person who grows up without the advantages you and I were fortunate enough to enjoy, doesn't become—" he hesitated.

"A murderer," she said. "Of course. I know that. But I object to the word *fortunate*. And even though what you say is true, that doesn't mean that the murder Ed committed—that he bears the entire responsibility for it, or even the largest responsibility."

The lawyer pursed his lips, and clasped and unclasped his hands. "That could be demonstrated," he said, "philosophically, I suppose."

"Not philosophically, Mr. Farmer," she said with heat. "Scientifically."

. . . While Ed was talking, she had thought, This is worse than I thought it would be. I don't know what I expected— I've seen plenty of moving pictures, but the idea never penetrated. But a man in a cage! A man inside a cage, eight feet by four feet. Once a week, he had said, they let him walk to the end of the larger room, take a showerbath, and shave his face. They watched him while he did these things. The toilet seat was inside the tiny cell, and the cot and the chair and the small table he had managed somehow to get took up all the room. You could take, perhaps, four steps in either direction.

She looked at him through the bars. Farmer had considerately engaged the sheriff's wife in conversation a few feet away, so that they could talk in low tones without being overheard. She watched his face and heard him say again, "I'm sorry, your seein' me here."

"It's not where you are, Ed," she said, "it's what you are. You're going to have to get a hold of yourself now. You must understand what's happened."

"Yes?" he said. "I understand."

There were still tears on his cheeks, and her own throat was full. He had wept when she took his hands through the bars, bowing his head onto her hand and sobbing. It had torn her so that she had felt she could not stay, but she had mastered herself. She had dressed herself carefully in her best dress, and she had even used some fingernail polish that Alice gave her, something she had never done in her life before.

He had noticed the nail polish and looked at her suspiciously, then looked more carefully at her. Her hair was neatly brushed and the new hat sat well on her head; he had not seen the coat before.

"You sure spruced up," he said. "You walkin' out?"

"Of course not," she said. She could not quite bring herself to say, I did it to cheer you up, to make you feel better, for you; because obviously it had affected him the wrong way. I couldn't have foreseen that, she thought. I had no way of knowing he would think I was dressed for someone else.

"Alice gave me the coat," she said, "and the hat. They've been terribly kind to us."

"You still there?"

"Yes," she said. "I'm looking for work. Every day I look for work, and Katey stays with Alice. I haven't found anything yet."

"You could mebbe go on the Relief," he said.

"No," she said. "I'd do it for a time if it were necessary, but even if I had to, I haven't established residence yet. I'll find something."

"How's Katey?"

"She's fine," she said. "Just fine. She asks for you."

"You didn't tell her?"

"I told her you went to camp, that you were drafted; she understands about the draft."

"I sure miss that kid," he said. Then he was silent for a time, looking at her. Then he took a deep breath and said, "I sure lied t' you."

"Did you?"

"I didn' mean to," he said. "It just come out. You oughtta know about me. I ain'—I mean I'm not nobody at all, like I said I was somebody. I never had no money like I said, I never had no house, I never had no brother that was my own brother, I was never a clown in Sells-Floto, I was never in Europe nor never in the Army Air Corps; I never went t' Alaska, nor owned no service station nor no auto agency, nor raced no cars nor drilled no oil wells like I said. There ain't really nothin' wrong with my eyes. I was never nobody like your husband was a World War ace an' learned scholars in the school, like Hogan writes books an' you bein' a school-marm too an' playin' the piano so pretty, I never was a test pilot—"

"That's all right," she said.

"No, it ain't," he said passionately. "Allus I wanted t' tell you the truth, but I didn' think you'd like me 'f I did. You went t' school an' speak good an' c'n read an' write an' got good manners. You know how t' hold a fork an' knife, you understand about pictures in books an' on the wall, an' you listen on the radio t' the simpany an' you understand the music like I don'. You understand t' speak t' people nice about important things an' understand them, politics an' books. I ain' so bright. I don' even know enough t' work an' keep you good after we got married."

She had placed her other hand over her face when he was talking and now she looked up at him, her lips sucked in between her teeth, and she pressed his hand. She considered a question, rejected it, then determined to ask it.

"You never flew an airplane, did you, Ed?"

"Yeh," he said. "I did. Not inna Army."

"You didn't crack up, your passenger wasn't killed?"

"I did," he said. "It wasn' bad; he wasn' hurt none but the ship was all washed up an' it ain' so that I got a piece o' steel in my head."

"You must tell the truth," she said, "even if it isn't easy; even if it isn't pleasant to you. It doesn't matter what it is to others. It doesn't matter, all the things you've just said, the things you haven't done. Believe me, Ed, it doesn't matter—not to me, not to anybody who can understand. What matters is that you never had a chance to do them. All that matters is the *truth*. You must tell Mr. Farmer everything, too; if there's anything you have to tell him before the Court opens, you *must* tell him."

"I did," he said. "There ain' nothin' else t' tell. Nothin' important."

"What do you mean, not important?"

"Somethin'," he said. "Mebbe it'll come out b'fore then. I can' tell now."

"What?"

"I can' tell."

"Don't you trust me, Ed?"

"Sure."

"Don't you trust Mr. Farmer?"

"I'd like to," he said. "I don' s'pose I do."

"I understand. But I think you can trust him, Ed. I'm sure you can. If there's anything to tell, now is the time for you to tell it."

"There ain' nothin' now," he said.

"You're sure of that?"

"Sure," he said. "What about Hogan?"

"What about him?"

"What they do t' him?"

"They didn't do anything to him; they released us both the first night. Ed," she said, suddenly remembering, "did you tell the police that Bill Hogan was with you, that he went upstate with you and that he did the shooting and you tried to stop him?"

"No, I never," he said.

"Are you sure?"

"Sure. First I said there was a aviator with me, name I thought up, an' that he did it; then I tol' the truth."

"Did they beat you?" she said.

"Sure. They allus do."

She closed her eyes but went on. "But what you told them was the truth?"

"Sure," he said.

"Will they let you have cigarettes? Is there anything I can send you?"

"I need t'bacco," he said. "It's good when you're alone. Mebbe you c'd send me a box o' paints like Katey's got." He laughed. "I'll paint you a picture like you got on the wall o' the fat ladies."

"I'll send some," she said. "Soon as I can get some money."

"That's mighty nice," he said. "When I was a kid, I never had no box o' paints."

. . . *11*

Of course, after the letter of dismissal came, she had asked for an interview with Mr. Fosdick, the superintendent of schools of Meadow County, and he had been most considerate. Nothing that he did, not so much as the flicker of an eyelash, could be adduced to indicate that he was saying anything more or less than he believed. It was simply the matter of the school board's appropriation, he said. There had been no complaint about the quality of her work; for a teacher without specialized training, her work was excellent. They had hoped to work her in as a full-time teacher, and they had exercised special consideration in view of her first husband's affiliation, realizing that she was a widow without means, with a child to support. "Perhaps it will be better now," he had said. "I understand you have remarried; congratulations." "Thanks," she had said.

Norah thought she had heard the word *first* emphasized slightly; it might have been imagination. Mr. Fosdick shook hands with her warmly and saw her to the door. He even patted her clumsily on the back, a familiarity he would never have dreamed of in the past, and assured her that if ever the appropriations were adequately enlarged, there would be room for her again.

"We must play politics with the legislature," he said in a way that was intended to indicate that he did not expect her to repeat this. "They're the boys who hold the purse strings." He laughed after he had said it, as though this were a condition he could lightly countenance and never question.

She caught the bus back to Polk and walked the mile and a half from the village to the house. She was disheartened; that was settled. Ed was working that day for Hortons' down the road. She had seen him in the field, cultivating, and he had waved at her, but she had pretended not to see him and she had not waved. She thought, when she got into the house, that that had been a niggardly thing for her to do. In what way could he be held responsible? The responsibility was hers. "You have to be practical," Bill Hogan had said. "You have not only yourself to consider."

Perhaps it was true that she had jeopardized Katey's security by her marriage, but everything in her rebelled at accepting or even considering the idea. When people are mature, she thought—any people—it's about time they learned to accept life. So what? So the educated widow of an educated man marries, after a reasonable and decorous interval, the uneducated farm hand of her neighbor. But most of these people were farmers, farm hands, agricultural laborers; they held—should hold—no prejudice against a member of their own class. That they did, when he married out of it, or when a member of the "upper classes" married into theirs, she regarded as a curiously inverted form of snobbism. Well, she thought, it's time they learned.

Katey came home from school with new pictures she had

painted and only augmented her mother's irritation. They did not allow the child a free rein for her imagination; the pictures she drew at home were infinitely more evocative than those she did in school. In school they put up pictures for the children to copy, or they arranged stupid still-life groups and had the children copy those. So when Ed came home tired, and washed at the pump outside the house, she was in a surly mood.

It was late in May and the weather was unseasonable. The oil range in the kitchen threw off a sweltering heat, and after she had returned from the county seat she had made herself do the week's laundry a day early, just in order to let off some steam. Then she had sent the child to play outdoors and started the supper. There wasn't very much to eat. She made a cabbage salad with a half-wilted head, some Mazola, salt and pepper and paprika. There were a few carrots to throw in and one tomato. She toasted bread and made a flour gravy. A working man needed more than this to eat, and so did a child.

She was annoyed by the way Ed looked at her when he sat at table, his hands and face washed, his dark, heavy hair slicked down with water. The lines of his face drooped with fatigue, but it was his eyes that annoyed her. There was patent adoration in his eyes and an expression of imminent fear she had never noticed before. Probably it had been there all the time, she thought, as she put the food on the table and took her place.

"Ain' there no meat t'night?" he said.

"You know there's not."

"It ain' very much t' eat, Mom."

"I know it."

He said no more but ate the toast and gravy and mopped the gravy up with more bread. He did a very careful job of sopping up the gravy, moving the bread in revolving circles on the plate, breaking off small pieces one at a time, so that the bread would last out the gravy and vice versa. Occasionally he looked at her, but she paid him no attention, and he felt a growing anger inside that he carefully controlled. It would not do to talk too much in front of the kid. She was all eyes and ears and asked too many questions.

"You can either go outdoors and play or play in your room," Norah said to Katey, and the child looked at her with astonishment.

"Aw, Mom," she said, "that's not fair."

"Mom's not feeling very well," she said. "I just don't want you making a lot of noise."

"I won't make any noise."

"I want you to play outdoors or go upstairs."

"May I stay downstairs if I don't make any noise?"

"Please, Katey," she said, "you're making Mom very angry."

"I didn't do anything," Katey said, her mouth puckering. "Honest I didn't."

"Katey!" she said and rose from the table, holding the paper napkin to her face. She left the room, and they heard her going up the stairs, heard the door slam.

Sloan and the child looked at one another. "What's the matter with Mom?" Katey said.

"Mom's not feelin' so good," he said. "She did a hard day's work, washin' an' all."

"She doesn't look any different," Katey said. "Maybe you should get the doctor from Polk."

"Be a good kid an' play outdoors," Sloan said. "I'll go an' cheer her up."

He sat and smoked a hand-rolled cigarette before he had made up his mind whether to go upstairs or not. When she was in these moods, he didn't know how to talk to her. She put up a wall between them that he could not climb, more because he felt she did not want him to than because he thought it could not be surmounted. She wants I should go away, he thought. Maybe I should. Or maybe it's because of what the school man told her; she didn't say. He pinched off the lighted end of the cigarette and put the butt in his pocket. Then he climbed the stairs and knocked timidly on the door. There was no answer. He knocked again and heard a vague sound that he interpreted as meaning to come in, and he turned the knob. The door stuck, and he thought, I'll have to sandpaper it. He pushed and the door opened, and he saw her lying face down on the bed.

"Mom," he said, "I'm sorry you're not feelin' good."

She didn't answer, and he put his hand on her back and gently pressed it. She rolled over then and looked at him, her face stained by tears, her lips trembling.

"You don't have to talk to me when I'm like this," she said.

"I said I'm sorry you're feelin' bad. What did the man at the school say?"

"He said nothing doing."

"T' hell with him," he said, smiling. "You don' want t' let that trouble you none. Even 'f he'd said yes, you wouldn' get no work till fall."

"You don't understand," she said. "Skip it."

"Why don' I understand?"

"You don't. Let it go." She turned back and lay on the bed. Then she got up and said, "How ridiculous, forgive me for acting like a child. Ed, there isn't any money; there isn't any food."

"I'm workin'," he said.

"How much do you earn? Twenty-five cents an hour, two fifty a day when you work? How long will you be working? Do you know?"

"When the job gives out there'll be another."

"Maybe."

"If there ain't another, I'll make one."

"Doing what? What about the back rent? What about the bills?"

"Let 'em wait. You been payin' bills hereabouts f'r years."

"That's the point," she said. "The last three years my credit hasn't been any too good, and right now it doesn't exist. The butcher in Polk, the grocer, the milkman want their money on time. They're small tradesmen themselves; they've had the squeeze put on them; they have to pay their own bills."

"If we can' pay 'em, we can' pay 'em."

"Very nice," she said, "very nice. If we don't pay them, we don't eat unless we pay cash."

She saw his face and she said, "I'm not blaming you, Ed, you're doing the best you can. I'll keep pulling too; I'll bake some pies and cakes and try peddling them again, and some preserves and things. I was just feeling low, forgive me."

"F'r what?" he said. "F'r havin' a man that can' keep you good?"

"Shut up," she said. There was a knock on the bedroom door.

"Come in."

Katey came in silently, with her hands behind her back. "You feeling better, Mom?" she said.

"Yes, darling," she said. "I'm sorry I was so cross."

"If you're not sick any more, I have a present for you," Katey said, bringing one hand out from behind her back.

She handed Norah a small bouquet of wild flowers and ran out of the room. They laughed and Norah called, "Come back, you monkey you, and I'll give you a kiss."

"Let's go downstairs, Mom," he said, "an' you play the piano."

"I don't feel much like it," she said, as they came down the stairs with their arms about each other.

With Katey sitting on his lap, Ed listened to the music. He could not resist asking her before she started the names of the pieces she was going to play, and she always kidded him about it.

"What difference does it make what the name is?" she said now.

"I like t' know the name," he said, "it makes it easier t' understand. Like you say 'The Blue Danube,' 'The Choc'late Soldier,' I c'n see 'em."

"Suppose I were to say Opus 25, Number 7?"

"That wouldn' mean nothin'," he said. "I ain' never heard of a opuss."

"You're a fool," she laughed and began to play.

"Opus means work," Katey said to Sloan, and he looked down at her.

"There ain' too much o' that," he said.

"Isn't," Katey said, and he laughed and started to tickle her. She squirmed in his arms and tried to get onto the floor, but he held onto her, tickling her ribs and poking her. She screamed, and Norah turned from the piano.

"If you two are going to keep that up," she said, "I'm not going to play."

"I can hear you, Mom," he said, grappling with the struggling child. "This li'l devil corrected my speakin' an' I'm punishin' her f'r bein' impolite."

"It's time for you to go to bed, Miss Gilbert," Norah said.

"Aw, Mom."

"Off with you," she said, "and don't forget to brush your teeth."

Miss Gilbert, he thought, that's *his* kid. Miss Sloan, Miz Sloan, Mister Sloan. Mister Sloan of Polk lives on the old Abbott place these days, has a wife and a ready-made family and no work to speak of. Miz Sloan don't have no money, and they owe for their rent and for their food and for wood from last winter when they weren't even married yet. March, April, May, only three months, he thought. Maybe she's going to have a kid that would be mine. He saw the little girl going upstairs, her small skirt hiked up in back, and he wondered if he would rather have a little girl or a little boy. He decided it would better be a boy that he could make it up to for what he didn't get when he was a kid.

He looked at Norah; she was playing. She was doing what she said was "improvising"; there was no tune that he could recognize, but her hands moved deftly on the keyboard, striking a chord now and then. Mostly when she improvised, the music was sad, and he thought, that's because she's mostly sad herself. Like as if she was sorry for what she done when she took up with me. He decided that some day he would ask her, right to her face he would ask and make her answer him. But first, he thought, there's a lot you'll have to tell her, a lot you ain't never told, so maybe you should begin it now.

He opened his mouth and said, "Norah," but she did not hear him. He said it louder, and she struck a low chord and turned and said, "Ed, what're we going to do?"

. . . Sloan moved up and down the rows of new tomato plants on the Horton place. Feeling the hoe in his hands, he moved it deftly around the roots of the plants that were tied by strings to their supporting sticks. He remembered having set out the plants several weeks before, transplanting them with care from the bright tin cans in which Ella had grown them indoors during January, February, and March. There had been a wonderful feeling doing that, tapping the cans gently with his fingers till they loosened from the packed earth inside, digging the holes with a small trowel, setting the plants into the holes, sifting the earth around them, and packing it down and watering each plant as it was set. It was best to transplant late in the afternoon, so the young plants had the cool night to get used to the earth before the hot morning sun arose.

Then as they had grown, he had brought sticks and tied each plant carefully to the stick set next to it. It had taken a long time—there were over three hundred plants—and his back ached when he was through. Now they were growing rapidly, and soon he would have to bring longer sticks and retie them. He bent to pick a potato bug off a plant and squeezed it between his fingers. He didn't like to do that. He examined the underside of the leaves for other beetles, for their eggs. It would be good to own a piece of land, he thought, a place of your own. It wasn't the same working for Hortons' folks as it would be working for yourself, for Norah and the kids. He always thought *kids*, not the kid, because he always thought of the kid that would come.

Now he leaned on the hoe and looked at the rich, dark earth under his feet. He noticed his arms, how strong they were, and he laughed, thinking of the way they had got so strong. He held out his arm and flexed the muscle, watching it bulge, and watching the prominent veins wind and twist below the skin. I feel good, he thought; I feel better than I ever felt in my life before. He remembered all the years gone by since he was a kid, and the every-morning feeling that he had always described as lousy. Every morning, for as long as he could remember, he had felt lousy. That feeling passed by afternoon, but now when he awoke in the mornings, now when he awoke feeling the woman's body beside him in the bed and touching it with something close to reverence and wonder, he felt good.

He felt, rising from the bed, as though there were nothing in the world he could not do if they gave him a chance to do it. It must be, he had thought, because now and for the first time, you got what you always wanted. It must be because you have come home now, to a place and a woman and a kid. And even though he knew that there was not much that he had learned, that there were very few things that he could do that would really bring in any money, he felt that he had only to take a slight step, a step through something he saw as a thin wall or a veil, that would mean the difference between poverty and security. It could be done; he knew it now. He was full of a sense of power and strength; you're a strong man, he thought, looking at his arms, feeling his legs reaching down and standing lightly but firmly on the soil. Go to it.

They had often talked of a place of their own since they were married. It was a game they played together, planning and speculating on the ways and means of getting such a place. No, it would not be in these parts. ("When I c'n rent a car agin," he said, "we'll see what we c'n do over t' Peekskill.") Just to make the game more real Norah had asked old Ella again whether she would sell the place and how much she would take. She wanted four thousand dollars; and where before she had offered Ben Gilbert a chance to buy the place on a monthly rental basis, now she wanted two thousand dollars down.

"Place ain' worth that much," Sloan said to Norah, and she laughed.

"What you laughin' at?" he said. "Tha's true. If it's worth a nickel, it might fetch fifteen hundred bucks, I wouldn' give a penny more."

Norah laughed until she bent double, and he finally caught on.

"You're right," he said. "Two thousan' might's well be twen'y thousan'."

"That's it," she said. "You hit it right smack on the head that time."

"What the hell," he said. "With you there ain' nothin' I couldn' do. Mebbe it would take a li'l time, but mebbe not so long's you think. I'm tired a livin' in a place where there's a hedgehog livin' under the outhouse. Like t' sit on him a dozen times a'ready."

She laughed. "Go to the bank," she said, "and draw the two thousand."

"Not a chance," he said. "I'm waitin' f'r a better offer. When you're buyin' real estate, you don' pay the askin' price, never."

"All right," she laughed, "I trust your judgment. But in the meantime you better shoot that porcupine."

It was lots of fun to play that game, and the game was not spoiled by their mutual recognition that it was only a game. Making dinner these days, doing the sheets and the clothes, darning his socks, Norah felt much the way Ed felt when he was working in the fields for Hortons' folks. There wasn't enough money to do with, for he only brought in two fifty a day when he was working steady six days a week. She was able, during May and June, to average about five dollars a week more, baking cakes and pies, selling the preserves she had made last fall. But the twenty dollars was a basic minimum; you couldn't go beyond it either way. Just the same, doing the housework in the house she didn't own; making the beds and conjuring up nutritious if monotonous meals out of the few staples they could afford to buy for cash, she enjoyed a sense of self-possession she had never felt before.

All my life before, she thought, all my life with Ben, I was only playing at living. I did the work and cooked the meals and mended the clothes and washed the linen in an automatic fashion. Now, and for once, it's a pleasure to be busy; there's a sense of accomplishment; the sense of working, even if only imperceptibly, toward a goal. The goal of security might be far away, but it was visible. The means for its attainment might be uncertain, but the sense of mechanical behavior no longer existed. It was real. It was good. It was solid.

She looked forward to seeing him come up the road at suppertime, and she made it a point to wash and change her dress before he came. She knew how depressed a man could be to find a messy house when he came home, a messy woman in the house, her face red with the heat of the stove, her hair unbrushed and stringy, the child's play toys scattered on the floor. So after she had set the supper on the range, she freshened up and went out with Katey on the front lawn behind the low stone wall to wait for him. These hot days she always had a pitcher of iced tea ready, and she made him sit in the other old deck chair on the grass and drink the tea and smoke a cigarette, even before he had washed up. Those times, the game went on, and they both sat imagining—though they rarely mentioned it—that this was their home; this was their place and now they were at home. *"J'y suis, j'y reste,"* Ben Gilbert used to say, but for him it meant something else.

It was astonishing to her how little jealousy Ed felt for her dead husband. It would have been only masculine for him to have felt some slight resentment for the ghost, for Norah never made any particular effort to suppress mention of Ben. She had told Ed a great deal about him since their marriage, had shown him the souvenirs that he had kept from the World War, the broken propeller and the helmet and goggles, the insignia from the skin of the crashed German airplane.

Ed had looked at the picture of Ben in his uniform, the second time she showed it to him—or rather, he had noticed it when she was looking for a handkerchief in her drawer. He had reached in and taken the picture in his hand and said, "That's a right nice photo. You ought t' put it on the table where the little girl c'n see it. He was her dad." She had done that, and the photograph stood on the table.

"That's quite a gat he's got there," he had said.

"Gat?" she said.

"The pistol hangin' on his belt."

"Oh, yes," she said. "It was a German pistol he brought back. Belonged to a German pilot who was shot down and made a prisoner in France. I used to have it here."

"Where's it now?"

"At Hogans'," she said. "I asked Bill to keep it when Ben died. I was always afraid of the thing, afraid Katey would get hold of it. Ben was a funny guy," she said. "He always kept it loaded."

"Might be a good thing t' use on that hedgehog," he said.

She had moved the radio from downstairs up to the bed table in their room, and evenings when Katey had gone to sleep, they spent a lot of time lying on the bed listening to it. Ed liked to listen to the Lone Ranger, and to Bing

Crosby singing from the Hollywood Hotel. "I'm headed for the laaaaaast round-up," he used to sing, "git along li'l dogey git along git along," and Ed had learned the words from the radio. They listened to Charlie McCarthy, but they also listened to the news. The Nazis had invaded Denmark and overrun Norway; they had rolled over Belgium and Holland, and the Belgian troops had been nearly decimated trying to give the British a chance to evacuate the mainland. Then the Nazis had outflanked the Maginot Line and poured into France.

"Sounds bad," said Norah. "They were sold out, every one of them."

"Don' make no sense t' me," said Sloan. "Movie I saw once a long time ago, there was a soldier said somethin' about a idee t' end the war. Think he was a German soldier, feller with a broad puss an' a busted nose. Said, 'The way I see it, let all them guys that wants t' fight, the kings an' the generals, git in a big ring all around with barb wire, an' fight it out.' Or somethin' like that. Seems t' me like he had the right idee."

"It isn't as simple as all that," Norah said.

"Song we used t' sing," said Sloan, "goes, 'Yore inna army now, yore not behind a plow, you'll never git rich you sonofabitch, you're inna army now.' Inna army you don' get much chance t' say what you want; you damn well do what they tell you."

On the Fourth of July the Hogans came to spend the day, but Ed had to stick with the first haying of the season. He came into the yard several times during the afternoon after they had made a load, and they pitched the hay into the barn beyond the house. Bill thought he'd like to get some exercise, and the men gave him a pitchfork, but he gave it up after about an hour's work.

"Had no idea what a tough job that was," he said, laughing. "I used to help with the haying when I was a kid, but that was a long time ago."

"You should have had more sense," said Alice. "You're going to have to drive back."

"I didn't do *that* much work," he laughed. He turned to Norah and slapped her on the back. "Well, kid," he said, "*comment ça va?*"

"It goes," she said. "It could go better."

"Could you use a piece of change?"

"Always could use a piece of change," she said. "But this time I'm not going to accept it."

"Why not?"

"Keep my credit fresh with you," she said. "Not that I've ever been able to pay you anything back, but if I don't borrow for a time—"

The three of them laughed together, and Norah thought, It's good to have such friends. Bill still feels sort of foolish about that time last March when he came up alone; he's bending over backward to compensate for it. She saw Alice looking at her and smiled at her.

"You guys ought to have another kid," she said, and saw Alice's eyebrows rise. "No, no," she said swiftly, "*I'm* not; not yet at any rate, but I'm thinking about it."

"This's a hell of a world to bring up kids," said Bill.

"I'd think a long time before I had another," Alice said. "The way the world is going."

"Fiddlesticks," said Norah. "You've got to live as though you were going to live forever; you've got to live as though everything were going to be all right."

"If you don't mind my saying so," said Alice, "I think that's a pretty romantic way of looking at things."

"I'm a romantic gal," said Norah.

"No, by God," said Bill, "but Norah's right."

"Oh, nuts," said Alice, "you're the one who gave me these ideas. First it was the children in Spain; then the children in Austria and Czechoslovakia, in Poland, Norway —millions on the roads with nowhere to go and bombers overhead. Now it's the children in France. Maybe I feel worse about them than I do about the rest. I've been to France. I've seen those children."

"They'll really go to town on England soon," said Bill. "You can count on it. And we'll get in. The conscription bill's going to pass, you know."

"Sure," Norah said, earnestly, "but you've got to take a long look ahead, and then you've got to live from day to day. Otherwise it doesn't make any sense. Otherwise you'll get so low you'll be useless when the time comes."

"Oh, ho," said Bill. "You admit the time is coming?"

"Sure," she said. "Didn't you tell me once that nothing's static, everything's in a process of becoming?"

"I might have," said Bill. "I'm partial to quotations."

"That's not a quotation," Norah said. "That's a fact. If you take any other attitude, you're licked before you start."

"Hi," said Ed. He was streaked with sweat, and there was hay in his hair. He mopped his face. "Sun's pretty hot t'day," he said.

"You through?"

"Yeh, f'r t'day," he said. "On'y a couple more days hayin'."

"There's some cold beer in the ice box," Hogan said.

"I'll bring it out in a pitcher," said Norah. "You guys sit and soak up the sun."

"Not me," said Ed. "You city folks try t' get the sun; me, I try t' keep outta it." He followed Norah to the kitchen and washed just outside the door in a pail of water.

—— 169 ——

"Where's Katey and little Bill?" she said.

"They went back down the road inna wagon," he said. "They'll be back."

"What're you going to do after the haying's done?"

"Dunno," he said. "They didn' say nothin'."

He came into the kitchen and put his arms around her. "Hello, pussycat," he said, squeezing her.

"Hello, tom."

"You like me?" he said.

"Sorta; sometimes yes, sometimes no."

"No t'day?"

"No, yes today."

"Which d'ya mean," he said, "yes or no?"

"No and yes."

"I'm not so smart like y'r city friends."

"Oh, cut it out," she said. "I don't like to hear you say that."

"Mebbe I'll write a book some day m'self," he said, "after you git through learnin'—teachin' me t' read an' write. You been fergettin' my lessons."

"I'm not the one who forgets the lessons," she said. "You're the one."

She had the pitcher full and set it on the tray with the glasses, picked up the tray. He stood in front of the door and barred her way, his arms outstretched.

"Get out of the way, dope," she said.

"Kiss me first."

"I can't kiss you with the tray in my hands."

"Then put it down."

"I won't."

"Then I won' let you out," he said.

"Get the hell out of the way," she said.

"The hell I will," he said. "Not till you kiss me."

She turned and set the tray down and came up to him. He took her in his arms, and crushed her to him till he could feel her large breasts firm against his chest.

"You're hurting me!" she said. "Ouch!" she said, "you need a shave!"

"You used my razor-blade on y'r corns," he said.

"I never did, I don't have any corns."

"You want I should show 'em to ya?" he said. "I wake up inna middle o' the night an' count 'em. I c'n see 'em growin'. Ev'ry night they sprout, an' they keep me awake, they tickle me."

"Let me go, you dope," she said, "what will Bill and Alice think?"

"Mebbe they'll think we went upstairs."

"Shut up," she said, and slapped his face gently.

"Mebbe we *should* go," he said and winked his eye.

"Don't you ever get tired?" she said.

She picked up the tray again and started for the door.

"Mom," he said, and she turned and saw him smiling "D'you mind if I ask Bill t' bring that gat the next time he comes up?"

"Bring what?"

"You know," he said, "the gun Ben—y'r husband used t' have."

"What do you want it for?"

"Dunno," he said. "It'd be handy t' have aroun' the house."

"You know what I think about that," she said, her brow furrowed, her eyes steady.

"Don' worry none," he said. "I won' shoot ya with it."

She went down to the lawn with the tray, and he followed her.

"It took you long enough," said Bill. "What were you up to?"

Ed winked at him, and Bill laughed. "Thought you guys were going to move to Peekskill," he said. "Whatever happened about that house?"

"I ain' made up my mind about it," said Sloan, and Norah thought, That's funny, I almost forgot about that house; he never mentions it any more. She looked at him, and he was aware that she was looking at him.

"Couldn' a moved 'f we'd a mind to," Ed said. "I had steady work hereabouts since you was up last. Thinkin' o' maybe takin' a job up in Deerfield makin' airplane engines."

"Hornets?" Hogan said. "They must be looking for mechanics these days."

"Yeh," said Sloan. "Ads in the papers."

"Why don't you reapply for the Air Corps?" Bill said and almost bit his tongue when he remembered.

"They wouldn' have me," said Sloan. "I ain' fit."

There was a pause and they drank their beer. Sloan looked up again and said, "Frien' o' mine in town says it looks like they're gonna pass conscription."

"Looks that way," said Bill. "How old are you?"

"Thir'y-four."

"They'll get you," Bill said happily, "don't think they won't. It makes me feel good to know I'm over forty." He rubbed his hands together with mock maliciousness. "Make a man of you, Ed," he said, "build you up, join the Army and see the world."

"That's a Navy," Sloan said with a smile.

"Better learn to speak Spanish," Bill said. "Learn French and German too, not to mention Japanese."

"You really think they'll git me?" Sloan said, and Bill wiped the smile off his face. The man's worried, he thought;

maybe there's something in that business; maybe they're really looking for him.

"Hell, no," he said, "at least not at first. You're in the age limit, but you've got a dependent wife and kid to support."

"There ain' nobody I want t' fight," Sloan laughed. "I ain' mad at nobody. 'Cept mebbe the guys that hounds us f'r the bills. "

. . . In late July the Hortons hired a man with a Fordson tractor to pull the disk harrow, and Ella told Sloan she wouldn't need him any more.

He went upstairs to see the old man and said, "Look, Pop, I c'n run that cat well's the guy you got."

"You're forgettin' the tractor belongs t' him," the old man said with a sly grin. "It's hisn, so he gits the job."

"Them things puts lots o' guys outta work," said Sloan.

"I can't help that none," Sam Horton said. "Mebbe you should talk t' old Hennery Ford about it."

He started back to the house, then decided, Well, it's come and you gotta do something about it. He walked down to the main road, to the crossroads where he'd stood that night in March and waited for a night driver to pick him up. He decided that he would go from town to town and ask for work. If there weren't any farmers in the neighborhood who needed a hired man to drive a team or hoe the garden or do the chores, there might be some work in town.

He picked up a ride with a traveling salesman, who talked all the way into Polk. Sloan looked at him and thought about him. Here was a man who had a car of his own, could go where he pleased on wheels, wore good clothes and made a living.

"I don't get to see my wife very often," the salesman said. "They keep me on the road all the time; but the country's full of women. How's crops?"

"Fair hereabouts," said Sloan.

"Wish I could live in the country all year 'round," the salesman said. "When the Nastys come bombing us it'll be a good place t' be. Where you going?"

"I'm lookin' f'r work," Sloan said. "You don' know of any?"

"Hell, no," the salesman said, "I thought you lived here."

In Polk Ed talked to the man who owned the red front store.

"I'm Sloan," he said. "Me an' my wife owe you f'r stuff."

"That's right, Mr. Sloan," the grocer said.

"Ain' much chance o' settlin' the bill right now," Sloan said, "but I thought how mebbe you might need a man t' help aroun', deliver mebbe, wait on the trade. Thought mebbe I c'd earn a bit here, work off the bill."

The grocer looked at Sloan curiously and laughed. "Why, man," he said, "if all the folks hereabouts that owe me money was to come in and ask f'r jobs, where'd I be?"

"Dunno," Sloan said. "You don' have no job?"

"No," the man said.

"Thanks."

"Hi, just a minute," said the grocer. "I hate t' mention this, but you think maybe you could pay a little on the bill?"

He got a ride from Polk to Coney and talked to the man at the gas pump. He talked to the blacksmith, who offered him a job in exchange for meals. He talked to the garage man, who said he had all the help that he could use and couldn't even pay the two men he had.

"Didn' you never hear tell of this here de-pression we got?" He laughed. "Used to be it was a de-pression, then it was a re-cession, dunno what they call it now, but everybody's plumb broke. Maybe you should talk to Harker at the Plymouth agency."

Harker looked him up and down, noting the shabby clothes. "What can you do, buddy?" he said.

"I c'n drive any car you got," said Sloan. "I c'n make repairs."

"You a mechanic?"

"Yeh."

"Ever work in a auto agency before?"

"No," said Sloan, "but I worked in garages, places."

"Ever work for a auto company, factory, I mean?"

"No," he said.

"Maybe I could use you," the man said, spitting. "Come around in a couple months and talk to me again."

"Thanks," said Ed.

From Coney he got a ride on the good highway into Glover, where he inquired his way to the shoe factory and saw the sign NO HELP WANTED. Glover was such a big town that he didn't know where to go to ask for work, but he went up and down Main Street, in and out of the stores, asking in each store. In every store they made him aware of his shabby clothes. In each place they asked for references, and he invented the names of places he had worked in various towns throughout New England. One man told him to join the Army; but none of them had any work, and he caught a ride from Glover down to Low Hill and spoke to the garage men, the blacksmith, the Ford and Buick agents, the sawyer and the local mason. From Low Hill he came back to Polk by way of Stiles, and it was late afternoon.

"I was worried about you," Norah said, and he smiled, showing his uneven teeth.

"You got good reason t' be worried," he said, "but not about me. I been huntin' work. Went over t' Polk, Coney, Glover, Low Hill, Stiles. No soap. Covered over fifty miles."

"Cheer up," she said.

"I ain' downhearted, not yet," he said. "But it don' look easy."

The last week in July and the first two weeks in August he made the rounds of every town in the neighborhood, of almost all the farms. He hitched as far as Shoreline in one direction, to Deerfield in another, then back to the countryside around Morrisford in the western part of the state, where he had lived when he was a child. Norah made sandwiches for him to take on his trips, but he never had more than a half dollar or a dollar in his pocket.

She wrote to all the teachers' agencies she knew about and received application blanks in return. Since all of them asked details of normal-school training and she had none, she did not fill them out. She wrote to Mr. Fosdick, asking frankly whether he knew of some small town in Meadow County that needed a country school teacher for the lower grades. He did not answer. She wrote to Bill Hogan, asking for a loan, and he replied. But she didn't tell Ed that she had written.

Christ, Bill's note said, *but you hit us exactly the wrong time. I haven't sold a line in months now, and we're living on our fat like the proverbial camel, or whatever it is. The market's closing down, you know; magazines aren't buying very much. But the minute we get something in, it goes to you. Keep your nose down,* he wrote, *and hold the fort, if you don't mind mixed metaphors. Reinforcements are coming up, and I'm considering going into the cloak-and-suit business. Fic-*

tion? Coming events cast their shadows, you have heard. They want war stuff now. A few months ago you couldn't sell them a line about the war—"controversial." Now that we know which way the wind is blowing, they want it, and how! The sheets are full of it. Fiction utilizing the fall of France is appearing daily, stories about the heavy raids on London that only happened two weeks ago! Stories about the retreat from Dunkerque. And so far as articles are concerned, it's getting more and more difficult to place one that even questions the advisability of our entering this great crusade. The President is out to save the British Empire again. Well, I think you know I'm not a pacifist; Hitler has got to be stopped. I supported Spain and I support China, and I think I'd support any war that was a real antifascist war. The German people will have to take care of Hitler in the end. But it won't be easy. They'll have to get some help from people who really want to help.

It won't be easy, she thought. "Ed," she said, "you know we're in a spot."

"I know it."

"There hasn't been any orange juice for Katey the last couple of weeks."

She wanted to say that she had skimped on food for both of them so Katey would be sure to have enough to eat, but somehow she couldn't bring herself to mention it. He probably knows it anyhow, she thought.

"Listen, Mom," he said. "You think you c'd make out better 'f I went away?"

"Don't be a fool," she said. "At least not any more of a fool than you have to be."

"You think I'm a fool?" he said solemnly.

"Of course not. Don't be such a nut."

He suddenly had an idea. So he looked at her and said, "You know, it don' make no difference t' me 'f you think I'm a fool."

"What're you talking about?"

"I said it don' make no difference t' me what you think about me."

"Doesn't it?" she said, smiling.

"No, it don't!" he shouted.

"It doesn't," she said. "I thought I'd *learned* you not to say don't instead of doesn't."

"I'll say don't any time I got a mind to," he said, his eyes snapping. "I know I ain' so educated like you, but 'f you don' like the way I talk, I c'n go away, like I done before."

"Did before," she said, smiling.

"I done it b'fore," he said, "an' I c'n do it agin. I seen you look at me," he said. "Specially when you got y'r fine educated friends from New York. I see how you look at me like you was ashamed o' me because I ain' got no schoolin' like you got."

"Stop it," she said.

"I'm gettin' mighty sick o' it," he said. "I may not know how t' read an' write good, but I'm a human bein', I got feelin's, you may not think so 'cause you an' y'r high-falutin' friends—"

"Stop it right away," she said.

"Nuts," he said. "I'm sick of it all. I'm good an' sick of it."

He recognized now that if, when he had started this conversation, he had been trying to get her angry for a purpose, for her own good, he was now good and angry himself.

"One night w'en you got me t' stay here, w'en I tol' you I was through at Hortons', I got t' thinkin' late at night that I don' belong here. Well, I don'. You ain' my kind an' I ain' your kind. I don' want you should feel sorry f'r me. I'm just as good as you are, even if I don' speak good an' y'r kid c'n tell me not t' say this an' that, jus' like you do. T' hell with it," he said, his face convulsed, his fists clenched. "I say t' *hell* with it!"

"If that's the way you feel about it, Ed," she said, "I suppose that's the way it is."

"Tha's the way it is," he said. "If you don' like it, you c'n lump it."

"I'll lump it," she said, and turned on her heel and walked away. She heard the door slam, and she wanted to go to the window to look, but she didn't. Instead, she went upstairs to see whether Katey was covered by the sheet, and then she lay face down on the bed and wept. It was a mistake, she thought, then sat up on the bed and said, "No."

You're not licked yet, she thought. He'll come back. He's *got* to come back. Don't be so sure, she thought; don't be so sure of yourself. What he said was true, you know. There *is* an element in you, an element of condescension, of Christian moral uplift. That's bad, she thought; that's snobbery; that sort of snobbery is just as bad as the neighbors on the party line. Take a good look at yourself, she thought, and make up your mind. Why do you—she couldn't quite say love—why do you like this man, why are you interested in him? Is it because he's a person in his own right, or is it because you *do* feel sorry for him, because you don't think he ever had a chance and you would like to right a wrong? Which is it, Lady Bountiful; are you trying to help the man because he's starved, or are you the one who's starved yourself?

She had two days to think this over, because he didn't come back for two days. Then she was standing in the kitchen, stirring an oatmeal supper for Katey, and he put his hands over her eyes like a child who says, Guess who? Suddenly she went all to pieces and turned into his arms and sobbed loudly. He patted her shoulder clumsily and stroked her hair.

"Mom," he said quietly, "I want you should f'rgive me."

"Forgive *me*," she said. "I've been a fool."

"No, it ain' you. I'll try harder."

She looked up into his face and said, "Did you really go away that time last winter? Did you really?"

"Yeh," he said, "I did."

"You never told me."

"Nah."

"Why didn't you tell me?"

"W'at was the sense o' tellin' you," he said. "When I come right back agin?"

. . . "Altogether a little over four hundred dollars," Norah said, looking up from her account book.

Ed whistled. He wet his lips and said, "W'at c'n they do t' you?"

"Nothing."

"Nothin'?" he said, his brows wrinkled. They could put her in jail, he thought; she ain't telling me the truth.

"Well," she said, "of course, they can sue me and they can probably get a judgment against me for the money; but we have no income to amount to anything, and they'd have a hard time collecting it."

"But they *could* collect it?"

"They could collect it," she said, "if we ever earned

enough for them to be *able* to collect it. They get what's called a garnishee, a percentage of your earnings."

She laughed and said, "Didn't I tell you you'd got into something, brother? You know, under the law, a husband's legally responsible for his wife's debts. Maybe that will teach you a lesson."

"Sure does," he said. "If I'd a knowed that I wouldn' a married with you." He slapped her on the back and laughed at her. "No crap," he said. "Whatta you think we ought t' do?"

"I think I'll let you worry about it, Ed," she said with a smile.

He laughed too, and they both laughed, and it was fun. She watched his face and saw that he was taking it with a sense of humor, but soberly as well. Then she grew serious, and said, "Well, darling, what *is* there to do except to keep on trying? I'm writing to all the school superintendents in the state, and we're in good company. Something's bound to turn up sooner or later."

"I couldn' allow t' have you keep me," he said, "even 'f you got a job o' teachin'."

"Why not?"

"I jus' couldn'," he said. "It wouldn' be right nohow."

"Nuts," she said. "You'd support *me* if you had the money, wouldn't you?"

"Sure Mike."

"Well, what's the difference?"

"It's diff'rent."

"I don't see it, Ed. You don't really believe there's that much difference between men and women, do you?"

"Heard tell there was a diff'rence," he said. "Like in the ol' joke. How the preacher said, 'An' God created Man in

—— 181 ——

His own image, an' He created women too, on'y with a diff'rence,' an'—"

Norah held her nose.

Katey came running in, shouting, "Bill's here, Bill's here!" and they both felt a sudden access of energy, of hopefulness, and came to the kitchen door to watch him drive in. He was in a brand-new car, a Ford convertible, and Alice and Bill, Jr., were with him. They were all waving, and Bill was shouting, "Tally-*ho*, YOICKS! Tally-*ho*, YOICKS!" as they came up the driveway, the horn tooting.

"Where'd you get it?" Norah said, and Bill said, "A small thing, but mine own, how you like? No more borrowing cars for the Hogans till they repossess *this* one."

"Nice, nice," said Norah, "you must have struck oil."

"Not quite," said Alice. "Now we belong to the finance company." She shook her head. "This dope sold an article, and we're buying the jallopy on the installment plan."

They all climbed out and stood around, looking at the new Ford.

"This's Labor Day," said Bill. "This," indicating the car, "is the fruit of my labor. Only, as you may have learned by now, nothing as expensive as this comes through honest toil. You have to sell yourself. I have *sold*," he said, mock solemnly.

From the back of the car they brought cartons of food and bottles of beer, canned soup and chicken-and-noodle dinners, fresh vegetables and an enormous sirloin steak, siz dozen oranges and grapefruit, Shredded Wheat and other cereals, potatoes (white and sweet), two cartons of Camels, sweet corn, a quart of whisky and some ginger ale.

"We will celebrate my prostitution," Hogan said, "as befits."

"What's he talking about?" Norah laughed, and Ed stood beside her grinning.

"Don't mind him," Alice said. "He's done nothing wrong, but he enjoys tormenting himself about it. He wrote a piece for *Collier's* about the new Air Corps we're building, the new planes. He's considered an expert because he flew in the last war, so they paid well—fifteen hundred bucks."

"Wow!" said Norah. "Blood money!"

"You said it," Hogan said, setting the carton on the kitchen table. "Why do you suppose they wanted such a piece? I'm no expert anyhow. I'm a fraud."

Alice frowned. "There was nothing in your piece to be ashamed of, and you know it."

"Balls," said Hogan. "Look. I'm a World War Ace, what Ben used to call an *as-s-s-s*. That's French," he said. "So they say, Hogan old ace old ass, go look over the new ships we've got and tell us the difference between the ones we got now and the bird cages you Knights of the Air used to fly in the olden days. So I visit Mitchell Field and they hop me in the Boeing XB-15, and I tell how it can decimate the enemy or make ice cubes, fly over three thousand miles nonstop or run its own electric light plant, turn up 4200 horsepower or heat a can of soup. They take me up in the Vultee V-12 and they let me sit in the Curtiss P-40 and I tell how if we'd had this sort of stuff in the olden days we could have wiped out the Imperial Armies in thirty minutes flat, and now that we've got this stuff—by implication—we're going to clean up the panzer divisions in nine point five seconds. Rue with a difference."

"Thank God for the difference," Norah said, and Bill said, "Pardon me?"

"A private joke we have."

"It's no private joke," said Bill. "It's a public calamity."

—— 183 ——

"You'll do it again," Alice said, and Bill said, "The hell I will."

"Oh, yes, you will," she said. "It's about time you made some use of what you like to call your brains."

They drank the beer, which was cold, and sat around on the lawn watching the children in the swings and on the seesaw.

"I brought you each a present," Bill said. He went to the car and came back with two boxes used for mailing books. They were both wrapped in Christmas paper and tied with ribbons. There were stickers on them that said *Do Not Open Till Xmas*, but he said it would be all right to open them.

Ed and Norah sat in the grass, the boxes in their laps, their faces smiling, opening the packages. In hers, Norah found a book titled *One Thousand Ways to Make Money*. She laughed and tossed it aside on the grass, and Bill said solemnly, "Don't lose that book, lady; it's worth a lot of money."

"I'll study it," she said.

"Start tonight," he said. "Start tonight, and study it carefully. You'll find something in Chapter Six that will meet your needs."

He looked at Sloan, who had his box open. Ed's face was solemn, and he looked up at Hogan.

"What's the matter?" said Bill. "That's what you asked for, isn't it?"

Sloan closed the box again, saying, "Yeh."

"Come on," said Bill, "I'll show you how to use it."

"What is it?" Norah said, and Bill said, "Ben's pistol. I'm glad to get rid of it," he said. "You know, we have a Sullivan Law in New York State. I've often wondered what the hell I'd say if anybody found the thing."

"There's been some skunks an' hedgehogs 'round here lately," Sloan said, and Hogan laughed. "If you can hit a skunk with a .38, you're a dead shot."

Sloan didn't answer, but Bill got the German pistol out of the box, released the clip that held the magazine and pulled back the breech-block.

"Be careful with that thing," Alice said, and Bill's face assumed an expression of patient resignation.

"My wife's a back-seat driver," he said. "Nothing worse. Times I've hopped her in airplanes she even says, 'Don't go so high, don't go so fast.' "

He loaded the clip from the box of cartridges in the cardboard box and said, "Where's a tin can?" He called to Bill, Jr., and said, "Come on, son, I'll teach you how to shoot."

Norah and Ed stood in the kitchen door with Alice, watching Hogan and the children, whom he had instructed to stand behind him. He placed the tin can on a rock some fifty feet away and aimed at it. There was a sharp report, and the can showed a hole. Alice looked at Norah and saw Ed's face. It was grim; his teeth were set, and the lines in his cheeks seemed more prominent. There was an expression in his eyes she could not have described, but it made her feel distinctly uneasy. She heard Bill calling her.

"Come on and shoot!" he said. He had given the large pistol to little Bill and was standing behind him, directing his hand. The fool, she thought. Bill, Jr., squeezed the trigger, and the can jumped off of the rock.

"Bravo!" Hogan said. "It runs in the family." He loaded the gun again for Alice and stood behind her while she fired. She hated the thing, but she fired it because she knew that somehow or other she stood higher in her husband's estimation when she showed no fear. Norah consented to fire a clip, and Bill fired one himself, then put the gun in his back pocket.

"I want to shoot," said Katey.

In the house again they were all silent as Bill sat at the long table in the dining room and stripped the gun. He laughed.

"This'll come in handy, Ed," he said. "From the way they're talking on the radio these days, you can expect parachute troops to be dropping in your dooryard any minute. Defend the home!" he said, carefully wiping the inside mechanism of the pistol.

"Beautiful thing, isn't it?" he said to Sloan, who was sitting next to him, watching him reassemble the gun.

Sloan smiled and shook his head. "Don' like the things," he said.

12

. ▪ ▪ ▪

IN THE COURT OF OYER AND TERMINER
OF BACONSFIELD COUNTY
(No. 1, March Term, 1941)

The State

vs.

Edwin Alberts Sloan, alias Edwin Alberts

Charge: Murder
Plea: Guilty

March 3, 1941, this case came on for trial, indictment having been found a true bill for murder at January Sessions, 1941. John A. Cobb, District Attorney, representing the State, and Burton Farmer, representing the defendant, all of whom being present in Court.

For the State:

They let her sit at the counsel table, and Norah felt slightly ill. When she had entered the courtroom, she saw and felt what she had expected to see and feel—an enormous throng for a small country town; the curious, the morbid, the vindictive, come to see a murderer receive his just deserts. Many were personally acquainted with the dead man, who was referred to by the local newspapers as a "pillar of society." He had been the owner of a small flour mill; he had employed a hundred people, which meant that perhaps three or four hundred people were dependent upon him. His son, in mourning, had shut down the flour mill temporarily; the workers had been thrown out of employment. Many of them were present in the court.

There was a continuous hum and buzz of conversation; it was an ominous sound. There was an overtone of vengeance and of that enjoyment of other people's misfortunes that is the hallmark of the self-righteous. They nudged each other and pointed at her, and when Ed was led into the court by the sheriff there was a mounting angry mumur. He was freshly shaved and wore a clean white shirt under a clean white sweater. His eyes moved from side to side; he was afraid, she felt. He smiled at her, and when the sheriff indicated that she might sit inside the rail at the counsel table, it was a pleasure and a relief to sit and hold Ed's hand. He pressed her hand almost continuously, and she returned the pressure to give him confidence.

During the two visits she had made to see him in the Baconsfield prison, when she stayed with Farmer and his wife, she had come to like the attorney. He was a true humanitarian, she felt, and whatever doubts he had originally entertained about taking the case he had overcome himself. He was actively interested in the defense, and although he held out little hope of anything better than a life sentence, she had enlisted his sympathy in her husband to a larger degree than she had at first believed possible.

"I don't understand the nature of this procedure," she had said. "Isn't he entitled to a jury trial?"

"In this State," Farmer said, "they will accept a plea of guilty to a capital offense. Some States don't, you know; New York, for instance. But Ed confessed to the crime, and the State will accept the plea. In order to have a jury trial he would have to repudiate the confession. I don't think that's advisable right now. What happens now is that evidence is taken to substantiate his confession, and the Court will fix the degree and determine the sentence."

"Is the death sentence mandatory?"

"No," he said. "There's precedent for leniency; it's entirely up to the judge and his two lay associates."

"What do you think of the judge?"

"I know him well," Farmer said. "He's kind; he's intelligent."

She saw him on the bench, a gentle man in appearance, well past fifty. On either side of him sat the two lay judges. One held his head slightly on one side and had a sensitive face. The other was a stolid-looking individual who, Farmer said, was a local merchant. He had no expression on his face.

"You may stand, Edwin Sloan," said the clerk of the Court. He cleared his throat. "Hearken unto an indictment, presented by the Grand Inquest of the State, inquiring for the County of Baconsfield.

"*In the Court of Quarter Sessions of the Peace for the County of Baconsfield,*
"*Number 8, March Sessions, A.D. 1941,*
"*County of Baconsfield, ss:*

"*The Grand Inquest for the State, inquiring for the County of Baconsfield, upon their respective oaths and*

affirmations do present that Edwin Sloan: alias Edwin
Alberts: late of the county aforesaid, Yeoman, on the
First day of December, in the year one thousand nine
hundred and forty, in the County aforesaid, and within
the jurisdiction of this Court, with force and arms etc.
in and upon the body of one, James T. Baldwin, in the
peace of God and the said State, then and there being,
did feloniously, willfully, and of his malice aforethought, make an assault, and him, the said James T.
Baldwin, then and there, feloniously, willfully and of
his malice aforethought, did kill and murder, contrary
to the form of the Act of the General Assembly in such
case made and provided, and against the peace and
dignity of the State.

> (Signed) John A. Cobb,
> District Attorney of Baconsfield County.

"To this indictment, how say you— 'Guilty' or 'Not
Guilty'?"

"Guilty," said Ed.

The judge leaned slightly forward and said, "Let the
record show the defendant, being arraigned, pleads guilty
generally."

Mr. Cobb, the District Attorney, spoke. "If Your Honor
please, up to this time the State has had no knowledge of
whether there would be a plea of guilty or not guilty, and I
would like to have a few minutes to consult as to procedure."

When they resumed, the State opened its case with a
parade of motor policemen Norah had met before. They
were the men who had arrested Ed, the men who had questioned her and Bill Hogan; Private Joe Reilly and Corporal
Slattery, the short, thin man with the soft brown eyes; Cap-

tain Fenster; these three men were from the Low Hill barracks. Lieutenant Partrick of Baconsfield followed them —he still had a toothpick in his mouth, which he removed and held in his hand when he took the stand, and all four men testified to witnessing Ed's statement in the Baconsfield Courthouse after he had been removed from the Low Hill county jail. The old sheriff of Baconsfield was also a witness to the confession. What they said was identical, and Farmer did not cross-examine any of them. There was a phrase that the District Attorney, Cobb, kept repeating. He was an intense man, very thin, with black hair that stood up on his head. His grammar was none too good, and he had an abbreviated way of speaking that at first amused Norah, then annoyed her.

"Whether there were any promises of any kind whatsoever offered to the defendant to make a statement?"

"No promises whatsoever."

"Whether there were any threats of any kind made; was any inducement of any kind made to the defendant for making the statement?"

"No."

"How and by whom was this statement taken?"

"By Miss Folsom here, direct, the Court Stenographer."

"By direct, do you mean on the typewriter?"

"That's right."

"Were there several sheets of paper?"

"They was."

"Were they fastened together?"

"They was."

Then there was a son-in-law of Baldwin, the murdered man, who said that he had last seen him at noon on the first of December; he was employed by his father-in-law. He was questioned by Judge Horan.

"Is he living or dead?"

"He's dead now."

"Did you attend his funeral?"

"Yes."

"Did you see him after he was dead?"

"Yes."

Mr. Cobb: "When did you attend the funeral?

"I'm not good on dates, I don't just remember." (No cross-examination.)

Then there was the coroner of the county, who used a great many anatomical terms in describing the condition of the body; he testified to its appearance when it was found, to its condition when he examined it in the morgue. Norah was made slightly ill by his description of the wounds.

A photographer identified pictures he had taken of the scene where the body was found, and then Lieutenant Partrick, the man with the cold eyes and the toothpick and the beaked nose, was recalled to describe the finding of the body, relative to the pictures the photographer had taken of the scene.

There was a recess for fifteen minutes while the judge and his associates left the courtroom, the judge holding one of his associates by the arm, and Norah began to sense and almost feel in her body the operations of a machine at work. She could understand the logic of the inquiry and the way it was put together; it was dull and repetitious but impressive. Ed sat quietly by her side, holding steadily to her hand (she could feel the perspiration in his palm); she had the impression of a child holding her hand for comfort and for courage. She thought of Katey back in New York with the Hogans and of Bill, who had told her that he would have liked to attend the trial.

"My lawyer told me," he said, "that it would be a good idea for me to keep out of the State."

Perhaps it would, she thought, but he must be definitely afraid of being involved. I can understand that, she thought. I have been afraid myself. She realized that in a very real sense she had been afraid for a long time—long before this thing had happened.

"Mr. Partrick," said Cobb, "did you know James T. Baldwin?"

"I did."

"And was this body you found there under this bridge, as you have described it, the body of James T. Baldwin?"

"It was."

"To what extent was the body in the water? Whether or not it was face down?"

"The body was laying on its left side submerged under the water."

Mr. Farmer cross-examined Partrick.

"What was the width of the stream at the point where the body lay?" he said.

"I judge about six feet from bank to bank," the Lieutenant said, reaching in his pocket for another toothpick.

"Was the body on the upper or the lower side of the middle of the bridge?"

Norah began to understand the reason for the cross-examination. She remembered that the confession had stated explicitly that Ed had placed the body on the edge of a steep bank beside the road, which fell off to a tiny stream. The police insisted that the body had been found below that point, not on the bank, but in the stream itself, face down and under a culvert. The stream was too shallow for the body to have floated down it, even though it might have rolled down the embankment into the water. But Farmer could not shake the Lieutenant's statement that it had been found under the culvert.

At this point Mr. Cobb introduced the full confession. It covered some twenty-four pages of legal foolscap and had been dictated in two parts, and Mr. Cobb read it so slowly and with such emphasis upon the significant admissions that it took two full hours for him to read it. Court was then adjourned until the next day, and Ed was led back to his cell. The reporters from the neighborhood papers questioned Mr. Farmer.

"Are you going to put Sloan on the stand?" they said.

"I think so," Farmer said.

"How do you feel about this, Mrs. Sloan?" they said sympathetically. She didn't reply. She was still too stunned by the repetitious horror of the confession, which she had read in January, the first time she had visited the defense attorney in his home. It was horrible and it was incredible, and it was at the same time thoroughly understandable. It was a damning indictment, she felt, and as Cobb had read it in the courtroom, she could actually feel the pressure of the crowd of people behind her.

She could feel their eyes on her back, although they probably were not even looking at her. She could sense their condemnation and their horror as the sharply accented voice went on, lingering on the more hideous details and pointing the more incriminating admissions. They could be a lynch mob, she thought, as easily as not. They might be decent people, honest people, kindly people, and still turn into a lynch mob in a moment, if opportunity were provided. She could hear them murmur and gasp; she could hear a woman sobbing.

SLOAN GOING ON WITNESS STAND
Killer of Baldwin
Pleads Guilty But
Wife Stands By

HIS ALLEGED CONFESSION IS REVEALED

Farmer read the paper sitting in a chair across from Norah. She had another copy of the paper, and she had to make a definite effort to read it.

Baconsfield, Mar. 3—Edwin A. Sloan, 34-year-old confessed killer of James T. Baldwin, prominent Morrisford flour miller, pleaded guilty to a charge of murder when arraigned in Baconsfield County court today, and by so doing placed his fate in the hands of Judge F. X. Horan and his two associates, Miller and Washburn.

Defense counsel Burton Farmer of Baconsfield indicated that Sloan will take the stand as the principal defense witness, with the possibility that his wife will also testify. Mrs. Sloan was in court throughout the day, much of the time holding the hand of her husband, whom she married only nine months before his arrest for homicide. When the prisoner entered the crowded courtroom there came an immediate hush. He glanced rapidly over the throng and his eyes came to rest on his wife, sitting in the front row of spectators. He tried to smile but it apparently was difficult and as he took his seat he sobbed. For a time he seemed to have trouble in getting his breath and his chest heaved convulsively.

*At a signal from Sheriff Edwin Fisher that it would
be permissible, Mrs. Sloan made her way to the defense table and sat down beside her husband, gathering
his right hand in both of hers and giving him a reas-
suring smile. He seemed to calm himself then but as
his name was called and he was ordered to stand before
the bar of justice, a mist again came into his eyes and
he wiped them with a clean, neatly folded handkerchief.*

It seemed surprisingly sympathetic, Norah thought. She
noticed such phrases as *On her left hand was her wedding
ring which she fondled when not gripping Sloan's hand,*
and, *As the day wore on, certain bits of testimony brought
tears to her eyes and she bowed her head and covered her
face with her hands. When Sloan noticed it he would grab
her hand nearest him and squeeze it.* Norah had to force
herself to continue reading when she saw that the bulk of
the news story contained long excerpts from the confession
itself.

The next day at one-thirty, the parade of State's witnesses began again. They took, for the most part, only a
few minutes each, but what they had to say was perfectly
selected to substantiate the major admissions Ed had made
to the police.

A hotel clerk in Lebanon said Ed had rented a room
from him for overnight, inquired as to whether there was
another exit to the hotel, jumped his bill the next morning.
That was on November 28. He had signed his real name
and given Polk as his address. (No cross-examination.)

George Goreski, ex-felon of Charlesville, told of Ed's
meeting him on the twenty-ninth, when Goreski was working on the roads. Sloan came home with him. He exhibited

a pistol, stayed that night and the next day and night. He helped to build a chicken coop, and took part in practice with a .22 rifle. He told a lot of lies about where he was going, said he was working and had left his wife in Morrisford, where their car, a Buick, had broken down. He left the morning of the first. Goreski had known Sloan in the Deerfield penitentiary in 1931, where he used to write letters for him to Ed's relatives. (No cross-examination.) "That punk. . . ." Ed said to Norah, and she looked up at the man on the stand, where he sat self-consciously, but with the smug expression of a righteous citizen who is helping the law to see that justice is done.

On the morning of the first, a clerk in Morrisford. sold Sloan a pack of matches.

Old Mr. Forsythe of Morrisford confirmed the fact that he operated a store there, had known Ed Sloan since he was a child.

"Did you use to give him candy when he was a child?" said Mr. Cobb.

"I did, sir, many times," Mr. Forsythe said. "The family was poor."

A truck driver had picked him up near Morrisford at noon of the first, given him a ride for three and a half miles in the direction of Sheba. A farmer had given him a ride about five miles in the opposite direction half an hour later.

Two women who knew Baldwin said they had seen him in his blue Chrysler sedan at one o'clock that day.

"Was there anyone in the car with him?" Cobb asked them both.

"Yes, sir."

"Do you know who it was?"

"No, sir." (No cross-examination.)

At four o'clock on the first, a country-store proprietor

sold Sloan a pair of rubbers and socks and filled his car with gasoline.

"What kind of car was this?"

"A 1940 Chrysler."

"What color?"

"Blue."

"Dark blue?"

"Right."

"Did you know whose car it was?"

"It looked like Jim Baldwin's but—"

"Was Mr. Baldwin driving it?"

"No."

"Did the man get out of the car?"

"No."

"Did you see his feet?"

"No." (No cross-examination.)

A little after four o'clock a gas-station proprietor directed Sloan to Dr. Pincus of Lemmon, said Sloan was riding in a car.

"What kind of car was it?"

"Blue Chrysler sedan."

"Have you seen it since?"

"No." (No cross-examination.)

Dr. Pincus said, "When I entered my office, the waiting-room door was open, and as I walked in Sloan was stroking the head of my little two-year-old boy and remarked that he (the boy) liked him and smiled about it. I asked him to come into the office, and on the way he said he had just had a narrow escape. He said he was sitting in the kitchen of his home and his brother, who was cleaning a rifle upstairs, accidentally discharged it and the bullet had come down through the ceiling, injuring his foot."

"Did he pay you?" said Mr. Cobb.

"Yes."

"How much?"

"Five dollars."

"What time did he leave your office?"

"After five."

At half-past six a young man employed by his father in a diner on the road between Lebanon and Morrisford made supper for Sloan and changed another five-dollar bill. He noticed that Sloan was wearing a rubber overshoe on one foot and was told it had been run over by a truck. When Ed left, said the young man, he had difficulty starting his car; it took him twenty minutes. The young man, who had become suspicious, and was going in to town to the movies, followed Sloan.

"He drove so slow, he forced me to pass," the young man said. He stopped his car and looked back, saw that the blue Chrysler was off the road. "He was racing the motor, I could hear, and couldn't get back on the road. A Model-A coach come up the road and slowed down to assist this gentleman, but before he could get stopped he got the car back on the road and started toward Lebanon."

"Did you think there was anything strange about this?" said Mr. Cobb.

"Yes, sir."

"What?"

"He asked me the way to Morrisford, the other direction." (No cross-examination.)

A storekeeper in Charlesville sold him a pair of sneakers and socks at seven-thirty that night.

"What color was the socks?"

"White."

"Will you examine these sneaks, then tell us whether or

not these are the sneaks or just like those you sold to him at that time?"

"They look just like them."

"And the size, do you recall?"

"Ten."

"And what size is this pair of sneaks?"

"Size ten." (Cross-examination by Farmer merely corroborated the statement.)

Norah felt dizzy. Ed was still holding her hand, and when she looked at him he smiled wanly. She released her hand for a moment, patted the back of his hand. She was thirsty; her throat was dry, as though she had run a mile under a burning sun. There was a woman on the stand now, who ran a combination gasoline station and diner. At eight o'clock on the night of the first, she had made dinner for Ed. She described his car, said he was limping, and told that he had said he'd had a couple of toes cut off. He had on a pair of new sneakers, said he had just got out of the hospital and was on his way to Peekskill. He gave her a ten-dollar bill, and he had a lot of money in a roll.

"Do you know which way he went when he left your place?"

"Toward Lebanon from our place."

"Is that the way toward Peekskill?"

"You can go that way."

After a recess at three o'clock, Joe Reilly and Gordon Slattery told how they had arrested Sloan on the eighth of December. Slattery reported the fact that the blue Chrysler carried a tag on its license plate, such as the Blue Sunoco gasoline people sold for a few cents. The tag bore the initials E.A.S. He identified the license plates the car had originally carried, which had been found by the police under the barn on the old Abbott place. Lieutenant Partrick followed him, told how they had traced Ed's journey from the finding of Baldwin's body to the arrest, that Ed had gone over to Peekskill the night of the first, driving all night, and the next day had purchased an old Ford in Peekskill for seventy-five dollars, obtained New York plates for it, left the Ford to be repainted, then switched the plates onto the Chrysler.

A deep and respectful hush fell over the courtroom as James Baldwin, Jr., the son of the murdered miller, was called to the stand. He wore a black arm band.

"What was your father's age?"

"Fifty-six." He identified the license plates from his father's car.

"When did you last see your father?"

"On a Friday before the first of December."

Slattery, recalled, identified the original plates young Baldwin had said belonged to his father. They were the same plates that had been found under the barn at Sloan's farmhouse. Another photographer, who was also a member of the State Police, identified photographs he had taken of the inside of the car, exhibiting what he said were blood stains. An attempt had been made to wash them out.

"Did you make any chemical or other analysis or examination of these stains to determine what their actual composition was?" said Farmer.

"There was no examination made other than their appearance, and it is from that—"

"And it is from that you testify that they appear to be blood stains?"

"Yes, sir."

Slattery was recalled again to testify as to the pistol. "That is known as the 9 millimeter, which is the same as a .38 American make. It is a German-make gun, called a

Luger." He went on to tell his version of the original conversation he had had with Sloan in the Low Hill county jail.

"At first he started off to tell about a man by the name of Logan or Hogan, accompanying him on the trip and after I checked him—"

"What do you mean by checked him?" Farmer asked in cross-examination.

"I says, just wait a minute. Something like that."

Blood-stained posters were placed in evidence. They had been in the car since before Election Day, and Cobb held them up. Vote for Willkie, they said.

"About Sloan's admissions to you in the Low Hill jail," said Cobb on redirect examination. "Did he express any regret for what he had done?"

"No."

"Did he shed any tears?"

"He did when he met his wife."

"But not at those times?"

"No."

The stenographer, Miss Folsom, identified the statement she had typed. The old sheriff, Ed Fisher, as well as Slattery and Fenster stated that in bringing Ed from Low Hill to Baconsfield they had asked him what he would have done if he had been stopped by a police car when he was riding in the Chrysler. " 'Only thing left for me to do,' " Fenster quoted him as saying, " 'shoot it out.' "

Norah was biting her lips. She was thinking of the State's exhibits, the blood-stained Willkie posters, the two sets of license plates, the pistol and the sock, the shoe, the sneaks, the clothing Baldwin had worn when he was killed, the photographs of the car, the body, the place where the body was found, the rubbers Ed had bought. It seemed hopeless;

it was open and shut; there was a confession and it was "inadvisable at this time" to repudiate the confession, even though Ed had said he had been beaten before he made it. What was there that could be done now? What could be said that would alter the picture or mitigate the offense? It was cut and dried. Homicide in the commission of a felony —automatically first-degree murder. First-degree murder would mean a death sentence unless the judges felt there were mitigating circumstances. What mitigating circumstances were there? Was the man insane? No.

The State rested its case with testimony as to the photographs of Mr. Baldwin's body, made in the "mortician's" establishment. There was something funny about the word *mortician*, but Norah could not smile. The trial was adjourned for the day.

Ed smiled at her before he was led from the courtroom and said, "Don' worry none, Mom. We on'y just started t' fight."

13

THE HUNDRED DOLLARS
Bill Hogan had given them on Labor Day did not last more
than a day or so. They had found it the same night facing
page 100 in the silly book Bill had left, *One Thousand
Ways to Make Money*. They had laughed until their sides
ached, and they had danced around the bed, Norah waving
the bill and Ed clapping for her, until Katey woke up in
her room and said, "What's the matter?"

The next day they went into Polk in the same old Dodge
Ed had borrowed for their wedding day, and they paid off
some of the smaller bills, paid the milkman in full and gave
twenty dollars to the grocers, forty dollars to Ella Horton
for the July and August rent. That left September due, and
the fact that September was due and that some two hundred dollars more were still owed in Coney, Stiles, and
Polk sobered them. It was astonishing how small an amount
of money could be called a hundred dollars.

Ed had steady work that month and part of October,
cutting and sawing wood, drawing it. But the time was past

when any country school might be appointing a teacher for the fall semester, and the cakes and preserves Norah had made didn't sell very well. There was wood to be laid in against the winter; there were potatoes to be bought, and Ed succeeded in picking some on shares with Hortons' folks. That way he got about ten bushels (which they figured ought to last them through the winter), without having to pay more than a week of his labor.

But on October first Ella came up the road to see them, and her face was firm.

"I need t' have my rent," she said. "I know you folks 're hard pressed, but this can't go on forever."

"I'm sorry," Norah said. "You know that if we had it, you'd get it. We've made barely enough to live on, Ella."

"I got a offer to buy the place," the woman said.

"Then you ought to sell it."

Ella blushed and said, "Well, you see what you c'n do. It don't pay me t' rent the house f'r nothing."

"Ella, I've been here since 1935; five years, Ella, and I think you ought to know by this time I'm a responsible person."

"I reckon you are," Ella said, glancing at Ed. "All right, I'll have t' wait, I guess." She went.

You'll have to wait, Norah said under her breath. She looked at Ed, who was sitting in the armchair, his elbows on his knees, his face in his hands. "Cheer up," she said.

"Mom," he said, "I gotta do somethin'."

"Hurray," she said. "What do you plan to do? Come to the rescue, pal."

"Dunno," he said. "But somethin' gotta be done."

"Now you've got it, pal," she said. "It sure has."

"Mebbe I'll take a run over Peekskill way, see what I c'n do 'bout that house."

"Anything you say."

He said no more about it for a week or so, for he was working steadily again on the road scraper and helping fill the holes in the town roads before the winter rains came on. But the bills continued to mount. She counted them. September and October rent, $40; milkman, $11.50; groceries, $13 in Coney, $8 in Polk; wood for the furnace, $14 for two cords; butchers that came to the door, $19.25; the Raleigh man, $3.00; the My-T-Fine man, $4; butter and eggs from Ella Horton, $4.25; kerosene oil, $2.75; telephone $14.50; fresh vegetables, $1.50—that was well over a hundred dollars by itself. Not counting the old bills that had been hanging on for years, it seemed, for some furnishings she had bought just before Ben died, installment payments due on the vacuum cleaner and the range, the washing machine, loans (she regarded them as such) from Hogan. There seemed to be no way out of this mess. Then the November rent was almost due, which would add another twenty to the growing sum.

"You got a dollar, Mom?" he said.

"I suppose."

"I gotta go over int' town, get somethin'."

He walked out without so much as kissing her, and she sat down at the table in the living room and sulked. How can he ask for a dollar like that, she thought, when he should know how hard he works to get the money? Probably he's going to get drunk; well, I wouldn't blame him, she thought, but I hope he's got sense enough to bring a little home, so I can get plastered too.

But there were Katey's teeth to fix and her own, which were surely going to pieces. Ed's headaches seemed to grow worse as time went on; he needed glasses, if he didn't need an operation to remove that piece of steel in his head. *I'm* the one who got into something, she thought, but what could I have done without him? What you could have done, her mind replied, was to have held onto your job, which you wouldn't have lost if you hadn't married him. Nuts, she thought, you're thinking like a quitter. Sit down and make a plan, as Bill would say. True course, variation, magnetic course, deviation, compass course. Yes, she thought—what kind of a plan? . . .

. . . Sloan got into Polk and went to the garage. He walked through into the shop where they did most of the repairs, and he found what he was looking for. There were three men crouched in a corner behind a rack of tires, shooting craps.

"Hi, Joe," Sloan said, and Joe said, "Hi."

Sloan crouched on the asphalt floor and, dropping the dollar in the center, said, "Shoot a quarter."

"You're faded," Joe said. "Take the dice."

Ed spit on his right hand and shook it near his head. "Let it come," he said under his breath and rolled a four. "Come four," he said, "baby needs a pair of shoes."

"That's a hard 'un t' make," the other man said. "You'll never make it."

"You don' know me, bud," said Sloan. "I allus make m' points."

He rolled a six, an eight, and then the four came up again. "Shoot the half," he said.

He got home late and found her still sitting at the table. She had a writing tablet in front of her, and she had torn off a dozen sheets. They were covered with figures, and there were unpaid bills lying on the table, on the floor.

"What you doin', Mom?" he said.

"What does it look like, Ed? While you were in town,

having yourself a time, I've been trying to make head or tail out of this mess."

"That so?" he said. He smiled, but when he saw that her face was serious, he stopped smiling.

"Where's your sense of responsibility?" she said. "What's the point of gallivanting around town, spending money you can't afford to spend?"

"Ain' no sense at all," he said, fishing in his pocket. He dropped the bill on the table. "Here's y'r dollar," he said. "I was hopin' there'd be another t' put with it, on'y there ain'."

She looked at him and stretching out her hand, laid it on top of his. "What have you been up to?"

"Shootin' craps," he said.

She laughed. Then she said, "Forgive me for laughing, I didn't mean to."

"Tha's all right. There ain' nothin' I know how t' do t' bring home the bacon, seems."

"You're all right."

"No I ain'," he said.

"You're doing fine. I'm the one who should be ashamed," she said. "I had an expensive education, but you'd never know it. I've been all over the country and seen a lot of things; I ought to be able to put it to some good account. But if anything, I know less than you do, brother." She laughed. "So we're both in the same boat."

"Si' down," he said. "Quit rockin' it."

He saw a face in front of him, not hers. It was a face in his mind's eye, and he was trying to place it. It was a hard face, and the mouth moved in a peculiar way when it was speaking. The mouth said, *There ain't nothin' to it. You c'n do it easy. Sometimes they catch you*—he remembered now. It was a guy he'd known in the pen, years before.

—— 208 ——

What was his name? Bogard? Loger? Sure, sometimes they catch you and then you land right here. Right there. Where he was; where I was, too. He dismissed the face from his mind and looked at his wife.

"Don' you worry none," he said. "I'll think o' somethin' yet. There's more work comin' up on the road machine. But mebbe you c'd ask Bill—"

"I'd hate to."

"I get you, Mom," he said. "You're right."

She didn't sleep well at night any more. He lay awake long after she fell asleep, and she stirred restlessly, sometimes awoke screaming. At such times he clasped her in his arms to quiet her, saying, "What's a matter, Mom? It's me, I'm here." She wept in his arms, saying, "I had a bad dream, it was nothing. But golly, it *was* a bad dream." Then she fell asleep again, moving frequently in her sleep, her arms suddenly thrashing out.

It was hard for him to sleep himself. He was bewildered. The road commissioner had kept his word to give him steady work, but it seemed that the harder he worked—ten and twelve hours a day at two bits an hour—the worse in a hole they got. That didn't make much sense, but he figured that it wasn't really the way it seemed. It was just that there had been so many bills, even before he came along, that there was no catching up to them. Why, he thought, I never even paid that minister, what was his name, Halstead over to Polk, for marrying us. From this day forward . . . till death. I gotta do that, he thought, and wondered how much would be right to pay a minister, two dollars, five? Why, that was almost nine months ago, nine months come the first week in November.

He had registered for the draft at the little schoolhouse where Katey went to school. (That kid is positively skinny, he thought.) And they had told him he would get a questionnaire to fill out before very long. What're you gonna do about *that?* he wondered now, lying in bed, listening to Norah's heavy breathing. They won't never take you, but that ain't the important thing.

No, he thought, it's best to wait. Maybe when his name went into the board, they'd know about him and not even send a question sheet. But a day or so later Norah called his attention to the questionnaire, a facsimile of which had been published in the Shoreline paper.

"Hasn't it come yet?" she said.

"Nah," he said. "Read it out t' me, what the questions are."

"You ought to try to read it yourself, Ed," she said. "You're not getting enough practice reading these days."

"Read it jus' this time."

"All right," she said. She read him the list of questions, name, address, place of birth, color, parents, nearest relatives, married or single, dependents and their names, previous military experience—she looked up at him and saw that his face was sober. She continued, saying, "Have you ever been convicted of any crime?"

"Don' read no more," he said. She looked at him.

"Reckon I'm up the crick without a paddle, Mom."

"Why?" she said. "You've got a dependent wife and child; you're almost thirty-five—oh, I see," she said. "You mean about the Air Corps, and your taking a run-out powder from the hospital. That's what's worrying you, isn't it?"

He thought a moment and cursed himself for not being able to say, No—I'm an ex-con, I been in jail on and off since I was fourteen years old, for burning down a schoolhouse, for breaking and entering, for jumping my parole, for sassing a judge, and for stealing a car.

Then he said, "Yeh."

"Don't worry, kid," she said. "Maybe it's not as bad as you think. We'll cross that bridge when we come to it."

"O.K.," he said, but he thought, You'd better cross it first, yourself, before it comes to you. He smiled at that idea, of a bridge coming to him.

"That's the ticket," she said. "I like to see you smile. You have a sweet smile, Ed."

"I got crooked teeth."

"Never mind," she laughed. "When we get Katey's teeth plugged up, we'll get yours all pulled out and—"

"What!" he said, "draw all my teeth; the hell you will!"

"Wouldn't you like a brand-new set of store teeth, that you could take out every night and put in a glass of water on the night-table, like my Aunt Clara used to do?"

"The hell I would!"

"Well," she said, "I'm telling you; if I don't get mine tended to pretty soon, that's what's going to happen to me. I'd much rather have a couple of plates than the toothaches I get once in a while."

"You'll git 'em fixed, Mom, 'f it's the last thing you do."

"It probably will be at that," she said. "Look; Katey'll be home from school pretty soon. Keep an eye peeled for her. I'm going to take that ten dollars we scraped up down to Ella before she tosses us out on our ear. The November rent's due tomorrow morning. That'll make sixty dollars, less this ten. It's known as maintaining your creditor's good will."

She went down the road, and he walked upstairs to change into the old sneakers he had in the closet. He sat on the edge of the bed and eased off the shoes, pulled out the toes of the socks. Them shoes she give me are getting pretty old, he thought, over a year now and curling up. He wiggled his feet and looked at the worn-out socks; four toes were out; you could only darn them so many times.

Where's your sense of responsibility? she said. Yeh, he thought, where is it? You think you can keep them going on what you make, two-fifty a day, with almost three hundred bucks in bills again? And the telephone coming out tomorrow? And if the kid gets sick, not even a telephone to call a doctor? Funny she forgot what I told her, he thought. Like her saying, Oh, I see, it's about running out of the hospital that's got you worried. But I *did* tell her, he thought; I told her long ago I had trouble with the law, and she didn't ask no questions. She said, I don't want to hear about it if you don't want to tell me. And I said, I don't mind telling, it was nothing much; it was when I was a little kid. That was when you should of told her, he thought. That was when you should of told her the whole damned story, from beginning to the end. And because you couldn't tell her then, and didn't tell her, maybe that's why you could never tell her afterwards.

But you're a goddamned liar, he thought. Always have been, too. You tell her, It wasn't nothing much, it was when I was a kid, and leave out all the rest. You take a look at the picture of her husband in his uniform, and you say you was an Army aviator. Couldn't you of told her, Sure, I was a flier once, I flew a plane once or twice and cracked one up a little? No, you get an idea from the picture, and you tell her you was inna Army Air Corps and you been a test pilot (like that guy what did she say his name was, Jimmy Collins), and went to Europe and seen Hitler and Mussolini, and you go to Alaska, and you make out the crash was a hell of a thing, and your observer—that's a hot one—

he was killed, and you was months in a hospital, what crap!

An idea came to him in the form of an image. He could see the picture of Ben Gilbert that was downstairs on the bookshelves, but the face wasn't Ben's, it was the same face he had seen a while back, the face of the guy in the pen (what the hell was his name? Bogan?), and the guy was saying, *That's some gat he's got there, hangin' on his belt.* And the face was saying, *It's a cinch; sometimes they catch you but mostly they don't.* You thought of that before, he thought; so cut it out. You thought of going back over Morrisford way and sticking up old Forsythe that used to give you candy when you was a kid. You thought about it even that time last summer when you was looking for work and walked through Morrisford and saw the store he had there, right where it always was, way on the edge of town where there ain't many people going by. All-day suckers and licorice shoestrings and candy bananas.

He went into the closet and put his hand up onto the shelf. Under the felt hat there was the box, where he had put it the night the Hogans went back to New York, Labor Day. He brought the box down and untied the string. The gun, sheathed in its leather holster, was wrapped neatly in cloth, and he unwrapped it on the bed, took it out of the holster, and handled it. It was big as a cannon and heavy. He weighed it in his hand and thought, That would be one hell of a thing to do, hold up old man Forsythe; why, he was the only guy you can remember that was ever halfway decent to you, excepting maybe the sheriff and his wife in the Baconsfield County jail. Forsythe was the guy who sent you there, matter of fact. He said, I'm gonna send him down to the county jail; it'll be a better home than he's got now. And he did. If you gotta hold somebody up, then make it somebody else, he thought.

But who says you gotta hold somebody up? You'd never get away with it. All right, he thought; tell me where you're gonna get this money? Well, you're *not*, that's plain. The guy said it was a cinch. Yeh, I suppose that's why he was in stir, because it was such a cinch! He saw the man's face plainer now. I was only maybe nineteen myself, he thought. You live with those mugs, you hang around with them and know them after you get out, like Goreski, who still lives up Charlesville way, and you get to *be* like them. They stick together; they know the score. They're a tough bunch of mugs, he thought; would knock off a guy for a nickel. You never stuck nobody up, and you're not gonna do it now.

He held the gun in his hand and pointed it at himself in the mirror. He said, "Bang!" out loud, let his arm drop to his side, then slowly brought it up again to his hip and pointed it at the mirror. Hogan said, Beautiful, ain't it? He looked at it. The handle was long and strong and firm and fit his hand perfectly. The barrel was long and the metalwork was dark blue and gleamed with a thin film of oil. Hogan had oiled it. There were some words on it in German, *Erfurt*, it said, and *Gesichert*. He turned it over in his hand and examined it, pushed the catch, and the magazine fell out into his hand. He tried that once or twice; it was clever the way, when you pressed the catch, the magazine fell right out into your hand. It was empty.

There was a box of fat cartridges in the cardboard box, and he opened it, took some out and slipped them one by one into the clip the way Hogan had done it, against the strong spring of the magazine. They'd slap a hole in a guy the size of a walnut, he thought. Eight of them fit in neatly, and he marveled at how well the thing was machined. That was what Hogan meant, he figured, Beautiful, ain't it, the tooling. Watch out, he thought, the thing's loaded now; better take them bullets out.

There must be thousands of stickups all over the country every day, he thought, and I'll bet not one out of ten of them gets nabbed. Well, maybe one out of three. He had listened to a lot of detective stories and seen a few moving pictures. What's the motive? he thought. The motive's robbery. To get some money. O.K., that's a clue to the guy who done it. A guy done it who needed the money. But there was millions of guys who needed money, and if a guy was to take a gun and go a long way from his home place with it and stick up somebody that never saw him in his life before and get away fast—in a automobile, maybe—how could they find him out of all the millions of people in the country? Would they think to look for him a long way away from where it happened, or would they think to look for him near by? Near by, of course. So you didn't let the guy see you in the car, if you had a car. You parked the car beyond where you were going to do it, and you left the motor running, and walked back fast. Then you stuck the guy up and took the money and locked him in a back room where you were sure there wasn't a phone and he couldn't see you out of the window, and you got the hell out of there as fast as you could. And then you ditched the car somewhere.

He heard Katey downstairs, shouting, "Mommy, Mommy!"

"Mom's down at Hortons' folks, Katey," he shouted and hastily put the gun into its leather holster, wrapped it in the cloth, stuck the bundle in the box, and tied it loosely with the string. The box he slipped back on the shelf under his hat. He came downstairs and saw the child standing in the kitchen.

"I'm hungry, Ed," she said.

"I'll make you up a nice bowl o' Wheaties," he said, and the child made a long face.

"Aw," she said, "I don't like Wheaties. All I get is Wheaties. I want an orange."

"Don' think there's any oranges, Kit," he said. He looked in the icebox. There wasn't very much in it of any kind of thing to eat.

"Let me stir you up a nice bowl o' Wheaties," he said. "Don' you listen to the radio, where it says alla time how good Wheaties are?"

"That's only a advert-ise-ment," Katey said, and he laughed. "They say a lot of things on the radio that are fibs," she said. "Mommy told me. But I like Pepsi-Cola. It hits the spot."

"What spot?" said Sloan.

"I don't know," she said. "Ed, who're you going to vote for, President Roosevelt or President Willkie?"

"Don' know that I'm gonna vote f'r neither of 'em," he replied. "Who d' you think I should vote f'r?"

"I don't know," said Katey. "You vote at my school, the teacher said to tell you. We have vacation when you vote."

"Mebbe I'll vote f'r Santy Claus," he said.

"There *is* no Santa Claus," Katey said solemnly. "It's your father and mother. *I* know *that*."

Norah came back from Ella's with a broiler the older woman had given her. She held it up by the legs, and Ed said, "I be dog, she broke her heart."

"Don't be a cat," Norah said. "The old gal has a good heart. She was feeling sort of cheap about the scene she put on last month. It did her good to give the chicken."

This won't help much, he thought at table. It won't do no good to have Hogan giving us a hundred bucks and Ella

Horton giving us a chicken. That's charity, and it don't last long nohow. You gotta do something that'll mean something. You up and marry a woman you can't take good care of, with a kid to boot, and you sit on your tail and wait for something to happen. What do you think's going to happen? Maybe Hogan will send another hundred, maybe Ella Horton'll give you rent free, the hell she will, and then where will you be? The Reverend Proctor said, he remembered it, You gotta have more sticktoitiveness, you gotta know what you want and then go out and get it. Yeh, he thought, but he didn't mean *that*.

"What're you thinking about, Ed?"

"Nothin'."

"Golly I was hungry," Katey said, and they both looked at her. Ed looked at Norah and then down into his plate.

"Mom, you got an orange?"

"No, dear," Norah said. "Oranges are pretty expensive these days."

"Then why don't you just buy some oranges?" said Katey.

Norah laughed and said, "If you haven't any money, Katey, you can't buy any oranges."

"Then why don't you just go to the store and buy some money?"

"You don' buy money, Kit," said Sloan. "You gotta earn it."

"Then why—"

"Katey!" Norah said, "Eat your food and stop asking so many questions." She sighed.

They sat in the living room after the child had gone to bed, and for the first time in weeks they were silent for half an hour at a time. Ed had it in mind to go for a walk by himself, but he figured that would only make Norah feel lonely, so he sat and watched her reading.

"Read t' me, Mom," he finally said.

She looked at him, and he knew by the way she looked that she was reading the sort of book she had often read before—the sort of book he wouldn't understand, and he felt lonely.

He rose and went upstairs and turned on the radio. He didn't listen to it after he had turned it on but lay on his back with his hands behind his head and thought about what he could do to help. There didn't seem to be anything he could do, and he said to himself, "There's nothin' you c'n do." Well, if there was nothing you could do, then you couldn't do anything. That's a hot one, he thought; that's an easy way out of it. It's your own fault, you know, he thought. If you hadn't moved in here, if you hadn't married her, then she would still have a job and the kid wouldn't be hungry, and the rent would even be paid. Or would it? She didn't have any too much even last spring; how could she of got through the summer with what she had, less'n I helped her out with what I could earn?

Yeh, he thought, but if you hadn't been here, then she wouldn't of had to spend half of what she got on you. Yeh, but if I hadn't been here, he thought, then there wouldn't of been as much as there was. And you can't run away no more, he thought, so put that out of mind. You was thinking about that, wasn't you? That's like you; you was thinking you'd run away again, like you done last time, only you know better now. You wouldn't do a thing like that no more. She learned you better. She learned you, when you got a problem, face it and work it out, and if you can't work it out, if it licks you, it won't be for not trying. No.

I can lick it, he thought, but I need some help. Who's gonna help you? Norah can't; you gotta do it by your own self. He felt slightly dizzy now and put his hand up to his head. My head's going round and round like a top, he thought, but I got a job to do and I gotta do it. You're in a spot, didn't she say it? Didn't she say, You don't know what you got into this time, brother? *Face* it, she said lots of times. But how can you lick it, he thought, if there ain't any work and you can't get none, and she can't get any neither? Nobody's going to dish it out to you; you have to go out and get it by yourself. How?

I don't want to *do* that, he thought miserably, and the voice said, *It's a cinch.* There's a gun in the closet, he thought. You take that gun and you point it at somebody and say, Stick 'em up! and you go through their pockets with one hand, or you go through their till and they stand there with their arms hoisted—Reach! you say, and they reach, 'cause who wouldn't if you stuck a gun in their belly?—and you go through the till and scram. Yeh, he thought, and the bulls catch up to you and go to work on you, and you're in the can again. That's a nutty idea, he thought. You get ideas like that because you been in stir and listened to those guys talk and that's all they talk *about,* about the jobs they cased and the jobs they pulled and how much there was in it and how they spent it on liquor and the gals and running around the country, but they always catch up to them, don't they? Crime don't pay, everybody knows that.

That's what the coppers say, he thought. The big shots with the coconuts and the big cars, they say that, too. They say it because they want you should know, We got the stuff but if you try and take it away from us, we'll get you for that, we'll stick you in the cooler and you'll stay there till you get over taking things away from other folks. Yeh, he thought, but the right guys say it too. But those that got it, he thought, they don't *need* to take it away from those that ain't. Ask and they will give it to you, knock and they will open the door, that's what the Reverend Proctor read to me out of the book, only it's a lot of bushwa. Who ever give you anything? Except maybe Norah, but she's different.

In the morning he went to work on the road scraper, and they kept him on till the rains set in, late in November. Hogan sent a check for ten dollars with a note saying, *Buy yourself a toikey, and give thanks you're not in Coventry.* They didn't buy a turkey with it; there were too many places the money had to go, and when Sloan gave the milkman two dollars of it, the man said, "Do you mind coming out here a minute?"

They stood by the truck, and the milkman said, "Look, Mr. Sloan, the bill's over fifteen dollars, and you've only give me two dollars on account."

"I know it," Sloan said. "But I can' give you no more than that right now."

"I understand," the milkman said, "but you've got to see my position. I don't own this business; I'm just the driver. If you don't pay the bill, it comes outta my pocket. The boss said to tell you folks that if you can't pay at least a half the bill, cash, he can't let you have no more milk."

"Can' do it, bud," said Sloan. "We don' have that much cash."

"Look," the milkman said. "I got a couple kids myself; kids have gotta have milk. Maybe I could let you have a quart a day for the kid, if you could be sure to pay me every day."

"I'd try," said Sloan. "I couldn' say; I ain' sure of it. There's whole weeks sometimes we don' have a nickel in the house. Last couple weeks we been gettin' a average of two bucks, when I was workin' on the roads. Now that job's done, I'm lookin' f'r another. Right now I got thirty cents, you give me a quart o' milk t'day."

"All right," the driver said, "but you see my position."

"Yeh," said Sloan, "I see." That guy's at least got a steady job, he thought, even if he don' get chicken feed.

He walked back to the house and told Norah about his conversation.

"Maybe it's just to throw a scare into us," she said.

"You can' tell," Sloan said. "The driver, he's a right guy; he'd even give it to us outta his own pocket, I'd bet, but the guy that runs the dairy, I don' know—"

He suddenly had an idea. "How much money you got in your pocketbook?" he said.

"About four dollars."

"Be all right 'f Katey an' me, we walk into town?"

"Sure," she said. "Why not?"

With the child holding his hand, he started walking the mile and a half into Polk. The question sheet from the draft board had come that morning and was lying on her desk. He had to walk slowly into town, and he was thinking of the other letter—the one she had received that morning. She tries to put a good face on everything, he thought. She don't want me to think she's scared. But he remembered that letter. It was from that lawyer in Coney, and it said:

> . . . has called this matter to your attention any number of times. Surely you knew when you purchased these articles that they would require to be paid for, and it is an evidence of bad faith on your part that you have not paid more than five dollars on account in the past year, and that many months ago. This is to inform

you that I have been authorized to start legal action if the balance is not paid in full within a week from date. . . .

That's the business, he thought, and she can't fool me no more by smiling that pretty smile of hers and saying, Let 'em bring suit . . .

■ ■ ■ ■ *14*

For the Defendant:

Mr. Farmer: "If the Court please, it is all before the Court, and the Court knows what the case is all about. We will put the defendant on the stand and examine him as to the entire background that might have a controlling influence with the Court in disposing of the whole question."

The Court: "We feel that we not only want, but we require every possible detail that will be informative of this man's state physically and mentally and his background. We would like to look into that. It is the duty of the Court to know those things in fixing its final judgment."

There was a loud murmur when Ed took the stand and, being sworn, sat down. Norah thought she had never seen him look so well or so confident. He smiled at her from the stand and she gathered her hand into a fist and jerked it toward her, as though to say, Buck up, speak your piece, don't be afraid.

Mr. Farmer: "Now Ed, we're going to ask you some questions."

The Court (addressing the witness): "How old are you, Ed?"

Defendant: "Thirty-four goin' on thirty-five."

"Where were you born?"

"Near Morrisford."

Mr. Farmer: "Ed, how old were you when your father died?"

"Accordin' t' my mother, three days ol'."

"What did your mother do after your father's death?"

"She put the rest o' the children exceptin' me in diff'rent homes 'round about in the county an' we went t' the County Poor Home."

"How many other children were there?"

(Hesitating a few seconds): "Four, 'f I'm not mistaken."

"They were all older than you, were they?"

"Yeh."

"And after your mother took you with her to the Poor Home, what was the next thing that happened that affected your life?"

"Accordin' t' my mother, we was took out of the Poor Home by some people into their home."

The Court (addressing the witness): "Where was that?"

"In Baconsfield County, 'bout three miles from Morrisford."

Mr. Farmer: "Did she marry again?"

"Yeh."

"And whom did she marry?"

"Jed Alberts."

"How old were you when she remarried, do you know?"

"Between a year an' two year ol'."

"Is that why you're sometimes known by the name of Alberts as well as by the name of Sloan?"

"I allus went by the name o' Alberts. I allus thought my stepsister was my sister till I was aroun' twen'y-one."

The Court (addressing the witness): "Morrisford is where Forsythe's store is, is that right?"

"Yeh."

Mr. Farmer: "Ed, how long did you live in that place?"

"Lived there I'd say three 'r four year."

"And then where did you move?"

"Moved then t' what's known as the ol' Ogden place near the New School House."

"Ed, were there any other children in the family of this man Alberts your mother married and with whom you went to live?"

"You mean stayed at home?"

"Yes."

"No, sir."

"Did he have other children?"

"Yeh, three."

"Were they grown children?"

"Yeh, an' moved away fr'm home."

"Did they live near by?"

"Yeh."

"What were their names?"

"Joe Alberts, Bill Alberts. They was the two livin' there close. Ben Irwin, he lived in Charlesville."

"Was it Ben Irwin's wife that was Albert's daughter?"

"Yeh."

"Her name was what?"

"Nancy."

"Did your mother and stepfather have any children after they were married?"

"They had one. That died jus' a few days after it was born."

"And your earliest recollection of living in that— withdraw the question.

"Now, Ed, what sort of man was this stepfather Alberts? What was his treatment of you as a child in the home? Whether he was kind to you or harsh and cruel?"

"I never have no remembrance o' his bein' very kind t' me."

"Then what did he do?"

"In my own way, he was very mean t' me; beat me quite often. Any time I done anything outta the way I allus got a beatin' f'r it an' sent t' bed without no dinner or supper, whichever it was. I been beat so I couldn' sit down in school. I remember one schoolmarm brought a pillow f'r me t' sit down on, I'd been beat so bad I couldn' sit down."

"What did he use to beat you with?"

"Sometimes a rubber hose, sometimes a wire 'r steel rod."

"Did he express any sympathy for you or give you kindly treatment of any kind?"

"No."

"Would he when you did something that was good, did he recognize it and commend you?"

"No."

"Did he make any manifestation at all when you did what was right?"

"No."

"When you did anything that was wrong, what happened?"

"Allus got a beatin' f'r it."

"These times for which you got beatings, were they always things which were wrong, or what were some of the things for which he would beat you?"

"They wasn' exac'ly right, but sometimes I shouldn' of got a beatin' f'r it."

"Do you recall one instance?"

"I recall one time I couldn' of been but five minutes late comin' home fr'm school. I was playin' along with the rest o' the school kids. It was the on'y time I c'd get t' play, I allus had t' hurry home. I hardly ever got out with any o' the neighbors t' play. I never had nothin' 'round home t' play with."

"Did you have to work and help with the chores around the farm?"

"Ay-eh."

"At about what age did that start if you recall?"

"I wouldn' be able t' say exac'ly. Long's I c'n remember."

"And if you didn't do the work?"

"I was beat an' sent t' bed."

"Did he at any time that you can recall exhibit any kindness or sympathy toward you?"

"Yeh. One time he'd beat me an' my mother an' she left an' took me t' Charlesville or where my sister lived at that time I don' recollect, an' when he come down an' wanted her t' come back he was very kind t' both o' us, an' very kind f'r some weeks after we come back."

"Then did the same kind of treatment as before resume?"

"Yeh."

"Ed, what was your stepfather Alberts' treatment of your mother?"

"He allus treated her very mean 's far 's I c'n recollect."

"Did he do physical violence to her? Did he strike her?"

"Yeh an' beat her."

"How did he talk to her in the home, nice or otherwise?"

Mr. Cobb: "I object as incompetent in this case. I think the manner in which he treated someone else is incompetent."

The Court: "Overrule the objection. He was a child brought up under the supervision of somebody whose influence learned counsel is trying to develop, and we think it has bearing upon this man's life, and we are going to hear about it."

The Court (addressing the witness): "What kind of language did he use?"

"I will say it in my own way. If ever she put up any opposition t' his mean treatment o' me he would allus turn on her an' use mean treatment, an' they were a lotta cussin' in the home when they was nobody 'round. As I remember very distinctly o' one o' the neighbors sayin' that the on'y time they was any religion in the home was when somebody was there. But still in all my young days I was sent t' Sunday school."

Mr. Farmer: "Ed, did your mother attempt to interfere in your punishment?"

"F'r quite some time, yeh."

"And with what result?"

"I'd say it had no effect at all, on'y made things worse. She saw it on'y made things worse an' she quit tryin'."

"She stopped trying?"

"Yeh, an' she wasn't well at the time this happened."

"Whether to your knowledge your stepfather ever inflicted any violent bodily or physical injuries on your mother?"

"Whatta you mean, hit her?"

The Court (addressing the witness): "Did he beat your mother?"

"Yeh."

Mr. Farmer: "Did he beat your mother so as to injure her?"

"Yeh. She hadda scar one time—I think over the right eye, from a dish he'd throwed at her."

"Did he ever beat her so as to cause internal injuries?"

"Tha's what the doctors said down t' the Charlesville hospital, that somebody had."

"Do you recall any instance in which he may have hit her or kicked her out of the house?"

"Yeh, I do. One time he kicked her out while we lived near the New School House an' he kicked her outta the door an' down offa the porch, an' when she went t' go off the porch she tried t' catch the porch an' she fell an' hurt herself."

"Did she require the services of a doctor at that time?"

"Yeh, they was broken bones, I don' jus' recall what they was now."

"Now, Ed, you say you went to school. How long did you go to school? How many years? Do you remember how long?"

"I'd say between three an' four years."

"And in that time how far did you advance in your studies, in what grade?"

"Third."

"Did you ever have any further schooling of any kind after this four years you talk about at home?"

"No, sir."

The Court (addressing the witness): "Back to the father again. Did he ever beat you about the head?"

"A couple o' times he has throwed things at me that I still got scars on my head. He hit me with diff'rent things."

"What?"

"Once I was hit with a glass pitcher an' it made a cut

over my forehead. I got another scar from a piece o' wire over the eye."

Mr. Farmer: "Did he ever hit you with a pitchfork?"

"Yeh."

"Where?"

"Across the forehead, here jus' below my eye."

"Under what circumstances did that happen?"

"I said somethin' I don' recall just now, somethin' over feedin'—I was doin' the feedin' o' the sheep."

"And would he fly up suddenly?"

"Yeh, he was very quick-tempered. He cracked me across the head with a glass pitcher an' he hit me with a pitchfork an' the blood started an' I come near bleedin' t' death an' Dr. Mercer was here in Baconsfield an' he was out there f'r one night an' half the day b'fore he got the blood stopped."

"Do you remember how old you were at that time?"

"Between six an' seven."

"What were the financial circumstances of your stepfather, did he have any money?"

"He was a Spanish War vet'ran an' drew a pension."

"Did he work his farm?"

"Yeh."

"Was he a good farmer?"

"He never sold very much."

"Was there always plenty to eat?"

"Yeh, there was allus plenty t' eat then. Later there wasn'."

"Did you have any money to spend?"

"No, I never had no money."

"Did you ever run away from home?"

"Yeh."

"How many times?"

"Three times that I c'n recollect."

"And why did you run away from home?"

"Because I got a beatin'."

"Were you brought back each time?"

"Yeh."

"And was the treatment any different after you came back?"

"One time, yeh."

"Tell us about that."

"Once I was brought back by somebody from down near Morrisford. I don' recollect who the people was but I had marks on my back an' they tol' him if they heard of it agin they'd have him arrested, an' f'r some time he was very kind t' me."

"Ed, what happened about the schoolhouse when you were about thirteen years of age?"

"Me an' a fellow by the name o' Tim Fowler, he was goin' to a Christmas party an' I wanted t' go t' this party, but the old man said I couldn' go, so—"

"What do you mean by the old man?"

"My stepfather. I'm likely t' call him anything—excuse me. My stepfather wouldn' let me go so when he was out t' the barn I slipped out an' went with this Tim Fowler an' he says on the way over the fields, Let's set fire t' the schoolhouse. I says, No. He says, You stand here at the end o' the yard an' whistle if anybody comes an' I'll go inna schoolhouse. He goes inna schoolhouse—I didn' go in with him. I don' know what he done until the following Sunday mornin'—an' then we went t' this party, an' I come home afterwards after the party was over, an' the next mornin' the old man was waitin' f'r me an' he give me an awful beatin'. The followin' Monday—I think it was—I was arrested f'r it an' brought before Mr. Forsythe, who was a judge I think. He had a hearin' an' I explained there jus' how the thing was an' the old man said that they should kill me instead o' sendin' me t' jail 'r anything. Mr. Forsythe stated, I'm gonna send him down t' the County Jail, I think that would be a better home than he had."

"And you were sent to the jail here, in Baconsfield?"

"Yeh."

"Was the other boy sent with you to jail?"

"No."

"What happened when you came here to jail?"

"I stayed at the jail down here from I think after Christmas till April."

"And then what took place?"

"I come up here an' plead guilty t' the charge. I liked it here down in the County Jail, it was real comfortable an' they was very kind t' me. The sheriff Fisher an' his wife was kind an' I went all over the town. It was really the first home I ever had. I really liked it here, so when I come up f'r trial—b'fore we come up, Tim Fowler an' his sister come down t' the jail an' tol' me his mother was sick an' everything an' I tol' him, Well, don' worry none, I'm gonna take the rap. I got nothin' t' lose. I ruther be here 'r any other place than where I come from. I said, Don' worry none, I'm gonna plead guilty, an' I was sentenced t' the reform school over t' Edom.

"How long were you at the Edom reform school?"

" 'Bout five years."

"How were you treated when you were there?"

"The treatment—"

"First, how old were you when you were sent there?"

"B'tween thirteen an' fourteen."

"And you stayed there five years?"

"Yeh."

"What sort of treatment did you receive while you were there?"

"The treatment at that time was kind o' what you'd call a sorta military school. The treatment was very bad there, but I'll say it in my own way. A good deal of it was my fault. I knew the rules an' regulations. I was tol' that. My not obeyin' the rules caused me very great punishment. The punishment used t' be f'r runnin' away. They used t' beat you in the basement floor. The beatin' was, that was a long rod made outta bamboo like a fishin' rod but not as big aroun', like my little finger. They take 'em an' soak 'em in a barrel o' vinegar which makes 'em very limber an' they stan' back from you 'bout thirty feet an' a guy takes a run. If you stand up after, you're a better man than I ever seen them do. I've come outta that basement with blood runnin' down my legs. But it was due t' the fact that I didn' like the place an' I run away several times."

"That happened more than once?"

"Ay-eh."

"Ed, when you got out of the reform school, you were between eighteen and nineteen years, were you not?"

"Yeh."

"What did you do then?"

"I went back home. I was paroled t' my stepfather."

"What were the conditions when you got back home? Were they any different?"

"They was f'r a time."

"Was his treatment of you any better?"

"F'r a time."

"For how long?"

"A week 'r two."

"And then what? Did he go back to the same kind of treatment again?"

—— 232 ——

"He did."

"How long did you stay at home?"

"A very short time after he started his beatin'. It was while we was loadin' hay that somethin' I done, I don' recall what I done. I tol' him I couldn' reach the top o' the load an' he says I didn' try. I tol' him I was tryin' the best I knew. He got mad an' hit me over the shoulder with the pitchfork. The guy on top o' the load tol' him if he used the pitchfork on me any more he'd break it up on him. He stopped an' that night I left home."

"Did you ever go back to live at home again?"

"Never t' stay. Jus' t' visit."

"Where did you go and what did you do after you left home?"

"I left an' went down t' Rockwell."

"Did you get work there?"

"Yeh."

"What was the next time you had any difficulty with the law?"

"That was in 1926."

"Where were you staying at that time? What were you doing?"

"In Charlesville, stayin' with my stepfather's daughter an' husband."

"Would that be Ben Irwin's wife?"

"Yeh."

"Were you working anywhere?"

"Yeh."

"And what happened?"

"I broke inna cellar that they was movin' the house—we was movin'. I was helpin' 'em move, an' that night I come back an' went into the cellar o' the house an' took some home brew."

"Was anyone living in the house?"

"No. They hadn' moved all the stuff they was movin'."

"Had you been helping them with the moving?"

"Yeh."

"Did you stay in the house?"

"Yeh, all night."

"In other words, you went in the house which you had first helped them move and stayed there over night and took some of the home brew, and what happened?"

"I lef' the next mornin'."

"Were you arrested?"

"Yeh, later."

"Who had you arrested?"

"Breakin' an' enterin'."

"Who?"

"I don' know, I think Ben Irwin."

"Your stepbrother-in-law?"

"Yeh."

"And what happened as a result of that arrest?"

"I was sentenced t' six months inna County Jail."

"Any further punishment?"

"Yeh. I told the judge goin' outta the courtroom, I said, I ruther be dead than be in this place. He said, You're one o' these smart guys, I'm gonna send you down t' the state penitentiary at Deerfield f'r an indefinite period."

"How long were you in the state penitentiary?"

"Two an' a half, three years, aroun' there."

"What were the conditions there, were you treated well?"

"When I behaved myself."

Mr. Cobb: "I object as incompetent."

The Court: "That is a state institution. He said he was treated well as long as he behaved himself."

Mr. Farmer: "Ed, was there any change in your family during the time you were in the County Jail?"

"Just b'fore I went t' Deerfield my mother died while I was inna County Jail."

"Did you ever go back after you got out and live with your stepfather again?"

"No."

"Did you ever see any of your mother's children after you and she went to the County Poor Farm?"

"No."

"Do you know where they are?"

"No."

"When you came out of Deerfield—where did you go?"

"T' Armonk in York State."

"What did you do there?"

"Worked at the airport, mechanic, an' learned t' fly there."

"How long did that keep up?"

"Aroun' six 'r seven months."

"What happened to terminate that employment?"

"I flew a guy down South an' cracked up inna mountains in Kentucky."

"Was it a bad accident?"

"No."

"Was the plane badly damaged?"

"The plane was."

"Were you injured?"

"Slightly injured in my right foot."

"Then what did you do?"

"Went t' work in Kentucky inna coal mines."

"Did you work there any length of time?"

"Quite a time."

"After that where did you go and what did you do?"

"I come back up here aroun'."

"What did you do up here?"

"Worked on a farm, an' doin' carpenter work by the day whenever I c'd get it."

The Court (addressing the witness): "When was this?"

"Aroun' 1930."

Mr. Farmer: "Did you have any further trouble at this time?"

"Yeh."

"What was that?"

"My sister had left Irwin, was keepin' house f'r a fellow name o' Reilly. We went out to a party one night an' when we come back we had all been drinkin'—Reilly couldn' drive the car, I was drivin'—he sent me after more t' drink. I took the car an' went after some stuff t' drink. I got the stuff an' kep' on goin'. I went t' Massachusetts, 'round Williamstown I think it was.

"What happened?"

"I wrecked the car up there an' I sent Reilly a telegram an' I said I had the car an' had wrecked it an' I'd bring it back the followin' Saturday, an' he waited till he had the car insured, then he went an' turned the telegram over t' the State Troopers an' they sent word up there an' they had me locked up."

The Court (addressing the witness): "Where was that now?"

"Williamstown, Massachusetts."

Mr. Farmer: "And was there any prosecution brought against you as a result of that?"

"Yeh, I got five years."

"Where?"

"Massachusetts State Prison."

"How long did you serve?"

"Three an' a half."

"And then what happened?"

"I was pardoned."

"Did this crime for which you were sentenced in Massachusetts, this automobile case, did it have any effect on your parole?"

"I broke my parole. After I was pardoned from Massachusetts, I come back here t' get work, an' they took me back t' the pen t' finish my sentence, a year an' a half."

The Court (addressing the witness): "Didn't you try to find work in Massachusetts while you were on parole?"

"Yeh, I did."

"Did you find any?"

"No, sir."

Mr. Farmer: "Is that why you came back here, because you couldn't find any work?"

"Ay-eh."

The Court (addressing the witness): "When were you finally released?"

"You mean the las' time?"

"Yes."

"Late 1937."

Mr. Farmer: "Now, Ed, when you got out in late 1937, what did you do?"

"Tried t' get work in Massachusetts, Great Barrington, Pittsfield, all over."

"Did you get any work?"

"No, sir."

"How long was it before you got any work?"

"I didn' get no work up in Massachusetts."

"How long was it before you got any work of any kind?"

"It was a year."

"What did you do in the meantime?"

"I come back here an' stayed at the Y.M.C.A. in Deerfield an' went on the Relief."

"Did you make numerous efforts to get work?"

"Yes."

"With what results?"

"The results allus it was where I worked las'. What recommendations I had."

"Did you tell them?"

"No, I didn' tell them. I hadn' worked nowhere las'. I'd been in prison."

"Did you tell them you had been in prison?"

"No."

"When did you finally get work in 1938?"

"Up near Polk, b'tween Polk an' Coney."

"What kind of work?"

"On a chicken farm."

"What wages did you get at that time?"

"From two an' a half t' four a week."

"How long did that continue?"

"That lasted till spring, 1939."

"Then what happened?"

"Man went outta business."

"Then did you seek other employment?"

"Yeh, got work with Hortons' over t' Polk right away."

"How much did these people pay you?"

"Fifteen a month."

"Did you have any promise of better work the spring of 1939?"

"Yeh, over t' the Glover airport, mechanic."

"Did you get this work?"

"No."

"Why not?"

"I was turned down 'cause they foun' my pas' record was bad."

"Ed, when were you married?"

"March 1940."

"And were you able to secure work—other employment—after your marriage?"

"No, not steady, jus' a day's work here an' there, cuttin' an' drawin' wood, hayin' f'r Hortons', cultivatin', road work an' such."

"What was your home life after you were married?"

"Very good."

"Did you have a real good home at last?"

"Yeh."

"Were there any children in the home?"

"Yeh, one little girl, was five 'r six near 's I c'n remember."

"And did you enjoy having this child around?"

"I certainly did."

The Court (addressing the witness): "What are your habits as to the use of intoxicants?"

"You mean drinkin'? I never drank none till 1929. I smoked long 's I c'n remember, since I was a small kid. I remember sneakin' off away from home whenever I could an' smoking."

"Since 1929 have you been a heavy drinker?"

"No, sir."

"How about the last few months since you have been married?"

"No, sir. On'y a couple times I've touched any since I was married."

Mr. Farmer: "What were your financial circumstances after your marriage? I am speaking now of last spring after you were married. Did you have much money?"

—— 239 ——

"My wife was fired from her teachin' the scholars in Olds after she married me. No, we didn' have no money."

"You said you had occasional jobs. Did you get much pay for these jobs?"

"Twen'y-five cents an hour."

"Did you have much money to do with and keep house with?"

"No."

"In November 1940, did you get a letter or see a letter addressed to your wife with any threats in it?"

"I did."

"What were the nature of these threats?"

"It was a letter from a lawyer f'r a bill she owed in Coney."

"Did they threaten legal proceedings?"

"Yeh, threatened suin' her."

The Court (addressing the witness): "I believe you testified that you could not read very well."

"She read it t' me."

Mr. Farmer: "What was your reaction to this letter?"

"I got very worried 'cause I didn' want my wife—I figgered when they sue they'd put her in jail. I knew she didn' have no money t' pay the bill an' I didn' have no money t' pay the bill an' couldn' get it."

"And was that when you decided to get the money somehow to pay the bill?"

"Ay-eh."

"Was that what you meant, you made up your mind to get the money somehow if you had to get it to meet that bill?"

"Yeh."

"You believed, did you, that if your wife were sued she might be put in jail?

"Yeh. I didn' know it wasn' so that way."

"Did you ask her if this was true?"

"No."

"Why not?"

"I thought it was true; I didn' want t' let her knew I was scared."

"Did she seem worried about this?"

"She tried t' make out like she wasn' worried, an' so did I, so we didn' talk 'bout it none, but I figgered she was doin' it b'cause she was scared she would be put in jail an' didn' want me t' know it."

"Ed, have you ever had much experience with firearms?"

"No."

"Had you ever owned a gun?"

"No."

"Did you ever shoot a gun much?"

"No, I think on'y three times in my life."

"Do you know the difference between an automatic and a revolver?"

"No, I don' think I c'd tell the diff'rence."

"You saw the pistol that was introduced in evidence yesterday. Will you tell us what kind of a pistol that was, whether it was an automatic or a revolver?"

"I been tol' it was a automatic."

"Ed, without going into the details that have been so thoroughly reviewed in your confession that was read here yesterday, I want to ask you what your mental impressions —what was your attitude at the time of the commission of the crime for which you are here charged? At the very moment when you fired the first shot? Why did you shoot?"

"I don' know."

"What was your state of mind?"

"All I was tryin' t' do, I wanted the car."

"What—"

"I wasn' figgering on my shootin' 'r anything when he grabbed my wrist, I was tryin' t' get outta the car myself. I would like t' of got outta the car myself but he was hangin' onto me an' I started t' fire. I don' know why. I can' give no explanation."

"Were you frightened?"

"Yes."

"Had you ever robbed anyone before?"

"No."

"Had you, as testified to in your statement, previously that morning tried to get up your courage to take two other men's cars away from them?"

"Yes."

"Why didn't you take the other men's cars?"

"I don' know. I just couldn' get the nerve."

"In any of your law violations, in any of the things which you have testified about here for which you have served sentence, did any of them ever involve the injury of a person?"

"No."

"Did any of them ever involve any violence?"

"No."

"Have you ever had fights?"

"No."

"Did you ever before in your life carry a weapon?"

"No."

"Ed, did you feel badly having done it?"

"Yes, I did."

"Are you sorry for what happened?"

"Yes."

"Did you feel remorse for what happened?"

(Sobbing): "Oh, yes."

When the recess was announced and Sloan stepped down from the stand, there was a great collective sigh, a sigh that rose from the crowded courtroom as though on cue. Norah could hear a woman sobbing; she looked around and saw several women, even some men with handkerchiefs to their eyes. There was a different air in the room, a different quality in the atmosphere. There was almost a feeling of—she tried to formulate a word, and *sprightliness* was the word that came to mind. As though an enormous burden had been lifted from the shoulders of the throng; as though now that they understood something of the man they had come to see justly punished, they were more hopeful, were almost happier.

There was a sense of pause in the room; they seemed to be holding their breath. Norah felt tears come into her own eyes, tears of gratitude and good cheer; and, too, tears of humiliation for having so grossly mistrusted these people.

Ed was back on the stand again, his face worried as the prosecutor, Cobb, faced him and began the cross-examination. The story can't be shaken, she thought; it was the *truth*. It should make a difference; the very people in the room had not been insensible to the story, to his simplicity in telling it, to his directness, his honesty.

Cobb led Sloan back over the entire story he had related under direct examination by his attorney, point by point. Nor was it very long before the "line" of his examination became patent. He was trying to establish the fact that Ed knew the difference between right and wrong, for Cobb had learned that Dr. Pincus had unexpectedly offered his services as a defense witness, and he anticipated testimony that might try to establish mental incompetence. That's ridiculous, Norah thought; there can be no doubt of his mental

— 243 —

competence, of his sanity. Of course he knows the difference between right and wrong.

"Now," said Cobb in his sharply accented voice, "you knew when you took this car of Mr. Reilly and went up to Massachusetts with it, you knew that was wrong?"

"I took his car lots o' times," Ed said, "an' went diff'rent places with it."

"How far is it from where you were in this state to Williamstown in Massachusetts?"

"Mebbe a hundred fifty miles."

"Do you think that was the right thing for you to do, take his car a hundred and fifty miles away?"

"I took it further than that often."

"Nevertheless," Cobb shouted, "you were placed under arrest!"

"Yeh."

"And you pleaded guilty to the crime of taking it?"

"Yeh."

"If you pleaded guilty to the crime of taking the car, you knew what you did was wrong, didn't you?"

"I don' know as it was so wrong."

"Would you plead guilty to something you didn't think was wrong?"

"I didn' plead exac'ly guilty," Sloan said. "I explained how it was and everythin' t' the judge."

"Mr. Sloan, do you mean to tell me that you were sentenced to five years in the State of Massachusetts without your being convicted by a jury or a plea of guilty?"

"I tol' the judge exac'ly how the circumstances was, an' I tol' him I knew I shouldn' of took the automobile."

"You told the judge that, and you knew it was wrong?"

"Yeh, I also tol' the judge I had took it lots o' times b'fore."

Cobb dropped the subject with the statement, "At any rate, you were sentenced to five years and then for violation of your parole you were sent back again?"

"Yes."

The prosecutor then took up Sloan's marriage and developed the stories he had told his wife. "You told your wife you owned certain property in the State of New York, and you told her you were going to place a mortgage on it and buy a farm, didn't you?"

"Yeh."

"What was your purpose in telling that to your wife?" he sneered.

"I s'pose," Ed said, "it was through some questions that she may of asked me that I decided t' ease her mind."

"Didn't you try to create the impression that you owned some property and told her that story?"

"Yeh."

"And you told her that *before* you married her, didn't you?"

"I don' recall that I told her b'fore or afterwards."

"You come to a point when a letter was received and you say that letter worried you?"

"Yes."

"And then you decided to go out and stick up somebody as you said in the confession?"

"Yes."

Cobb pointed his finger at Sloan, who was gripping the arms of the witness chair. "Did that worry you?"

"What?"

"Going out and *sticking somebody up?*"

"Yeh, it did."

"You knew *that* was wrong, didn't you?"

"Yeh, I knew it was wrong."

"Then why did you do it?"

"Because I didn' want my wife t' go t' jail. I love my wife an' had a very happy life."

The prosecutor put both hands on his hips and smiled at the people in the courtroom. Then he whirled on Sloan and, pointing his finger at him again, said, "Did you think it was all right then if you believed your wife would go to jail, it would be all right for you to go and take a gun and stick somebody up to get the money to pay the bill!"

"I knew it was wrong, yeh, I knew it was."

"A gun had been brought to your home by a friend of your wife's former husband, had it not?" Cobb asked.

"Yeh."

Cobb suddenly produced the gun from behind his back and shoved it under Sloan's nose. Ed turned his head.

"Mr. Sloan," Cobb said, "I show you State's exhibit G, being a gun, and ask if that is the gun from which you fired the bullets into the body of James T. Baldwin!"

Ed burst into tears and sobbed, "Yes."

"And you had fired this gun before," Cobb said. "I believe you testified that you had fired a gun before."

"Not this one, no."

"I believe you testified in the presence of Corporal Slattery, Captain Fenster and Sheriff Fisher that you and your wife and Mr. Hogan, the friend of her first husband, had fired this gun at a mark at your home in Polk, Meadow County."

"I don' remember of makin' that statement," Sloan said. "I was there, but I didn' fire the gun. I remember that they was there an' he used the gun and Norah—that's my wife— she fired it, but I never fired the gun. I don' remember the statement f'r all I might of made it."

Norah could see that he was sweating; the lines of his

face were more tightly drawn, and his dark hair was damp and hung over his forehead. He leaned forward in the chair, and the prosecutor continued relentlessly, pounding on the fact that he had lied to the police at first and then told the truth. Why?

He had lied to his wife and he had lied to the police—

"At first you told them that this shooting had been committed by a man named Logan?"

"I think that was the name I used."

"Who was that party?"

"I don' think such a party existed."

"You did not mean Mr. Hogan, your wife's *friend?*"

"No."

"Was there any party by the name of Logan in the penitentiary when you were there?"

"Not as I knew. A man's name inna penitentiary is seldom used. They go by numbers."

He had lied to the police and he had cheated the hotel clerk in Lebanon; he had lied to his ex-convict friend Goreski about his trip and about the gun that Goreski wanted to buy and about a job he didn't have.

"And you say that while you were at Goreski's, what we call the clip of this gun was taken out? Who took it out?"

"I did."

"And who put it back in when you left there?"

"I did."

"Then you *knew* how to take out the clip and put it back in the gun?"

"Yeh, I had been showed."

Cobb held the transcript of the confession in his hand and followed it as he questioned Sloan, marking with his voice every point that tended to show that Sloan knew exactly what he was doing, was afraid of being caught with the gun when a State trooper's car passed him, threw the gun in the bushes when another car came along that he *thought* was a trooper's car, got the gun again, tried to take two other cars, finally was picked up by Baldwin.

"And what did you say to him when you told him to stop the car?"

"I jus' tol' him t' stop the car an' get out."

"Then what did he do?"

"He grabbed my wrist."

Cobb hammered away at the details of the killing, how Sloan had fired and Baldwin still held him by the wrist and dragged him from the car, and Sloan fired till he fell, and Sloan looked around to see if anyone had seen this trouble, "And why did you do *that?* Was it not because you realized what you had *done*, Mr. Sloan?"

"I realized I done somethin' I shouldn' of done."

Cobb dropped his voice. "You realized you had committed murder, had you not!"

"Yes," said Ed in a faint voice, and Norah covered her face with her hands. She felt Burton Farmer put his hand on her shoulder, and she straightened up. It went on, endlessly, she felt, on and on, hammering and pounding. It was like a physical beating he was taking. He had killed a man and carried the body in the car and disposed of it and stolen the money from the corpse, and he had lied and lied. He had lied to the gas-station man and to the young man in the diner, he had lied to the doctor who treated his foot and to the car dealer in Peekskill, to his wife and to the police.

"And you *say* you had intended to take the man to a doctor, and yet you decided, Mr. Sloan, so long as the man was *dead*, there was no use in taking the man to a doctor.

Wasn't this the real reason, that you knew you would be implicated if you took his body to some doctor?"

"No," said Ed, "I didn' even think o' that."

Cobb spoke of the days before Ed was arrested, in particular of that day in the new Chrysler when they had been driving in to Shoreline, and Norah could vividly see the image. They were approaching the top of a hill in a long line of cars, and the car ahead stopped before it reached the crest. In the rear-vision mirror, Ed had seen the police car, and she saw that he had become intensely nervous. His face grew white and he pulled on the brake and the motor stalled. He worked feverishly to start the motor again, and finally the car up ahead got going, and Ed got the Chrysler going, looking continuously into the mirror over the windshield and working his hands and feet with frantic speed.

She had thought about this at the time, and later that night he had said to her, "Mom, you look worried," and she had gone over to him and sat beside him and said, "Ed, what were you so rattled about this afternoon when we were going up that hill? I never saw you behave like that before."

"Why," he said, "that car up ahead was rollin' back down, an' I was scared it would hit us, an' it ain' my car, it's my brother's car."

She had accepted the explanation, but now she recognized that if she had been mildly concerned before and slightly puzzled, that was the moment when she had become actively worried, certain—but unwilling to admit the idea to consciousness—that something was wrong; something.

Mr. Farmer was speaking. "Ed," he said, "you testified in your answer to questions by Mr. Cobb that you had pleaded guilty in previous crimes. Did you not, as a matter of fact, plead guilty in all your previous crimes?"

"Ay-eh."

"Were you represented by counsel in any of them?"

"No, sir."

"Ed, can you read and write?"

"No, sir, not very much."

"Have you learned to write your name?"

"Yeh."

"Can you write anything other than your name?"

"Very little."

"To what extent are you able to read?"

"Well, very small words."

Mr. Cobb took over again, trying to inquire into Sloan's education in the reformatory.

"No schooling of any kind there?" he said incredulously.

"No, sir."

"That is all," said Cobb.

Then Horan, the chief judge, resumed the questioning himself, tracing Ed's movements from the moment after the crime to his apprehension in Polk.

"Weren't you afraid of being caught in a holdup?" he asked.

"T' tell you the truth," said Ed, "I didn' think about it."

"You remember Mr. Forsythe very well?"

"Yes, very well."

"Hadn't he been kind to you?"

"Allus very kind, ev'ry time I come in the store he used t' give me candy."

"You liked him, didn't you?"

"Yeh."

"Then why did you pick him out to hold up and rob?"

"I don' know why I did it."

"It wasn't anything you had against him because he was the judge who sent you to the county jail?"

"No sir, he had never done nothin' agains' me in any way."

"Then your only objective was to get money, is that right?"

"Yeh."

"Had you made any arrangement to cover your face up when you entered his store?"

"No, sir."

"You also figured you had to have a car to get away in?"

"Yeh."

"And that's the reason you made this plan to get a ride with somebody and take the car away from him?"

"I hadn' figgered on gettin' a ride, I figgered on gettin' a car in Morrisford, an' I got this ride. I was figgerin' on goin' into town an' pickin' one up onna street there; folks leave their keys in cars; I didn' want t' hurt nobody."

"You didn't know Mr. Baldwin?"

"No."

"Never saw him before?"

"Never saw him b'fore in my life."

"Now you have told us about your hard upbringing when you were a small child; how were things at your home before you departed and came up here, were you happy there?"

"Very happy."

"Did it occur to you that that happiness was very apt to be destroyed by this act which you had in mind to do?"

"Yes, I knew that. I had been so happy in the few months we was married that I figgered anythin' I c'd do t' help the wife an' the kid out would be worth what I would get outta it."

"In other words, you were willing to take a chance with the law to do something for them?"

"Yeh."

"Didn't it occur to you that the police would be looking for this car immediately?"

"Yeh. After the man got killed—I didn' plan t' do that—I expected t' be picked up in a very short time b'cause I guess I left everythin' wide open. So I expected t' be picked up in two 'r three days."

"You say Mr. Forsythe gave you candy and was kind to you and you liked him?"

"Ay-eh."

"When you were debating about robbing him didn't it occur to you that you might better rob someone who *hadn't* been kind to you? Did that occur to you? Did the fact that he had been kind to you occur to you at that time?"

"Yeh."

"Didn't that restrain you?"

"Quite a lot. I thought about it quite a lot b'fore an' that was one reason I didn' come up long b'fore I did, jus' f'r that reason."

"You're very fond of your wife, are you?"

"Yes."

"You love the child?"

"Yes."

"Well, did you know when you killed this man, or when you got the idea of robbing Mr. Forsythe, that you would surely be taken away from your wife and child?"

"Yeh, I knew."

"You were willing to make that sacrifice?"

"Yeh. You see, Y'r Honor, there was not only these bills but the milkman threatened t' cut the milk out on the kid if we didn' git some money f'r him too."

"Didn't it occur to you that this money you contemplated taking—that it would be gone soon after you got it, and then what would you do?"

"Yeh, I did. But I didn' know what t' do. What I mean— we *had* t' have some money, an' there was no way o' gittin' it, an' even when I thought it would be gone fast, I still didn' know what t' do if I couldn' git it so I knew I hadda git it nohow, an' I figgered mebbe it would give us a start, a chance t' start till I foun' a good job 'r we could move somewhere 'r somethin'."

"Ed, do you mind talking to me?" said the judge.

"No, not a bit."

"You know what revenge is—hatred?"

"Yeh, I know what it is."

"Is there anyone in the world that you would rather have killed than Mr. Baldwin whom you didn't know, in view of the fact that someone had to be killed, or someone *was* killed, would you rather it had been someone else?"

"No," said Sloan, "I don' think o' nobody else outside o' myself."

When Norah was called to the stand, there was a distinct murmur in the courtroom and the chief judge, Horan, had to bang his gavel on the bench. She could see all the eyes, and she felt slightly like the time, years before, when she had thought she might be an actress. Her throat was dry, and she licked her lips.

"Mrs. Sloan," said Farmer, "when were you married to Edwin Sloan?"

"Last March 1st, 1940."

"Had you known him very long before that?"

"Well, I hadn't known him well, but he had worked on the farm for the people from whom I rented my house, for about eight or nine months previously."

"The only opportunity you had to know and observe him

was in the nine months prior to your marriage, and the short time you were married?"

"That is right."

"You have one child?"

"Yes."

"What, Mrs. Sloan, was the attitude of your husband, Edwin Sloan, toward that child?"

"Well, I first noticed it from observing him working during the summer before. I had barely known him, but my daughter was not in school at that time, and she used to follow him into the fields when he was working there. That was probably how I got to know him, and I saw the way he worked, eight, ten, fourteen hours a day sometimes, six days a week, and he was always very quiet and very kind to the child."

"Did you ever at any time discover any trait of viciousness or meanness in this man?"

"No, on the contrary, at times when I'm sure I would have provoked anybody to lose his patience, he was always very well under control. I have never seen any signs of meanness in him."

"Was he always kind and quiet with the child?"

"Yes. She was very fond of him."

"Did he play with her?"

"Yes, as any parent who loves his child would play with it."

"Mrs. Sloan," said Farmer, "prior to your marriage to Edwin did he tell you he had been in prison?"

"I believe he told me he had been in prison once."

"Did he tell you of all these prison sentences which you now know about?"

"No, he didn't, though later on I realized he possibly

—— 254 ——

wanted to tell me everything in the beginning. I look back and see that before we were married, he wanted dreadfully to tell me. I can well understand why he wasn't able to, but he didn't."

"Did you know of his lack of formal education?"

"I gathered that."

"Did you know—did he try to conceal the fact that he could not read or write?"

"I wouldn't say he pretended he knew, but he managed not to let me know for a time that he didn't know how. But that fact and his lack of education wouldn't have influenced me in any event."

"Has he at any time since expressed a desire to learn to read and write?"

"Yes, and I have helped him; both during our marriage and since he has been in prison. Before then, when I taught him, I tried not to hurt his feelings. He was very nice about it, but a little rebellious. He would like to have broken down then and let me help him. You see, he was thrown into an environment which he had never come in contact with before."

"In relation to the events that have been testified to here, did you have any previous knowledge of these facts, before your husband was arrested?"

"No previous knowledge." (There was no cross-examination.)

Then Dr. Pincus, who had volunteered to take the stand as a defense witness, spoke, relating his experience with Sloan, both immediately after the crime and in prison, where he had treated him again for his injured foot. He gave it as his considered opinion that Sloan was essentially a kindly person, who had not had a chance to develop his better qualities. He believed that he was truly remorseful and quoted evidences of his remorse and his essential honesty.

"I think he's an unfortunate product of an abject home environment during those very early impressionable years. I think that at heart he's honest, but I think his good qualities haven't been developed and cultivated. He's not to be condemned. Criticism should be leveled at those who have failed to provide him with an emotional training, and I think society in general—which is accountable largely for the failure to develop those qualities that most of us have at birth—is culpable throughout."

Norah remembered Farmer saying, "A victim of society" and intertwining his fingers. "The usual defense," he had said. . . .

"Well, gentlemen," said the judge, "what do you have in mind? That this record should be written up and arguments made?"

Farmer rose. "I do now move that this case be continued until April 3, 1941, at nine o'clock a.m., in order that the record may be transcribed and counsel be given an opportunity to make a brief."

That was a month ahead, and they took Ed back to his cell, and one of the local newspaper reporters offered to drive Norah to the bus station after she had said good-by to Ed and promised to be back to visit him before the day for final arguments, and after she had said good-by to Mr. Farmer.

In the car driving over to Morrisford, the reporter talked to her very kindly and asked her many questions about herself and Sloan.

"Would you mind if I wrote an interview with you?" he

said, and she said, "I'd rather you didn't. I'm not important here, unless you think it would do some good."

"It might help people to understand," the reporter said, and she looked up at the man who was driving, perhaps for the first time. He had a good face, she thought, and she asked if he was the man who had written the story she had read after the first day of the trial.

"Yes," he said.

She had an hour and a half to wait for the bus, and fifteen minutes before it was due he came rushing into the bus station with a sheaf of papers in his hand.

"Would you mind reading this?" he said. "I'd rather you O.K.'d it before I go to press."

She was exhausted, both physically and mentally, but she consented to glance over the interview he had written, and he said he would send her printed copies later that night.

When she first came to Baconsfield to see Ed after his arrest, the story read, she said he asked: "Do you want a divorce? You can get one easily." But that, she assured him, was farthest from her thoughts. One could easily see that she was sincere as she went through the grueling experience of days in the crowded, stuffy courtroom—the center of all eyes as she sat beside her husband and tried to bolster him for the ordeal of a struggle to prove the right to life. Told that she had the sympathy of many because of the bitter experience, she spoke up bravely: "I don't need sympathy. He does not need it. He needs to understand himself. People need to understand how these things happen, and why." The spirit of the woman in standing by a man who has admitted murder and faces pos-

sible electrocution, gripped the imagination of the huge crowd that jammed into the stuffy courtroom. Even District Attorney John A. Cobb shook hands with her as the session ended and expressed his sympathy for her.

Norah smiled. "Did you know that Mr. Baldwin's son nodded to me and smiled when I passed him?"

"Did he?" said the reporter. "May I use that?"

"Certainly," Norah sighed.

But she was not terribly shocked when the newspaper arrived at the Hogans' house a day or so later, and she saw the interview headed by the boxed caption:

> Can Anyone Still
> LOVE
> A Mate Found to Be
> A MURDERER?
>
> Read One Woman's Re-
> Action on Page 6 Today!

That was not the reporter's work, she knew. That was the work of an editor who had his eye on the box office.

15

ALICE WATCHED HER
packing. "Are you worried?" she said.

"Pretty much." Norah looked up from the bag. "It's
hard to say," she said. "I never expected the judge to be
so sympathetic, or the crowd. We're likely to underesti-
mate people, their understanding. They'd come to see him
lynched; they changed their minds. If it had happened in
New York, I imagine, with Ed being the man he is—a nobody, a bum, with a record—it would have been pretty cut
and dried."

"From what you told me," said Alice, "I'd say he stood a
chance."

"Quit kidding me," said Norah. "I'm prepared for the
worst, you know. Farmer told me as much."

"There's something else that's worrying you," Alice said,
sitting down on the bed next to her friend.

"Lots of things, kid," said Norah. "Lots of things. For
one—I've been here since the first of December and now it's
the end of March."

"Forget it."

"No, I can't forget it," she said. "Even if Bill *is* making a little money these days, nobody can be his brother's or sister's keeper. I'm on the track of a job, but there won't be anything definite for a week or so."

"You can forget it," Alice said. "You know you can stay here as long as you need to, and as long as we've got a dime it's yours. You'd do the same. I know you. You've got a heart bigger than a house."

"Maybe that's what's wrong with me," Norah said. She doesn't know what I mean, she thought, but *I* do; oh, boy, do I know what I mean!

"Look, darling," Alice said. "I'm off to get Junior from his school. Bill wants to talk to you before you hop the bus; be nice to him, will you? He's in a terrible stew."

"Sure," said Norah, thinking, I know what's worrying him. He's still ashamed of the day he spent with Ella Horton and of playing *deus ex machina*. And if I weren't ashamed of thinking so, I might even feel that he'd sort of like me to be hauling my ashes.

She found Hogan in what Alice called his "study," sitting before the typewriter with that expression of small-boy worriment on his round face that had always amused her. When she came in the room he tore the sheets out of the machine and crumpled them and threw them on the floor with a curse.

"Take it easy, boy," she said. "You'll live longer." She recalled having said that once before and tried to place the time.

He smiled and bent toward her, clasping his hands between his knees. "I wish to hell I could drive you up, Norah," he said, "but I still think it's better for me to keep out of that State."

"You're probably right," she said. "There's no reason for you guys to be any more involved than you are already."

"No," he said, irrelevantly, apparently thinking of something else. "Norah," he said. "I—this may seem a cruel thing for me to say, but I hope you don't expect too much."

Suddenly she remembered where and when she had said it. She could see Ed's face, the boyish bustle he was in, see him getting into his coat, pulling on the cap. That was when she had said it. That was when she also had said, "Haven't you forgotten something?" and he had scratched his head and said, "Don' think so; so long Mom, see you tomorrow or the day after."

"I don't," she said. "I expect nothing."

"You *mustn't*," he said earnestly. "I want to get this off my chest," he said. "To begin with, as you probably know, I was pretty sore about it all—I wasn't too sympathetic. I'm ashamed; I've wanted to tell you that. I was a snob, as you said I was; I didn't have any real understanding of this situation, of Ed. I thought he'd told the police—they *told* me so—that I was with him. I'm sure now that he never did."

"He didn't," Norah said, wondering, How can you be so sure? he might have.

"I'm sure he didn't," Hogan said, clasping and unclasping his hands. "But I want you to know that I feel responsible for all this—"

"How, for God's sake?"

Hogan's jaw dropped and he sighed. "I provided the weapon," he said. "I didn't use my head. If I'd used my head, I would never have brought the gun, and if I hadn't brought the gun—"

"That's nonsense," Norah said. "That was pure coincidence. You mustn't feel that way."

"I can't help it," he said. "I was so bound up at the time in the fact that I was making a little money for a change, selling an article at a good price, buying a car on the installment plan; I was so preoccupied with myself that I never used my head at all."

"It was an accident," Norah said. "You can't consider yourself responsible in any way, any more than I consider myself responsible."

Hogan looked up at her, his brow furrowed, and said, "Do you really believe that? After all, there was no other gun around, was there?"

"That's not the point," Norah said. "Forget it." She went over to Bill and put her hand on his shoulder. "Forget it, pal," she said.

"I can't," he said miserably. "I keep thinking that if I hadn't brought the gun, this never would have happened. If there's anything I can *do*, if the decision goes adversely; if there's anything I can *write* to anyone, or appear before anyone, or what have you—"

"Thanks," Norah said. "How do you think I feel, brother? If I hadn't met Ed myself, if we hadn't married— You musn't allow yourself to feel so damned important. Life isn't as simple as all that. People have complex motives."

On the bus to Morrisford she got to thinking of what she had said to Bill. If I hadn't met Ed . . . any more than I consider myself responsible . . . life isn't as simple as that. Was that true? Aren't you avoiding the contemplation of your actual responsibility? Wasn't it you who were the prime mover in all this? Wasn't it you who held the trump card? Didn't you hold the possibility in your hand of calling it all off at a particular time when Ed would have gone away and this might never have happened? Didn't you deliberately prevent him from going away, for your own purposes—playing on his own hunger—because you were lonely and needed a man, because you cherished illusions and fostered them? And even then? And didn't you realize the position in which you were placing him? Didn't you understand that Bill was right when he said, "He hasn't the *means* to help you; he can't keep up to you"?

Didn't you put this man—a man who had had no training or opportunity or experience, in the position of being suddenly a husband, a father, a bread winner? And wasn't it exactly this that broke him? That made him turn to the only choice that was open to him in order to shoulder his new responsibilities? Certainly it wasn't your fault that he had neither the training nor the opportunity nor the experience in handling responsibility; but if he hadn't been forced to shoulder it, then what? And after that, what about after that? Couldn't you have stopped this at the point when he said, "Do you mind if I ask Bill to bring that gun?" And after that, when the gun had come and when you felt uneasy? Couldn't you have taken the gun, as you had in mind to do at least once, and buried it where it never would have been found again?

Who's oversimplifying now? she thought. It isn't as easy as that. No single individual's influence is ever so controlling. It's not true that life is what you make it; it *is* true that you 're what life makes you. The time you live in, the place, the form of your society. That's first, she thought; that comes first. The man is made by his life; his ideas, his actions grow out of the conditions of his life. People aren't helpless victims of circumstance. People aren't the puppets of the gods, any more than they are the gods themselves. Certainly the society makes the man; then the man turns around and acts upon his society. But his actions, his ideas are also limited by the circumstances that make him react in the first place. Could Leonardo da Vinci have invented the airplane? He could not, no matter how he tried.

From the window of the bus she watched the Westchester countryside move by. It was a bright spring day; the sun was hot and the light on the land was brilliant; the neat little houses and the low, rolling hills spoke of life, of people living their lives in security, in comfort. The earth was new again and bubbling with energy. Once you said you weren't an intellectual, she thought; you told Bill Hogan. "I'm a simple gal," you said. But you've been sitting here working this out in your head as though it were a problem in design. She closed her eyes. The contrast was too great; the blossoming hills and the light over the blooming land. Your life with Ed is over; *his* life is over. It started, and now it's ended. She saw the deep-lined face, the gray eyes, the strong hands. This is the ruin of what you thought you had when you made your first decision—to make him stay awhile, "just a little while," you thought, "see what happens." Now you know what happened; the house is empty. She could remember looking back at it in the reflection of the headlights on Bill Hogan's car. She remembered the cat whose eyes had flashed in the beam of the lights, and the cat had leaped into the brush. Now you know . . .

. . . Sloan moved up and down in the narrow cell. If I hadn't been in stir before, got sort of used to the idea, I'd be batty by now, he thought. With his thumbnail he had marked the days upon the brick wall under the high, small window that let in the only daylight he ever saw. Since he had been brought there in December of the year before, he had been out of the cell only once a week, to walk, escorted, down the corridor to the shower bath, the toilet where they let him shave. It was April now, the first of April. April Fool's Day, he thought. I remember what she said.

"Do you know what day this is?"

"No," I said.

"It's April Fool's Day," she said, and I didn't get it at first. I thought she meant that she was really going to be the principal in the academy over Olds-way. Then I thought she meant the letter she was reading, that fired her, was a made-up letter and she was kidding me. I was dumb. *I'm the April fool,* he thought.

Pretty soon it will be all over. Pretty soon it will be all decided. Day after tomorrow. Day after tomorrow they were going to make their final arguments, and then the old judge Horan and the guy with the stiff neck and the other sourpuss would speak their piece. They got it all decided now, he thought, no matter what the lawyers say. The prosecutor, Cobb, he'll shout, his face red and shaking a finger at the air. *The most brutal crime in the history of this county!* he'll yell, just like they do in the moving pictures. *The State demands the life of this brutal criminal, this cold-blooded, blood-thirsty man who cut down the life of his fellow human being.* A lot he knows, Sloan thought.

"Hi, Ed," one of the other men said, walking past his cell. There were two other men in jail now, a Negro and another. The Negro was in for being drunk and disorderly; the other for a crap game. Bad business, Sloan thought. Those sure are crimes. He remembered that day.

"Hi," Sloan said.

"Yore woman comin' up t'day, I hear," the Negro said.

"Yeh," said Sloan.

"Wish you luck, 'bo."

"Thanks," said Sloan.

He envied that man, and the other. They could walk around in the jail; they could even go outside when the sheriff let them and play ball on the grass in the yard. He had heard them playing ball, and the lawyer, Farmer, had told him that sometimes they played catch with the State troopers who were quartered in the county courthouse. I'd like to see the sky, Sloan thought. I ain't seen the sky since I come in here. Nothing but the bars of this cell and the light burning all the time in the cell and in the corridor outside.

Norah had mailed him a box of water colors, and he had sent her back a lot of pictures he had painted. Mostly he painted pictures of the house over in Polk, Katey swinging under the big maple and Norah and Ed standing in the doorway holding hands. Or he painted a picture of a big red car in the dooryard (he never made it blue), with Ed sitting at the wheel and Norah and Katey coming out of the house all dressed up. He was very careful with these pictures. He put in every clapboard and every shingle on the roof, the exact number of windows and the way the branches on the maple grew and twisted out of the trunk. They looked like the pictures Katey painted herself, and he laughed at them. But it was nice to do; it gave him a good feeling, and Norah had written back to say that he had a good sense of colors. That pleased him.

At first he had had the sheriff write to her, dictating what he wanted to say, but later, with hard work, he had been learning to write himself. She had sent him exercises to copy and to read, and he had copied pieces out of aviation magazines to improve his handwriting and to improve his understanding of the words. So that now he generally wrote himself, painstakingly forming the letters like a small child, his hand cramped, his tongue stuck between his lips. And he was able to understand almost everything she wrote. She writes simple, he thought, so I'll understand. She don't use the big words. But she had also sent him a small dictionary so he could look up words, and he sometimes spent hours reading the dictionary, page by page, and he had even started to write the story of his life, but it wasn't very long. He had only written five pages, and it made him tired even to think of writing more. It ain't good writing, he thought, and so many things happened, I wouldn't know how to put them all down or where they should go in the story. But this much was sure; now he was beginning to understand why he was in the jail and why he had been in jail before, beginning with the first time, and where he had got some of the whacky ideas he had got and why he had never learned any more than he had learned.

But most of all, he felt that it wasn't all his fault that he didn't know anything, and by searching himself he had come to a conclusion he could not shake, that he had never really meant any harm to anyone. Then how was it that he had really killed a man? There's something about a gun, he thought, like when Hogan said, "Beautiful, ain't it?" He knew now what Hogan meant when he said that. A gun wasn't really beautiful, but in a way it was. It was made so good; it was put together so good, clever, he would say, and the tooling was tricky. He stopped thinking about that, except to record once more the feeling of being strong that it gave to have it in your hand, to feel the hard firm stock and see the dull blue glint of the metal. That's moving picture stuff, he thought.

It was all like a moving picture that had happened to somebody else. It wasn't really him, Ed Sloan, that it had happened to, even if it was. He could see himself after, like in a picture. He could see himself with the brand-new car, driving Norah and the kid all over the place, once he had got the hang of the machine, and he lay back now on the cot with his hands behind his head, his eyes closed, seeing himself. He could feel the money he had in his pocket—what a drip you were, he thought, not to know that if they caught up to you, all the money you paid on the bills would be taken back again, the telephone and the grocer and the meat man, the milkman and the wood and coal, the new coal stove would be taken back and everything, and she would owe just as much as she owed before.

But he could still feel the money that didn't belong to him and the sense of strength it had given him to have it in his pocket. Three hundred dollars! And the business of peeling off a fresh, stiff bill and paying for gas and things and knowing there was a lot more where it came from. You never had that much money before in your whole life, he thought. But he worked for it, that guy Baldwin, he thought; it was coming to him. Maybe that was only right, because he was the manager, wasn't he? And the Chrysler he had, the 1940 sedan, with all its shining lights and little gadgets and levers, and its silent motor humming along the road, fast, fast. It was a lot better car than most folks could ever buy, even if there was a lot of them on the roads. To see the new cars rolling by, he thought, you'd think they come with every pack of chewing gum, but it ain't so. There's millions of people in this country, he thought, and maybe in his life he had met thousands of them (not to know well, of course), but there wasn't one out of a hundred of them that had a new Chrysler like that, or even an old one, but they could almost all of them drive.

He lay there savoring with his body the feel of that car, as he had driven Norah and Katey up to Vermont and over to York State and east to Rhode Island. It was swell, feeling the heavy machine rolling under him, feeling in his hands the very slightest tremor of the body, enjoying the sensation when the fancy new-fangled gear shift, once he got the hang of it, clicked neatly into place, no, *slid* was the word, and the car moved into higher or lower gear. And the comfortable seats in it, and the sense of flying it gave. And the wonderful feeling the times he had picked up hitch hikers, driving with Norah and Katey, young kids hitting the road from here to there. He had made it a point to pick up every hitch hiker that thumbed him when he was driving in it. And one of them he had taken far out of his own way home, and he gave the kid two dollars for his bus fare, saying, "Don' worry none about it, 'bo; I hit the road plenty myself! I know what it's like."

And he had tried hard all that week, after he came back, not to think of what he had done, but how could you forget you had killed a man? And he knew they were on his trail even then. That was why I had to be on the go all the time and why I got the jitters that day in Shoreline when the prowl car was in back of me on the hill and the dame in front started to slide back down the hill. And why I got sore at Norah that time when she asked what was in the little pocket on the dashboard, and I said, I don't know, I'd lost the key to it. The gun was in it then; I hadn't taken it back into the house. And the plates of the car was in it, too; that was before I hid them under the barn. That's what they call a guilty conscience, he thought.

But you thought you could get away with sticking up old Forsythe's store, didn't you? he thought. You had a bum steer there, brother. Maybe you could of got away with the holdup if you'd done what you thought to do and if you hadn't met this guy Baldwin on the road. Maybe you could of pulled off the holdup and got clean away without hurting nobody, the way you intended, and they never would of caught up to you at all, and the money would of paid off the bills, and everything would of been O.K., and you could of got rid of that car—no, you wouldn't of *had* that car if the holdup had come off—I'm all mixed up, he thought. But it would of been better if you'd never come back after it happened—like you meant to do at first—because then Norah wouldn't of got in so much trouble, and the kid and that guy Hogan. To hell with him, he thought; he's a screwball. But once it happened, you knew you didn't stand the chance of a snowball in hell, so what's the odds? So you come back with the money and paid off all the bills and then what?

Then it was more like it was in the movies than ever. He could see himself again, taking Norah and the kid for rides, starting early every morning and not coming back till after dark and driving slowly up the road from Hortons' place with his eyes peeled to see if there was maybe a prowl car parked in the dooryard. And he was nervous and Norah got mad with him, and a couple of times she said, Ed, I never seen you like this before, what's eating you? and I said, Nothing. But there was plenty eating you. Even if you liked the feeling of taking them for dinner or lunch in roadhouses along the way, getting good dinners with fried chicken and French fries and ice cream for the kid every day and knowing you could almost buy them anything they wanted, for a week, you knew the money you was spending wasn't your money, and it come off a dead man's body and you could see that body with the blood—he stopped thinking of that now, and immediately saw himself after they had come back from one of the trips—to York State or Rhode Island or Massachusetts. He had stopped at a couple of airports to look at the planes and even sent Norah and the kid up in one of them. But always when he came back he went upstairs immediately and switched on the radio while Norah was making dinner and switched it onto the short-wave police calls and listened.

He expected at any moment to hear them saying, Calling all cars in Meadow County, proceed at once to the old Abbott place out of Polk, and pick up Ed Sloan, wanted for murder in Baconsfield County. Tall, dark, heavy-set, last seen with a bullet wound in his left foot and driving a 1940 blue Chrysler sedan with New York plates. But he never heard that. And anyhow, they wouldn't of said that; they used signals, because lots of people listened in to the police calls, and to say that would of been to tip off the guy maybe who did it—Sloan. Why did you switch the plates? they said in court, Wasn't it because you wanted to throw the police off your trail? No, I said, I never thought of that, and it was *true*, but they didn't believe it. I wasn't worried so much about their catching up to me, which I knew they would do anyhow, as because of Norah. If I said my brother in New York loaned me the car, then it would of looked funny to her to see a New York car with plates on it from this State, and that's why I done it. Did it.

So he had lain there listening to the radio, and sure enough, they come to the house before the radio said anything at all. Only five days it took them. They were smart that way; they knew how to do it. But you left the trail wide open, he thought. It was easy to follow you. You give your right name wherever you went, and why not? That's my name, I said, he ast my name and that's my name. I ain't no gunman, he thought, that goes under another name. I never meant to hurt nobody. But it's too late to think about that now, because now they made up their minds and you're going to burn for this. He remembered his stepfather saying, They oughtta kill the brat instead a sending him to the county jail, and old Mr. Forsythe saying, I'm gonna send him down to the county jail, it will be a better home than he had before, and that's the way it started. Maybe it would of been better if there'd been a jury, he thought. Maybe on the jury they would of put a few stiffs like me, that know a thing or two. Like the colored fellow in the bull pen and the other guy in the crap game; or just some working stiffs that would know what it was about, maybe.

You never was a *real* working stiff, he thought, like the others. You always been separate from them. You ever done any real hard manual labor? the judge said, and I said, Sure, and that was true. Where? he says, and I said, I worked in the coal mines down in Kentucky, and in the pen you do plenty of hard work in the jute mill or working on the roads or making little ones outta big ones. That's real hard work. But that ain't what he meant; he meant working hard a long time at a time, like the other working guys that go to work and eat their lunch out of a pail and come home all knocked out with only enough gumption left to maybe read a newspaper and then fall in bed like a log with their mouth open and snore until the whistle blows and it's time to get up and go to work again. I never held no real job long enough at a time to be called a real working man that way. I always had a rolling stone in my pocket; I was never satisfied to stay no place long at a time. But what chance did you have, he thought, to stay any one place at a time? In and out. In at fourteen and out at eighteen; in at twenty and out at twenty-three; in at twenty-six and out at twenty-nine; in at thirty and out at thirty-two and in at thirty-four and never out again, 'bo, never out again.

He opened his eyes and looked up at the ceiling of the cell, which was made of the same latticework bars that formed the three sides. I seen *it* lots of times in the movies, and I heard tell about *it* lots of times in the can, working in the jute mill or on the rock pile they tell about *it*, and the grapevine picks up lots of news that would surprise anybody that don't know how it's done. (In again out again gone again Finnegan.) But those are the kind of guys that would maybe understand, he thought, the working guys.

But they ain't on the juries often, they say, and you didn't *have* no jury—I always plead guilty, he thought, and I never had no lawyer—and what difference can it make now? And he remembered how they talked about *it*; you walked the last mile and there was a little green door, but it really wasn't green, and the chair itself, the hot seat, was maybe painted brown, and they sat you down, but first they shaved the top of your head and they split the pants' leg and they strapped you in, but first there was a preacher walking with you and you talking after him, saying I am the resurrection and the life, he that believes in me, even if he dies yet shall he live or something. And they said it didn't hurt at all, it was like getting conked on the head with a sledge hammer, and you went out like a light so fast you never knew what hit you, and they give you a chance— the guy who was a trusty at Deerfield told me that, he seen it, he was in the room—they give you a chance to talk first, but sometimes they cut you off right in the middle of it, so you don't know when they're gonna throw the switch, and this guy said the stiff jumps right against the straps, it would jump right outta the chair he said, if there wasn't the straps to hold it in, and a little steam comes up outta the seat of the chair where the guy pisses when the first shock hits him, but he never feels it, he said, he never feels it *at* all; but to prove he ain't dead yet, the next shock does the same thing and the stiff jumps against the straps, and the preacher is mumbling and praying all the time like the Reverend Proctor did with me that time at Deerfield

—— 273 ——

Y.M.C.A. when I visited with him, and he says, Ed, I'm reading the Scriptures now and I'd like for you to read with me, repeat after me, he says, and I remember what he was reading, because he made me repeat it after him. He says, This is the most beautiful part of the Holy Scriptures, he said, where Our Lord walks up on the mountain and talks to the people, the carpenters and the fishermen and all, the poor people that followed Him and believed on Him, because the rich didn't, and He says to them, what did he say? Repeat after me, Ed, the Reverend Proctor said. So I did, and he said, Give not what is holy to the dogs, or cast pearls before swine, I forget it, Sloan thought. No, then he says, Ask and they will give it to you and look and you will find it and knock and they will open the door. *That's* the way it went. And, oh, yes, for everybody that asks gets it and him that looks for it will find it and if you knock the door will be opened. And, oh, yes. Or what man is there, he says, that if his son asks for bread, he will give him a stone, or if he asks for a fish, will he give him a serpent?

All the time the preacher is praying and the people in the room, the guy says, they never look at it, the warden or the preacher or even the newspaper reporters, only I looked, the guy says, I seen it all. And then the doctor comes up—the damned thing takes so much juice that when they throw the switch all the lights all over the pen go dim, so the other guys in the cells, they know what's happening, and you'd be surprised, the guy says, how many of them get down on their knees and pray when it's going on, because they're lots of them good guys, and they're thinking when the lights go down, There I go, that's me frying in the hot seat, it might just as well be me, even if they're not all in for murder.

But then the lights go down all over the pen and the lights go up again and the doctor comes up and puts his thing against the man's chest and he looks up, and he says to the people sitting there, the warden and the newspaper reporters and the minister and the screws, he looks up and he says, "This man is dead."

. . . Norah went directly from the bus stop to the Bacons-field County jail. She found Mrs. Fisher, the sheriff's wife, in a surly mood.

"Don't know why you come here any more," the woman said. "There ain't nothing you can do for him. He never was no good."

Norah looked at her with astonishment but asked whether she could see Ed, and the woman said, "Come along." She sat on a stool down the corridor, where she could keep an eye on Norah and hear the conversation without too much difficulty.

Ed looked bad; he was thin and pale, and the old clothes she had managed to send him a week or so before hung on his body as though they had been draped.

"You look fine," she said.

"I'm O.K." He grinned and glanced over his head at the bars that formed the roof of the cell. He jumped up and caught the bars and chinned himself as far as he could without bumping his head.

"I do this couple times a day," he said, "an' bendin' exercises, like you said. It keeps me feelin' pretty fit."

Then he sat down on the chair he had inside the cell, and Norah sat on hers, and they looked at one another. She could see that he had made an attempt to decorate the cell; he had torn some airplane pictures out of aviation magazines and rotogravure sections, and he had a snapshot she had sent him of Katey and herself, stuck to the wall with some chewing gum. She put her left hand through the bars, and he held it in both of his. If only they would let me in the cell with him, she thought; if only I could put my arms around him; it might give him a little strength; he must ache for someone to put her arms around him. She looked at him; he was holding her hand and fingering the wedding ring.

He looked up at her. "Reckon you put this on jus' t' come up here," he said bitterly.

"I've never had it off since you put it on my finger on the first of last March," she said. "Even to wash my hands."

"No crap?" he said, smiling.

"No crap," she said, and he laughed.

"How's Katey?"

"She's fine, just fine. I entered her in school; it's a terribly big school, hundreds of children, and it frightened her at first, but she's getting used to it."

"Mebbe you should be teachin' the scholars, Mom," he said.

"No," she said, "that's out of the question. But I'm on the track of a job."

"What doin'?"

"In a department store," she said. "Selling dishes."

"That ain' no job f'r a educated woman like you."

"It's the only one I've been able to find," she said.

"Did you read Katey the letter I writ?" he said and watched her face. He saw immediately that she was embarrassed and knew that she had not read the letter and changed the subject.

"I got a letter my own self," he said. "Want t' see it?"

"Who's it from?"

"I tol' you about the Rev'rend Proctor, he's at the Deerfield Y.M.C.A. Time was I used t' live there, when I was broke an' outta work an' on relief, an' because he knew I used t' go t' Sunday school when I was a kid, he sorta took an interest in me."

"I'd like to see it," she said, thinking, It's good he has an outside interest like that.

He sighed. "This here letter," he said. "It let me down." He bent under the bed and brought out a cardboard box, in which there was a pile of old detective and aviation magazines and all the letters she had written to him. He brought out a letter and handed it to her through the bars.

Dear Edwin (the letter read)

I am in receipt of your letter, and it moved me exceedingly. Of course, you must know that I was aware of this thing, and it is true what the police told you; that I was, in a sense, instrumental in helping them apprehend you. I had read of the crime in the Deerfield papers. But I have searched my conscience, and I can find nothing with which to reproach myself, and I think that if you were now to do the same, you would agree with me that I could have done no other thing than what I did.

Many times in past years you have come to me for advice, and I have tried to give it. I have assured you that God loved you, and surely you must know that He has never failed you when you needed help. In my humble way, I have tried to help you, and it seems to me that with the knowledge of these facts, you should have placed your faith more in God than you have. Therefore I am at a loss to understand how you could have done this terrible thing.

I do not wish to preach to you, for I am certain that God himself has been speaking to you since your arrest, and I trust that by now you have found with Him the peace that you require.

You are a confessed murderer, and you must know that your crime is considered by men to be one of the most heinous and unforgivable of all crimes. And therefore it seems to me—in view of the circumstances —that man is not likely to be merciful enough to do more than condemn you to the extreme penalty. You must expect this.

But if you will take your Bible in hand and read the Ten Commandments again (Deuteronomy V, 16-21), you will notice that the phrase "Thou shalt not kill" is not emphasized any more than the other crimes against God's law therein set down. God does not consider your crime as being any more heinous or severe than the other crimes he expressly forbids, such as adultery, theft, covetousness, bearing false witness and the like.

Try to keep this significant fact in mind, and remember that Jesus has said He had not been sent into the world to condemn the world, but that the world through Him might have everlasting life. Herein, Edwin, lies your great hope of salvation, and I want you to contemplate the significance of this great message. For the Father who is in Heaven is even more conscious of your failures and your sins than the most merciful of men could be, and since He is not a God of Vengeance, but a God of Mercy and Righteousness, He will take your failures and your sins into account in passing His judgment upon you.

But it is also true—

Norah looked up at Ed and saw that he was watching her face, watching it intently to read in it what she might be feeling, so she was careful to show nothing in her face. She smiled at him and continued to read—

—that God will not forgive you just because you might be afraid for what you have done, just because you are afraid of suffering the penalty for your sins. Before you contemplated this horrible crime against Him and against man, you should have thought of this. For I distinctly remember telling you that, in respect of death and the life after death, sinful man could offer only one plea for mercy—and that is the plea that Jesus Christ has paid the penalty for his sins upon the Cross. Don't you remember that I told you this? How could you ever have forgotten it? Do you remember my reading to you the words of the Christ, where He says, "I am the resurrection, and the life: he that believeth in me, though he were dead, yet shall he live"? This is the great truth on which you must fix your mind.

For if you are condemned to death, the only peace and comfort you will find will be for your remaining days to strive to find the Christ. To understand that He willingly laid down His life under a far more barbarous means of execution than will be used in taking yours. He did this willingly because He loved you, and so great was His heart that He knew, when He was dying upon Golgotha, that He was expiating all the sins of man to come—even the great sin which you, Edwin Sloan, were to commit so many scores of years later.

For, as I have told you many times, there can be no

salvation for any man who cannot see in Christ that He is both the Son of God and man's only comfort and salvation. You did not recall this, Edwin; you did not try to guide your life by this great precept. Now, before it is too late, you must cast aside all cares for this world and strive by might and main to find Christ —you must find Him and know Him, and be assured that when you do God will forgive your great sins if you make Him an honest confession, for His Son has promised us that whosoever confesses Him before men, He will confess before His Father.

I am afraid that my heavy responsibilities here may prevent me from coming to see you, but rest assured that there will be fervent supplications for your soul.

Sincerely yours,

Elwood Proctor, D.D.

"You see what I mean, it let me down?" Ed said.

"I see."

"That's all a load o' crap," he said. "I don' believe no part of it."

"If you could believe it, Ed," she said, "it would bring you a lot of comfort."

"D' you?"

"In a different way, perhaps, yes," she said. "I'll read the Bible for you when I get home. I'll send you some passages I think might mean more to you than what the Reverend Proctor said."

She looked up at him and he said, "You're worried, Mom."

"Are you, Ed?"

"No," he said, "I ain'—excuse me, not."

"I'm glad you're not," she said. "I think you've done marvelous things with yourself since you've been here. I was afraid for you. I don't know how I could take it myself, being shut up like this."

"It ain' bad here," he said. "There're some good guys in here now, a colored feller, another guy. They know the score. They know what it's all about, like lots of preachers don'."

"What do you mean?" she said.

"I mean, I met lots o' folks in my time. Most of 'em were good folks; they wouldn' harm a fly. I allus liked folks, but it was hard f'r me t' get next to 'em an' it was hard f'r them t' get next t' me. Somehow I was allus feelin' diff'rent from 'em, mebbe because they had a home an' I didn'—I was allus a friend o' the fam'ly, or a boarder or a hired man. Diff'rent because they had somethin' an' I didn'."

"That keeps people apart a lot," she said.

"It kept me away from 'em, an' they must o' thought I was a queer lot," he said. "I was allus on the go; I was never stayin' nowhere. I don' know why, but mebbe because I never had no reason t' stay nowhere—till I met you," he said.

She bowed her head so he couldn't see the tears that were forming in her eyes. She nodded for him to continue.

"When I met you, I knew I'd come home," he said. "There was that about you, somethin' homey-like, mebbe. I dunno. But you made me feel like I was somebody, an' I never felt like that before."

His lined face screwed up, the lines deepened and he said, "But don' you worry none. Even if they say thumbs down, that ain' the end."

"You mustn't kid yourself, Ed," she said soberly.

"I tol' you I might have somethin' t' say," he said, "but I ain' said it yet."

"What do you mean?"

"You gotta swear t' me you won' tell nobody," he said excitedly.

"I won't."

"You gotta swear it."

"I swear it."

"The story I tol' on the stand ain' exactly all the truth," he said.

"It's not!" she said, lifting her brows.

"No. What I did, I didn' do it the way I said. I did it all right, I ain' denyin' that; but it didn' happen the way I said it happened, an' it didn' happen inna same place I said."

"Where did it happen? How?"

"I can' tell that," he said. "Not yet I can'."

"Ed," she said, "do you realize what you're saying? Are you telling me the truth?"

"Yeh."

"Why didn't you say this before?"

"The time wasn' ripe, I reckon."

"Have you told Farmer?"

"No, I ain'. Christ knows I wanted to, but I couldn'—you mustn' tell him neither."

"Why?" she said. "I don't understand! If it puts a different light on the crime—it means the difference between life—"

"No," he said. "You swore you wouldn' tell. I got people workin' on the outside," he said earnestly. "I'm waitin'. Even if they give me the chair, that ain' the end. I'll wait.

I'll wait till it's almos' time, mebbe, an' then 'f nothin' happens, I'll talk, but not b'fore."

Has the man's mind gone? she wondered. Has he lost his mind, or is he lying? He saw what she was thinking and gripped her hand.

"You promised," he said.

"I'll keep my promise," she said. "But can't you even trust me, Ed? I could understand if you didn't trust Farmer, after your experience with the law, but you must know how deeply you've hurt me by not trusting me."

"I trus' you, Mom," he said. "Now you trus' me. I c'n on'y say, there's folks on the outside knows the score. They're workin'. There's a guy they're tryin' t' find."

"A witness?" She saw that his face was pink, suffused with blood.

"Yeh."

"A man who saw it happen?"

His eyes gleamed. "Yeh."

"You mean Goreski!"

"I can' say," he said, "you mustn' ask me."

"Whom are you protecting, Ed?" she said. "Are you protecting anybody?"

He shook his head, and she couldn't tell whether he meant he was not protecting someone or that he wasn't going to say. She looked at his gray eyes, and he smiled at her.

"Trus' me," he said. "I don' wanna die no more'n you want me to. If I did—" he gestured at the sheet on the bed. "I'm not whacky," he said. "I know what I'm doin'."

"All right," she said. An idea had struck her. "Did it happen in self-defense?"

She thought of the bullet wound in his foot; it had

—— 283 ——

always struck her as strange that he could have been wounded in the foot if, as it seemed, he had had the initiative from the beginning.

"That's right," he said nervously.

"Ed!" she said. "Do you realize this makes the difference between first-degree murder and manslaughter!"

"I sure do," he said. "But you're not gonna say nothin', are you? You swore." His voice was urgent; it almost cracked.

"I swore," she said with a sigh, and turning her head she noticed that Mrs. Fisher was watching her. . . .

. . . She sat for an hour in the little Coffee Pot and thought about it before she went to Farmer's office. She had the uneasy feeling that the man who ran the Coffee Pot recognized her and was watching her, but she put it out of mind. On the face of it, the story was fantastic—but then there had been so many discrepancies in the evidence adduced at the trial. Well, somebody might be lying, or somebody might be wrong, and probably neither fact was important.

But why hadn't he told all this to Farmer? If he *had* shot in self-defense you'd think this would have been the first story he'd have told. Self-defense is something else again from murder. If he hadn't told Farmer, why hadn't he told her? Who in the world could a man be protecting at the expense of his own life? Only someone very close to him. Who was close to him? Certainly not Goreski, whom he had not seen in years—or *was* it Goreski, and *was* he close to him, and *had* he seen him? She recalled the image of the iceberg—the bulk of it lying below water. There's so much I don't know about this man, she thought; and he's told so many lies, so many lies. Or were they lies?

It suddenly occurred to her, with a pounding heart, that perhaps *she* was the one—she and Katey were the people he might be protecting. How? Suppose he had been involved with a gang? Suppose he *had* shot in self-defense, or maybe not even shot at all, but whatever—and suppose the gang had said to him, You'll take this rap or we'll get after your wife and kid? This could be a long-term threat, even if he went to his death and the story only came out afterward. That might be possible, she thought, but it's too much like a moving picture.

And I don't believe it, she thought; it doesn't make any sense. There was no evidence, not a bit of it, that anyone else might have been implicated in the actual crime. If there had been, wouldn't the police have brought them in? If Goreski had been involved—and he an ex-convict who had even been so stupid as to try to buy a revolver— wouldn't he have been arrested, if only on suspicion of complicity? The police are thorough, she thought, oh, how thorough! They had trapped him in a week, although there had not been a single witness. Or perhaps there *had* been a witness and the police were protecting him in exchange for information. Goreski? But didn't Ed say at first that another man had done the shooting, and he had tried to stop the man?

That was the first story he told them, and perhaps when they had beaten him—if they did, because they didn't believe the story—he decided to conceal part of the truth. Wouldn't a man of his experience of the law almost automatically conceal the truth, or tell as little of it as was necessary? But this means his *life!* she thought, if his story's true.

I have to know, she thought; I *have* to know. What makes you think it's not the truth, she thought—because you already *feel* it's not the truth? It's pretty feeble; no details are mentioned. Why? Because there are none? If it's not the truth why did he say it? You say, you think of how he lied, and you instinctively use the word *lie*. Has he ever lied, really *lied?* The stories he told you—the Army Air Corps and the crash, the dead observer, the trips to Europe and Alaska, Hitler, Mussolini, the multiplicity of well-paid jobs he said he'd held, the filling station and the auto agency, the brother in New York, the racing cars, the oil wells, the home he owned, the trade he was about to make, the mortgage he was going to place, the place he actually showed you—the other one he showed Bill Hogan, too—the circus he had worked in as a clown, were these deliberate lies, told to deceive you? For what purpose?

On the face of them, she thought, they were lies. They deceived me. But did he *tell* them to deceive me, or did he tell them to make himself more attractive in my eyes, or—what I know in my heart is true—did he tell them to deceive *himself?* To make himself more important in his own eyes; to make himself believe what was not true; to *create* himself?

That's it, she thought. I've even done it myself. Everyone has done it. Everyone does it daily, from the small child, like Katey, who comes home from school with the most outlandish stories of seeing a dragon on the way, a real dragon breathing smoke and flame, and tells the story with such realistic histrionic talent as to completely deceive herself for the moment. From the child to the adult—the man in Gorky's diary of his college days, remember him? The man who took off his shoes every night and set them on the floor and said to them, "Now walk!" And when the shoes didn't walk, he said, "You see, you can't do a thing without me!" What *is* this? she thought. The child relieves his fairy-tales; he *lives* them; his toy soldiers are armies that fight and bleed and die.

But is Ed a child? No, she thought; he has the total emotional equipment of a man. Is he a liar? A psychopath? The idea struck her with repulsion. Does he know that the stories he has told aren't true? Of course he does. Why does he tell them? Better still, why does he *have* to tell them?

This man, she thought. At no point in his life has he been allowed to express himself—the natural, simple efflorescence of his imagination; of the imagination every single one of us possesses at his birth. He could have become many things, many men. He has a gift for handicraft but has used it for the first time in his life in prison. He could have been a pilot, a father of children, a mechanic, a carpenter, a farmer who tills the soil and watches his creative mind, his love, blossom in the form of blooming crops. Look around, she thought—the people everywhere are fighting for their very lives.

The war that destroyed my first husband, that destroyed his friend, was fought for nothing. The wars in Spain, in China, were something else; wars of the *people* for their freedom, the freedom our own people have always believed in. I supported them, she thought; I gave money that I could not afford, to help the people fight; I'll do it again. But when will they put an end to it?

What has this to do with Ed? I *love* that guy, she thought, and she could see his face again; the lined face and the deep gray eyes, the large muscular hands grasping the bars as he had said, "You gotta swear it," and she had said, "I swear." Swear what? she thought; only to understand him; that's what he meant, although he didn't say it. To understand him and to make the link; he's fighting for his life; they're fighting for their lives. His life is their life, and theirs is his. They're being destroyed and they continue to fight, and he was destroyed long since, but he's still fighting. The fabric of imagination he had constructed for so long—because he had nothing and wanted something—had been destroyed by the cold facts of his arrest and his confession to the crime. The structure he had erected, by which he bolstered his self-esteem, had collapsed around him; and the reason you believed, for a moment in the jail, that there might be some validity to the new story, was because you *wanted* to believe it, because you're his wife and you love him and you want to save his life. It was tragic that that story had—she felt—no actual basis; for it might have saved his life. But it was still more tragic that a man, *any* man, had had to create himself so desperately because his life had left him so long uncreated. And what he was doing now, instinctively, was to re-create himself in a *new* pattern; he was doing it, she knew, not only to leave in her mind—in case the story never should come out (and she was certain that it never would)—the impression that he might be dying for a better reason than that he had killed a man; he was doing it in order to *live* until he died.

She walked to Farmer's office, thinking, But I have to know, I *have* to know. It was a refrain in her mind all the way to the little frame building, and it persisted on the stairs, I *have* to *know*. Farmer smiled when she entered and rose from his chair. He had a long typescript on legal foolscap in one hand and a pencil in the other, and he had to put the pencil down to shake her hand. He saw that her face was serious and he waited for her to open the conversation.

"I'm not at all certain," she said, "that we know everything there is to know. I'm not certain the entire truth has come out yet."

"What do you mean?"

"There're so many discrepancies in the evidence," she said. "You'll remember." She cited the discrepancies and saw that he nodded his head, whether in agreement or just to encourage her, she couldn't tell. She had changed her mind again, however; she had decided not, for the moment, to tell him what Ed had told her in the jail but merely to hint at it. He indicated that he understood what she was driving at, but both of them avoided any statement that could have been considered explicit. Both of them skirted the issue; Norah, because she had made up her mind to wait a little longer; Farmer, because (she felt) he was, in a sense, afraid of uncovering more than he already knew.

He was a good guy, she decided. He was a liberal lawyer; the same sort of lawyer that Clarence Darrow might have been, but probably of lesser caliber. He's still young in many ways, she decided; his development is still ahead of him. Yet Darrow himself, who had consistently defended the underdog, had defended him not out of any radical desire to change the world, but out of an emotional understanding of people who had never had a chance. This, she could not help feeling, was the wrong approach. Today the honest human being *had* to be a radical. You cannot say, Have mercy! You *must* say, Let there be justice! and anything that obstructed or subverted justice, *anything*—whether it were laziness, misunderstanding, ignorance or prejudice, or pure malevolence and greed—would have to be outlawed. There's a wall here, she remembered thinking, a wall through which we'll have to break.

"I want to know where we stand," she said. "You needn't spare my feelings."

Farmer had been watching her; she's grasping at straws, he felt; she must not do that.

"Well, Mrs. Sloan," he said. "To tell the truth, I don't think we'll get a favorable decision. That's why I'm preparing an appeal."

He lifted the long sheets of legal cap that lay on his desk. "I'm preparing an appeal because I feel the decision's going to go against us. I'm basing it on the presumption of a reasonable doubt. And I'm basing it on the evironmental factor. I don't think there was a person in court that day who wasn't moved by his testimony, including at least two of the judges, Horan and Washburn. I know Washburn; he's acute; I know he would incline to leniency; the other one I'm not at all sure about. He's a hard-boiled businessman."

He handed her the brief he had outlined, and she glanced over it. It was, he explained to her, naturally subject to considerable revision, but he felt he could almost predict the basis for the Court's decision. The appeal opened with a statement of questions involved:

1—*Was the learned Court below justified in finding the defendant guilty of first-degree murder when the uncontradicted testimony of the defendant showed:*

a—That he had abandoned his attempt to rob the deceased and was attempting to flee when the fatal shots were fired?

b—That after abandoning his attempt to rob the deceased, the defendant fired the fatal shots without malice aforethought, but rather as a spasmodic muscular reflex of pain and terror caused by the physical violence inflicted upon the defendant by the deceased in an attempt to secure possession of defendant's pistol?

2—Was the learned Court below justified in sentencing the defendant to death rather than life imprisonment because it believed that the murder was committed in the attempt to perpetrate robbery, even though there is evidence to show as mitigating circumstances:

a—That the defendant had abandoned his attempt to rob the deceased and was trying to escape when the shots were fired?

b—That the shots were fired without willful, deliberate premeditated intention to kill, but in the struggle for possession of the pistol?

Norah glanced through the pages, noting a phrase here and a phrase there; for some reason she did not feel like reading it all consecutively, but she did notice that the argument was based on what she felt were purely legal technicalities—the business of a reasonable doubt; the justification of the death sentence when there was precedent for life imprisonment; the testimony of Dr. Pincus that Ed was "the product of an abject home environment"— upon this, apparently, rested less weight in the final determination, than upon whether there was a precedent for commutation of the sentence to life imprisonment. It was a plea for clemency, and she supposed that it could be no other under the circumstances.

Life imprisonment! she thought. Would any person pre-fer life imprisonment to a swift and painless death? Would *you?* she thought. I have no way of knowing. Now, today, I would say yes—but I am I. Another person might readily say no, and for as valid reasons. It depends on who is im-prisoned and what reasons he has for wanting to live. Political prisoners, it seemed, preserved their integrity, their sanity, their determination to live out their lives longer than the "common" criminal. And she recalled reading of a political prisoner in Poland, an antifascist poet, who had been released from prison after eight years and who, six months later, published an epic poem he had composed and memorized in prison, where he had had no access to paper or a pencil! That man, she thought, had a reason to live. Would such a man as Ed? Not until he was able to face himself; to know himself; to finally create himself correctly.

She reread one passage that seemed to be the crux of Farmer's appeal for clemency:

Certainly if clemency is ever to be extended in any case involving robbery, the case at bar presents a most appropriate instance for its exercise. We have here a man who, according to the evidence of both the prosecution and the defense, was impelled to commit the proposed robbery, not from the depraved motives of an antisocial disposition, nor from the sordid im-pulse of personal greed or desire, but purely from his natural desire to provide for and protect his loved ones. The fact that through lack of judgment, or inability to reason along the lines of an average person, he acted upon a mistaken impulse, and employed a method wholly wrong in the eyes of the law, does not deprive his generous impulse of its full appeal to human sympathy. None but the most heartless person could say he was wrong in his impulse to protect his wife from what he believed to be the shame and disgrace of a possible jail sentence, and the child whom he loved as his own, from hunger and want. He was unquestionably acting under the impulsion of the most compelling necessity when he determined to rob the only friend he could remember from his miserable boyhood days. Like Robin Hood, the hero of childish imagination, who utilized the principle of self-help to overcome injustice and oppression, he found justification in taking from those who had plenty, to assist those who were destitute. . . .

Could anyone with such a background as the defendant has so candidly revealed under both direct and cross-examination be expected to react normally when faced with a situation surcharged with such strong emotional impulses, feelings plumbing the very depths of a soul which had just found, and fought to preserve the first real love for which it had been starved so long? The pattern of his later years, cross-barred as it was by one prison term after another, none of which were for crimes that denote depravity of heart, or confirmed wickedness of mind, is not one to stimulate normal mental and intellectual development. Taken together, they give ample reason for the psychology of concealment, the fear of society that caused an active imagination to build a protective shell around a sensitive mind. The lack of education and of normal outlets for emotion and imagination would result naturally in mental instability, wish fulfillment, and flights of fancy inconceivable to a person of normal experience. Weighing

*right and wrong as he knew them with his smaller
than average range of selectivity, it is not surprising
that he felt that he must do the thing that involved
some abstract wrong to society in order to save those
he loved best from great hardship and suffering that
was close and personal to him. There is not in any of
the testimony, even a suggestion that he wanted the
money for himself alone. . . .*

She looked up at Farmer, who was sitting with his hands
folded in his familiar way, watching her, and she smiled.

"I'll cross this bridge when we come to it," she said.

"That's right."

"What happens now?"

"We make our final argument, and Cobb will make his.
The Court will then impose its sentence."

"And if it goes the wrong way?"

Farmer indicated the appeal, which was still in Norah's
hands. "It goes to the Supreme Court of the State."

"What're they likely to do?"

"That's hard to say," he said. "They seldom reverse the
trial courts in cases such as this, but they may."

"If they don't? I take it you don't think they will?"

"We can go to the Governor, no higher."

She realized that she was grasping at straws when she
said, "Would there be any point in a psychiatric examination—even if it cost a lot of money, I could find some way
to raise it. I'd *have* to."

Farmer shook his head. "There can't be any doubt of
the man's sanity," he said. "He's as sane as you or I."

She wondered whether she should bring out the story Ed
had told her, and she determined to remain silent for the
time being. You're getting hysterical, she thought. The

appeal will automatically stay execution of the sentence. I'll wait; I'll find out; I have to know.

"We want you to stay with us tonight and tomorrow, Mrs. Sloan," Farmer said. "My wife's anxious to have you with us, and you'll be able to see Ed again tomorrow."

"Thanks," she said.

"My dear," he said. "I say I don't expect too much, and that's true. But neither of us should prejudge the case. I've learned a great deal since I undertook Ed's defense; things I never knew before. I know this—that if I were the judge in place of Horan, and with what I've learned and heard in court, I'd recommend leniency."

"Thanks for the kind words," she said. . . .

. . . The day was unseasonably hot for so early in April, and the small courtroom was jammed to the doors long before Ed was brought in. She was sitting at the counsel table when he came in with the sheriff, and she heard the crowd murmur and stir. He seemed composed; his hair was neatly combed, his face shaved. He wore a clean white shirt without a tie under the familiar white pullover sweater. He smiled and took his seat by her side.

They sat holding each other by the hand, and he said, "How you feel, Mom?"

"All right," she said.

"I feel fine," he said and squeezed her hand. "Slept good."

Now is the time, she thought. Yesterday, when she had visited him twice, neither of them had mentioned the "new" story; it was as though they had arrived by common consent at an agreement not to mention it until the time was right. But she knew she couldn't wait any longer, and she turned to him and took both his hands.

—— 295 ——

"Ed," she said, "I'm going to ask you a question, and you're going to tell me the truth."

"Sure, Mom," he said.

She caught her breath but controlled her nervousness. So much depended on his answer, and she wasn't at all sure that this was the time to ask the question. He had had only a day to think over what he had told her the day before yesterday, and it might be best to wait a little while. But she decided to take that risk.

"The story you told me Thursday, the day I came up—"

"Yeh," he said.

"—that was a story, Ed; it wasn't the truth, was it? It was a story you were making up. You were whistling in the dark. Look at me, pal," she said, and he lifted his head. She saw him swallow.

"I—," he said and paused.

"Don't be afraid, Ed," she said. "Don't be afraid of *anything*."

"It ain' the truth," he said. "I made it up. I—"

"You needn't tell me, darling," she said. She bit her lip. "Don't say any more. But I want you to know I'm prouder of you for saying that than I've ever been before, and I've been pretty proud of you, brother, pretty proud."

She felt his body tremble and looked up. The three judges had entered the courtroom, and the crowd stood. They took their seats, and Norah scanned their faces, the stolid face of the businessman, the old but kindly face of Horan, the judge, Washburn, who held his head inclined slightly to the side. Their faces revealed nothing to her. Then Cobb, the District Attorney, rose and began his summation. He put on the show Farmer had warned her to expect. He pointed at Sloan and shouted at the top of his lungs. He said that this was the most brutal crime that could ever have taken place in Baconsfield County. He spoke of the noble character of the deceased, of his grieving relatives and employees and friends, of his innocence of any wrongdoing, of his kindliness in picking up a shabby hitch hiker on the roads, of his cold-blooded murder. He referred to Ed constantly as "this hulking brute," "this confirmed criminal," "this sinister highwayman." He pled with the Court for a death sentence; he lowered his voice and whispered, then broadened it, spreading his arms, appealing, threatening, exhorting. His face dripped with perspiration, and he mopped it continuously. It was a performance, and Norah glanced at Farmer and caught a smile upon his face.

Cobb spoke for forty minutes, then took his seat. Farmer spoke as long, reading from notes in a quiet, yet insistent voice. Where Cobb was emotional, he was logical; where Cobb was oratorical, he maintained his dignity and composure. He reviewed most of the material with which Norah was already familiar from reading the drafted brief of his appeal; he quoted Ed, he quoted Norah, the police; he cited precedent for leniency in similar cases; he hammered on the question of reasonable doubt, and he extracted from Ed's personal history the more poignant episodes that might be felt to carry weight with the judge and his two lay assistants, incline them to clemency. When he had finished there was a recess till after lunch.

"You mean the Court will render its decision *now?*" Norah said with astonishment.

"Yes," said Farmer.

"But that means it had *arrived* at a decision before either you or Cobb presented your arguments."

"Yes."

"Then why the arguments?" she said.

He didn't answer.

When they were all seated again, she saw Horan look directly at her over his glasses. She knew what this meant, and her heart sank. He began to read from his opinion. He defined murder of the first and second degrees and stated their respective penalties.

"A large number of witnesses were heard on the part of the State," he said, "principally verifying the written, signed statement of defendant. The defendant, his wife, and Dr. Pincus were called by the defense."

He abstracted the principal facts as set forth in the statement Ed had signed and followed the course of the proceedings through his arrest and the appointment of Burton Farmer to defend him. Then he indicated the line of reasoning on which he had decided.

"After hearing defendant," he said, glancing over his glasses at Ed, "we could not question his soundness of mind and we are morally certain that he has complete knowledge of right and wrong. Although the degree of murder is fixed by the above Act of Assembly, it is our province to determine the degree, and we find defendant guilty of murder in the first degree."

He paused and looked up; there was a murmur in the courtroom, and Ed gripped her hand. She looked at him; he was smiling grimly.

Horan took a drink of water and continued.

"We have now a most solemn duty, to determine the penalty to be suffered by defendant. The act above quoted makes it discretionary with the Court, under these circumstances, to fix the penalty at death or imprisonment for life."

He quoted the testimony of Dr. Pincus relative to Ed's home environment and the factors that had shaped his early years. He went into this environment in considerable detail and related Ed's criminal record.

"It is contended by the defense counsel," he said, "that his history, his appearance, and testimony, with that of Dr. Pincus, show sufficient matters of mitigation to justify the sentence of life imprisonment rather than that of death."

Norah bowed her head; get it over with, she thought, get it over with.

"The Act of January 3, 1924, P.L. 821, as re-enacted by the Criminal Code of 1938 above quoted, wherein the court is given discretion to fix the penalty at life imprisonment or death, means that a sound discretion must be applied to the acts and circumstances of each case, although there are no fixed or arbitrary standards provided by law regulating the exercise of that discretion, State vs. Maybee, 211, page 96; State vs. Pindell, 218, page 126. In the case of the State vs. Inkster, 225, page 311, it was said, 'Murder of the first degree should not always be punished by death; when sufficient mitigating circumstances are present, the punishment should not exceed life imprisonment.' In State vs. Webb, page 11, the Court said, 'To determine whether the appropriate penalty was imposed, we must consider the history of the past life of the defendant, as well as the facts of the crime.' And again it said, 'He deliberately committed murder with the intent to perpetrate a robbery. It was not an abuse of discretion to impose the death penalty. It was the uniform penalty imposed by the law itself in all first-degree murder cases prior to the Act of January 3, 1924, P.L. 821, which vested in the court, when sufficient mitigating circumstances are present, the power to impose a sentence of imprisonment for life.'"

Norah looked at Ed; his face was hard and determined;

the lines were more prominent; the lips were set. Farmer was looking at his hands, folded on the edge of the counsel table. Horan was speaking, quoting the opinion of a previous justice to the effect that the extreme penalty works a "deterrent effect, and therefore should be aimed against cases where a murder is committed from what might be called mental, rather than emotional, impulse . . ." He then indicated that his authority felt this was the case in such crimes as highway robbery, burglaries, and robberies committed by raids on banks, stores, and the like.

Judge Horan referred again to Dr. Pincus' opinion that Ed's range of selectivity in making choices had been narrowed by the circumstances of his life and said, "There is no lack of mental capacity evident, but there is evident a lack of shrewdness of plan and getaway. For instance, he registered his own name in the community where his criminal record was more or less known, and left the hotel without paying his lodging, which would tend to direct attention toward him. He had previously stayed around in the neighborhood of the crime for two days with a former convict; he committed the murder on one of the main highways; he stopped the car upon a bridge along the highway to make inquiry concerning a road; he laid the body out near the highway, where it could be seen, and then threw out posters that were covered with blood, where they could be readily observed. A short distance from the scene of the crime he stopped at a country store and made some small purchases, and then in the very shadow of this courthouse he inquired for a doctor. He told the doctor his correct name and such a false story concerning his residence and accident that it could be readily proved to be false."

Judge Horan cleared his throat. "We cannot conceive

of a person who testified as clearly as did the defendant, not knowing right from wrong. He has no appearance or expression of one we would call dull. To us the doctor's reaction that the defendant was essentially honest and kindly are inconceivable and have little bearing. Would anyone venture to say that society would be safe with defendant still living, considering his criminal history? What safety would there be for his guards, attendants, and fellow prisoners? What definite assurance have we that eventually he would not be turned loose upon society, if we should impose life imprisonment? It is well demonstrated that punishment has no salutary effect on him. It therefore remains for us to protect society and give it a stern, deterring example, that the majesty of the law requires the life of him, who, possessed of the clear knowledge of right and wrong and other qualities here noted, commits highway robbery and in doing so kills his victim."

Judge Horan looked over his spectacles and said, "Edwin Sloan, you may stand."

Norah felt Ed's hand withdrawn from hers, and he stood. She stood beside him. Behind her, the entire audience in the courtroom stood as one. There was a phrase going through her head, *the majesty of the law, the majesty of the law*. She saw, as if for the first time, the large American flag hanging on the wall behind the judges. Horan and his two associate judges stood.

He spoke. "Have you anything to say before sentence is pronounced?"

Ed shook his head and grasped Norah by the hand.

"And now, April 5, 1941, the sentence of the law is that you, Edwin Alberts Sloan, be taken hence by the Sheriff of Baconsfield County, to the jail of that county from whence you came, and from thence in due course of time to the penitentiary in Deerfield County, and that you there suffer death during the week fixed by the Governor of the State in a building erected for the purpose, on land owned by the State, such punishment being inflicted by either the warden, or deputy warden of the Deerfield Penitentiary, or by such person as the warden shall designate, by causing to pass through your body a current of electricity of intensity sufficient to cause death and the application of such current to be continued until you are dead." He paused. "And may God have mercy on your soul."

Norah opened her eyes and looked at her husband. He was standing firmly; there was no expression in his eyes. Just beyond, to his left, she could see old Ed Fisher, the sheriff; there were tears streaming down his face.

. . . . *16*

BURTON FARMER
COUNSELLOR-AT-LAW

Baconsfield, June 16, 1941

Dear Mrs. Sloan:

The delay in writing as I had promised on the telephone the other day was occasioned by the rush of work involved in placing the case before the Governor. This has now been done, and he should render a decision before the date that has been set for execution of the sentence.

I was not surprised by the Supreme Court's decision, although I was slightly surprised by the rapidity with which it was rendered. If they had decided otherwise they would have had to reverse a long line of other cases in which they have consistently held that the robbery element requires the maximum punishment.

The Court's opinion gave no more weight to the environmental factors than had the opinion of the trial court. Nor did they feel that the element of reasonable doubt had been proved beyond cavil. To the contrary, they cited the same grounds for disbelief as did the trial court; namely, that the carefully laid and executed plan and Ed's subsequent behavior negatived the truth of our contention that he had no intention of carrying out the felony.

(For what it might be worth to you, I have spoken to Horan since the case went to the Supreme Court and he indicated to me that he had found it extremely difficult to make up his mind. Washburn, as I had expected, inclined to leniency; the other did not.)

The Governor is the court of last resort. It rests entirely in his hands. No, I do not feel—as I believe you recently wrote me—that it would do any harm if Mr. Hogan were to write the Governor. Anything that anyone can do might help. But I feel that the hope of commutation is so slight as to be negligible, and I know you are prepared for this.

You may rest assured that until the very last, I shall bend every effort toward the best interests of your hus-

band and yourself. Mrs. Farmer asks to be remembered
kindly to you.

Most sincerely yours,

Burton Farmer

Mrs. Norah S. Sloan,
141 West 122nd Street,
New York City

■ ■ ■ ■ *17*

... THAT'S THE BUSINESS,
Sloan thought. They'll sue her and they'll law it and
they'll send her to the pen. He was holding Katey by the
hand, impatient that he had to walk so slowly into town.
Let 'em bring suit, she says. You can't get blood out of a
stone, she says. Maybe so. But you can't refuse to pay them
neither. If you could, who the hell would pay them? So
they got the law on their side, and she can't fool me none
about that neither. These lawyers and the police, I know
about them; I guess I oughtta know. She says they get out
a summons and you go to court, and they law it back and
forth, and they get out a judgment and they can collect it.
And suppose you say, I ain't got no money, so I can't pay
your judgment; what happens then? She lied to me, he

thought. These guys got protection from people that don't pay their bills. Why, they practically own the lawyers and the cops and the courts anyhow. They get a lawyer and they get the cops, and then where are you? You're in the coop.

O.K., he thought, that's where you come in. I have been authorized to start legal action . . . the boss said to tell you folks. . . . Nuts to them, he thought, I'll show them a thing or two. I'll go out and I'll get the money, and to hell with them. And if they won't give me a job and there ain't no jobs, then the next best thing to do is to take it away from somebody that's got it. And who's got it? Well, old man Forsythe has got it; I remember he used to go to the bank every Saturday morning with his money. Today's Thursday. You're crazy, he thought; what you got in mind to do is plumb crazy, and you'll find it out quick enough if you try to pull a stunt like that.

What's the odds? he thought. Is it better to take a chance or to have her in the coop and the kid with its ass sticking out? I know what *that's* like, I been that way all my life. *It's a cinch,* the voice said, and he tried to think of what he would do if he had a wad of dough and somebody stuck a pistol in his ribs. There's no arguing with a rod, he thought. Like the guys in stir used to say, A bullet ain't got no brains, it goes where you shoot it. But you don't even have to shoot it nowheres, he thought. All you got to do is point the gun and they'll reach. And if they don't, then you can start running like hell anyhow. But they'll reach, he thought; I'll show 'em. He could feel the gun in his hand now, the hard feel of it, the strength of it and the deep blue metal gleam. It was heavy in his hand, and he gripped it hard.

"Ouch!" Katey said, "you're hurting my hand," and he

released it. He grinned at her, and she said, "What did you do that for, Ed?" Her face was puckered up.

"I didn' mean t', babe," he said. "I wouldn' hurt you f'r nothin'."

He saw her smile and said, "How'd you like t' have a ice-cream cone? We'll stop at Joe's place an' git us one."

Katey nodded with delight.

He asked Joe for a bus schedule and looked it over. It didn't make any sense to him.

"You figger this out f'r me," he said. "How'd you git t' Peekskill from here?"

Joe puzzled over the bus schedule and said, "You c'n get a bus from Coney in a hour an' a half, change at Glover an' get another one there. The guy in the bus station in Glover will tell you."

That wouldn't leave much time, he thought. You'll have to get a hump on you. From Glover he could get a bus to Lebanon, he knew, and from there it was only seven miles to Morrisford. He started walking rapidly back down the road toward home, with Katey tagging along.

"Hurry up, Kit," he said, "I gotta git back t' the house."

"I can't go so fast," the child said. "I'm eating my ice-cream cone."

He bent and picked her up, and said, "Keep on eatin' it, but don' you get none of it on me, young woman."

He walked as rapidly as he could, carrying the child, thinking, Even if it's crazy you're gonna do it. And even if they pick you up, he thought, Norah and the kid can't be no worse off. Maybe they'll even be better off. It's a cinch, the voice said, stop worrying about it.

Old Forsythe, he thought, you better leave him alone, he'd know your face. That's crap, he thought, it's all of twenty years, and you didn't go in his store last summer.

He must be pretty old, but suppose he does know you and says, Why, Ed Sloan, you little devil you, I ain't seen you in a dog's age? Then you don't have to stick him up; you can just say, I want a pack of Camels, and pay for them and pass the time of day and go some place else. But he won't know you, never fear. You changed a lot in twenty years. But it's a lousy thing to do, he thought; you knew that a long time now.

"Golly," Katey said to Norah, "we walked so slow into Polk and we came back so fast Ed had to carry me." Norah could hear him moving around upstairs, and she came to the foot of the staircase and shouted to him.

"What's up?"

"I'm in a hurry, Mom," he said. "Goin' over Peekskill-way, see 'f I c'n raise some money on that house."

She started up the stairs, saying, "What's the rush?"

"Bus leavin' in a hour," he said, "from Coney."

She came into the room; he was putting on his jacket, and he kept moving around, finding a handkerchief, a cap in the closet, getting into the shabby overcoat Bill Hogan had sent, that was much too small for him. It was so small he had to hold it close around him.

She smiled at the bustle he was in, the small-boy excitement about him. He started out of the room and she said, "Do you really think you can raise some money on a mortgage?"

"Why not?" he said. "I reckon I'll be back with plenty."

"You better had," she said with a smile. "Otherwise I'll divorce you. Haven't you forgotten something?"

"What?"

She went to her bureau and brought out her purse. "What were you going to use for money for the bus?"

"Cripes!" he said, "I plumb forgot."

"Take it easy, pal; you'll live longer."

"Thanks," he said. "I'll give it back t' you with int'rest; be back tomorrow night, mebbe, Saturday night sure."

"Anything else you've forgotten?"

He pushed up his cap, scratched his head. "Don' think so," he said, his face flushed. "I'll be suin' ya." Then he was gone.

I know what she wanted, he thought; she wanted I should kiss her good-by. Couldn't take a chance on that, even if she got hurt feelings now; she'd of felt the gun in my pocket if she put her arms around me.

He caught a ride with the Raleigh man at the crossroads, who took him all the way into Coney and did not mention the bill. There he had to wait another half an hour for the bus, but he bought the ticket as soon as he got there, so he wouldn't change his mind and come back. He had thought of coming back the minute he started from the house. He had looked back at the house and a crazy idea sprang into his head. That's the end of that, he had thought; you'll never see that house again! That was a crazy idea all right. Keep your head, he thought; take it slow and easy and case it good.

He got on the bus when it came, and he had a seat just back of the driver. And immediately the bus got to rolling, he began to think again. What the hell are you doing? he thought. You got any idea at all what you're doing? This is pretty serious business you started out to do. Right now, if there was a bull to pick you up, you'd get a long stretch for toting a gun. You got no right to tote a gun unless you got a license for it. He kept his hand in his pocket on the gun, so the man who was sitting next to him might not bump against it when the bus rocked and feel the hardness of it and look at him.

I'm going to do a stickup, he thought. I never did a stickup in my life before, but I'm going to do it now. He was hungry. There was a dull ache in the pit of his stomach. When he came to think of it, he remembered that he had been more or less hungry all his life. There were times when there was plenty to eat, but there were long times when there just wasn't enough and you went around all the time with a dull ache in your stomach, because when you quit eating you wanted to eat more and there was none.

Think about *that*, his mind told him. Every day we been eating potatoes. Potatoes is good, but they ain't enough of the right kind of thing, not for her, not for the kid, not for you. You could eat a bushel of spuds every day, boiled or mashed or fried or hashbrown with or without gravy, but they ain't enough. You gotta have milk, like the kid, and meat to set your teeth into and greens, plenty of greens. You wouldn't think, with a whole countryside full of greens growing, that it would be so hard for a man that lived on a farm to get enough of them. Unless he had the time to put in a big garden, and to tend it proper, which we didn't. Well, you couldn't get what you needed less'n you had the money. Go to the store and buy some money, Katey said, that was pretty cute. Well, I'm going to the store.

The man next to him was reading a paper, and it was dark now and they had turned the lights on inside the bus. I'd sure like to drive a bus like this some time, he thought. That's my idea of a good steady job. These buses were pretty heavy and the boys that made 'em roll must get plenty for rolling 'em. He decided he would ask the driver what he got, but it might seem a queer thing to say to a guy you never met in your life before; and, besides, it would be a good idea not to call any attention to yourself.

He unconsciously pulled the peak of his cap down further over his face. A gunman, he thought, a highway robber. He smiled at the idea, but then it gave him a good feeling to hold onto the grips of the gun in his pocket, even if it was in the holster. It made him feel strong, like he felt that time with the hoe, working in Hortons' patch, and like the two times he drove the old Dodge over to Polk and Coney, but mostly like the time, so long ago, it seemed, that he had really flown an airplane.

Now that was something, he thought. That there is something for a man to *do*. He could remember it as though it were yesterday. You held the stick, only not so hard as he was holding the grips of the gun in his pocket, lightly, and with the other hand you pushed the throttle forward (that was funny, too, they called the throttle a *gun*), and when it was all the way forward it got to rolling and rolling, faster and faster, and you pushed the stick a little forward, not too much so it wouldn't go over on its nose or the prop hit the ground, but just so the nose come down to the sky line, and you held it there, kicking rudder left and right to keep it straight. Then you eased back a little on the stick, a little and a little more, and then gradually you could feel it coming off, you could *feel* that it wanted to lift, it *wanted* to fly, and sure enough, you could feel the seat under your pants pushing against you and the whole thing come away, and you pushed the stick forward again so as to fly level and pick up more speed over the ground, just over it, and then you pulled it back again and then, *boy*, did it want to climb! It began climbing and climbing and you could look down then, down and around and see the earth falling away, the ground and the trees and the houses getting smaller and smaller like toys, and then you were flying.

There was something in the rolling of the heavy bus that

gave him the feeling he was flying. It was like as if the bus would come off any minute now, and he watched the back of the driver's neck and could see how easy he was in the padded seat, just like the pilot in his plane, ship Bill Hogan said. (That's right, they call them ships.) But you gotta think, he thought; you only got so much time, the bus will get into Lebanon late tonight and then tomorrow will be Friday, and you could do it tomorrow and get back tomorrow night if it all came off all right, so you better figger it that way.

You go into Lebanon and you find a place to flop, because it will be too late then—but all he had was about fifty cents and that wasn't enough—anyhow, in the morning, you get a hitch to Morrisford, or maybe it would be a good idea to find out if Goreski was still living near Charlesville. To hell with him, he thought, I don't want to see him anyhow, but maybe. So, you're in Morrisford and you don't stay there too long, but you walk through the streets and look over the cars and see if somebody has left his key in, and then you just step into the car and start it going, like as if it was your own, and drive right out of town with it and around the other way—no, just right out on the hill road to Forsythe's store, and park it just beyond the store with the engine going, and you walk back fast and walk right in and what if he wasn't alone? Well, you could wait till the other customers went out, saying, Wait on the lady first, I can wait, and then when they go out you flash the gun and say, I want all the money you got and make it fast, 'cause I don't want to hurt nobody, but this gun goes off easy.

Maybe you ought to lay off the old man, account of he was good to you. Nuts, he thought. He's made a pile in his time, he's even a kind of judge, and you know the layout

—— 311 ——

there, you been over the place lots of times when you was a kid and the backrooms, and only last summer when you was looking for work you took a good look on the outside. Looking for work, he thought, that's a hot one.

O.K. it's the old man, he thought, unless you can find something better that looks easier. All you want is a wad of dough. So you get it and you get the hell out of there, and double around on the roads, this way and that way so if anybody saw you in the car, one of them would say, He went this way and one would say, No, he went the other. And when you get a good way from home, you ditch the car in the woods some place, right in the woods, drive it right off the road into the trees, and then you start walking. So you hitch one way, then you hitch the other; but longer each time in the direction of home. Or maybe it would be better to get into a town the opposite way from home, a *long* way, and take the bus back from a place you didn't go to. No, he thought, that might look funny if they got suspicious of you. You said you was going to Peekskill, so you go there. Afterwards, you get to Peekskill, and you come back from Peekskill. Right.

The bus got into Lebanon at one o'clock in the morning, and he walked down the street of the small town with his hand in his right-hand overcoat pocket, where the gun was, and he found the hotel easily. There was a young fellow on duty at the desk, and Sloan said:

"How much f'r the cheapest chamber?"

"A dollar," the fellow said. "How long you going to stay?"

"T'morrow night," said Sloan. He looked around; there was no other entrance to the place that he could see, so he said, "You got a fire 'scape here?"

"There's a rope in every room," the fellow said, "hangs right by the window."

"I was in a fire once," Sloan said. "Got scared bad that time." He laughed. He signed the register, Edwin Sloan, Polk.

"You don't need to worry none, mister," the young fellow said. "I'll take you up myself, show you how it works." When he was in the room and the door had closed, Sloan was suddenly exhausted. He threw off his clothes and took the pistol out of its holster, slipped it under the pillow. It was queer, getting into a strange bed. The bed was hard like in the pen. But after a while, when he couldn't sleep, he took the pistol out from under the pillow, and put it under the mattress. Then he took the pillow in both his arms, and it was easier to go to sleep. The softness of her, he thought, and will you touch her again? Women were strange critturs any way you looked at it; there was something mysterious about them, something a man could never get at, never touch. He thought about her and saw her wide smile and the large soft breasts he loved so much to put his face between. He felt that he was going to sleep soon.

Only when he slept, he had a bad dream. He was in a small house that he didn't recognize, and the State troopers were outside in the woods, and they were banging away at him with rifles and Tommy guns, and he was firing back at them with the pistol. He kept looking at the pistol, expecting it to be empty any minute, because it only held eight cartridges, and he knew he didn't have any more in his pockets. But the strange thing was that the pistol kept on firing. It was always full of shells, and yet he couldn't get used to the idea. He kept looking at it, expecting it to be empty, but it was always loaded. And he was saying to him-

—— 313 ——

self, Come and get me; I'll shoot it out with you guys any day; if you want me, you'll hadda come and get me. And then Norah was there, sitting in a rocking chair behind him, wearing steel-rimmed spectacles like his mother used to wear. She was rocking slowly back and forth, and she had a Bible in her hands, which she was reading to him. She said, "You never were no good nohow, Ed, and the Good Lord said, Ask and it will be given to you, and you were always a liar all your life, son, and Knock and they will open the door, do you think I'd wait for a jail bird like you, and Look and you will find it, and you have got to know what you want, saith the Good Lord, and go out and get it." "I'm tryin', Mom," he was saying, firing all the time, "I'm tryin', can' you see I'm tryin' hard?" "No," she said, "you're not really trying at all."

He awoke with a start early in the morning and dressed rapidly. He knew where he was going. He was going to look up George Goreski over to Charlesville and see what he could find. It was only seven miles. He only had fifty cents in his pocket, and he wanted to eat.

He walked downstairs slowly, his hand in his pocket on the gun, and saw there was somebody else at the desk. It was an old man this time, an old man with thick eyeglasses. Sloan walked up to the desk and said, "C'n you tell me when the next bus goes t' Glover?"

"Why," said the old man, "that won't be for three or four hours, I reckon."

"I'll get me a bite t' eat," Sloan said.

He walked toward the door, expecting that the old man would say, Hey, wait a minute, you ain't paid your room, but the old man didn't say anything, and Ed couldn't help grinning at the fact that he had got out of there so easily. That was a good sign, he figured. He started walking on the road toward Charlesville, and in a few minutes he was picked up by an oil truck.

"Tough goin'," the truckman said, and he said, "Yeh."

"Where you bound, Mac?"

"T' Charlesville."

"I'm only goin' a couple miles down the road," the driver said. "Makin' deliveries."

"That's O.K. with me," said Sloan. "You get paid much on this job?"

"Not much more 'n you could put in your eye without blinkin'," said the driver.

He walked two miles more. It was cold; there was a wind. Be December pretty soon, he thought, day after tomorrow. Hey, he thought, what's the big idea your going to Charlesville? That's the wrong way from Morrisford. Today's Friday; tomorrow the old man takes the money to the bank. Maybe I'll come back this afternoon, he thought. Maybe I'll come back tomorrow morning. Goreski would be sure to give him a meal if he still lived there, and there was plenty of time.

He got another ride with a salesman who was going into Charlesville. "You get much money on this job?" he asked, and the guy said, "Nothing to shout about, but you'd be surprised the tail I get." Walking out of town at the other end of Elm Street, Ed had a picture in his mind of the house where Goreski had lived some years before. It was at the edge of town, as he recalled it, all run down. Goreski had got married, he remembered, and when he came to the house, it looked exactly like he remembered it, except that it had a coat of cheap paint on it. An untidy woman with a round flat face came to the door suspiciously, and Sloan tipped his cap to her.

"You're Miz Goreski?" he said. "I'm Sloan."

"How do," she said.

"George t' home?"

"No," she said. "He's workin' up the road a piece." She pointed.

"I used t' know him, time was," Sloan said. "Mebbe I'll walk up the road."

She nodded, and he tipped the cap again and started walking. About a half mile up the road he saw a gang of men laying a drainage pipe, and he saw Goreski.

"Why, you punk," said Goreski. "When did you get out?"

"Long b'fore you," Sloan laughed, and Goreski glanced around and lowered his voice.

"What you doin' in these parts? Ain't seen you f'r a coon's age."

"Me an' my wife, our car bust down," said Ed. "She's over t' Morrisford, where it's laid up; in a hotel there."

"You married?"

"Yeh," he said. "Got a kid too."

"No crap! Goin' straight?"

"Sure Mike," said Sloan. "Makin' out good too. Our car, that's a Buick, busted down; broken ex; left her over there."

"Why didn' you bring your woman over? Shamed of your old pals?"

"Nah," said Ed. "She's not feelin' so good; got the kid along anyhow. Told her I'd run over t' see you, an' she says, 'Go ahead, have yourself a time.' That's a kind of a woman she is," said Sloan.

"Look," said Goreski. "I'll be through here at three. Why don't you run down the house, tell the woman t' feed your face. Wait f'r me."

"Don' mind 'f I do," said Sloan. "I'm a mite hungry."

Walking back, his hand still in his pocket, he thought,

Why don't you ditch this idea, look around hereabouts for a job? Nuts, he thought, there ain't no jobs here, any more than there's jobs back in Meadow County.

The woman was very cool to him at first, but gradually she warmed up, and she made him a nice mess of fried potatoes, eggs and coffee. By the time George got home from the job, they were pretty friendly.

"Your friend Sloan here," Martha said, "says he knew you up Deerfield-way."

"Sure," George laughed. "We did a stretch together, did he tell you? Boy, what a punk *he* was."

"No," she said. "Well, it don't pay none. George here's going straight, and I'm mighty glad t' hear you are too."

"Kee-rect," said George.

Sloan laughed. "Never hoped t' live t' see the day."

"Why don' you let us run over t' Morrisford, pick up y'r wife?" said George. "C'd get some beer and make a night of it."

"You save your money, George," the woman said. "You don't get too much."

"She's all right," said Sloan. "T' tell the truth, we had a kind of a spat; I'm lettin' her cool down a bit."

Goreski and his wife laughed, and he said, "I'm going t' fetch some beer anyhow, Marty. You don' like it, you c'n go roll your hoop."

He was back in half an hour, and they drank the beer while Goreski's wife made supper for them. They talked about the time they had done in Deerfield, the other cons and the screws there.

"Trouble with me," said George, "is I don't like t' work much. Doin' the same damn thing I did in stir—makin' little ones outta big ones." He laughed. "But it's better than coolin' y'r ass in the pen."

Sloan frowned. "I don' mind workin'," he said. "On'y I been outta work a long time till I met my woman. She's a great 'un; a pusher. Kept me straight an' she helped me an' I got a good job the last couple years."

"You been hitched two years?"

"Three."

"How old's the kid, what kind?"

"A gal," said Sloan. "She's—she's two."

"That's mighty nice," said Goreski. "I'd like a kid or two, but my wife says we can't afford it. Doses herself ev'ry month with all kinds of crap." He laughed. "Ever heard tell of a woman eatin' gin an' bitter apples? Ask Marty."

"Can' say I have."

They had a good dinner of stew meat and boiled potatoes, and afterwards they played some poker for match sticks. Ed reached back and switched on the radio, and the voice said, ". . . according to the local union leader, who said, and I quote, 'The charge that the Vultee strike was fomented or is dominated by Communists is—' "

"Turn off that crap," said Goreski, "an' get some music."

Ed reached in his side pocket, said, "Mebbe you'd like I should play you a tune on this baby?"

He dropped the pistol in its holster onto the card table, and Goreski whistled.

"What you doing with that?" Martha said.

Ed laughed at them. He took the gun out of the holster, pushed the catch, and the magazine fell out into his hand. He put it in his pocket and handed the pistol to Goreski.

"What the hell you doin' packin' a rod?"

"I got a license f'r it."

"Who ever heard of a ex-con with a license f'r a rod?"

"Take it easy," said Sloan. "I need it on my job; the

—— 318 ——

Shoreline Truckin' Company. We all carry guns. I'm bonded."

"What you do?"

"Drive truck," he said. "I'm on vacation now."

Goreski turned the gun over in his hand. "Nice job," he said. "How much you want f'r it?"

"George!" Martha said sharply. "You don't want no gun around this house."

"How much?" said George.

"I ain' sellin' it," said Sloan. "I tol' you it belongs t' my job."

"You put that thing away," Martha said.

"Mind 'f I stay here overnight?" said Ed.

"No," she said, "but you put that thing away." She reached over and took it away from her husband and went out of the room with it.

Sloan stayed overnight.

In the morning George said, "I got a rod myself." He laughed. "Want t' see it?" He went into a closet and brought out a .22 rifle.

The three of them walked over the fields toward a wooded hill, where they set up a row of tin cans and empty beer bottles and fired at them.

"Wanta try that pistol?" said George.

"You will not," said his wife. "I put it where you won't find it, mister." She looked at Ed angrily. "I'll give it back to you when you go."

"You want I should go now?" he said, and she didn't answer.

"The hell he will," said George. "Let his woman cool her heels till t'morrow. I want him t' help me with the chicken coop."

They came back to the house, and after lunch they built a coop.

"Ouch!" said Ed, who was holding a board for George to hammer. "Just because I'm helpin' you don' mean you gotta kill me." He sucked on his thumb and George laughed.

"Looka that," said Ed, showing the blood blister under his thumb nail. "See what you done t' me."

"Make a man outta you yet," he said. "What say we rustle some more beer?"

"Don' mind 'f I do," said Ed. "We ain' had enough money t' spend on things like be—"

Goreski looked at him with an incredulous grin. "Thought you said you had such a good job?"

"My wife don' approve," said Sloan. "She's right at that; poisons y'r system."

Goreski roared with laughter. "Poison y'r system," he shouted; "I been poisoned since I was knee high t' this here coop."

I better get going, Sloan thought; I better get going before I lose my nerve about this job. He told Goreski that he wouldn't stay that night, but George said to hell with that, if he was worried about his wife, he could go in to Charlesville and telephone her at the hotel in Morrisford.

"Let 'er have a little fun," he said.

"Ain' much fun just mindin' o' the kid."

"You don' know women," said Goreski, laughing. "She'll find herself a little fun."

"I'll hadda get goin' in the mornin' early," said Sloan.

"That's O.K. with me," said George.

They sat up most of the night playing poker for match sticks, drinking beer, and listening to jazz music on the radio. About two in the morning, George insisted that they should go for a ride in his old car, and they racketed up the road toward Massachusetts, crossed the border and had a hamburger with coffee in Sheffield, turned around, and came back south. Ed was feeling uncomfortable; he wanted to get away, and when they told him to sleep on the couch and went upstairs to bed, he lay awake most of the rest of the night.

Tomorrow's Sunday, he thought. It's Sunday now. Maybe old Forsythe's store will be closed. Maybe I'll change my mind about the whole business, he thought, go back down home and get Norah to fill out that question-thing from the draft board. That's the best way, he thought. She'll know about it then; the whole thing will be out, you won't be hiding nothing from her. Yeh, he thought, and *then* what will she say? And then what will you do? They won't take you in the Army, where you could send most of your twenty-one a month back home. Instead, you'll be on her hands, and she'll be sorry she ever saw your face. And even if she ain't, even if she forgives you for what you been all your life, a jailbird, a liar, what chance will you have to get a job, to pay off those bills? None. Because like in every small town. Because they know already that you got a bad name, and once the draft board sees your record, it'll be all over town, if it ain't already.

What you got in mind to do is the best thing, he thought. Only you use your bean and do it right. He was dressed before George or his wife woke up, and he poked up the fire and laid on wood, put the kettle on to boil. He made coffee for them, and they heard him rattling around in the kitchen and came downstairs.

"Well," said George, "will you look what's gettin' breakfast! Maybe we should take him on f'r a hired hand."

"I'm on my way," said Ed. "I don' want no breakfast."

"Don't be such a punk," said George. "Nobody lays over at my house an' goes off inna mornin' without his breakfast."

He ate the breakfast, but he was extraordinarily nervous, and they noticed it.

"What's the matter?" Martha said. "You afraid of going back to your wife?"

"Nah," said Ed. "I'm not feelin' so good today. I'll take that gun, if you don' mind."

"I don' mind at all," she said and left the room and came back with it. Ed cheered up and grinned when he saw it. He took it, reached into his pocket, and brought out the magazine. He inserted it into the handle, heard it click, then pulled back the breech-block, and a cartridge slipped into the chamber.

"Stick 'em up," he said with a grin.

"F'r Christ *sake!*" said Goreski. "Put that thing in y'r pocket. Stop bein' a Boy Scout all your life."

Ed put it in the holster in his pocket.

"That's a foreign make," said Goreski. "You sure you don' want t' sell it t' me?"

"No," said Ed.

"That's right," said Martha. "Damn you," she said to her husband, "don't you have no brains at all?"

Ed walked half of the fourteen miles into Morrisford, his hand in his pocket. He heard a car coming behind him, and looking over his shoulder, he saw that it was a white police car. There were two troopers in it, and he kept on walking, his face to the front. His heart pounded against his ribs, and he wondered whether they would see him if he were to throw the gun in the bushes alongside the road. He decided they would and kept on walking.

Out of the corner of his eye, he saw the car pass him,

and he kept his eyes on the road. But he could still see that one of the cops was looking through the back window at him, and then the car was gone. He sat down along the side of the road and his chest heaved. He felt slightly sick to his stomach, so he rolled a cigarette. There was only one match in his pocket, and he had a hard time getting a light from it, his hands shook so badly. He sucked hard on the butt, and finally the tobacco caught on one side of the cigarette and drew unevenly. He took deep drags and drew the smoke down into his lungs until his nerves were steadier. Then he got up and started to walk more slowly.

You got the guts of a louse, he thought. What the hell are you ascared of? How's a cop riding in a prowl car to know that a guy walking down the road has got a rod in his pocket? The roads are full of guys walking, and what if they never saw you around these parts before, does that matter? You might be anybody at all; a 'bo on the hoof, a farm hand in the neighborhood, walking into town for Sunday services. He heard the church bells in Morrisford ringing, and he laughed. That's a hot one, he thought.

He came into town and walked down the main street. It was a small town, and the wooded hills were right behind it. He remembered it well from his childhood, and he thought maybe it would be a good idea to go back up the hill road and look over the old home place. He decided not to do that; it was a waste of time. What you got to do, he thought, is to look around for a car. This is as good a time as any; some folks were still in church; he could hear the organ playing and the voices singing. I heard that one before, he thought, what were the words to it? Oh yes, Bringing in the sheaves, bring-ing in the sheaves, we will come rejoic-ing, bring-ing in the sheaves. That was a song they sang come harvest time, a time for making merry because the crops was good. I used to sing that myself, he thought, when I was a kid in Sunday school, but the crops was never very good.

He looked carefully at the few people who were on the streets, to see if there was anyone he could remember from his childhood, but more especially to see if anyone would recognize him. Don't be a sap, he thought; it's twenty years, even if you was back around these parts early last summer hunting for a job. You didn't ask in town. Maybe that's what you should do *now*, he thought and said to himself, I said before and I said it now, I *ain't* going to look for no work because there *ain't* no work that they would give me. I got that through my head now. And I ain't going back home till I can go back with a wad of dough in my pocket, and I don't care how I get it.

Only it wouldn't be so smart to take a car here. It wouldn't be smart because if they know back in Polk that I got a bad name, if they suspicion it, then they know here that Goreski's got a record too, and if a car was missing they'd know to go right to his house and ask about it, and he'd be sure to say, Yeh, Sloan was here and he had a gat with him! So it wouldn't be smart to take a car so close to where Goreski lives. What the hell was I doing, he thought, flashing a gun in front of Goreski? That was a smart trick all right! You don't know *what* you're doing, he decided, that's the answer to that one, and you better be watching your step.

He went into a small store that was open and bought a pack of matches for a penny. Boy, he thought, it's a good thing George didn't expect me to pay nothing on the beer he bought, I'd of been up the crick without a paddle, with only fifty cents in my jeans. The woman gave him his change and he said, "Nice day," and walked out. He started up the road that led to the gray hills back of town until he came within sight of Forsythe's store. He walked slowly by it to the covered bridge, and saw that the store was still closed. The old man ain't been down yet, he thought. Or maybe he ain't going to open up on Sunday morning. He sat under the covered bridge, smoking, then he started back into town again and walked out onto the Sheba road.

I'll get to Sheba, he thought, and pick me up a car there. Then I'll come back down here by the hill road and drive past the store. By that time he ought to be opened up. But if he's took his money to the bank, like he used to do on Saturday, then I'm sunk; then I'll have to get going fast and get to a bigger town and try it somewhere else. Maybe over in York State. Maybe that would be better to do anyhow, he thought. He's sure to of took his money to the bank. What did you stay at Goreski's for last night, you damn fool, he thought. Now you missed your chance at Forsythe's and maybe you won't get nothing out of this at all. Tomorrow's Monday and no storekeeper that's got the sense God give geese is going to start the week with a pile of dough in his till. And what's Norah thinking, with you saying you'd be back last night the latest? Well, he thought, hearing the car behind him, it's too late now crying over spilled milk.

He thumbed the truck, which was piled high with lumber, and it slowed down for him.

"Which way t' Sheba?" he asked the driver.

"The way you're goin'," the driver said and started to put his truck in gear again. Sloan didn't wait to be invited but got into the cab with the man.

"You work on Sundays, Bud?" he said.

"Work any day there *is* work."

"This your rig?" said Sloan. He had made up his mind to

take it from the man, and he put his hand in the right side pocket of his overcoat, where he had the gun.

"Naw," said the man. "Guy I work for."

It was a slow truck, and Sloan figured that with such a heavy load on, he couldn't move it along very fast. He changed his mind.

"I'm going as far as Sheba," the driver said, "but I'm stopping about three miles down the road t' see a friend."

"That's O.K. with me," said Sloan. "Rather ride than walk three miles any day."

They were silent after that, and Sloan gripped the gun in his pocket, then let it go. He felt good about having decided not to stick up the truckman. He relaxed in the seat, rolled a cigarette, and handed it to the driver.

"I licked it," he said.

"Thanks," the man said.

"You don' know where there's any work a man c'd do in these parts?"

"No."

The fellow obviously didn't want to talk, so Sloan didn't try to make any further conversation. He sat quietly in the jolting cab, and when the man turned off the road into a driveway and stopped, he said, "Obliged."

"That's all right," the driver said.

Sloan was walking toward Sheba when he heard another car behind him. He glanced around and saw that it was white, and immediately he got the gun, which was strapped into its holster, out of his pocket, and with a flip of his wrist he tossed it into the bushes on the right side of the road and kept on walking. The car went past him and he stopped dead when he saw that it wasn't a troopers' prowl car after all, but a milk truck. You leave that gun right there, he thought, and kept on walking. That's the best place for it. He walked on, but his steps became shorter and slower, and he turned around and walked back along the left side of the road, looking for the gun. He found it easily and put it in his pocket. What were you trying to do? he thought, talk yourself out of doing this job?

He kept walking toward Sheba, then stopped on the side of the road and sat down with his feet in the ditch. It was getting warmer, and he wished he hadn't worn the old overcoat; it was hot and heavy. He rolled another cigarette and noticed that his hands were still shaking. Get going, he thought; you're not getting nowhere at all. He was hungry already and wondered whether he should stop somewhere and buy a sandwich. No, he decided, you already showed your face too many places. Ain't it a fact that the crooks out to do a job don't show themselves no place, and it's sure they don't flash guns neither. And what were you doing staying there? That's an easy one, he thought. I was staying there as long as I did because I didn't want to do this job.

He heard a car coming from the direction of Sheba, and he crossed the road onto the other side, where it would pass him. He started walking back toward Morrisford, and an old Model-A Ford drove up alongside him, with a very old man driving it. It rattled like a tin can, and the old man leaned out and said, "Goin' my way, son?"

"Thanks," said Sloan, climbing into the seat. Never mind that he's old, he thought. That only makes it easy. If you're going to do a holdup you can't slop over like a baby. He looked at the old man, who was smiling at him, and he reached into his pocket and fumbled with the catch on the leather holster. It came loose, and his hand closed around the grips of the gun. Immediately his heart started to pound against his ribs, and he let the gun slip from his fingers.

"Where you headin'?" the old farmer said.

"Lookin' f'r work," said Sloan with relief. He leaned back in the seat.

"Now that's a shame," the farmer said. "Ef I'd a met up with you a week back, mebbe I could of put you on. I took a man," he said, "an' he's a humdinger. Married an' with a fam'ly too."

"That so?" said Sloan.

"Work's hard t' come by these days," the farmer said. "I can't really afford to keep a hired man, but I figger the more work you can give, the better it is f'r everybody."

"That's mighty kind o' you," said Sloan. "There ain' many folks like you, I reckon. I been huntin' work all this summer an' fall, an' I ain' found none yet."

"You live around these parts?"

"Time was I did," said Sloan.

They drove straight through Morrisford and out the other side toward Charlesville, and a mile beyond the town the farmer slowed his car and said, "This 's as far 's I go."

"Thanks," said Sloan.

"You might inquire t' Perkins up the road a piece; he's figgering to cut some wood."

"I thank you kindly."

"It must be dinner time," the farmer said. "If you're tramping the roads, you must be kinda hungry."

"Thank you kindly," said Sloan. "I had a big breakfas' with a friend."

"Be mighty proud to have you in," the old man said.

Sloan recognized the road and kept on walking for a few minutes. Cutting wood rates thirty cents an hour, he thought. Then he sat down by the side of the road. What makes me so all-fired tuckered out? he wondered. There were no houses he could see in either direction, and the hills rose from either side of the road.

Here I am, he thought, right back where I started from this morning. Goreski's only just the other side of Charlesville. Maybe you should go on back there and see him when his wife ain't around and sell him the damn gun. No, he thought. You never finished nothing you ever started—except the time you run away from Norah and come back home again. He stood up and started walking. The next car that comes along, he thought, I'm gonna take it. I'll take it and I'll drive right back through Morrisford to Sheba or wherever and stick up the first store that's a bit out of the way that looks like there was money there. To hell with Forsythe. This is too close to Morrisford. Best to take the car a good ten miles away before you try, he thought; or maybe not, because that would give the guy time to make a phone call and put the troopers on the lookout. Well, he thought, we'll see. But this time you do it, he thought, this time you don't fool around, no matter what.

He hadn't walked more than a few minutes when he heard the purring sound of a high-powered car behind him. He glanced around and saw a deep blue Chrysler coming toward him fast; it had yellow fog lights on the front fender, and the polished metalwork glinted in the sun. The hell with you and your swanky car, he thought, and he didn't thumb it, for he knew that kind of car rarely stopped to pick up strangers on the road. It roared past him and came to a sudden silent stop with a bounce. He kept on walking, and when he came abreast of it, the man who was driving had opened the right-hand front door and was leaning across the seat. He had white hair and a deeply tanned face; he was wearing a brown leather jacket.

"Hop in, brother," the man said, and Sloan got into the seat alongside the man. He looked at him. He had on a pair of old trousers. The car itself was something to see. The dashboard was polished like a plate; it had all sorts of push buttons and gadgets on it. There were two cigarette lighters and two ashtrays; a radio. The seats were covered with a straw matting; the clock on the dash said 12:55. No wonder I'm hungry, Ed thought, and felt that the man was looking at him. He turned his head, and the man said, "Baldwin's the name; James T."

"My name's Sloan."

"Howdy," the man said. "I allus pick up folks on the road; make a point of it."

"That's right kind of you," said Sloan.

"Figger if I was walking, I'd appreciate a ride myself. Run the flour mill back there"—he nodded toward Morrisford—"on the Sheba road."

"I used t' live in Morrisford," said Sloan. "Don' remember y'r mill."

"When was that?" the man said and paid no attention to the reply. They were rounding a bend in the road, and two women were standing on the side of the road to let the car pass. Baldwin waved his hand to the women.

"What you say?" he said.

"Said I lived in these parts when I was a kid, left over twen'y years ago."

"Built the mill in '25," said Baldwin.

"You wouldn' have a job f'r a man?" said Sloan, and Baldwin turned to look at him.

"Might," he said. "What c'n you do?"

"Most anything; I been lookin' a long time."

"Live hereabouts? I don't seem to remember your face."

"No," said Ed, "I moved away a long time back."

"Oh, yeh," said Baldwin. "I recollect you said that."

"I'm a pretty fair mechanic," Sloan said. "C'n do most kind o' repairs, done farmin', road work, ev'rything."

"How come you ain't found any work?"

"There ain' no work."

Baldwin laughed. "Hell, man," he said, "there's work f'r any mother's son that wants it bad enough."

"I been lookin' most all summer an' fall."

"You don't look like a cripple," Baldwin said. "What's wrong? Where you say you lived?"

"Meadow County, outta Polk."

"Married?"

"Yeh."

"Kids?"

"One, little gal."

"Trouble is," said Baldwin, "this damn New Deal." He looked at Sloan and offered him a cigarette. Ed shook his head.

"Who'd you vote for this election?"

"Didn' vote."

"Why not?"

"Dunno," he said. "I ain' never voted. Never saw no sense to it."

"Why, man," said Baldwin, "you're a citizen?"

"Sure thing."

"It's a citizen's duty t' vote," said Baldwin. "Who'd you of voted for, if you had?"

"Neither," said Sloan. "I didn' see much difference between the two, six o' one, half a dozen o' the other."

Baldwin's face flushed, and he slowed the car. "You'd a voted f'r Willkie, you'd have a job by now."

"Dunno," said Sloan. "Heard 'em both talkin' on the radio; they said the same."

"You're crazy, brother," Baldwin smiled. He suddenly had an idea. "I'd bet you was on this WPA."

"No," said Sloan, "I never."

"How come?" said Baldwin. "That's the way this administration got its votes."

"That so?" said Sloan, "I didn' know that."

"Why," said Baldwin, "Roosevelt and these women he's got in office are running the country to the dogs. Take it from me, I *know*. I'm in business; built it up my own-self from nothing. I see what's happening to business, taxing the life outta it. This used t' be a white-man's country," he said. "You take it from me—I mill flour, sell it. Can't afford t' pay the farmer enough t' grow it; not an' make an honest dollar yourself."

"I wouldn' know," said Ed, "I don' un'erstand this politics."

"You got a duty t' understand it, brother," Baldwin said. "Take me. I'm all f'r the workin' man. So's Willkie. He's a farm boy hisself. Have a cigarette."

Ed took the cigarette and reached for a match in his right-hand pocket. He grasped the gun; it was loose in the holster, and he took a deep breath and clenched his teeth. The cigarette fell out of his mouth and he bent to pick it up. He put it back between his lips, reached into his pocket, and brought the gun out onto the broad seat next to him.

"There's a lighter," Baldwin said, nodding at it.

Sloan said nothing but pointed the gun at the man and said, "Stop the car."

Baldwin looked at him and saw the gun. "What the hell!" he said.

"Stop the car," said Sloan. "I don' wanna hurt you none."

Baldwin stepped on the brake so fast the motor stalled. He looked at Sloan and saw that he was nervous; the cigarette was quivering between his lips, his eyelids were fluttering. Baldwin relaxed in the seat, took his hands off the wheel and reached carefully toward his left, feeling for the handle to the door. He looked Sloan in the eyes.

"You bastard," he said slowly, "you god damned lousy son of a bitch."

"Get out," said Sloan.

Baldwin looked at him and said nothing. He carefully controlled himself and sat back further in his seat, his feet off the brake and clutch pedals so he could move fast if he had to. His fingers touched the door handle, but Sloan was looking at his face, not his hands. Sloan saw that the man was determined, not afraid.

"Get out," said Sloan unsteadily, "an' make it quick."

"Looking for work," said Baldwin with a grin. He leaned toward Sloan. "You pr——"

With his right hand that held the pistol, Ed made a sudden lunge for the door handle on his side and turned it. He felt the man grab his left wrist and twist it, and he groaned. He turned to face the man, his right hand swinging around, and he saw the man's face. Baldwin's teeth were clenched, and with one hand he was twisting the skin of Ed's wrist. Ed pointed the pistol at him and it went off. Baldwin swung the door open and stumbled out, pulling Ed with him. He held onto the wrist with both hands now and twisted for all he was worth, shouting at the top of his lungs, "God damn you, you son of a bitching bastard!"

Ed could feel the gun firing; it was leaping and jerking in his hand as Baldwin pulled on him, dragging him toward the rear of the car. The gun was still firing when Baldwin released his grip and fell onto the road. His legs kicked and he threw one arm up above his head. Ed heard the silence and the echo and looked at the gun; it was open; the block was jerked back and the chamber was open and he knew that it was empty. He put it in his pocket and looked at the

—— 333 ——

man. He looked up and around; there was nothing to be seen. There was a house, but nobody was near it. He listened; the echoes were dying away and then it was silent. His ears were ringing. He listened hard, but he could hear nothing coming.

On the road Baldwin was still lying on his back; his legs moved slightly and his eyes were wide open, staring at Ed. There was a red gash on the side of his face, and a sound came out of him. Ed came toward him and grabbed him by one arm and dragged him around back of the car. The body resisted him; it was enormously heavy; the other arm and the legs stirred, and the noise continued. Ed yanked on the body until it lay in the ditch alongside the road; then he walked around to the other side of the car and slammed the left-hand door.

He came back to where Baldwin was lying just as a truck came down the road from Morrisford and passed him. For a moment it looked as though the truck might slow down but it continued and went out of sight around the bend. Ed opened the right-hand rear door and pulled on Baldwin's body, hauling it toward the car. Dead weight, dead weight. Leave him, his mind said, *leave* him and get the hell out of here. All the time his mind was saying leave him, he was pulling and dragging at the heavy man, and he got him halfway into the back part of the car. But he felt sick when he saw that the man's hands were gripped against the door sills, and he had to yank his hands away from them. He climbed into the front seat and over it into the back, got a grip on the body and hauled it into the rear of the car. One leg stuck up and could be seen from the rear through the window, and he bent the leg down. He got Baldwin onto the floor and noticed that his head was lying on some old posters. —for *Willkie*, they said, and Ed was surprised that there seemed to be no blood. He pulled the back cushion out and dropped it onto the body.

He slammed the rear door and climbed into the front seat. He was shaking all over as though he were freezing, and he was aware that his left foot hurt. It burned. He looked for the switch and couldn't find it. There was a new-fangled gear-shift lever on the steering column, and he knew he'd never worked one of them before. He pulled out all the buttons on the dashboard and pushed them in again, one at a time. His hands were shaking and he could feel his feet tapping and pushing at the accelerator and the brake pedal. Nothing happened. "Take it easy," he was saying aloud, over and over again, "take it easy." He worked on the buttons again, and suddenly the engine started with a roar; the car moved forward and he pulled on the emergency brake at his left, and the motor stalled again. He fiddled with the gear-shift lever and got the thing started again, the motor roaring like an airplane engine. He pushed the gear-shift lever forward and back, lifted it and depressed it, gradually letting the clutch in a little at a time, and the car started forward slowly.

It picked up speed and he figured he must have put it into high. Only a good car like this would do that, he thought, and looked into the mirror over the windshield. He couldn't see anything in back, so he kept his foot down on the accelerator and the car moved swiftly and silently along the blacktop road. What the hell're you doing, he thought, carrying that guy in the back? What're you going to do now? From the top of the wooded hill, he could see the town of Lebanon ahead of him, and he braked carefully going down the hill. His foot burned like fire, and he wondered what was wrong with it. Don't want to stall it again, he thought; you'll never get it started. Christ! he thought, there's a traffic light in the middle of Lebanon. He watched for a side road that would lead off to the left or right so he could avoid the town, but there was none, and he came down the hill into the town itself and kept on going at about thirty-five miles an hour. He saw the traffic light in the middle of the road ahead, and it was green, so he stepped on the accelerator and went right through it and out of town the other side, toward Charlesville.

Just beyond the town a dirt road turned off at a hairpin angle to the right and there was a bridge across a little creek leading into the road. He saw a sign "WPA" and some men working on the bridge, and slowed the car down, leaning out the window.

"Hey, Bud," he shouted, "where's this road go?" He figured that he was hopelessly lost, but when the man said, "Freshet," he knew where he was, or thereabouts. He stepped hard on the accelerator and the car leaped ahead. That guy looked at me queer, he thought. Maybe he knows this Baldwin. He stepped down hard on the accelerator, leaning forward in the seat and staring through the windshield at the narrow road ahead. On his left, he could see the river below him, glinting through the trees, and when he glanced into the mirror he could see that he was raising a cloud of dust behind.

Maybe you shouldn't drive so fast, he thought; people will suspicion you. Now you done it, he thought, now you *done* it, and his mind kept saying that over and over as the car moved through the light woods on either side of the road. What you going to do now? Get him to a doctor, he thought. Get him to where there's a doctor and tell them the whole business. He kept on going, and then he saw a sign that pointed ahead, *Freshet, 1 mile.* He went right through Freshet, that was only a post office and general store and a few houses, and a mile beyond it a sign pointed to a road leading off to the right. *Lemmon*, the sign said. Now I know where I am, he thought; this's the State forest. He braked the car suddenly and almost groaned with pain. He had accidentally stepped on the clutch also, and he thought, I'll have to look at that foot. There was a still narrower road that led off to the left straight into the State forest, and he took that turn, climbing.

He climbed swiftly for about a mile and a half until the car crossed a little culvert over a creek, and he stopped it. It stalled. He climbed out and looked at the road; there were no signs of recent tire tracks in the dirt, and the woods were pretty thick. This is the place to look at that foot, he thought, and he sat down on the bank of the creek, which was steep, and pulled off his shoe with a groan. The shoe was full of blood and the sock was soaked too. He pulled the sock off and stuck his foot in the creek. It burned like fire and he pulled it right out and looked at it. There was an oozing hole in his foot, a bullet hole. He wondered how that had happened, but he got a handkerchief out of his back pocket and wrapped the foot up tight. There was no time to fool around.

He climbed the bank and opened the back door nearest him, pulling the seat off the man. Baldwin's head was toward him, and he noticed that there was a thin spot in the middle of his whitish hair. The man's face was a queer color, and he came out of the car a lot easier than he had gone into it. Sloan put his hand inside the man's shirt, but he could feel nothing. He felt his wrist and slapped his face. The mouth hung open and the eyes were glazed. This guy's dead, he thought; you knocked him off. He pulled on the body till it was at the edge of the bank and felt it all over. He put his head on the man's chest and listened but could hear a pounding in his ears that he figured must be his own heart. He's croaked, he thought; and suddenly he was sick. He rose from leaning over the man and, bending away, he vomited. It kept coming in wave after wave, and it was bitter in his mouth.

When he had stopped vomiting and wiped his face on his sleeve, he bent over the man again. He felt him all over, hoping that the man would move or make a sound, but he didn't; the face was a strange grayish color under the heavy tan, and the mouth was open wider. There was pink spittle in the corners of his mouth. He felt a bulge in the man's back trouser pocket and putting his hand into it, pulled out a wallet. It was tight. Money, he thought. He looked around him, up and down the road and listened. You started out to get money, and you found it. Go to the store, Katey said, and buy— He looked hastily into the wallet and saw the bills. There were more than he could count, but he saw that there were fives and tens, a twenty and a fifty. His mouth was dry, and he wet his lips. His throat was burning, and he thought of taking a drink and remembered he had left his shoe and his sock down by the creek. He limped down the bank and found them, washed the sock out in the stream, and put it on over the handkerchief he had bound around his foot. The handkerchief was soaked through.

When he had struggled to the top of the bank again, he avoided looking at the body but climbed into the front seat where he had thrown the wallet. He tossed the shoe in the back and saw the posters, so he climbed out again and pulled the posters out and threw them on the side of the road. There was a little blood on them. There was blood on the rubber flooring of the car, a little of it, and he got a handful of leaves from the side of the road and scrubbed at the matting under the clutch pedal and in the back of the car. The blood in the back had begun to congeal and it quivered like jelly, and he felt sick again.

It was hard to get the car going again, but once he got it started he kept on through the State forest, up and down hill, and was relieved that no car passed him while he was in it. Where the hell you going now? he thought, and what's the sense of going anywhere? It occurred to him that it would be a good idea to get the car going fast, as fast as it would go, and then close his eyes and let the damn thing run. Then it would be all over and there wouldn't be anything to worry about. That was a way to get out of it, but he thought, No, you *done* it now and you got to see it through. You got the money you went out—he stopped the car carefully, and it didn't stall. He examined the wallet and started to count the money. There was a lot of it, he could see, but he couldn't count it accurately. There was more than a couple hundred dollars; there must be three hundred or four hundred maybe. What would a guy be doing with so much money on a Sunday?

He took the money out of the wallet and put it in his pocket, and when he had the car going again he tossed the wallet far out of the window into the second-growth trees on the side of the road. They'll get you for this, he thought; you'll burn for this, don't make no mistake about it, Mr. Sloan. They'll hadda catch me first, he thought, and I can go a long way in a car this fast with this much money. I could maybe get to Canada before tomorrow night and disappear. Yeh, he thought, fat chance.

No, he thought, now you gotta finish it. It'll be a long time before they find that guy, maybe a whole day. You gotta keep on going now. He sat back in the seat and felt the car moving with him; it moved swiftly and silently, now that he was back on the blacktop. What have you got to do before they catch up to you? You started out to get some money. You got the money. Now you gotta take that money home.

You're a cool customer, he thought. That's what you'd like to think, a mug, a tough guy. Don't you know what it *is* you done, or are you scared to think about it? I'll think about it, he thought; and then he saw the man's face again, gray under the tan and the bald spot in the middle of the white hair and the queer way his body was lying on the road, as though it was hugging the road, as though there was no bones in it at all. You never saw a man dead like that before, and now you done it. You pumped the life outta the man; you plugged him full of holes, another man, a guy just like you, not so very different, where he was going somewhere. And now you done it. Think about it, his mind said; it's done. It's done and you're done. You start out to do a stickup, but don't hurt nobody, you say, and you start out with a loaded gun and you don't unload it, instead you cock it and you don't uncock it, and then you stick it at the guy and say, Get out, and he shows fight and you kill him and take his car. What the hell else did you think was going to happen when you walked outta the house with a loaded gun in your pocket? He was alive and fighting like hell and then he was dead. You took the car, he thought; you killed the man and toted his dead body in the back of his own car and dumped him like he was a crittur on the side of the road, and he's lying there now. He could see the eyes again, looking at him but not looking at him. I won't think about it no more now, he thought. I can't think about it, I got the job to finish. There'll be lots of time to think about it after they come and bring you in and you're waiting for *them* to finish the job. Then you can think about it plenty.

So he focused his eyes on the road ahead, and he glanced

around the car. This is some car, he thought; this is the kind of a car you wanted all your life. He looked at the dashboard and admired the shining knobs and the instruments. He put his hand on the gear-shift lever and noticed the little lever under it and wondered what it did. He pushed it and a light blinked on the panel, a green arrow pointed to the left; he pulled it down and a green arrow pointed to the right. Must be that showed you what was happening behind; it told the guy behind that you were going to turn. No, he thought, now you got to go back home to Polk, and make it fast. But you've got to think up a story so Norah won't be worried. And you've got to see a doctor about your foot before you get there, so you won't lose too much blood and he will bind it up and she won't see the hole in your foot where the bullet—

He stopped the car again and it pleased him to see that he was getting the hang of it. It didn't stall when he stopped it. He took the key out of the ignition switch and opened the dashboard compartment with it. There were some maps inside, a pair of sun glasses, a handkerchief, and a tire gauge. He put the pistol into the compartment and snapped it closed again. You put that pistol right back where you found it, he thought; you clean it up and put it back and tie it up again and put it on the shelf, and don't let Norah see it.

But what about the car? Well, he thought, it belongs to my brother that I never had who's at the Coast Guard airport in New York; and he left it with me because he went away on active service. But that's New York; you gotta switch the plates. All right, you can run over to York State, where you said you was going, and pick up some plates at night on the street; no, better to buy a cheap jallopy and get plates for it and put them on this car. York

State plates. Then you can stop at a Blue Sunoco place—he glanced at the gas gauge and saw that it was low, he'd have to get some gas—you can stop at a Blue Sunoco place and get some of them little tags with initials on them and stick them on the license plates—E.A.S., that would be. My initials, like the car was my own. Then Norah wouldn't suspicion where the car come from, till they come to get me anyhow. And they'll come; never fear that, he thought. They'll be coming soon, and they'll come in some day and say, Sloan, you're under arrest for the murder of Baldwin. And maybe I can tell when they're coming by listening to the police signals on the short wave; they'd say, Calling all cars, proceed at once to the old Abbott place out of Polk and arrest Edwin Sloan for the murder of Baldwin, or would they put a thing like that on the radio, or would they use a code signal instead? But maybe you could give yourself up before then and say to them, Please don't tell my wife; she don't know nothing about it; just let her think I took it on the lam, that I up and left her. They never would, he decided; they're just a bunch of mugs.

But they'll come, and they'll take you and you'll burn for it, don't worry. He saw a little country store up the road and drew up in front of the gas pump, within reach of the hose. A man came out and said, "Afternoon, friend."

"Fill 'er up," said Sloan. "High test."

"Yes, sir," the man said. "Pretty warm we're having it for December. Green Christmas a full graveyard, folks say."

Sloan didn't answer but watched the man in the rear-vision mirror. He filled the tank and came around to the side Sloan was sitting on. "Check your oil, water?"

"No, thanks," said Sloan. "This car don' hardly use none."

"That'll be two-ten with the tax," the man said.

"You got any high-top rubbers?"

"Why, I think so. Want to step into the store?"

"No," said Sloan, "I'm in a swivet. Think size ten shoes is about right, an' I want a pair o' white wool socks."

The man looked at him curiously and went back into his store.

When he got going again, Sloan thought, That guy looked at me queer. You can't get away with murder, he thought; ain't no way of doing it. But before I go to Peekskill I got to find me a doctor to get this foot fixed up. What you going to tell the doctor? They know a bullet hole when they see one. Well, that was easy; it was a bullet hole; that would be a cinch. All right. Then you study the map and you get to Peekskill; it's a good long haul, and you buy the cheap car and get tags and switch the tags, and you go back home to Norah. She must be worried stiff, he thought. And what if she wonders about the gun and goes and hefts the box? It's a good thing, he thought, you didn't take more bullets and put the kid's toy pistol in the box, so it would be heavy.

Remember what the old man said, the old skunk, he thought, It'd be better to kill the brat, he said, than send him to the county jail, and old Forsythe said . . . Yeh, but maybe the old man was right at that. 'Cause if they'd of killed me then they wouldn't need to kill me now, which is what they're gonna do.

But no, you'll get back home and you'll say you put a mortgage on the house and you'll hand her over every cent, or you'll pay the bills yourself. You'll pay the Reverend Halstead over Polk-way, four dollars or maybe five would be enough, and you'll get the telephone turned on, and pay the milkman and say, Now you gonna shut the milk off, you punk—not the driver, he thought; he's a right guy, but you go right to the dairy to the guy himself, and you say, Shut the milk off on little kids, will you, you slug? Well, here's your money and you know where you can stick it. Then you go to the lawyer over Coney that's gonna lock her up and you give him the money and you say, Here it is, and you can call off the dogs, and you pay the grocer there and the butcher and you pay the Raleigh man and the My-T-Fine man and the lumber over in Shoreline and anybody else that needs to be paid, and you get their teeth fixed, and you buy them clothes, shoes for the kid and warm clothes for the two of them, and you buy a coal stove for the living room and lay in a big supply of canned goods and vegetables of every kind and fruit juice in cans and bottles and pay Ella Horton the rent a couple months in advance, but particular lay in a big stock of wood and coal and food and clothes and pay anybody else that needs to be paid. And *then* you'll see 'em, he thought, the fat-bellied bastards, saying, Yes, Miz Sloan, and No, Miz Sloan, and Thank you, m'am, and Come again, m'am, and Always pleased to serve you, m'am, and Excuse it please, m'am, but you understand how it is.

Yeh, he thought, I understand how it is, I ought to understand because I seen it everywhere, and Baldwin says, Hell man, there's work for every mother's son that wants it bad, and *did* I want it bad? Didn't I say so and didn't I mean it and wouldn't I do it even now if I hadn't knocked off a man and they wasn't going to come and pick me up? Because what I done ain't no good, it's bad; it ain't the way. But maybe they won't come, he thought, the dumb lugs. Maybe they won't find the guy till spring, but don't kid yourself. They'll come, and you're just as good as dead right now, he thought.

Because there ain't no place for you now, and there

never was, and it was pretty dumb of you to think that you could do it—be a husband, be a father, bring home the bacon; it was too much for you, too good for you, you didn't have it in you to do. But it ain't her fault, he thought; she did her best. She took you in and she got you warm, and she was good to you—not like that gal so many years ago just before I took Reilly's car and smashed it up, and she knew about it and she said, "I'll wait for you, Ed, I'll write to you and I'll be waiting," and when I come out of Massachusetts State Prison, she says, "Did you think I'd wait for you, you jailbird you? You never was no good," and *that* was true. But Norah would never do a thing like that; she'd stand by you, no matter what you done; don't be so sure. You never did trust nobody, you never did tell nobody about yourself, and you never found nobody you could talk to, not even Norah. But Norah never knew about that gal, he thought. I never told her. And she took you in out of the cold and she made you warm and she gave you to eat and look and you will find it, and I found it. For a minute I found it.

But I *found* it, he thought, so the preacher he was right. And now I'm all alone again. He saw a gas station ahead and thought, I'll ask there where I can find a doctor, and I'll get this thing fixed up. He saw Baldwin's eyes looking at him and he shut his own for a moment. He's dead, he thought, and so are you. You been dead, really, all your born days and you only just come to life again when you met her and she said, what did she say? "I didn't ask for no shingles," she said. "I didn't order no shingles." And I said, "These was layin' 'round the place an' not doin' nobody no good," so I said, "We'll put 'em on y'r roof," and she laughed. I remember her laughing; when she laughed she opened her mouth wide, and I remember other things about her too. I remember her laying next to me and her big breasts and—and so does Katey too, he thought, open her mouth wide when she laughs, just like Norah. Don't say don't, she said, and she learned me.

He drove up to the gas station, and there didn't seem to be anybody around, so he honked the horn. There was a big steel ring on the steering wheel that honked the horn when he pushed it. Some car, he thought, it ain't your car. It was a funny idea, going to a doctor to get your foot fixed up, when soon enough they're going to knock you off for what you done. Because they're *going* to, he thought, and have no fear. Only you won't be able to put up no fight. Like Baldwin did. He was scrapping like hell, and then all of a sudden he was dead. You been dead all your life since you was born, he thought, except for maybe a little time between, nine months, and now you're dead.